TIDES OF DARKNESS

Andrew Van Wey

TIDES OF DARKNESS

BEYOND THE LOST COAST
BOOK TWO

ANDREW VAN WEY

TENTACLE PRESS

Copyright © 2024 by **Andrew Van Wey**

Cover Design: Damonza | Damonza.com
Editing: Bodie Dykstra | Bdediting.com
ISBN-13: 978-1-956050-10-3 (hardcover)
ISBN-13: 978-1-956050-11-0 (paperback)

V.7.11.24

Visit the author online: andrewvanwey.com

PART I

WHISPERS IN WINTER

As winter settles across my fog-shrouded shore, the roots of isolation grow deep in my heart.
   Her tortuous gift, gratefully accepted.

—Arthur Cummings, 1823

1

The darkness hadn't frightened Ben Thomas since he was a child. Twenty-nine years of experience had softened his fears, quashing superstition with science and research. He knew the world and how it worked. Even three months after completing his PhD in physics, the only thing that still scared him was his thesis advisor's red pen.

Until tonight.

Because there was something about the inky shadows inside the lighthouse that knotted his stomach. Something *wrong*.

He steadied himself at the top of the spiral stairs where the lantern room glowed. He told himself the spotty light was just his overworked mind. Days alone on this rocky shoal played hell on his thoughts and teased his senses. The rumbling waves deep in the night. The wind through the cracks in the old structure. The groan of the motor as it turned the lamp and illuminated the coast.

Days...

How many days had he been here? Several at least. Or maybe longer.

He pushed that thought aside. For now, the lantern room had his attention. Shouldn't that light be a warmer hue?

He paced the room, the windows to his left with their view of the

Pacific, deep blue beneath a canopy of stars. To the east, vineyards and estates twinkled atop cliffs and rocky beaches that formed the northern edge of Greywood Bay. And south, the twinkling pier where he'd had four dates with Janice, and soon a fifth.

But for now, he turned to the lens.

Looming at twelve feet and weighing nine and a half tons, the hyper-radial Fresnel lens was a sight to behold. Concentric circled glass focused light across twenty-six miles, through clear skies and fog, stormy weather and calm nights. But now, shadows bloomed within the glass, spotty and mold-like.

"Shit," he muttered.

If something broke, there'd be hell to pay. His research, his funding, it might all fall apart.

He squeezed through the service area beneath the lens, checking power cords and humming motors. Sometimes this structure's history staggered him. How many keepers had crouched here over the last century and a half? How many men had wound gears, swapped out springs, and lit wicks so ships could sail safe in the night?

It was all automated now. The intricate clockwork had become simple motors. The lanterns became electric lights. The Historical Society had even helped him procure funding to ensure it was Y2K compliant.

And now that work was coming apart.

Smokey ribbons fled from the cooling unit's exhaust. Something sizzled inside the Gateway computer. Next came what he feared most: a flash of diodes, a flicker from the lens, and then darkness swallowed the tower.

Silence. Even the waves seemed to pause. Only his heart drummed in the shadowy depths. This was it: the end of his research and funding. His reputation. Because when people learned he'd assisted in the renovation of a historical treasure that broke on his watch, well, he could almost hear the doors slamming.

Unless...

"The backup, right."

He stumbled through the darkness until he found a flashlight. A few clicks confirmed the worst: it wasn't working. And yet he was certain the batteries were fresh when...

When he came here, he thought.

But when was that, exactly?

No, he had work to do. He found the railing in the darkness and the first step.

Point Greywood wasn't the tallest lighthouse on the western seaboard—that went to Point Arena some forty miles south. Still, at 110 feet from foundation to crown, even a small tumble could be fatal.

He clutched the handrail and started down, counting each step. Fifteen per half-floor rotation, then the landing. Another fifteen, another landing.

After months of studying the Lost Coast's unique terrain and light, he knew every bush and turd-spattered rock of this shoal's windy nine acres.

Point Greywood. Shit. It might end his career before it started.

Another landing. Another fifteen steps. Another and another and...

"What the hell?"

His voice echoed through the darkness. He should be near the engine room now. Yes, he should have passed the bedroom at least. He glanced back up, squinting at the lantern room bathed in dim moonlight.

He'd only descended a single floor.

"No, that's not... possible."

Even the high window he watched birds from was a floor below.

So he descended again through the darkness, fingers on the rail. He focused on the window. Fifteen steps. Seven. Then the landing. Another fifteen and it would be there on his left: the moonlight through the glass and a view of the coast.

Then something licked his palm.

The scream exploded from his lungs and fled past his lips. A single squeal that took on an embarrassing echo.

"*What the hell? Hell... hell...*"

Clutching his damp palm, he studied the handrail. Had it wriggled in the shadows? Was it now damp and glistening? And were there little blinking beads within the metal and a milky-thin membrane?

Eyes.

No. No, no, no. He braced himself against the wall. It was the darkness and his imagination. It was the stress and isolation. Why the hell had he agreed to stay here alone?

Because you needed the money for your research, he told himself.

Because no one funds a postdoc with such unusual theories.

Because you know the truth: this stretch of odd coast is the only place to study that anomaly in the sky.

A star that only appears in certain conditions.

Breath in. Breath out. *This is just a lighthouse*, he told himself. Brick and concrete reinforced with iron. One hundred and sixty-five steps, from crown to foundation.

But the window...

It was—impossibly—almost a full floor below yet again. He'd taken his eye off it when the wet rail touched his palm.

Licked.

"No, that's not... It can't be."

Listen to yourself, Ben. *Truly listen. Windows can't move and handrails don't have tongues. Stairs only lead up or down. The isolation's playing tricks on your mind. Cabin fever, that's what they call it.*

And yet...

He kept his hand on the wall, the cracked plaster and bricks beneath decades of gray paint. His fingers traced the comforting weight of the ages. If this lighthouse withstood the centuries and the sea, so could he.

Fifteen steps. Then the landing. Another fifteen. Another landing.

The window was before him now, and he laughed. There was no impossible architecture, no stairs that descended forever. There were the sturdy walls and this thick salted glass with a view of the southern coastline.

Except...

The lights of Greywood Bay were gone.

The glimmering Ferris wheel at Coogan's Wharf. The noisy amusements and souvenir shops along the pier. Even the nearby bluffs with the fancy cliffside estates.

It was all gone.

Not hidden behind a misty veil or swaddled in fog. Not concealed by a curtain of rain. The night was so clear and the waters so calm he felt like he was looking upon a pane of black glass, polished to a horizonless reflection.

"What... the fuck?"

He wiped the window and yet it remained: an endless dark void.

There had to be an explanation. Was this what the old sailors felt when they truly died and the waters grew still? Yes, it was just a convergence of low-pressure surfaces and warm air, a phenomenon well-known and studied. He comforted himself with this fact for three flights of stairs.

Until he saw the star in the sky.

His star.

The one that had eluded his attempts to capture it, to measure it, to document its presence.

Here, it glowed bright in the inky heavens, a colossus wreathed in black-violet light. As the other stars faded, his star rotated, turning amidst an emptying sky. Because it wasn't a star, he realized, but an eye.

And it opened.

Ben Thomas, who could list each element on the periodic table. Who knew every constellation. Who once pointed them out to his date as they stood at their pier, wondering if anything else might be looking back. He now saw it: a star that had no business existing.

So he did something he hadn't done since he was a child.

He ran.

Screaming, he clamored down the stairs as the lighthouse shivered around him. Step by impossible step, the stairs stretched and distorted. Brick by brick, the walls expanded. Undulating flesh, scarred and necrotic, bloomed between growing cracks. Railings slithered and pipes twisted while windows offered flip-book glimpses beyond: a maelstrom of tendrils descending from the sky.

And the light...

No, he would not look at it because he knew—instinctually—that the star's black-violet glow saw him. Through the bricks and mortar. Through his sweat-stained clothes. Through his weak, simple flesh. That the black-violet stared into him—into his very memories—and it hungered.

Knees wobbling, feet burning, Ben took the steps three and four at a time. Then he came upon the engine room with the generator. And there in the corner: the fuel canisters. Only enough to run the lighthouse through the night if needed. But that was enough to power the radio and call for help.

Because he needed more help than ever.

The star... It beheld him.

Sloshing, hands shaking, he poured the fuel into the generator. He set the choke to the closed position. Then he gave the pull-start a tug.

"C'mon... C'mon!"

It didn't start on the first try, nor the fifth. By the eighth yank, his shoulder ached and sweat dripped down his brow. His vision shook with an adrenaline haze.

"Please!"

No, he shouldn't be here. He should have turned down the funding and gone to the movies with Janice. He should have had a fifth date, then a sixth, then maybe a lifetime together.

"PLEASE!"

The engine rumbled and rotated. The throttle took over. All at once, a dozen diodes flickered. First, the generator. Then, the entire room.

Light. Beautiful, honeyed light from industrial-grade bulbs. Incandescent fixtures buzzed with that cozy hue he knew well: 2700 to 3000 kelvin.

It was the color of safety. The color of sanity and science.

The bricks no longer shifted. The pipes and railings didn't slither. And that vast space beyond—that terrible stretching as if the world was being pulled from its corners—it all snapped back to unyielding structure.

Safety. Sanity.

He collapsed against the cool wall of the radio room, sweat-soaked and gasping. He started laughing. It built from a low rumble, and then an airy guffaw, and finally left his mouth in a grateful wheeze. Only the sputtering generators replied.

Yes, nothing had been there beyond the walls of the lighthouse, beyond the edge of reality itself. To think otherwise was foolish, child-ish, absurd.

But the power...

He'd need to call the Coast Guard and the mainland. They'd need to know the restoration wasn't complete. Not any longer.

Chuckling to himself, he crossed the radio room, relieved no one had witnessed his little freakout. Even the fears of the past ten minutes receded with each breath. He made a mental note to have the place checked for carbon monoxide pockets or black mold. Who knew how much could grow in this old structure?

He found the radio and powered it on switch by switch. His mind was already elsewhere, thinking of the dinner he owed Janice. Maybe steak at the pier where they could watch the migrating birds. Maybe he'd tell her how he really felt. How coming to Greywood Bay had been the best decision he'd made.

Yes, he'd never been good with words, but he'd try. He'd say every-thing soon.

"Base, this is Point Greywood. Do you copy? Point Greywood to base. Over."

He was smiling to himself, thumbing the receiver when he saw it: a series of lines scratched into the wall's dry paint. He counted them up. Seven groups of five. Thirty-five. Written below in charcoal:

I don't know when I got here... do you?

"Uh, base, this is Point Greywood. Do you copy?"

The reply came in a low, resonant hum laced with static. Not one voice, but many.

"Glima dilim, sky'une vok'arr zathule n'gä vey'eel."

"Base, this is Point Greywood." He swallowed. "How long have I been here?"

The voices grew. Louder. Stronger. The static gave way to hyper clarity beyond the radio's simple speaker.

The voices, they were chanting.

"Verin zār'hane v'ghara'lor thraa'le dūr za'rik'rind dak'hal nakte."

He slammed the receiver, switched off the radio. Silence. Peaceful silence.

Then came the rumble of waves and the moan of the wind. The soft crackle as bricks shifted in their mortar. The buzz of a lightbulb, its amber giving way to oozing black-violet as shadows grew from every corner.

All the while, the chanting returned. *"Zhal ghis skre'mskhane d'lure vzaruke, sklar'leen dorle skfeele zur thakün."*

Ben covered his ears, but still it came. He stuffed his fingers deep into the canals, poking and pushing, squishing his very eardrums until hot wetness dripped down his cheeks. Yet the voices burrowed, worms in his ear, in his skull, in the cracks of reality itself.

He shielded his eyes, too, but the black-violet light seared through his skin like an X-ray. He blinked with eyelids that no longer worked.

He saw the pipes and the rebar of the lighthouse. The very struts long buried in stone. And he saw *beyond*. To a place of stars and sand—a beach where masked figures stood in a circle around a man strapped to a black slab.

That was him.

And they chanted, *"J'HARR! J'HARR! J'HARR!"*

He wasn't sure what broke first: the walls or his sanity itself. Brick by brick, the lighthouse whirled itself apart until he hung among a chanting void, infinite and violet, ravenous and echoing.

But not alone.

When they came for him—the mewling creatures and their chitinous shells, the tendrils and claws—he knew only that he was screaming loudest of all.

He had always been screaming.

2

On the first Thursday in December, the night of her fourteenth birthday, Zelda Ruiz decided she'd had enough with wrestling. It wasn't the twisting or tumbling or the bruises that followed. Nor was it her record this season: five losses and zero wins. It wasn't even the crowds filling the gymnasium with cheers for her opponent, who executed a near-perfect single-leg takedown that brought Zelda's skinny body crashing down onto the mat.

Mostly, it was the armpits.

Clamped between Arianna Chang's biceps and her ribs, Zelda struggled for air. She tried to calm her thoughts and count each breath as Coach Howard had taught her. One. Two. A deep inhale, then a counter.

Twisting from her hips, Zelda wriggled her fingers inside Arianna's grip, and something loosened. The two girls grunted, sweat-slicked and trembling. Zelda dug her knee into the mat and forced Arianna to adjust her stance. In an instant, they were both rising, rising...

And then air—precious, clean air—filled Zelda's lungs and sharpened her thoughts. She twisted out from Arianna's grasp and gathered her bearings.

There was the boundary line mere feet behind her. The referee circled to her left. On her right, Coach Howard gestured to press the offensive. Straight ahead, Arianna closed in, her mouthguard turning her smile into an orange sneer. God, she was solid for the weight class.

"Zelda-rooni, you got this!" someone shouted from the bleachers. "Go for her left tit. That's her weakness! Just latch a nipple and twist!"

The boy shouting was Ali Hadid, her classmate. Seven months ago they'd met during summer school and fast became friends. A self-diagnosed verbal learner, Ali was lanky and awkward, a puppy with his proportions all out of whack.

"Shut up before you get her DQ'd." The big girl beside Ali elbowed him.

"Ah, my ribs," he moaned. "Why is your love language so aggressive?"

Maura Goodman-Kerns—the big girl—ignored Ali and rose to her feet. "Sweep her leg when she closes in! Use your reach, like we practiced!"

My reach? Zelda's thoughts crashed through the past three months spent on the mats. All those afternoon practices. All those new words and new moves. Maura, always there to walk her through each pivot and twist.

Yet the moment Zelda stepped into the ring, her body forgot it all. Her mind locked. All she could taste was the adrenaline and sticky sweat. And the armpits, most of all.

She was certain Arianna had skipped deodorant today.

"Forty-five seconds, ladies," Coach Howard called out from the side. Zelda caught a glimpse beyond, her uncle Mark and Stacey Layne at the edge of their seats. Her uncle locked eyes with her, nodding and mouthing, *You've got this.*

And that was all it took. She met Arianna's glare and locked her grip. She used her reach to execute an ankle pick. The floor rumbled as the two girls hit the mat.

Yeah, Zelda thought, she had this alright.

Until she didn't.

Whatever move Arianna did, it twisted her in a way she hadn't anticipated, buckled her feet, and suddenly the world spun on a new axis. She was beneath her again. Pressed against sticky skin and that heaving chest. Arianna's sharp chin dug into the soft meat of her shoulder. How the hell did she keep losing so fast?

"Mmm... There you are," whispered a frigid voice in her ear.

A voice Zelda hadn't heard in several months.

First came the stench from Arianna's mouth, rotting flesh in the cold depths of space. Then the dry taste of mud. And the smokey tang of plastic and hairs, wooden structures and trees all burning around them.

"Look at you, child. Such a weak little thing, all tender muscle and bone. So easily twisted and broken and... bent."

That voice...

J'harr...

Zelda's eyes fluttered as each breath thickened.

This summer, she and her friends had earned the ire of an entity fueled by torment and destruction. She wasn't quite sure what J'harr actually was. Perhaps a ghost or a demon, an alien or a curse. Whatever she was, J'harr was outside Zelda's comprehension. Like an ant trying to understand the workings of a nuclear submarine, Zelda's mind had simply collapsed.

But not before she stood up to J'harr.

Helped her neighbors escape from the fire of Raven's Valley.

Denied J'harr's pups a feast of pain.

"Mmm... You could have been more, Zelda Ruiz. Become so much stronger. You could have ascended, *like many before you."*

"Shut... up," Zelda grunted. Over the past several months, she had consigned J'harr's cosmic voice to the back of her mind. Quarantined it, telling herself it would slowly fade.

And for a while, it had.

Now, her heart raced and her body trembled as those words dripped into her ear, sibilant and taunting. *"Oh, you tried, little girl, yes you did. But your neighbors burned all the same. Eleven screaming and dead. Eleven souls for my forge. I can still help—"*

"I don't want... your help." Zelda tongued her mouthguard aside and shifted beneath Arianna's grasp. She stretched her left leg out, used it to squirm free. No good. Arianna had a tight hold and pressed her down into the mat.

Little room to move.

Less space to breathe.

This was it, loss number six. Hell, it was probably a school record.

Another twist, and she could see the crowd through a gap in Arianna's hold.

A middle-aged man sat in the bleachers, his body a cracked map of charred flesh. One row back stood a man in melted joggers, his eyes two smoldering hollows where embers crackled and popped. Two rows behind him, a seared woman clutched an ashen baby to her ruined breast.

"Mmm... there they are. How can you help yourself if you can't guard your own mind?"

Arianna's left arm slid over Zelda's mouth while her right arm squeezed the air from her chest. That arm, she realized, was blackened and smoldering. Flaky skin slid over cooked muscles and bones. Bitter ash bloomed on Zelda's lips as her mouthguard slid loose.

"This town... will watch you... CRUMBLE!"

"I said... shut... UP."

As Zelda's world stretched to a pinprick at the end of a dark tunnel, a curdled eye opened within the charred arm. This was it, she realized. No more air. In a panicked twist, she did the only thing she could think of.

She bit down on that burned skin.

There was a loosening and then a scream. Not J'harr's honeyed murmur, but Arianna's shrill voice, distant and pained. The tunnel filled with light as Zelda's face hit the mat. A gasping heave, and she sucked in air—sweet, clean air—while the gymnasium lights whirled above.

"What the actual fuck?" Arianna shouted.

Distantly, Zelda realized the referee was blowing his whistle as Coach Howard hurried over. A pair of parents—Arianna's, she suspected—scampered from the bleachers and onto the ring. Maura and Ali, her uncle Mark and Stacey Layne, they all rose.

"She bit me." Arianna clutched her forearm as her eyes filled with tears. "That psycho bitch. She bit my arm."

And Zelda, still on her back, found her tongue tracing circles around her teeth, the salty metallic tang of blood on her lips.

3

The first thing Mark Fitzsimmons thought when he saw the balloons and the cake in the near-empty pizzeria was that he needed a drink. A big old pint of a pretentious craft beer, the kind Greywood Bay was known for. Something stout and foamy, loaded with enough alcohol by volume to calm his nerves and put a bounce in his step.

As he held the pizzeria's door open, he let his mind wrestle with that craving. Then he pushed it away.

Because the next thing he thought of was his niece.

"Whoa, where is everyone?" Maura asked, filing in through the door with Ali and Zelda.

For a moment, the three kids just stood there, studying the quiet restaurant—the tables arranged banquet style in the corner, the cakes already set out, the sign reading *RESERVED FOR PARTY* beneath colorful balloons, one tied to each empty chair.

Mark's stomach dropped as he checked his watch: 6:45. The guests should have arrived. Yet he saw only a group of college students by the window and an elderly couple in a corner booth, eating pizza with a fork and a knife.

Stacey touched his elbow and whispered, "I thought thirty people RSVP'd?"

"They did," he muttered.

"You sure you put down the right date?"

He checked the meetup app on his phone. The date was correct. Beneath an animated banner listing *ZELDA'S 14th BIRTHDAY PARTY*, forty invitations had gone out to her classmates, teammates, and former neighbors. Thirty-one had responded *YES!*

And none had shown up.

Shit.

"Pity party, table for five," Ali said. "At least Elliot didn't come. That fool always steals my cake. Okay, let's peep the lineup: vanilla with strawberries, fudge roll and cookies. Oh! Is that mint chocolate chip?"

While Ali perused the desserts, and Zelda and Maura took their seats, Stacey discretely tilted her phone toward Mark.

At first, he wasn't sure what he was looking at. Instagram or TikTok or whatever the latest app every teenager was on. A video played, shot from the stands of the wrestling match and looking out at the mats.

There was Arianna, pinning Zelda to the floor. An animated sticker pulsed over Arianna's face as she screamed, like some Japanese cartoon, red in the cheeks.

And then came Zelda.

The filter rendered her into a cadaver, skin blue and necrotic, teeth bloodied. The text read, *TFW when ur opponent has rabies. Go Bayview Broncos!* A hashtag flashed underneath: #ZombieZelda.

There were over four hundred likes and thirty reactions. The most recent comment: *total psycho. stay away from her b-day or she'll bite.*

Mark rubbed his temple. Fuck.

Stacey gave him a look that he understood: he'd need to say something to his niece.

He squeezed past Ali, who was taking photos of different slices of pizza.

"*Pepperoni pizza,*" his phone announced. "*Calories: 350. Fat: 15 grams. Cholesterol: 30 milligrams.*"

"Dude, your ChatGPT is worthless," Maura said. "That's sausage and mushroom."

"It's not ChatGPT," Ali said. "It's a custom LLM, and his name is Elrond, so apology accepted. Plus, he needs way more data to learn, but check this." Ali raised his phone to his mouth. "Elrond, tell Maura a joke."

The phone screen flashed for a moment, an animated thought bubble becoming a speech bubble. Then:

"Knock knock."

Ali grinned and held the phone out to Maura. She said, "Uh, who's there?"

"A Vietnamese cowboy named Yu."

"Yu who?"

"Fuck you and the horse you rode in on."

"Ali!" Stacey gave his shoulder a gentle smack as she squeezed past him. "What'd you train it on, 4chan? I don't want to hear that at school, got it?"

Ali nodded, dejected, and took the phone back from Maura.

"Plus, that joke doesn't even make sense," she said. "Wake me up when he can draw hands."

As Ali and Maura's banter continued and Stacey fetched napkins, Mark leaned toward Zelda. She'd been quiet after the wrestling match, but silence was her default setting. "Hey, Zelda, you hanging in there?"

She nodded. He mentally kicked himself for asking a teenager a yes/no question.

"Look, I'm sorry more people didn't show up," he said. "It's my fault. I should've booked the party on the weekend."

Zelda shrugged. "It's fine."

"I mean, who throws a pizza party on a Thursday, you know? That was stupid. My bad."

"No worries." She reached for a slice of pesto as two more pizzas arrived. They'd be eating leftovers for weeks. "Really, it's okay."

Mark wanted to believe her, but the truth was things were far from okay. Five months after the fire consumed the subdivision of Raven's Valley, they were living in a two-bedroom apartment off the coastal highway. They were waiting for the city and the developers, the insurance agencies, and a small army of attorneys to agree on some sort of payout or plan. Money was tight.

And the Ruizes—Zelda's paternal grandparents—were still contesting the will that had designated Mark as her guardian. They claimed he wasn't fit to take care of her. Some days, he agreed. He could barely take care of himself.

But he also suspected there was more. Perhaps they were after Zelda's inheritance. Perhaps they were wounded. For now, the family court sided with Mark. It was what Zelda's parents had wanted.

Still, the costs added up. Attorney fees and court-ordered therapy. The monthly check-in with the judge that always bristled Mark's spine and quickened his pulse. And of course, the cost of caring for a teenage girl. Sometimes he was shocked how many boba teas she could drink.

Now, watching the kids dig into pizza and cake, he realized she hadn't really made any new friends since the summer. The video making the rounds wouldn't help. He was glad he grew up before phones and social media, all the technological horrors modern teens had to face.

And yet, Zelda's first semester of high school at Neumann Prep had been uneventful. She'd joined a few clubs. She spent some afternoons at the skate park, which made Mark's back hurt just to watch. Her GPA lingered in the low-B's.

But it was the words at the bottom of the report cards that concerned him. Comments about a young girl, quiet and kind, yet unfocused and prone to distraction.

A girl who sometimes muttered to herself.

No, things didn't feel okay. Not lately. Even his alcohol cravings were stronger, little claws in his subconscious. He found himself scanning the menu's wine list, wondering what to pair with the pizza. A Sangiovese? A Cabernet Franc? Perhaps a Syrah with a slice of pepperoni.

"Try the ginger lemonade," Stacey said. She gave his hand a squeeze that tamped down his cravings.

"PDA, gross." Ali eyed their hands and snapped another picture of a slice. "I thought it was illegal for teachers to hook up. Like, isn't that a conflict of interest?"

"Wow, that's a big phrase," Stacey said. "No, Ali, it's not illegal. And we're not hooking up."

Mark raised an eyebrow. "We're not?"

"Of course not. We're not sixteen and you didn't get me a promise ring and a Snapple. Or did you?" She gave him a wink and flagged down the waiter.

Mark liked Stacey. She was smart, career-focused, and she cared about the students. As an addict in recovery, she understood his drift toward liquor. She even got him jogging twice a week, encouraging him despite his slow pace.

She ordered their drinks, giving his knee a reassuring pat as he closed the wine list.

The only thing that frustrated him was Stacey's insistence on keeping things casual, though he understood her reasons. Last year, her decade-long marriage ended in a messy divorce. She didn't talk about it and he didn't ask. Still, he'd caught wind of the rumors. Apparently, her ex-husband had been quite the Don Juan on the sly.

Mark couldn't wrap his mind around it. The few times they'd slept together, he'd stayed up half the night ruminating on how she was clearly out of his league.

Perhaps she saw a fixer-upper in him.

Perhaps her ex-husband never knew what a good thing he'd lost.

When the drinks arrived, she crinkled her straw and blew it at Ali.

"Ma'am, that's abuse," the boy said between bites of pizza.

Damn, Mark thought. He really was taking a shine to her.

Was this how Rosalia once thought of him? Rosy, his neighbor in Spain and his occasional fling. Rosy, a remnant of what he'd left back in Madrid. That old life in Europe, so distant now, ended by a midnight phone call.

And a vision of his dead sister.

Don't let them put maggots in her heart.

He pushed that uncomfortable memory away and embraced this moment: Ali poking Maura with a pizza crust, Stacey and Zelda talking —bonding, perhaps, as much as a fourteen-year-old girl could. In these simple things, he found a smile tugging at his lips.

Stacey caught his look and asked, "What is it?"

"Nothing," he lied.

Yeah, maybe some things weren't okay. But maybe that was life in all its chaotic glory. Maybe building something together didn't come with instructions.

He heard the jingle of the bell as the pizzeria's door opened. A crisp wind followed and sent a chill up his spine. The conversations came to a hush.

Because of the old man standing in the doorway.

4

His aching bones didn't feel the cold of the fog or the bite of the wind. Nor did they register the warmth of the winter jacket that Mark insisted on wrapping around his skinny shoulders. Chester Halgrove didn't feel much these days besides his tired heart ticking away like an old clock with rusty gears.

What Chester did feel—and what he saw the moment he entered the pizzeria—was the black-violet enveloping that young woman. The dark glare of J'harr. It suffused Zelda's skin and mottled her eyes, turning her youthful, sweet features into a misty inkblot.

Of course, no one noticed but him.

So, it was as he feared: the dead star was back in motion. What foul plans did she have?

Zelda offered him a place at the table. "Mr. Halgrove, please—"

"Chester," he corrected.

"Chester, right. Please, have a seat."

The salty tang of melted cheese, meats, and fresh tomato sauce filled his nose. Pizza and cake. Yeah, that was what people ate at a party.

As the guests forced back their disbelief, that teacher woman, Stacey, filled his plate. Maura, the girl he'd met on his doorstep this past summer, passed him a slice of cake. He nodded his thanks. He didn't have the heart to tell them he couldn't keep sweets down for more than a few minutes.

Not with the cancer growing like weeds in his chest.

J'harr had taken a lot from him. But he'd be damned if he let her steal as much from the girl.

"You got the invitation," Mark said. "Good. Zelda wanted to hand it off in person, but the caregiver said you were sleeping."

"Mmm-hmm," Chester grunted. Invitation, right. Most people left messages and sent letters. They didn't follow dark omens like an old hound on a scent. They didn't sneak out through... alternative means.

"Mister... *Chester*," Zelda said. "I'm glad you came. It's been a while and, well, you look good."

Another grumble tickled his dry throat. He didn't need to read her aura to know she was lying. Sure, the words he'd carved on his face this summer were healing, and his beard covered the worst of the scars. Still, he knew his reflection and what it showed: an eighty-one-year-old with a dying soul. He looked like what the town had always called him.

A madman.

"I... brought you something." He reached into his jacket and withdrew a piece of folded newspaper. The guests squinted and tilted their heads as he unfolded it. Blue glass glimmered in the light.

"I had a twin sister," he continued. "I think you read about her. Like you, she was... *unique*. She made things. Trinkets, jewelry, art. She told me they kept her safe. I don't know if it did, but it also made her happy and, well, that's important. Anyway... happy birthday."

He slid the newspaper to Zelda. She lifted it, studying the chain and the blue disk as the restaurant's light played over its surface. It was the size of a quarter, and yet with each shimmer, the black-violet shadows thinned and receded.

Perhaps Mabel had been onto something. It was too bad he couldn't talk to her.

"Mmm... I can arrange such a meeting."

"Quiet, you." Chester realized he'd spoken a little too loud. The whole table of people—the *normies*—stared back, confusion in their eyes.

But not Zelda. No, she knew. She understood. Which meant—

"So, like, what kind of gemstone is that?" Ali asked. "Sapphire? Aquamarine? Hold up, I got it: a turquoise spinel."

"Ali." Maura nudged him under the table. "You don't ask."

"What? I'm just curious. My grandma was watching *Antiques Road-show* and this lady had this suuuuuper ugly old earring—not saying *that's* ugly or anything. Anyway, she thought it was just agate, but you know what it was? Blue diamond. That's, like, ultra rare."

The boy's enthusiasm was giving Chester a headache. He pinched his neck and said, "It's bottle glass."

Ali cocked his head. "Is that like lapis lazuli—"

"Bottle... glass," Chester repeated. "Take a bottle, break the glass, throw it in the ocean. Wait a few decades and this washes up."

"Oh." Disappointment tugged Ali's lips. "But that's pretty cool, I guess."

"It's beautiful," Zelda said. "I really like it. It's just..."

He was old, but he wasn't an old fool. He could sense her choosing her words. "It's not your style," he said. "I understand."

"No, no, it's not that. It's... Well, it's a family heirloom, right? It should stay with you."

Humble girl. What she really meant, he suspected, was that she didn't feel worthy to wear it.

"Fair enough." He coughed. "But do me a favor, okay? It's been a while since it's touched another's skin. Go ahead, try it on."

Zelda nodded and unclasped the chain. After a moment of fumbling with it, her uncle reached around her neck. A twist, and then the chain hung, not too tight and not too loose. The blue glass rested near a freckle below her throat.

It looked good on her, Chester thought. Simple and strong, with a twinkle of brightness beneath the scratches and scuffs.

Just like her.

"I'll take it back," he said. "I'm not offended."

Zelda reached around, fumbling with the chain and the clasp. Again, her uncle helped her with it, but a scowl soon furrowed his face.

"Huh, that's funny," he said. "It's, um... It's not coming unclasped."

"You need a woman's touch," Stacey said.

Like Mark, her fingers worked at the back of Zelda's neck and her face scrunched in confusion. Zelda cast a glance back, waiting, wondering what was going on.

Then her eyes returned to Chester. A smirk formed on her lips as gold spiked in her aura. Chester thought it might be the most beautiful light he'd ever seen. A smile, just for him.

She asked, "It's not coming off, is it?"

"It will when it's ready." He gave her a wink.

"That's not creepy at all," Ali coughed. "Tracking chips. Traaaacking chips."

The pizzeria's bell jingled, and all eyes turned from Chester. "There you are, Mr. Halgrove," squeaked a voice he dreaded.

Ms. Tan worked at the Pacific Manor, the assisted living facility he'd been remanded to since the summer. In theory, he was free to come and go as he pleased; that's what the brochure promised. In practice, he was a prisoner. His activities were as regulated as the medication they fed him. He couldn't take a dump in a different wing without permission.

Yet sometimes he found a window or a door to unlock. He still had a few tricks up his sleeve.

"You gave Ms. Tan here a real scare, Mr. Halgrove." That was Mr. Comerford, a near-hairless stump of a man, all biceps and neck. "You know how worried she gets when you don't sign out."

"We tore half the place apart just looking for you." Ms. Tan flashed her best Sunday school smile. "To think you walked all this way? Your poor, poor feet. And those slippers... My goodness."

Chester glanced down. Three miles of strolling along the coastal highway at night had turned the cream cotton slippers a rancid brown. No wonder people on Main Street had looked at him funny.

"We'll get you taken care of, don't you worry." A massive hand fell on his shoulder as Mr. Comerford played friendly for the others. "Folks, I'm sorry to crash the party, but resident safety is a priority."

Resident. Chester's laugh turned into a cough.

"Come, Mr. Halgrove," Ms. Tan chirped. "We've got the van all cozy and warm."

Mr. Comerford's massive hand squeezed Chester's shoulder, just strong enough to let him know he was in trouble. Goodness, Shakespeare was really onto something. Infants and the elderly all wound up in the same place: manhandled, spoken over, and ignored.

"Yeah, s'pose we should go," Chester said.

Zelda whispered something to her uncle that made him nod. "We'll drive him back," he said. "It's no problem. We're actually quite glad he could make it."

Ms. Tan pursed her lips. "Oh, that's kind of you, but we have... *procedures* to follow. And it's after eight. Another time, perhaps."

Chester sensed a darker truth: there may not be another time. Not after this evening's wandering. Ms. Tan and Mr. Comerford would see to that. There was a sickness inside them, a pustulant shadow that fed off control over others.

Were they a pair of J'harr's minions?

No. Probably not. Some people were cruel enough on their own.

His knees wobbled as he rose, and Zelda stood to help him. "Thank you," he said. "Walk me to the van, and I'll see if we can't get that silly thing off your neck."

She might have dressed in a baggy hoodie and torn jeans, but Zelda's manners pleased him. Within seconds, she had his elbow, helping him walk. First to the pizzeria's door, and then to the Pacific Manor van idling in a handicap spot. They hadn't spoken in months, but they didn't need to. He'd left a little piece of his mind inside hers on the night of the fire.

An ember that hadn't flared up until tonight.

Ms. Tan walked around to the driver's side while Mr. Comerford slid the van door open. The dim interior greeted Chester, seats redolent of stale farts and Febreze. He pointed inside. "Help me in for a moment, would you?"

Zelda climbed in and Chester followed. Good. He glanced outside at Mr. Comerford, distracted by a group of teenagers biking down Main Street. Even better.

In a lash of his hand, Chester slid the door shut and slammed the lock. He breathed on the window, fogging up a patch of glass.

"Look at it, quick," he said. "Do you see it?"

Another quick gesture, and he swiped four lines in the condensation, forming something like a *not equal* sign above a crescent. Zelda's eyes widened. She recognized that script, even if she didn't know its meaning.

"What is that?" she asked.

"Lesson one: a glimpse of the *All Tongue*, the language of the Nether. This one means—"

"Mr. Halgrove?" Mr. Comerford rattled the side door. "Mr. Halgrove, please open the door. Mr. Halgrove?"

Ms. Tan clicked the fob and fumbled with the handles to no avail. "Mr. Halgrove! Mr. Halgrove, this isn't funny!"

Chester ignored them, tapping the damp glass and the fading symbol. "This one means 'to lock or unlock something of value.'"

"What is it?" Zelda asked. "Like, a magic spell or—"

"No," Chester scoffed. "More like a command or an order. Lesson two—"

"Hold on. Just wait, please." Zelda's eyes darted about as she took it in. "*All Tongue*? I don't understand—"

"You don't have time to understand it," he said. "You just need to remember. J'harr, her gaze is shifting. Scouring this town from beyond. You've felt her stirring, haven't you?"

She swallowed and nodded. "I think so."

"Mr. Halgrove! Mr. Halgrove!" Ms. Tan and Mr. Comerford were both banging now, really pulling at the handles. But from the inside, they might as well be banging on stone.

Chester took another wheezing breath and fogged up a second patch. He scribbled something like a spiral bisected by an unfinished diamond.

"Lesson two: light isn't always our friend."

A faint click and then a buzz from above as the dome lights dimmed. Darkness spread, thick and inky, as Mr. Comerford and Ms. Tan mutely banged on the windows. With a low hum, the corners of the van stretched, pinched and pulled from its corners as the very space around Chester and Zelda expanded.

"What's happening?" she asked.

He could see fear and confusion in her eyes. Yes, he was going too fast, telling her too much. Her mind was doing what fourteen years of life had taught it to do: fight back and deny it, swim back to reality's safe shores. And yes, he should go slower for sanity's sake—he wanted to.

But they didn't have time.

"Lesson three," he said. "Sometimes the fastest path is a shadow."

A third breath. A third scribble on the damp glass—something like a triangle inside a circle and aligned with three dots in the center.

He grabbed her wrist. "Apologies, but this is going to feel weird."

5

Zelda knew something was happening. Not to her or Chester, but to the surrounding world. It began with a stretching. Like the van had become a slab of taffy. Like something had seized the vehicle and tugged.

Next came the shimmer. Black-violet bubbled beneath every surface and blistered out. The frozen faces of Mr. Comerford and Ms. Tan. The paused bodies of Uncle Mark and Stacey stepping out from the pizzeria. The air glistened as the world compressed to a flat layer and peeled itself back.

Because that's what it was, she realized. A peeling of reality itself.

And beneath it...

No. Her mind flinched and her body shuddered. She turned away as the nausea roiled up in her gut.

Six months ago, the ghost of Ms. Saperstein had shown her a glimpse of destruction. A vision of Raven's Valley on the night of the fire.

The feast J'harr had planned for her pups.

Now, something similar bled in behind the world that Zelda knew. Her downtown Greywood Bay—this town of cute shops and wide sidewalks, of verdant trees and crisp, salty air—was replaced by something else.

A forlorn street of confusion emerged before her. Sickly willows and oaks drooped in a stale breeze. Brickwork buildings leaned, vine-covered and forlorn. Fissures split the dusty sidewalk. From these simmering cracks, black-violet mist rose skyward, twisting reed-like among a twilight haze.

Looming above the town, nestled within a bed of dark clouds and auroras: J'harr.

She took up the western edge of the sky, a writhing star of blackened flesh and broken bones. Of claws rending at each other, and furious mouths gnashing in the cold darkness of space. Of eyes. So many eyes peering in every direction. Numbly, Zelda realized the glimmering auroras—the one beautiful thing in that wretched sky—was the twinkle of J'harr's terrible glare.

"Welcome to the *All*," said a voice beside her.

Chester gripped her wrist so tight she thought her bones might just shatter. And yet she sensed that if he let go, she might fly off. Thrown into this dark world with no way home.

"The... All?" Her voice was weak as she fought back the nausea.

"All things scoured by her deeds," he said. "People. Places. Moments in time. All of it, overlapping here for her torment. Her feeding grounds."

Zelda didn't remember stepping out of the van, but here they were on the sidewalk, the door open and the vehicle behind them. Dust dimmed its windows and rust speckled its doors. Tires sagged on cracked, brittle rubber.

"The All," she repeated. The simple word felt heavy on her tongue and slippery in her mind.

Chester led her down the sidewalk. There was something odd about him, too. A spring to his step and a straightness to his back. As he turned, she caught a glimpse of his face.

He was younger. Not in years, but in decades. A shimmer of youth danced over his old skin like a transparent mask. And the hand gripping her wrist, gone were his age spots and yellow fingernails worn down to the quick.

He was handsome and healthy, she realized. Or he had been, once, long ago.

"So are we, like, time traveling or something?" she asked.

"Time traveling," he scoffed. "You're serious?"

"Like, the buildings are old and your face is way young. Plus, there haven't been redwoods downtown since the eighties. I saw the pictures."

"I'm younger, you say?" His eyes sparkled as she nodded. "Funny. From where I'm looking, your reflection's a bit older yourself."

"My reflection?" Zelda stopped walking. "What do I look like?"

"Ask me another time. For now..." He studied the sky as a layer of fog darkened the All. "Okay. She's distracted. We need to go."

"What about Uncle Mark and—"

"They're not going anywhere. C'mon."

Guiding Zelda by her wrist, he continued down this confused version of Main Street. Past an old bus that rested on its side, shattered and broken by some ancient collision. Past a moss-covered phone booth tilting on the corner. Alongside a dark pharmacy—Rutherford's Remedies & Soda Pop—where bullet holes dotted dim walls and frayed stools lined a sinking counter.

Chester paused, reaching through a broken window and snatching a mixing bowl off a table.

"What's that for?" she asked.

He ignored her, his unfaltering grip guiding her further down the street.

At the end of Main—or what had perhaps been a different street altogether—a rickety wooden structure groaned in the stale breeze. Makeshift beams and stairs led up to a platform where frayed ropes swayed.

Gallows, she realized.

"If this isn't time traveling," she said, "then what do you call it?"

"Sneaking," he said. "Investigating. Poking around. It's like... You know how an LP has grooves and notes that make up the song?"

"Like a vinyl record?"

"Yeah, sure, whatever it's called."

Her father J.C. had collected classic rock albums. Sometimes they'd stop by Amoeba Music in the city and spend an afternoon scouring the bins. She was always surprised by how few songs could fit on that plastic disc and how heavy it was.

Her heart warmed at the memory.

"The record spins," Chester continued. "The notes make the song. But the music's already there. All those notes exist on the record. They're just... waiting."

They passed a group of metal benches and something like a hitching post. Above, streetlamps twisted around each other. Some buzzing electric. Some flickering gas. Some little more than sconces for long-melted candles. On the corner sat an old Buick, its classic wide body and fins rusting beneath dry cobwebs and fungi.

She said, "So this is, like, all the notes at once?"

"Something like that. At least, all the notes that she's touched."

Zelda glanced up at the sky, where clouds still concealed that horrible star. "And she can't see us?"

"If she could, then she would have. But she didn't, which means she can't."

Zelda blinked. "That's... really confusing."

"It's a paradox. You'll get used to it. It's this next part that's unpleasant."

"What part?"

"The part where we find out where she's going."

With his left hand, he gave the old Buick's side mirror a hard twist— far harder than his years seemed capable of. A low crackle echoed down the dead thoroughfare, where several birds took flight.

"Whoa. There are other things here?"

"Mmm-hmm," Chester grunted. "She keeps it well stocked. Some of it's benign. Some isn't. Those ones you don't want to meet."

Using his thumb, Chester popped the side mirror free from its casing. Then he stomped it, shattering it into a dozen shards. A few feet away, he found an old pitcher pump. He raised and lowered the rusty handle, filling the bowl with cold water. Keeping one hand on her wrist, he placed the mirror's shards in the bowl. He grouped the large ones at the base first. Next came the smaller pieces in the gaps. They formed something that—oddly enough—reminded Zelda of a reflective satellite dish.

She asked, "What are you doing?"

"Scrying," he said. "But I'm not doing it. You are."

"I am?"

"J'harr turned her dark glare on you," he said. "You carry the light; that's how it works. You can use it, Zelda. For ill or for goodness, but they both incur debts. Remember what I told you?"

"We help each other," she said. "Like links in a chain, all stronger together."

"Right. My watch is ending and my eyes are cloudy. But I can still sense her. In time, you'll learn to spot the omens, too. But for now, I'll need your eyes to find them."

"Like this summer?"

He nodded. Sometimes her memories of Raven's Valley felt impossibly distant, like a dream from another life that borrowed her voice. Yet in moments, she could still feel the metal sculptures shivering to life under their shared touch—hers and Chester's.

"J'harr." The name clung to her tongue, bitter and heavy. "She burned down Raven's Valley. And that mudslide at West Pine, she killed all those people."

"Far more than you can imagine."

Something hardened inside Zelda, a memory of all the bullies she'd met. All the times she'd swallowed her pride or bit her tongue and said nothing. Those that used power not as a shield but a sword.

"Then fuck her," she said. "Let's smoke the bitch out and crash her party."

"Funny. I think I always knew that's what you'd say." For a moment, a smile turned his dry lips upward, then ended. "I'm sorry about this."

"About what?"

His hand shot out and seized the back of her neck, forcing her face down, down, and into the bowl. The water hit her cheeks, so cold it stole her breath. She fought back on instinct, but his grip was impossibly strong against her neck. His other hand squeezed her wrist, pinning her. Mirrored shards scratched at her cheeks as a scream exploded from her throat.

No, this wasn't right. She'd made some terrible mistake. Trusted the wrong person and—

And then... light.

She saw the mirrors. Impossibly, she saw the shards spinning and her face shaking among a tempest of reflections. There she was, fourteen and shrieking as a madman drowned her in inches of water.

And then there was another reflection. Chester's octogenarian eyes looking back from her own face—*through* it. Blue eyes and brown eyes set within youthful skin.

The tempest quickened until the shards spun outward, flung to the far corners of the darkness. Zelda saw. Once again, she saw *beyond*.

A moon in the darkening sky, now sliding before a warm sun.

A wreath of black-violet light blooming at its lunar edges.

Burned wood and twisted metal, the wreckage of houses lying in endless damp piles.

A scuttling crab emerging from the sand.

Silken robes sliding down goose-pimpled skin. Trembling hands clasping together. And a chorus of overlapping voices, like the Mongolian throat singers she'd heard in music class.

"Mmm... You've learned a new trick, little one. Yes, a curious skill indeed. And how brave to venture so far from your home."

That voice. J'harr. She was closer than ever now.

Zelda's heart drummed faster and faster. She breathed in, the frigid water surging into her mouth. Bitter shadows scraped their way down her throat. This was it. She was going to drown here, in a bowl, in some limbo realm she hardly understood.

Lost in the All.

"Ah, but it's not only you looking out, little thing? I wonder... what did the broken man promise? A chance to sneak by and catch a glimpse of my plans?"

The visions split, spun, and tumbled outward, flung by the vortex as new horrors assaulted her eyes.

Maura, her gaze upturned toward the sky as her eyes bubbled and melted and dripped down blistering cheeks.

"Zelda..."

Then Ali, a manic smile stretching his mouth so wide crimson fissures split his face.

"Zelda?"

And Uncle Mark, eyes red and wet as he cupped a handful of white pills. Uncle Mark, sobbing as he swallowed them and chased them with a bottle of scotch. Uncle Mark, curling up as black-violet foam dripped from his lips.

"See, that's the thing about plans. Mine were set in motion before your stars ignited. You... Can... STOP... NOTHING!"

She squeezed her eyes shut, but still they came.

Her mother's hand against the window as the car slid down the cliff.

Her father's final hours, intubated and murmuring from a chemical haze.

The sickly sweet smell of organ failure as his broken body shut down.

Zelda was tumbling now, down through a spinning void. And then a hand snatched at her, warm and filled with life and strength. A new world snapped into sharp focus.

"ZELDA!"

Then she was lurching down the sidewalk—the *right* sidewalk—a place of nighttime conversations and warm winter lights. Main Street in Greywood Bay. Uncle Mark tugged her by the wrist, pulling her away from the van, Mr. Comerford and Ms. Tan beside it.

"Zelda?" Uncle Mark shouted. "Hey, look at me. You alright?"

She was the center of a great focus, not of some terrible eye and its cruel gaze, but a dozen faces filled with worry for their friend, their class-mate, their niece. She blinked away the confusion.

"Yeah," she coughed. "I'm okay."

In the dark van, Chester cast a nervous glance in her direction. "Please," he said. "Tell me what you saw."

She swallowed. The briny taste of saltwater and mud on her lips and tongue. Then they were gone. The images that had assaulted her. The fear that had quickened her heart. The All. It held the loose tatters of a half-remembered dream, fading just as fast.

"Zelda," Chester shouted. "What did you see?"

The answers never left her lips. She had no words to shape the sticky horrors retreating into the locked rooms of her mind.

"What did you see?"

"I don't know," she said. "I don't know. I don't..."

It was the truth. Or as much as her mind could assemble.

Uncle Mark pulled her close while the caretakers apologized. Then the van doors slammed shut. Chester's anxious gaze pierced the window as half-formed symbols vanished upon the damp glass.

6

As he pulled the car up to the driveway, Mark could hear his teeth grinding in the silence. He was so mad he'd hardly spoken since the pizzeria.

"Well, that was an interesting evening." Stacey opened the door and offered a comforting smile, her eyes flicking to his niece in the back seat. "And happy birthday, Zelda."

In the shadows, Zelda nodded.

He walked Stacey to the front door, a two-bedroom duplex she shared with Pavarti, another teacher from Neumann Prep. Like most of the Raven's Valley homeowners, Stacey was stuck in limbo, waiting for the courts and lawyers to figure out who owed her a house. On most nights, Mark might come in for a coffee or tea.

But he needed to have a chat with his niece.

"So we'll see you at the town hall?" Stacey asked.

"And miss a chance to do my civic duty? Yeah, I'll be there. I'm making it a field trip for my seniors."

"How'd you spin that?"

"Entrepreneurs need to learn systems before they disrupt them."

Stacey smiled. He liked how it wrinkled the corners of her eyes.

"Look at you, bringing that Silicon Valley hustle to our backwater town."

"Probably the last thing it needs."

"I'll settle for more housing." She gave him a soft kiss and a squeeze on his waist. "G'night, Mark."

Even a few months into their relationship, he still got goosebumps. It was funny, he thought, how he was more nervous in his forties than all the years before. Maybe there was more riding on it all. Or maybe it was the knowledge that he wasn't getting any younger.

He climbed into the car, disappointed that Zelda hadn't moved up front. He drove two blocks in silence before he worked up the courage. "You know I like Mr. Halgrove, right? He helped a lot of people. And I know you care about him. But I don't think you should see him anymore."

In the shadows, a puff of air left Zelda's lips. "What?"

"You heard me."

He merged onto the crosstown expressway, accelerating past a billboard for the now-defunct Hawk's Hollow development. Someone had graffitied CROOK! over the name Strathmore and Daniels.

"He means well," Mark continued. "At least, I think he does. But the thing is, people can have good intentions and still cause harm. Mr. Halgrove—"

"Chester. He likes being called Chester."

"Chester, right. He's... Well, Chester's unwell. Like, mentally sick and... People sick like that can be a danger. To themselves, sure, but also to others."

Zelda speared him with a glare from the back seat. "I'm not a kid, Uncle Mark."

"No, no, of course not. Sorry."

Still, he couldn't help but think of the girl he'd visited on those trips home from Spain. How each Christmas her presents had changed. Socks and sticker packs becoming band T-shirts and YA books. How her music had taken on a brooding, mumbling edge. And now, when she looked at him, he saw eyes older and hardened by life.

Like darkness shrouded her, visible only at certain angles.

"I'm sorry," he said. "But I just don't think that he's safe."

"He didn't do anything. It was just a misunderstanding."

"Right." Mark studied her in the rearview. He wanted to believe her, yet something had come between them lately. A wall, silently constructed while he was looking elsewhere these past few months.

Or maybe that was the natural ebb and flow of adolescence. It'd been so long since he'd been there himself. Memories of an absentee father and a mother doing her best to pick up the slack. Microwave dinners and MTV. Coupons clipped and hung on the fridge. And Maya, of course. All the scary movies rented while their mother worked another double shift on the weekend.

Goodness, it sometimes planted a seed of panic in his chest: he was really caring for his dead sister's daughter. He checked the car's speed.

"But if he did do something..." he said. "If Chester, you know, tried to touch you or—"

"He didn't." There was a barb in her voice.

"I'm just saying you could tell me. Or Dr. Rhonda, if you wanted. You trust her?"

Even in the darkness, he could sense Zelda shrugging. That was as close to an affirmative answer as he'd get.

"Well, I trust her," he said. "For a shrink, she's pretty cool."

It wasn't a lie. Despite the court order, therapy had been helpful and he found himself looking forward to the biweekly sessions. Sure, Stacey might have given him the confidence to curb his drinking, but he couldn't burden her with all of his problems. And the only other people he knew were fellow teachers or former homeowners locked in litigation. Everyone said men needed to be more emotionally open. Yet nothing made someone look for the door faster than a man in his forties getting misty-eyed.

He sighed as they pulled off the expressway. "Zelda, why does it feel like you're not telling me everything?"

"Because it doesn't matter."

"What do you mean?"

A beat of silence. Her eyes flicked from the phone in her lap to the window, where the ocean emerged, cold and foggy along the dark coastal highway. "You always say you trust me, right? So trust me on this: Chester didn't do anything. He's just... old."

Mark considered it. Or rather, he gave her a moment to think that's what he was doing. The truth was, he'd decided the moment he stepped out of the pizzeria. The moment he saw Ms. Tan fumbling for the van's keys. And Mr. Comerford, banging on the window. And the interior, impossibly dark.

With his niece inside.

Fuck, how could he have let that happen?

He said, "The thing is, Chester displayed poor judgment tonight. Walking all the way to the restaurant—"

"We invited him."

"Not in his slippers. And that weird present that's stuck—"

"He showed me how to unlock it. See?"

He glanced into the rearview, where she held up the blue pendant. He didn't have the heart to tell her it looked like something made in arts and crafts.

"Locking the van, even if it was just for a moment, it's..." He could feel his knuckles clenching at the mention of it. "Look, I trust you, okay? But the bottom line is, I don't trust Chester. Not after tonight. Not around those that I care about."

He turned off the coastal highway, where the cheap neon glow of the Heartwood Apartments greeted them, warm among the fog. He waited for Zelda to say something, anything, but the silence stretched on until he killed the engine.

"We good?" he asked.

Her answer came not in words but the quick opening of the door followed by it slamming shut. This wasn't their first disagreement—far from it. Still, he sensed it would be a while before they made peace.

His phone chirped with a message from his lawyer, Ms. Phong. He blinked, stomach souring as he reread the text.

The Ruizes, it seemed, were coming to spend Christmas in Greywood Bay.

Christ, he was thirsty.

He turned the engine back on, rolled down the window, and called out, "Zelda! I just remembered: we're out of milk. Need anything from the store?"

She paused in the apartment's courtyard, that long hoodie with its distressed patterns over a pair of mismatched boots. Just a fourteen-year-old girl, small among the mists of winter. She shook her head.

And then she went in.

FIVE MINUTES LATER, MARK ROAMED THE AISLE OF THE QuickStop Market, a carton of milk in his basket and a shameful spring to his step. He scanned the refrigerated shelf, craft beers glistening. He'd made it forty-five days since his last relapse: a new record. He was proud of himself. Another five and he'd get a new coin at the meeting.

Or he could have a drink now.

Didn't he deserve one for his efforts? Self-care, yes, that's what Dr. Rhonda called it. A chance to unwind. And besides, he'd be sober with the Ruizes around.

He opened the cooler door, eyes caressing the beautiful bottles.

There was Flying Dog Imperial Porter, dark and aged in bourbon barrels for three months. There was North Coast Brewing Company's Red Seal Ale, strong and earthy. There was something called Fort Darrow's Finest, a stout featuring a whale and a squid fighting on the label.

But tonight he reached for his old favorite, Racer 5 IPA. He could almost taste the hops and piney undertones, crisp with a hint of citrus. His fingers locked around the bottle's neck, the last on the shelf.

Then a hand reached out from the darkness.

Mark didn't scream as the bottle broke on the floor. Nor when the damp fingers touched his own. He fell back onto his ass, onto the wet checkered floor as foamy beer soaked his ankles. He tried to form words with a limp tongue.

Because he knew the woman staring back from beyond the refrigerated shelves.

It was his sister.

"Maya?"

Her eyes blinked, dim and dry. At first, he thought it was the store's lighting that gave her skin such a sallow complexion. Or perhaps the shelf's deep shadows she crouched within.

Death, he realized.

A rigid pallor suffused her cheeks, tightening her jawline and curdling her eyes.

"My-uh," she repeated. "Yes, My-uh, that was... my name. Maya Fitz-sim-mons. Or was it once changed?"

Every ounce of Mark's sanity screamed, *Get up and go. Run away and never look back. This is all in your head.*

And yet he knew—instinctually, he *understood*—that his sister was here, now, and no matter the impossibility, these seconds were more real and precious than most hours he lived.

He willed his tongue to move and his mouth to find shape for his words. "Maya, what are you doing here?"

"I slipped through a wound only meant for one way." The dead flesh of her cheeks resisted the movement of life. "Maya, yes. Maya Ruiz... Maya Fitzsimmons. There was another name, too, one I loved most of all. Something like... mother." A smile pulled at the left side of her face. "How long has it been?"

"Nine months, sis," Mark choked.

"Nine months... Nine thousand years." She forced herself to blink and yet it hardly looked human. Like tight sheets stretched over rocks. "Time is all the same... from this side of the sea."

He didn't remember scooting forward, but here he was at the edge of the refrigerator, straining to look past the shelves of beers and see his sister's face. "I've missed you, baby sis. We've all missed you."

"We?" Another blink. Something sparkled in those dim eyes. "Ah... *We*. You and *her*. My sweet Zelda, the protector." Her stiff fingers gestured to her head. "It's muddled, all of it hazy and soft. All... fading. My heart no longer beats... but it still reaches... for you both."

"Maya, please—"

"There is another, a mother of hunger, the last of her kind. Even wounded, she draws strength from the deeds of the wicked. She is calling... Calling the mud and the flame. Calling... her debts."

Like frost in the warm morning light, every inch of her face crackled as she spoke. The muscle and sinew, the tight skin and white lips. Mark worried his sister's face might just crumble. And if it did, his mind would crack.

If it hadn't already.

Maya said, "It's coming: tides of darkness on her day of black night. Her wounds fester and widen. Ajar... Ajar... Ajar."

These were the last words his sister spoke before her face receded into the shadows beyond the shelves of cold bottles. Beyond his reach. Beyond.

Mark, sitting there on the wet floor, hardly recognized the cashier who stood over him now, mop in hand, asking if he was injured or needed help.

No. He wasn't injured, and he was beyond help indeed. Maya's words still echoed in his thoughts. Ajar, yes, a strange word indeed. Yet he sensed his mind had suppressed something deeper.

A word he heard one night months ago, in the final moments of the Raven's Valley fire. A word repeated by Zelda as she stared at the smokey sky and collapsed into his arms.

J'harr. J'harr. J'harr.

7

Stomach rumbling, Franklin Torres spooned the first bite of beef stroganoff into the collapsable dog bowl and placed it among the weeds. Scout ambled over, all six and a half pounds of her quivering with excitement. Yep, he was getting tired of these freeze-dried backpacking meals, but his four-legged companion didn't mind. Dogs. They always found the best in each moment.

While Scout buried her snout in the bowl, chewing and grunting and wagging that little curl of a tail, Franklin stretched his sore legs by the campfire. He inspected his boots, worn from the week's walking.

They'd spent the morning hiking the sandy coast south before cutting inland. They passed the afternoon weaving through redwood groves and skirting weed farms. The goal was to make it to West Pine or maybe Fort Darrow before sundown. He knew a good spot beneath the coastal highway to camp and clean up. He could spend a few days in town, busking outside the Whole Foods. Play some classics on the ukulele while Scout danced in little circles.

But if not, he could always find an empty vacation rental in the hills. Pick the lock, raid the pantry, and give Scout a good scrub in the shower. It wasn't fair that a pretty dog always ended up so dirty.

At least that was the plan.

Instead, here he sat, warming his sore legs by the campfire and feeling his age. Wondering wherever the *here* really was.

Some sort of landfill.

He shined his flashlight across the dark mounds where conflicting shapes leaned in the shadows. Blackened wood and scarred girders. Rebar splayed and twisted in piles. Dirty glass shards dimly glinted as rats scampered off.

A faded sign read *LARCHMONT CONSTRUCTION & DEMOLITION.*

Then he saw the refrigerator.

Over the summer, Franklin had worked construction up in Seattle, part of a ragtag crew building some posh CEO's third house in record time. He recognized this fridge, a Sub Zero Pro 48, stainless steel scuffed and its glass door cracked from some sort of trauma.

He drew in a deep breath. Cool air and trees, but something else, too. Fire.

So, that explained the lingering scent: burned metal and plastics. This wasn't a landfill or compost, but something else.

Homes.

He played his light over the remains of charred houses. Fire-scarred beams and gutted walls. Piles of brick mixed with charred furniture and melted appliances.

With a crack, something shifted inside a nearby pile, sending his heart leaping into his throat and loosing a squeak from Scout's lips. They both froze—a nervous dog and an itinerant, his flashlight shaking. Shit, he shouldn't be here. And he sure as hell couldn't get caught with an illegal fire.

He kicked the burning logs over and stomped out the embers, sparks dancing in the breeze. Then, a most curious thing.

It began as a thread of light, where a glowing filament moved through the shadows. It unfurled. First, as a finger, then a whole hand. For one glimmering second, Franklin was certain he saw fiery footprints bloom upon the weedy earth and race from the campfire.

Toward a charred mound of rubble.

Where something glowed deep inside.

Scout let out a series of barks and scooted behind Franklin. Heart drumming, he watched as a shape clattered down the ruined slope. With a metallic clang, it tumbled over boards and beams, down half-melted solar panels and curled shingles. A final *tong*, and the object came to rest at the edge of his dying campfire.

It was part of a sculpture, he realized. An arm forged out of metal. Ash filled grooves of bizarre symbols among castings and plate.

Franklin squatted, running a finger over the surface. Odd. It was warm to the touch.

Then a voice boomed from behind him. "You're not supposed to be here."

A beam of white light enveloped him. Two more beams converged and sent shadows stretching across the weeds. Raising a hand to his face, Franklin squinted.

Three young men stood at the edge of the same fence he'd climbed through. One carried a backpack, pliers and wire cutters hanging from his belt. Another swayed and twitched in the fog. The third spooled some sort of thin rope. They lacked the thick build of security guards or construction workers. Instead, they had sunken mouths and dark eyes and bony frames lost in baggy clothes.

Copper wiring, Franklin realized. They were thieves.

"I was just passing through," Franklin said. "Heading to Fort Darrow to meet my cousin. He's coming any minute now."

He wasn't sure why he lied, but he had a bad feeling about the men. Some instinct murmuring, *Get out. Go.*

Two of the men grumbled and lowered their flashlights. The third kept it trained on Franklin.

"Your cousin, huh?" The man scratched an unkempt goatee. "What's his name?"

"Barry," Franklin said. "Barry Barnes."

Goatee Man hesitated, rummaging through some list in his own head. Franklin stole a glance at the other two, both skinny as well. One had beady eyes that protruded like a squeezed rat. The other was young, with a wispy mustache and a gaunt neck rising from a parka a few sizes too large.

Then Franklin saw their teeth.

Tweakers, shit.

The history of the Lost Coast was entwined with altered states. From the pot farmers to hippy chemists and modern shamans peddling psychedelic vacations. Yep, Franklin had even fried his own brain over the years. But meth? Shit. He drew the line long before that.

"Barry Barnes from Fort Darrow," Goatee Man repeated. "That kind of sounds like a made-up name. I grew up there. I don't know any Barry Barnes."

"Bro, you don't even know the mailman," the beady-eyed man laughed.

"Or that nosy bitch neighbor," Wispy Mustache added. "Always complaining about the music, like she got better taste."

Franklin gave them an amiable laugh. Tweakers had the conversational focus of toddlers. If he could get them smiling, perhaps he could slip off.

"Neighbors, eh? They're the worst."

He was a few steps away, grabbing his backpack, when the light fell on him again. Goatee man said, "It's a bullshit name 'cause you're a bullshit drifter, ain't ya?"

A knot formed in Franklin's stomach. "Look, guys, I'm gonna be on my way—"

"You people," Goatee Man continued, aiming the flashlight in Franklin's face until the world became a curtain of light. "You and your *tents* and your *fucking gui-tars*. Think you can just camp anywhere, don't you? Just pop a squat and move right fuckin' in."

No, Franklin didn't think that, not exactly. But he knew plenty who did. He'd even been beaten up by a few buskers in Portland when he chose the wrong sidewalk.

"It's okay, fellas. I'm going, I'm going."

A yip pierced the night, pained and sudden as three flashlight beams fell to his feet. He'd stepped on Scout's paw.

"C'mon, girl, let's bounce."

But Scout wasn't bouncing or following, and her leash was buried in Franklin's pack. Instead, she ran in excited little circles around his legs, yipping and wagging her tail and kicking up a racket.

"Huh," Goatee Man said. "That a Yorkie?"

"Just some sort of mutt," Franklin said.

"Nah, fool." The tweaker squinted. "Looks like a Yorkie to me."

"The fuck does it matter?" Wispy Mustache asked.

"You know how much a Yorkshire Terrier is worth?"

"Well, she's not a Yorkie." Franklin sensed his shaky voice wasn't selling the lie. "And she's not for sale. If you'll excuse me..."

"Go on," Goatee Man said. "Grab that fucking dog."

It took Franklin a half beat to realize this was really happening; they wanted Scout. The tweakers moved like zombies, hesitant and confused. One shot a glance back at Goatee Man, who snarled, "You heard me. That's a prime fucking score, that dog."

Then they closed in.

Despite his sore legs and the miles they'd walked, Franklin's body moved quick. He bent, scooping Scout into his arms, and took off. His backpack rattled and a loose pan fell free.

He made it thirty steps before he felt a hand swiping at his pack. He looked back, and there was Beady Eyes, clawing at him. He didn't think of all the precious wet-weather gear he'd collected—the tarp and the hammock, the tent and its poles. He didn't think of his ukulele and all the songs it had played.

He thought only of Scout.

So he shrugged his shoulders and twisted, letting the backpack fall away. Beady Eyes tripped, spilling over all that Franklin owned in this world.

He raced on, past the mounds of burned homes and appliances. Around the dark rubble and ruins. He ignored his beating heart, his burning lungs. But he couldn't ignore Scout. She yipped and barked, really having a fun time. He tried to clamp her snout, but she just licked at his palm and wagged her tail against his chest.

He turned left at a pile of blackened boards. A right past a stack of melted TVs. Then a flashlight beam cut the darkness, and there was Wispy Mustache, huffing and glistening in the fog. He looked almost as scared as Franklin.

"Bro... just give us... the dog."

Franklin turned back, but another beam rounded the corner and blinded him. They were trapped.

Again, his instincts took over and he grabbed something heavy and flung it at Goatee Man. The brick grazed his leg, only aggravating him. "Oh man, I'm gonna punt that fucking rat dog!"

There was no winning against three tweakers. And no way out.

But there was a way up.

The embankment was thirty feet high, a dark lattice of burned wood that screamed of sharp edges and disease. Still, Franklin hurried up it, his feet somehow finding rickety notches. His left hand snatched at anything: cables and broken window frames, melted insulation and patches of mud. His right hand clutched Scout tight to his chest. If these tweakers wanted his dog, they'd have to go through him.

But first, they'd have to climb this whole teetering mess.

From the top, he watched three flashlight beams scanning the mound for a route.

"C'mon, you pussies," Goatee Man said. "Shawn, head left. G-dog, take right. I'm going up here."

So they had names, Franklin thought. And maybe a bit of humanity left in their meth-addled brains.

"Shawn," Franklin called out. "I don't have any beef with you. I just want to go home."

Shawn—the one with the thin mustache—slowed a third of the way up the mound. Loose debris rattled and fell with each step. He shot a nervous glance at their leader.

"And G-dog, is it?" Franklin shouted. "Listen, we didn't do anything to you. Just leave us alone."

G-dog looked up, and for a moment Franklin saw shame in those beady eyes.

"Nowhere left to fucking run," Goatee Man said. It horrified Franklin that he was right. The man was almost at the top now, scrambling so fast up the mound that loose boards and bricks slid away.

Like he was tearing the heap apart just to get to the top.

Then something *shifted*.

Because Franklin was wrong, he realized. The tweaker wasn't tearing it apart. The ruins were collapsing beneath him.

G-dog shouted, "Tim-Tam, look out!"

For the space of a breath, clarity flashed in the cruel eyes of Tim-Tam—the man with the goatee. He was sober and scared, his world coming apart underfoot. Then a glow flashed deep in the rubble. Amber and crimson lit up his legs.

Like that ribbon of fire, Franklin thought. The one he'd seen earlier and dismissed.

With a crunch of rocks, the snap of wood, and the low moan of metal, Tim-Tam's goateed mouth made an *oh shit* shape as he swiped at the air.

Then the mound opened up and the blackened ruins swallowed him whole.

8

S afe in his arms, Scout barked as the two tweakers reached the top of the rubble. Franklin no longer held their attention.

Because the scream coming from the hole before them was so specific—so *desperate*—that all other concerns fell away. Nothing good came from such cries.

Still, Franklin pushed his fear aside and doubled back. Splintered boards lined the hole like broken teeth. Rocks tumbled down a dark gullet, going *plinkity plink*.

From below, Tim-Tam's voice echoed out. "Help me! Help me, it hurts!"

"Sweet fuckin' Jesus," Shawn muttered. "Bro, you gotta help us."

He leaned over and stretched his arm into the hole. G-dog covered his mouth.

And Franklin—who had wished these men terrible fates only moments ago—found himself stumbling over, morbidly curious as to what lay within. Then he felt it: heat rising.

"Help me!" Tim-Tam cried. "GET ME OUT, YOU IDIOTS!"

As Franklin peered over, he understood the screaming. Tim-Tam's left arm was bent the wrong way. Half-melted fencing impaled his thighs, wrought iron spikes glistening red and wet in the flashlight's cold beam. At the sight of all the blood, G-dog stifled a gag and Shawn simply sputtered, "Oh fuck... oh fuck... oh fuck..."

It was Franklin who found his voice. "Hold on. I... I've got some ropes. Just... wait there!" Well, not exactly rope, he thought, but the hammock and straps were rated for three hundred pounds.

Scrambling down, he located his pack and dug the straps out. He hardly stopped to consider why he was helping this man—this tweaker —who had been chasing him not thirty seconds back. He should let the piece of shit rot.

And yet, it was the right thing to do. Hell, he'd been low in his own life and done questionable things. Maybe this could be the second chance these kids needed.

Franklin was at the bottom when it happened: another scream from inside the mound, followed by an odd flicker of light. Purple and oily and growing.

Melted chairs and sharp metal, loose bricks and dirt. They all fell as the hole yawned wide, wider, swallowing G-dog and Shawn.

Loose rocks rolled to his feet as a wave of dust hit his stunned cheeks. For a moment, the only sounds were the settling of earth and debris, all that burned lumber and metal moaning in the night.

Then came the cries of anguish, now a chorus.

Franklin climbed over the wreckage where the hole had become a cavernous mouth. Tim-Tam's broken arm jutted out beneath a slab of concrete, fingers twitching. The poor bastard was crushed.

G-dog was pinned between a dirty oven and a utility pole, mud dripping down his panicked face.

And Shawn—the luckiest of the three—simply lay near an exposed tunnel that descended deeper into the mound.

A tunnel pulsing with impossible shadows and light.

Franklin froze, unsure of what he was seeing. First, a thin, wispy figure bloomed from the dark passage. Sinuous fingers rose, like heat from a candle. Then two burning eyes opened over a face of swirling flames. A mouth lined with embers twisted in a grin.

Body locked, Franklin stared as the *thing*—a young man of fire— seized upon Shawn. Its searing grip sent up sparks and ignited the tweaker's jacket. In a whirl of cinders and smoke, it dragged Shawn backward, howling and burning, into the flickering depths.

"Help me, please!" G-dog screamed. "My leg, it's stuck."

No, it wasn't stuck, Franklin realized. At least not in the rubble.

An arm—a long, muddy arm with too many joints—stretched out from the damp earth and coiled around G-dog's waist. Yellowed pebbles sprouted from its hand. Teeth, Franklin realized. Those were rotten teeth.

As G-dog screamed, those dirty fingers groped their way to his lips and squirmed inside. G-dog's eyes bulged, two quivering moons that grew wider, wider. Then another muddy arm embraced G-dog. Loamy fingers and clicking teeth caressed his hair and covered his eyes, pulling him back into the flickering tunnel.

Slack-jawed and numb, Franklin stared at the rubble as a tendril of bizarre light rose skyward. With a flicker, black-violet carved a path through the winter clouds. In that momentary parting, something looked back.

Eyes in the sky.

Eyes rimmed with undulous flesh and canyons of fangs. Eyes, his mind told him, that he was never meant to behold.

Franklin might have stood there forever, waiting for the creatures of fire and mud to return. To drag him into their burrow. But it was Scout's yips that mended his madness. She was looking at him, letting him know it was time to go.

As Franklin blinked, those eyes in the sky winked back and faded, one by one. He squeezed Scout in his shivering arms, kissed her head gratefully. He put one foot before the other and took off, running into the night.

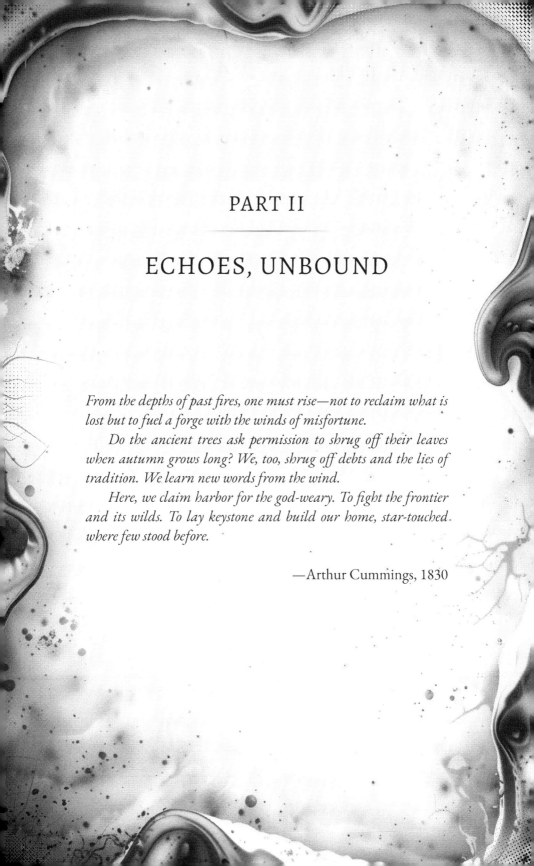

PART II

ECHOES, UNBOUND

From the depths of past fires, one must rise—not to reclaim what is lost but to fuel a forge with the winds of misfortune.

Do the ancient trees ask permission to shrug off their leaves when autumn grows long? We, too, shrug off debts and the lies of tradition. We learn new words from the wind.

Here, we claim harbor for the god-weary. To fight the frontier and its wilds. To lay keystone and build our home, star-touched where few stood before.

—Arthur Cummings, 1830

9

Ben Thomas held a shaking chisel in one hand and a hammer in the other when he realized he had no idea what he was doing. He took a step back, and then another. With each blink, the world came into focus.

This narrow room, cozy and oddly shaped.

The gray wall before him, textures rough and curved.

The briny air tickling his nose with each nervous breath.

Then a second fear replaced the first: he didn't know where he was.

His arms fell limp to his sides as his gaze swept the shapes chiseled into the plaster. Letters that spelled out two simple words.

"I can," he read aloud. "I can."

His words echoed in the damp air. *I can... I can...*

He turned to find the innermost wall forming something of a half donut where a rigid door stood in the center. The outer wall held a conical taper, suggesting some towering structure above and beyond. A wide rectangular window within, shuttered on the inside.

Where the hell was he and what was he doing?

Think, he told himself. *You're a physicist. You solve problems all the time. Okay, what do we know?*

He paced the room. This was some sort of workshop. Yes, there were hammers and pliers, wrenches and screwdrivers. A shelf of spare light-bulbs like the ones glowing overhead. Wires and rope hung from hooks, labeled and spooled. There was even a workbench where a bottle of wine sat, corked and dark.

New hypothesis: had he been drinking? It wouldn't have been the first time his mind spliced the tape.

He ran his thumb over the bottle's label, hoping to stir up a memory. The old, scabby paper flaked away at his touch. Whatever words it once held had long faded. No memory emerged.

And yet there was an odd heft to the bottle, the glass dark and thick. A curious indent marred the bottom, and he remembered something from a glassblowing elective he'd taken in undergrad.

That was a pontil scar.

Strange. Wine bottles hadn't been made using pontil rods in nearly a century.

He gave the cork a gentle pull, but it crumbled in his fingers, sand-like and brittle. The bottle's stench hit him: putrid mildew and vinegar, acidic rot and soured eggs. It all filled his nose and assaulted his senses. It drove him backward.

Gagging, he searched for something, anything, to clear the foul air.

The window.

He opened the shutters, noting how his fingers understood which latches to lift and which bolts to slide. As the hinges groaned and the shutters swung open, vertigo wobbled his legs. He was high up.

A sparkling dark sea spread out before him. There were distant white caps rising and falling. Swirling tendrils of fog that danced in the breeze. Starlight flirted with an inky surface, hinting at abyssal depths. A horizonless view, so clear his mind simply locked up. He stood, awestruck, beholding the sea from this rocky shoal, beautiful and terri-fying and infinite.

And most of all: familiar.

Yes, he knew this view just like he knew that the door behind him would lead to stairs spiraling both downward and up. There were metal posts lining the steps—a railing? Something about that word curled his fingers.

And at the top of the stairs?

A chill bristled his neck and glassy shards rattled behind his eyes. Somehow, the room felt a little brighter.

Lighter.

Lighthouse, yes. He sensed that's where he was. A structure built for nautical warnings and navigation.

And yet...

A flame sparkled far below, warm and orange and drifting across the calm waters. Then another flame. And another.

He wiped the window and pressed his face to the glass. That was some sort of rowboat down there. Dark shapes paddled through the starlit waves.

Why the hell were they holding lanterns?

A low rumble shook the room and rattled his bladder. Something felt more as a vibration and a battering of stone and wood. The lights blinked only once.

Then the room fell to darkness.

Ben stumbled through the shadows, fingers sweeping and brushing against objects. There had to be a flashlight somewhere. Then his knee struck something heavy, and the workbench wobbled. A second later, the bottle cracked and burst on the floor.

The stench of rotten wine returned, acrid and twisting his senses. Gagging, he stumbled through the foul shadows guided only by the dim stars from that window. He needed to get out, fast. His fingers found the door, and again they worked on instinct. A twist of the odd handle, then the door opened. He rushed forth as fresh air filled his heaving, grateful lungs.

He didn't see the railing in the darkness, but his body knew as they collided. His hands found the balusters, catching his balance. Another few inches, and he might have gone over.

He teetered, his echoing moan revealing the dark shaft. His eyes drew shapes from the shadows: steps and landings all spiraling down, an entryway where a door whistled with wind.

That door.

Why did he feel like he'd been through it before? Not once or dozens but *thousands* of times.

A boom shook his bones and rattled his teeth. Far below, a glow brightened beyond the door, sending orange rays through the cracks. Window by window, the flicker rose, golden fingers probing the stairs as a hazy tang filled the air: smoke.

Ben raced down the stairs, not sure why he was counting the landings and the steps in between. Only that the number fifteen felt pleasant to his mind.

He reached the foyer, the main door, and unlocked the heavy mechanisms that kept it shut. The breeze hit him.

A *hot* breeze.

Point Greywood was a scraggy patch of land, more boulder and wind-sculpted weeds than stable earth. The shoal felt like it could collapse at any moment. That the world might shrug and the sea would swallow it up, tide pools and rocks and all living things upon it.

But not the lighthouse.

There was strength to the structure. A tower, defiant in the face of nature itself. Lichen bloomed across its surface in patches. Moss hung from ventilation grilles. Shorebird nests dotted occasional sills and window ledges, sun-bleached branches cobwebbed and forgotten. And yet as he took in the lighthouse's size, he swore it was too small. The rooms inside seemed much larger than the outside.

A third boom and flash drew his attention beyond the tower, and his jaw fell open. "What the..."

A ship—a massive old schooner with canvas sails and wooden masts —tilted and rocked in the dark waters. Flames crawled their way up ropes and chewed through the sails. Embers swirled in the warm breeze. The entire deck was subsumed, long planks cracking open and belching black smoke.

And the people...

Ben estimated the ship was a quarter mile offshore. Yet their screams carried over the water and filled the smoky air. Scrambling bodies leaped from the decks. Others banged at portholes, desperate hands backlit by flames. A floating furnace burning to pieces over placid waters.

What the hell was such an old vessel doing here? Was there a festival for tall ships? And where were the flares and the Coast Guard?

Ben's eyes rose from the base of the lighthouse to the lantern room high atop.

When had the beam turned such a sick shade of purple?

Another shuddering rumble, low and subsonic, shifted rocks and reeds. That wasn't an explosion, he realized. It was something deeper. As if the lighthouse was drawing the world closer.

Swallowing.

No. No one was coming because no one had been called. He needed to find help.

The radio room.

As he raced to the lighthouse, an explosion tore the schooner in half. A glance back as the hot wind hit his face: hellish flames in oily waters, shrieking figures among the wreckage. In an echoing crack, one of the masts collapsed.

And that light—that sickly beam that swept over the sea—it *brightened* with each scream.

Dark ribbons unraveled from the deep purple. Sinuous tendrils unfurled from the beam's edges. No light could behave in such a manner; he knew this. It defied the very laws of physics.

He needed to get help. He needed to get away from this place.

Inside, that same sickly glow bathed the stairs. High above, the lantern room dripped shimmering darkness. Not a light but a liquid. Pouring. Oozing. Crawling down one step at a time.

He could have stared at it forever, mesmerized and marveling. Hadn't he come here to study such bizarre wonders?

But the ship, the people. The radio room, right.

He raced up the stairs, wondering, had he used the radio before? He must have, yet he couldn't remember when.

Before the radio room, he stole a glance upward. He wished he never had.

Because he was no longer looking up the shaft of a lighthouse but into a living throat. Meaty bones and curling tentacles replaced the railings and steps. Bricks drifted outward, revealing a membrane beneath, translucent and living, suckling and hungry.

Something that—*impossibly*—was devouring reality itself.

Ben slammed the radio room door shut. His shaking fingers squeezed the transmitter as he flipped switches, aware that he must have done this before, so many times.

He raised the microphone and spoke.

"Base, this is Point Greywood. Do you copy? Point Greywood to base. Over."

The response came at once, so clear he dropped the mic and fell back.

Chanting. Screaming. Sailors crying out. Voices shrieking across some infinite sea and right into his mind.

Their screams were in the wind and the waves. Carried in the salty air that he breathed. And he saw the letters on the wall now, chiseled in again and again. They filled the radio room, forming words that he knew.

I CAN
I CAN'T
I CANNOT LEAVE

Then it came: the grotesque light at the radio room's door. It bloomed inward, pouring over the walls and crawling across the ceiling. It stretched out lusty fingers of shadow. It delighted at his presence.

Most of all, it delighted at the chorus of screams. A chorus he was now leading.

It crested and washed over him, around him, and surged into him.

And like the ocean itself, it contained deep trenches squirming with life, alien and hungry.

10

D r. Rhonda St. James gave the clock on the wall a quick glance: 10:45, time to start wrapping up. As a therapist, she tried not to rush her patients. She trusted their stories would eventually connect. But as a type 2 diabetic in her early sixties, she was damn hungry. The granola and yogurt for breakfast had done little to hold her over.

So here she sat, trying to keep her mind from drifting to the Greek salad in the mini fridge while her patient beat around the bush. Teenagers. Sometimes it took the whole session to extract a few words.

Still, she liked the girl on the couch. There was something about her, a unique sort of *belle âme*, if one believed in such things.

And yet, after five months, she knew Zelda was holding back.

"I understand there was an incident at the wrestling match," Rhonda said. "And then something with an older man later that night?"

The black leather crinkled as Zelda shifted on the couch. "Uncle Mark told you that?"

"You know I can't discuss other patients." Even though Zelda wasn't looking at her, Rhonda smiled. It made her voice sound different. "But you're a smart girl. Care to talk about it?"

"Yeah, I think I'd rather eat glass."

"Fair enough. Feelings can be... difficult."

She clicked her pen so Zelda could see her put it away. Of course, she didn't always talk like this, but with clammy adolescents, techniques had to be applied, certain words used. It put them on the back foot. It *implied* things.

"Feelings," Zelda scoffed. "I'm not..."

"Not what?"

"It was nothing. The wrestling match, I mean. I just get scared in tight spaces."

Zelda pulled her feet up onto the couch and fidgeted with a pillow. Sometimes it was like prying a person from quicksand. The more Rhonda reached out and tried to connect, the deeper they sank.

"Forget it," Zelda said.

"Very well." Rhonda glanced at her notes. "But before we go, I wanted to touch on your grandparents."

Zelda stiffened. "What about them?"

Interesting. That was more of a reaction than she'd shown all session. "It's my understanding they'll be staying for Christmas. Are you looking forward to that?"

Zelda shrugged. "I don't know."

"You don't know," she repeated. "Well, family emotions are often conflicting, so that's a perfectly healthy response. Especially at your age. But, Zelda, you're not giving me much to work with. Want to toss me a softball so we can run out the clock?"

Zelda's eyes drifted to the coffee table and the objects Rhonda kept upon it. There were Slinkies, Silly Putty, a few magazines on art and music and urban design. Some of her patients found them calming and reached for them often.

Zelda did not.

Still, something softened beneath her face. "My grandparents. So, like, on the one hand, my *lito* is super sweet—"

"Your *lito*?"

"*Abuelito.* My grandpa. But on the other hand, my *abuela*—that's my grandma—she's... not. Like, she has super specific things that girls should or shouldn't do. She'll probably get me a long dress for

Christmas with, like, a doily around the neck. Or another bible. Or a dress with bible verses on it. We'll definitely go to church."

"I'm sensing a pattern. And you're not religious?"

"Not that kind. I mean, there's definitely something out there. It's just..."

She hesitated again. Maybe she thought she'd said too much. And yet her words tickled Rhonda's therapist senses.

There's definitely something out there.

That wasn't a phrase teenagers said very often. Not around here.

And with such conviction.

"Anyway, my grandmother," Zelda continued. "She used to call me things, like *machorra* or *marimacho* and—"

"Mary Macho?"

"Marimacho. It's like..." Zelda waved her hands. "Tomboy or butch or whatever, but not in a good way."

"Zelda, that's awful." Rhonda leaned in. "I'm sorry you had to deal with that. And your parents, did they know about this?"

Of course, she knew about Zelda's parents and the accident. The court had sent her a full briefing. Still, the subject was slippery, and Zelda often found ways to avoid bringing them up.

"My mom thought it was, like, a cute nickname or whatever. But my dad, when he heard it, oh man." She smiled and looked down at her ripped jeans. "He let my grandma have it, both barrels and all. It was pretty cool."

"Good," Dr. Rhonda said. "Good for him. Standing up to those you're closest to can be scary."

Zelda's gaze shifted to a painting hanging on the wall, some abstract landscape of pastels chosen for its calming qualities. She seemed anything but calm.

As she swung her legs over the carpet, Rhonda saw it all: the scared girl on the cusp of womanhood, the facade of indifference she armored herself in. But there was something else, wasn't there? Something chewing her up from the inside.

Her therapist instincts were lighting up now, a real storm. If she could just tease it out, maybe they could make some progress.

"Zelda, are you worried that without your parents around, no one will stick up for you?"

The girl met her gaze. No, that wasn't it, Rhonda realized. The secret was something deeper, something now receding like a spooked creature in the woods. Darn, she'd spoken too soon.

Zelda smiled. "No, I know Uncle Mark's got my back." Then she glanced at the clock high on the wall. "Looks like we're out of time."

Rhonda escorted her patient to the waiting room, where Mr. Fitzsimmons sat, a red pen dancing between his fingers as he graded essays. As usual, he stood to greet her.

"My turn for the old emotional tune-up, Doc?"

She smiled and opened the door. "I'll be with you in a moment, Mr. Fitzsimmons."

"Great," he said. "And I'll see you at the town hall?"

It took her a second to realize he was talking to his niece. "Right," Zelda said. "Five o'clock. City hall."

"Big white building, police station inside. I think we've seen it a few times." He headed into the office. From inside, he called out, "Doc, you mind if I play with some inkblot cards?"

"I don't have Rorschach tests, Mr. Fitzsimmons." She gave Zelda a wink. "But help yourself to the Silly Putty and stress balls."

Out in the hall, Zelda went left and Rhonda went right. Why did she always have a warm tingle when she saw these two patients? Like a familiar song had started up, yet she'd forgotten the words. Like the air took on a charge.

She shook it off and entered the building's shared kitchenette. She fished her Greek salad from the fridge. For a few minutes, she speared cucumbers and olives with her fork, savoring each bite.

She was grateful Mr. Fitzsimmons didn't pester her for information, as some parents did. What had their child said in the session? Were they okay in the head? Assuming she would trade the trust it took months to build for some on-the-spot analysis.

And, if she was being honest, the problems rarely began with the kids. One more fact the parents footing the bill never enjoyed hearing.

She swallowed the last bite of salad and washed the Tupperware in the sink. She checked her teeth in the mirror. A warbler landed outside the window behind her. She watched it hop on the tree branch, wings making weird circles as it pecked at its feathers.

Because something was tangled around the poor bird. Dark twine or thin strands of kelp.

No, she realized, not tangled but growing out from beneath its feathers like a mold. Oily roots and dendritic growths beaded with eyes.

No, that couldn't be...

Stomach souring, she watched the warbler spook and take off. It joined others in flight. Twisting and turning, rising and diving. One shape among hundreds now, the late morning light sheening on their sickly feathers as they flew into the haze.

11

O n the second Wednesday of December, the bells of Neumann Prep rang for the final time of the year. Teachers rushed to clarify holiday assignments. Students did their best to ignore them. And in room 212—the freshman bio classroom—a guest lecturer with an Irish accent struggled to wrap up his presentation.

"So, bottom line," McDermott said. "You want a career in the sciences? You need a hungry mind and a wolfhound's nose. Always be curious, and always be hunting for funding. Questions?"

Elliot's hand shot up. "So, can we go?"

Mr. Fitch, a man with broad shoulders and piercing eyes, sighed. "Not until we all give Dr. McDermott a round of applause for—"

The applause came quick and loud and ended even faster. Then the students were on their feet, rushing the door as a buzz grew in the hall. The slamming of lockers and laughter. The occasional whoop of excitement.

"Afraid we can't compete with vacation," Mr. Fitch told McDermott. "But thanks for trying."

In the rear, near a poster of Einstein sticking out his tongue, Zelda zipped up her backpack and shuffled to the door. A few students mumbled their goodbyes and hurried off.

"Hey, Zelda, hold up." Mr. Fitch's eyes always seemed to find her whenever she was trying to be unseen. "Got a moment?"

She nodded, sensing what was coming.

While McDermott left, Mr. Fitch straightened his desk and gathered papers. "Can I expect your report on the first day back?"

"Promise."

"Good." He zipped up his bag. "So, first semester down, how are we feeling?"

She ran her thumbs along her backpack straps. "Fine."

"Fine," he repeated. "I should ask more open-ended questions. Let's try it again, say, five words or more."

"I could have done better."

"Wow, right on the money. Impressive."

She glanced at the door, where two boys ran down the hall, pulling a third on a scooter. Tossed papers curled in the air behind them. A moment later, Coach Howard's whistle pierced the laughter and everyone scattered.

"Look, your uncle's a good guy, and I promised him I'd keep an eye on you. Let him know if you needed any extra help. So... what I'm trying to say is—"

"You have to tell him I'm bombing your class."

Mr. Fitch tilted his head. "You're not bombing it, not yet. But we both know you've got more potential than a C-minus, right?"

The P-word: potential. She really hated that one. Teachers had been using it a lot lately. She was smarter than this, they said. She could do better. They threw "potential" around like it was some secret key.

But the word did nothing to silence the cold whispers in her ear. J'harr murmuring at all the worst moments. Taunting her at the edge of her vision. Changing things no one else in the classroom could see.

Like the Einstein poster, now winking at her with cindering eyes and a tongue blackened and blistered.

"I'd roll my eyes, too," Mr. Fitch said. "Nothing worse than some old fart talking about potential."

"Sorry, I didn't mean to—"

"Relax. I was your age once, and teachers were about the lamest thing ever; I get it." He pointed to her skateboard, a Powell Peralta with the iconic Andy Anderson skull and helmet on the deck. "But I was more of a Tony Hawk guy myself."

She almost smiled but managed to hide it. "First one to land a 900."

"Yeah, he was." Mr. Fitch shut down the computer and raised the projector screen. "I saw the X Games in... '98, I think."

"Ninety-nine," she said.

"Right. Ancient history. So what are you working on? Kickflip?"

"Hardflip."

"Seriously?" He nodded, impressed. "That's a tough one."

"Gui Khury landed a 1080 at twelve with only a vert ramp, so..." She shrugged.

"Well, you'll get there, too. And hey, look at me. If you can master a kickflip, you can memorize Mendel and his fruit flies. Got it?"

She glanced at him, then scratched at a sticker on her board. She didn't have the heart to tell him Einstein's skin was bubbling and peeling.

"Alright, enough. Get out of here. Go practice your tricks. And remember what I said about the eclipse—"

"Don't look right at it, or you'll fry out your eyes."

"See you next year." She cringed inwardly. It was the same joke half the teachers said. She liked Mr. Fitch but often felt like she was being inspected. Like everyone knew her sad story and was checking her for cracks.

Or maybe it was like Uncle Mark liked to remind her: there were good people here in this town. People that cared.

Even if they forgot the bad things that happened.

OUTSIDE, STUDENTS STREAMED PAST ZELDA, CHARGED BY the final bell and the freedom it promised. Some rushed by in groups while others pedaled off alone on their bikes or buzzed along on electric scooters. Down the street, upperclassmen lingered by their cars, Range Rovers and BMWs and the occasional EV. Shiny reminders that Neumann Prep was a far cry from her old public school.

She hopped on her skateboard, wondering if she'd get a car at sixteen. Her parents had left her money; this much she knew. But the topic was confusing, spoken of quietly and handled by lawyers. What she did get was deposited biweekly into her debit card. The thought of driving felt so far away.

She found Ali and Maura past the senior lawn at the edge of campus, Ali pushing his bike while Maura walked hers beside him. She wore a sheepish look, like she was trying to make herself smaller.

"Yo, Z-dabs," Ali said. "What's the haps?"

Zelda studied the curious lean to his bike. "What's the haps with your wheels?"

"Oh, nothing. Someone accidentally let the air out of both of my tires."

"Yeah, 'accidentally.'" Maura gave Zelda a glance that said it all. "At least he's no longer getting stuffed into lockers."

"That stuffing has always been consensual."

Maura mouthed, *No, it hasn't.*

Wheels creaking, Ali shoved his bike onto the sidewalk. They were too slow to skateboard alongside, so Zelda walked with them, the breeze cool on her skin. It seemed like the whole town smelled like the ocean in winter.

"Yo, Ali!" Elliot biked up beside them, grinning. "Dude, that bike's flatter than your mom!"

"Knave!" Ali shouted. "I bite my thumb at thee!"

Elliot scrunched his face like he'd bitten something foul. "What are you on? Fucking weirdo." He pedaled off.

"Jesus, Ali," Maura muttered. "Could you be any more cringe?"

"Am I the only one that actually read *Romeo and Juliet*?" he said. "Biting your thumb is, like, super insulting. It's basically the middle finger. People have died over it."

"Like, back in the Stone Age."

"If you think Shakespeare was from the Stone Age, I pity you. Our education system has truly failed."

"Pity your shoulder." She gave him a solid thump that sent his hand to his triceps and made his bike wobble.

On most days their banter might have amused Zelda. Today, she barely noticed it. A group of odd birds fluttered between the trees, their wings shimmering in the cool light. She tried not to think of the poster of Einstein. Or the painting in Dr. Rhonda's office, and how it dripped past the frame. She just wanted a normal day. Was that too much to ask?

Her gaze fell to a group of upperclassmen lingering outside the baseball diamond, cars idling and music blasting. Her throat tightened.

"What's she doing here?" Zelda whispered.

"Who?" Ali asked. "There's like a dozen of 'em."

"Arianna," she said.

"Bayview got out last week," Maura said. "Plus, she's dating Finn from the soccer team."

"Eww, that junior?" Ali asked. "Why's he gotta poach girls from our grade?"

"Okay, first off, women aren't pheasants waiting to get poached— we have agency, right?" Maura held out her fist and Zelda bumped her knuckles. "Plus, he's cute AF."

"There it is," Ali said. "Pretty boy Finn cradle-robs freshmen, and he's an ally. But I hang out on the playground and I'm weird."

Maura ignored him. "And second, my dad's like eight years older than my mom; it's not weird."

"Yeah, totally normal in Shakespeare's day." He bit his thumb and dodged another punch.

As they drew closer, the bass of the upperclassmen's music drowned their conversation. Zelda shushed Ali, hoping they'd blend in with the other students. Just three freshmen on their way home.

She thought of Chester and the All, wondering if she could move through it like vapor. If she could avoid them all. At the thought, her fingers traced little circles and the world's volume grew distant.

"Mmm... a knock at my door. Be careful what answers."

Then Zelda blinked and Ali was standing by the cars—they all were —and he was saying, "Well, if you don't like charging, then why'd you get an EV?"

The upperclassman by the Tesla—Sam, Zelda remembered from some half-forgotten conversation—curled an eyebrow at Ali and said, "Bro, I'm sixteen. My parents just bought what was safest."

Cheeks flushed, Maura chuckled a little too loud. "Ignore him. It's his first day on earth."

"We should go," Zelda muttered.

Six pairs of eyes turned toward her. It was as if they hadn't noticed Zelda's presence until the sound left her lips. Here they were: guys on the cusp of adulthood, girls trying to look older and fashionable. Tina Jimenez from the volleyball team, and Sherri-Ann, who did a report on how European beaches were all topless.

And there was Arianna, on the other side of the Tesla, her hand playfully tugging at the zipper on Finn's hoodie.

Until she saw Zelda.

"Holy shit." Recognition flashed in Arianna's eyes. "Did you break out of your cage or do you always walk around without a rabies tag?"

A few confused chuckles from the upperclassmen and a scowl from Sam. They didn't quite understand her bitter words. Then:

"That crazy bitch gave me this." Arianna pulled down her sleeve, where a Band-Aid marred her forearm. "I almost had to get stitches."

Zelda felt herself folding and shrinking inward. She wanted to back into the bushes like that meme. But they were all looking at her and no one was speaking.

She swallowed and forced the words out. "I'm really sorry about what happened. I—"

"Yeah, you should be," Arianna said. "For real, who bites someone?"

Finn and Sam, Ali and Maura, all the others stared at the two girls. There was no going back.

"I didn't mean to," Zelda said. "It's just... I was in a car accident, and tight spaces... Look, you've got a killer arm bar and I really suck at wrestling. I sort of freaked out."

"You think?"

Zelda glanced at her shoes. Suddenly, the mismatched Chuck Taylors didn't seem so ironic and cool after all. And her jeans with the hole, the one she'd carefully scuffed with a cheese grater. God, was she a tryhard? Could everyone see right through her?

She said, "Anyway, I'm really sorry."

"Not yet... Not sorry enough... But one day..."

Sam brushed a curly lock of hair from his face and studied her, really seeing her for the first time. "Wait, you're that girl from the fire. Your dad made that game."

"She's a pretty big deal," Ali said. "Not Taylor Swift famous, but definitely above C-list."

Maura and Zelda both elbowed him at the same time.

Finn leaned close to Arianna, his dimpled cheeks moving smoothly as he whispered. It seemed so odd, Zelda thought, that someone only two grades ahead could look so much older. Move confidently and smooth. Like he glided over the world instead of stumbling through it.

Arianna's face softened as she nodded. "Yeah, you're right." She turned her gaze back to Zelda. "You know what? Don't worry about it, okay? For real, it's no biggie, sis."

Just like that, she waved it off.

Zelda studied Arianna, envious of how mature a little makeup and some tight clothes made her look. They were in the same weight class, both leggy and starting to fill out. And yet, Arianna was proud of her shape, comfortable and confident. Maybe Zelda could learn a thing or two from her.

Arianna raised a thin eyebrow. "So, like, do you guys party?"

"Hell yeah," Ali said. "My D&D campaigns are *epic*."

"He's joking," Maura said. "But yeah, we party. Like... big time."

"See?" Finn nudged Arianna. "Told you they were cool."

"And you know where Bottle Beach is, right?" Arianna asked.

"Mmm-hmm." Maura nodded.

"Fo' sho." Ali chuckled. "Who doesn't?"

Zelda caught herself before she shook her head. Wherever this beach was, she sensed it was some sort of test.

"Cool," Arianna said. "My brother's throwing a party Friday night. Bonfire, kegs, that kind of thing. You guys should come."

Again, it struck Zelda how casual Arianna said all this. A party. Kegs. Like these words were familiar and well-practiced.

"That'd be fun," Maura said. "I mean, I think we're probably free."

"Unless you're planning to turn us into vampires," Ali said. "'Cause I've seen that movie and I'm not falling for the old blood in the wine bottle switcheroo."

"You're funny," Sherri-Ann said and brushed something off Ali's shoulder. "Funny boy's pretty cute."

Ali blinked, face frozen in a grin. "He gets stuck buffering," Maura said and took him by the elbow. "Bottle Beach, kegs, Friday night. See you there."

They walked off, Ali pushing his bike, the flat tires creaking and clanking as Maura and Zelda did their best not to look back. The seconds stretched on and on.

When they passed the fire station and took a right at the hedges, Zelda finally said, "So, they're probably going to mess with us, aren't they?"

"Yeah, probably," Maura said. "But a party's a party. Now, does anyone actually know where Bottle Beach is?"

12

M ark gave the notecards a quick check before glancing back at the audience. There were the Montroses and the Kims, Pavarti and Mr. Weiland. The Taumalolo family and all their relatives took up nearly a whole row. All in all, nearly a hundred Raven's Valley homeowners filled out the chamber seats. And his students as well, twelve juniors and a few seniors from his entrepreneurship elective.

But the one person Mark needed most was a no-show.

At the podium in front of him, Mr. Abernathy mumbled into the microphone, berating the city council on their failure to take the exploding raccoon population seriously. Mark checked his watch: 5:27.

Damn, he really could have used Zelda's support. She was the reason so many people survived. Well, her and old Chester and those illegal tunnels under his house.

As grateful as Mark was for Mr. Halgrove, the man's verbal skills left something to be desired. Mark had stressed to his students that a core tenet of rhetoric was aligning the audience with your goal. Tonight, that goal was convincing the city council to fast-track permits for new homes.

"And that's to say nothing about the danger of their scat!" Mr.

Abernathy tapped the podium. "The average coon pellet harbors thousands of eggs that end up in our parks, our drinking water, even our stomachs. I know what you're thinking: raccoons might be cute. But there's nothing cute about roundworm. We need to judiciously—"

A sigh from the dais. "Thank you, Mr. Abernathy, but we're short on time as it is." That was Councilman Brand, a heavyset man in his sixties who looked like he'd rather be golfing. He motioned to the podium. "I believe Mr. Fitzgerald is next."

"Fitzsimmons," Mark corrected, waiting for Mr. Abernathy to shuffle off. With the podium clear, he pulled the microphone close. "Thank you, Councilman, Vice-Mayor, members of the planning committee. I appreciate you hearing us out today—"

A cough echoed out. He glanced back to see several people lined up behind him. And at the very back stood a woman in her seventies. Her hair was the first thing he noticed. A silver and brown bob cut, long in the front and fluffed up with spray, crowned her *Bless Your Heart* gaze. Pearl earrings glinted, bright as her teeth.

Mark's train of thought came to a halt. What was he saying? His notecards, right.

"The Raven's Valley fire didn't just darken the air; it displaced hundreds of families," he continued. "Business owners and health care providers. Sanitation workers that keep our town clean. Retirees hoping to live near their grandkids and take them to playgrounds. Even teachers, like myself or Ms. Layne over there."

He glanced at Stacey, who gave him a slight smile and a nod. It wasn't much, but it was enough to help him find his voice in the chamber.

"We lost more than just property. We lost our roots, our connection to the community. Some have lived here for years, while others—like me—are new to this town, but all of us have two things in common. We love Greywood Bay; we consider it home. But now we're scattered, living in apartments or Airbnbs. Listening to meeting after meeting passing blame. Watching lawyers rack up billable hours. Stuck in limbo while real solutions are kicked down the road. We've talked a lot, but talking doesn't put roofs over our heads. Actions do. The council can take action and—"

Another dry cough behind him. He glanced back, and there was that woman smiling her flat smile and waiting in line, much closer now. Several others before her were returning to their seats.

"Thank you, Mr. Fitzhugh," Councilman Brand said. "But I think your time is 'bout up."

Mark leaned into the microphone. "I'm almost finished—"

"Mr. Fitzhugh, sir—"

He ignored the councilman and plowed on, flipping to the last of his cards. "Each of you can approve the emergency ordinance. Two hundred and twenty-two permits, just like the homes that were lost. Councilman Brand, Vice-Mayor Barton..." He went on down the dais, addressing each of the members by name. "Your vote holds the power to heal our community. After all we've been through, doesn't everyone deserve a place to call home?"

The applause came fast and loud as he stepped back from the podium. Pavarti and Stacey, the Montroses and the Kims. Half the audience rose to their feet. One of his students even cupped his hands, shouting, "Fucking A, teach! You tell 'em!"

Smiling inwardly, Mark returned to his seat just as Zelda slipped in through a side door. He tried not to shoot her a disappointed look, but he could have used her five minutes ago.

As he sat, Stacey whispered, "Of course Bibi has to get the last word in."

Barbara Boyle—Bibi to the locals—waited at the podium with the white blazer and flat smile until the last set of hands stopped clapping.

Yeah, Mark had heard of Bibi. She co-owned an art gallery downtown that sold paintings in the style of Thomas Kinkade. Supposedly, she wrote books. She always seemed to be hosting a fundraiser for the birds or the seals at her family's vineyard. And lately, he'd seen her name on flyers and emails, opposing every measure for new construction.

With a squeak of the gooseneck, Bibi pulled the microphone close. She looked right at Mark and said three words. "No, they don't."

Silence hung in the chamber as hundreds of eyes blinked in confusion.

"Now I know that may come as a shock to some of the younger crowd in this room," she continued. "But no, not everyone deserves a home. Property is not a legal right. Homes are not guaranteed by our town's charter. Last I checked, we're all part of the free market. But being a part of Greywood Bay, that is a privilege. One that I fear many of us have forgotten."

Her bracelet glinted as she tapped her heart. This woman, Mark had to admit, she was well-versed in theatrics.

"We've built something here," she continued. "Something special and unique. And something delicate, too. We lose a little bit with each new Starbucks. Every tour bus chips away at our charm. All those houses rubber-stamped in the name of equity or inclusion or... whatever it is the young folks choose to call it."

Warmth spread up Mark's back and tightened his shoulders. He was forty-three. This was the first time someone had called him young in a decade. He'd almost forgotten how frustrating it was to have his opinion written off due to age.

"Friendly fascism," Stacey whispered and squeezed his hand. "Some people spend their whole lives climbing up ladders, then smile while kicking them down."

"As president of the Greywood Bay Historical Society," Bibi continued, "I speak for our members when I say we oppose any new construction. The fire was a tragedy, yes, but one ignited by greed. We need only to look at our own noble redwoods for guidance. When a forest grows too fast, what happens? It becomes crowded and weak. Eventually, it burns. That's nature's way of restoring balance."

"My neighbor died in that fire!" shouted Mr. Fox, the former head of Raven's Valley security. "You think that's balance, you leathery old bitch?"

Someone else stood up and shouted back. "Why do homeowners get handouts when the farmers are rationing water?"

Within seconds, a dozen voices argued and cursed, pointing at each other and shoving. As the council members begged for decorum, the vice-mayor slammed her gavel. "Order. Order, please!"

All the while, Bibi stood there, taking in the chaos with that sanguine, flat smile.

"And that's all, folks," Stacey said. "Another meeting where nothing gets done. We gave it our best."

Squeezing through the crowd, Mark joined Zelda near the back and they slipped out of the chamber together. As they made their way through the lobby, a familiar woman with dark hair and a blazer crossed their path. His heart rate doubled on reflex.

"Detective Brown," he said.

"Mr. Fitzsimmons." Debra Brown offered them as friendly a smile as a detective could give. "Evening, Zelda. Staying out of trouble, I hope?"

Zelda returned a meek nod. After a few run-ins this summer, they had last met with the detective on a hot August afternoon, two weeks after the Raven's Valley fire. She had questioned Zelda about how they escaped the inferno. Zelda claimed she wasn't sure; it was all a blur. Mark had never quite believed her, but he knew enough to keep his mouth shut.

They never charged Zelda or her friends with trespassing, either on Chester's property—which was remarkably unburnt—or at the hospital, which was packed with the injured. For a few weeks, she was a hero. According to their lawyers, the optics would have been awful.

"I'm glad to hear that," Detective Brown said. "After this meeting, I don't think our riot squad is ready for callout."

Mark wasn't sure if that was a joke or not, but he smiled and nodded. Thankfully, a policeman hurried over, whispering something into her ear that brought a scowl to her face.

"Duty calls," she said. "Good luck with the council. You've got my support."

She followed the policeman away, Mark's heart settling with each step. Still, frustration spiked his blood and tensed his jaw. He glared at Zelda. "Seriously, where the hell were you? You were supposed to be here."

"Sorry," she said. "I lost track of time."

"Unbelievable. What was the one thing I asked at Dr. Rhonda's?"

"I said I'm sorry."

"And you also said you'd be on time, so what good is your word?" The lobby whirled as he spoke. "We could have used you tonight. But I guess you lost track of time... or whatever."

Zelda stopped in her tracks, stunned and blinking. Even with the heated conversations around them, his sharp tone had carried across the lobby. He felt eyes upon them both.

Worse, Zelda flinched as she processed his words. First a glimmer of shock, then a flicker of pain.

She wasn't some homeowner dealing with insurance claims and loans.

She didn't have sets of lawyers fighting different legal battles and billing him biweekly.

She didn't know how low his bank account was, all the savings he'd drained, and the apartment in Madrid he was selling at a loss to keep them afloat.

How could she?

She was just a fourteen-year-old girl, here in her hoodie and jeans. Her biggest interests were music and memes. Her biggest worries were late assignments and what shitty rich kids wrote on social media.

And none of that excused what he'd said.

A deep breath. "Listen, that was incredibly rude of me—"

"I deserve it," she said.

"No, you don't and you didn't. I lost my cool and... It's just that you have a lot of social credibility, you know? Even a few words could have helped."

"I'm not your prop, Uncle Mark." She tugged at the thumbhole on her sleeve. "And you never asked me. Plus, I'm really not feeling crowds lately."

He thought back to their conversations. Damn, she was right. He'd just told her to be here at five, assuming they were both on the same page. He'd never asked.

He was echoing his mother's frustrations, a single parent some three decades back. He was fourteen, coming home after the streetlights turned on, wondering why she was mad. Back before iPhones and tracking apps. Back when the ten o'clock news reminded you to check in on your children. Just because the world was different now didn't mean kids had it easier.

It might even be the opposite.

So he inhaled and said something his mother rarely had. "You're absolutely right. I didn't ask. That was wrong of me, and I'm sorry. I hope you can forgive me."

She blinked. "No, it's... It's okay. I was late."

Maybe it was and maybe teenagers rebounded quick, but he still felt like he'd kicked a puppy.

My sweet Zelda, the protector, his sister's voice echoed. *They'll put maggots in her heart.*

"C'mere." Mark brought Zelda in close for a hug. That skinny body beneath the big hoody. Those stringy arms wrapping around him. "Your uncle's a big idiot, but he loves you. You know that, right?"

She nodded. And like most of her hugs, it was over too fast.

"That was quite the emotional roller coaster," Stacey said and opened the lobby door. "I might need a neck brace."

The night air hit them, moist and redolent of salt. Outside the vegan bakery, someone played "Jingle Bell Rock" on the accordion. The colorful lights of the wharf and the pier blinked as the Ferris wheel turned in the mist.

Mark asked, "Can I buy everyone's forgiveness with a churro and a hot chocolate?"

"Actually, I'm pretty sugared out," Zelda said. Her eyes shot down to her shoes as she asked, "But can I sleep over at Maura's on Friday?"

13

D etective Debra Brown's unmarked cruiser sped north along the coastal highway, the lights painting the fog and her instincts tingling. She liked Zelda Ruiz and her uncle Mark. She admired him for lighting a fire under the council's ass, so she wanted to catch up. And despite their first encounters, she nurtured a small crush on the guy.

Sure, she usually liked her men a little more put together, but Mark was friendly and well-meaning. And an outsider as well. At their ages, the pickings were slim.

But he was seeing that private school teacher; she had sussed it out from their body language in the lobby. Well, good for them.

Then came the call. Something about a transient out in county land. Something that didn't make any sense.

She thumbed the radio mic. "Dispatch, unit 12. I'm still waiting for the update. Please advise. Over."

"Sorry, unit 12. Details are still coming in." That was Barb running the radio tonight, her tempo never moving past a crawl. "Incident report includes a 10-54, 10-68, and a possible 187 out at Larchmont C&D. Be advised Fort Darrow PD is on scene and requesting assistance. Over."

"Copy that. Over."

Debra scanned the radio to Fort Darrow's police channel and listened in on the chatter. A 10-54 meant a dead body. A 10-68 meant it came in over the phone. And as rap music had taught her generation, a possible 187 meant a homicide.

So, something was really going down at the edge of Fort Darrow. No wonder the call kicked on over to her.

The town was hardly that, just a census-designated place with a few stoplights and enough sworn officers to be counted on one hand. And like West Pine and Greywood Bay, funding kept getting cut. Everyone seemed to hate the cops until they needed them. Recently, the three towns had signed a jurisdictional agreement to lighten the load.

Which meant here she was on her night off, parking at the graveled edge of Larchmont Construction & Demolition. Red and blue danced off a chain-link fence. Two cruisers idled by the gate.

Shivering, she met the deputy from West Pine, a baby-faced guy who introduced himself as Hansen. Inside the yard, the deputy from Fort Darrow handed out extra flashlights.

"Martinez, ma'am," the man said. "I took your workshop at county last spring. You probably don't remember me—"

"Crime scene procedure," she said. "You showed up prepared and asked good questions."

The deputy straightened up. "That's right. The seven steps. Wow, you remembered."

Hansen waved them deeper into the yard, where jagged mounds squatted in the shadows and the scent of burned wood suffused the mist. The husks of houses stretched into the darkness, all the hopes and dreams of those who had called Raven's Valley their home. Funny timing tonight.

A warm breeze brushed past her as Hansen led them between stacks of charred telephone poles. "So, walk me through it," she said. "Is that what this is, a crime scene? And if so, why haven't we established dimensions and security? Steps one and two."

"Detective, we don't know what this is," Hansen said.

"Or if it's anything, really," Martinez added.

"Okay, pause." Dry weeds crunched under her boots as she stopped.

"Dispatch indicated a dead body and a possible homicide. Martinez—" She snapped her finger. "Step three, hello?"

The deputy stammered. "Uh, create and communicate a clear plan."

"So, what's the plan?"

He glanced at Hansen. "Tell her what you told me."

"Right." Hansen cleared his throat. "This afternoon a call comes in, some vacation rental near the national forest with its silent alarm going off. I check it out, find this transient—Torres, that's his name—I find him washing up with his dog. I take him in, run him for priors, and nothing comes up—"

"Skip to the end," Martinez said.

"He's in holding for a few hours when he starts freaking out. I'm thinking detox, but we didn't find anything on him. He tells me how he needs to get out of the area. How these tweakers jumped him here a few nights before. And that something happened. Like they got hurt or... worse."

"Or worse?" Debra asked. "What, he did something to them?"

"You know how perps sometimes talk their way around a confession? '*If* someone looked under the floorboard, they *might* find the murder weapon.'"

Debra nodded. Depersonalization was a distancing technique she'd seen over the years, one she'd learned to exploit during questioning. Avoid the second person with touchy subjects. Never accuse someone of what you can't already prove. Use passive language.

Martinez said, "So Hansen calls me, and it just so happens I got a missing persons report last night from Mrs. Nesbit. Her son Shawn, she says he hasn't been seen in a few days—"

"Shawn's a local fuckup," Hansen added. "I booked him a few times for drug charges and check forgery."

Debra was struggling to keep it all straight. "So a crime might've been committed by Torres," she said. "And we're here, doing our due diligence. Fair enough. So, what, he wouldn't give us a walk-around?"

"Actually, he was keen not to come back." Hansen swallowed. "When I tried to take him, he, uh, well... He started clawing his eyes out."

Debra stopped by a half-melted stove and turned her flashlight on

Hansen. Had she heard that right? The glance that passed between the two deputies told her she had. "His eyes?"

"His face, technically," Martinez added. "He's at Greywood General. The doctors think they can save most of it."

Debra wasn't sure if it was the cold or that image that sent a shudder down her spine. Violent crime was rare in Greywood Bay and the surrounding towns. Break-ins and burglaries and kids drag racing down the coast.

And yet, every now and then, something happened that stunned her with its viciousness.

A bus driver plowing through the farmers market.

A mother shooting her husband and child because of messages in the TV.

And that kid in the summer, the one who killed several people and started the fire.

Why was it so hard to remember his name? Lester or Larry or...

Their beams panned and swept as they walked, stopping on the occasional out-of-place object. A dog's leash. A fallen flashlight. A worn duffel bag, some sort of coil sticking out.

Martinez unzipped it. "Copper wires."

So, a story was emerging. A chance encounter between two parties. The question was, how much matched up with what Torres had said?

Before he tried to tear out his eyes.

Hansen's beam stopped on the remains of a campfire. An empty pouch of freeze-dried beef stroganoff lay on the ground. The fire's ashes were cold, but it looked recent.

Lloyd, she thought. *That young man was Lloyd Betancourt.*

She wasn't sure why she'd suddenly remembered his name.

"Yep, it's all like Torres said it would be. Which means..." Hansen shined his light past the campfire, tracing a path between mounds of rubble. There, fifty feet away, one mound was different from the others.

The three of them stared at a sunken pile where a dark hole sat in the center. It reminded her of something like a collapsed anthill.

"In there?" Debra asked.

"In there," Hansen answered.

Wood and plastic, rebar and glass, it all crackled and shifted underfoot. Then they were at the edge of the hole, looking down into it.

"That's not that bad," Hansen said. "Dude made it sound like the Grand Canyon."

Sure enough, the hole was more of a slope that angled its way into the pile, twenty or thirty feet. Loose ground mixed with bricks and blackened beams. Jagged metal intersected splintered boards.

And mud, oddly enough.

Mud dripped down ruined lawn chairs and awnings. Mud oozed along half-buried sculptures. And mud pooled at the bottom, where their flashlight beams converged on three corpses swaddled in shadows.

"Fuck," Martinez mumbled.

The first body was impaled on rebar, half-crushed beneath an avalanche of debris. His pallid face stared up, a stiff mask of surprise.

The second corpse was hard to identify. A pair of burned boots and blackened jeans hinted at masculine form. Its clothes and skin had all been fused together. Charred, hollow eyes loomed above a lipless sneer.

However, it was the third person that spiked Debra's heart and caused her to take a sharp breath. He sat in the muddy soil, cross-legged and calm, like a Buddha beneath a tree. A pile of teeth lay in his open palm. His face was upturned to their flashlight, crimson lips and bloody gums stretched in a toothless smile.

Then he blinked, lifted his palm, and swallowed that handful of teeth.

14

The peach walls of the Pacific Manor held dozens of framed paintings. There were the soft watercolors of redwood groves and vineyards. The soothing pastels of spring meadows. There were comforting acrylics capturing coastal birds in migration and otters in play, scenes chosen to remind the elderly residents of a world beyond these halls.

But only one painting invaded the dreams of old Chester Halgrove.

Among the hard brushstrokes that formed a nocturnal ocean, a three-masted schooner fought a stormy tempest. Years of dust had dimmed the canvas's pigments. The ship's sails—the once-vibrant navy blue and purple of the Greywood Bay Trading Company—hung in muted ochre and salmon. Even the bolt of lightning backlighting the rocky shoal was little more than a hairline crack across shadowed canvas.

It was the lighthouse, however, that occasionally caught the old man's attention.

Some nights it blinked through the walls, taunting him at the edge of sleep.

Tonight, however, a different sense roused Chester. It crept up his skin, opening his eyes and starting a fast rhythm in his tired heart. It bloomed on his lips.

The taste of blood and sour earth.

"Mud," he muttered in the darkness of his room.

He spent several breaths staring at the ceiling, licking his lips and counting his teeth with his tongue. They were all there, good. Still, he couldn't shake the feeling he wasn't the only one waking up. Like the pressure of an oncoming storm rattling old bones, the trauma bonds of his past were tingling.

"Larchmont. Shit."

Chester detested how that name stole the moisture from his mouth. Yet, names had power. Names harbored memories. And memories were fickle things.

So, work to be done.

It took him twenty-five bone-creaking minutes to stretch out his limbs, get dressed in his winter clothes, and empty his bladder twice. It took him another ten minutes to pace the small apartment and count the steps. He ran his fingers along the paint, studying the color.

Three hundred and eighty-eight square feet wasn't much, but the suite offered Chester everything that he needed. A single bed, a bathroom, and a closet. There was a TV he never watched and plugins for the Internet he didn't care for. There was a kitchenette with a stove and a small oven. Above it all, the fire-suppression system. Important when residents fell asleep baking cookies or popping corn.

Tonight, however, his teeth hurt too much to think of sweets. He took a pen from the desk, slid his skinny arms into his jacket, and stepped out into the hall.

Midnight, the assisted living facility lay quieter than the cemeteries its residents eventually moved on to. Chester soaked in the silence as he shuffled down the hall. At the rec room, he paused to inspect that painting that mocked him.

Tonight, its waves stayed frozen in motion, its lighthouse dim. The old schooner didn't creak. But something new had emerged on the canvas since his last viewing.

A group of Indians danced around a bonfire on the shore. A closer look: those weren't burning logs, but bodies.

"You got your fingers in everything, don't ya?" he said to the painting.

The painting did not reply.

Down the hall, a TV glowed and murmured at the attendant's station. Legs propped against the desk, gray slacks ending in a pair of Oxfords. Mr. Comerford, wide awake and chatting on his phone.

"—girl, you have no idea. I've been hitting them planks hard just to keep pace. N'you know what? Not to brag, but my tongue game's on fire. I bet you're glad you swiped right."

Chester shivered. Not because of Mr. Comerford's gross words but because of the wind his frail body anticipated. He'd have to sneak out the back.

Retracing his path, he froze at the window with its view of the courtyard. Ms. Tan stood near the sculpture garden, staring back. For a beat, neither of them moved.

She took a moment to study her reflection and picked something from her teeth. Then she raised her vape pen, inhaled, and blew out a plume of vapor.

She couldn't see him in the dark hall. Good. Shadows were his friends.

He found the emergency door chained with a bike lock. Funny how it was always gone when the fire marshal made his walkthrough. But locks hadn't bothered Chester for years.

He placed his left hand against the door's cold glass and focused on his reflection. The sunken cheeks. The tired eyes. And the scars on his face, still red in a few places. He was grateful for these scars.

They gave him something to follow.

With the pen, he began tracing on his left cheek, a circle and two lines. Then his right cheek. Then three lines connected to his forehead and one down his chin, giving him the look of a cracked kabuki mask. Which was how he felt: a mask over a soul burned down to its embers.

But not extinguished. Not yet.

In a sudden shift, the frigid wind caressed him and he shivered.

Because he was on the other side of the door now, outside and looking in at an empty hallway. He let his hand fall from the glass. He gave the chain lock a wink.

Then he started off, down the sidewalk and away from Pacific Manor.

Forty-five minutes later, the wind-battered shape of Chester Halgrove emerged from the fog and shuffled through an empty parking lot. The Home Depot sign flickered above the store's creme-colored facade and locked doors. Darkness loomed within.

He paused at the lumber entrance as rattling coughs rocked his body for minutes.

"Ah, the old rat left his nest," J'harr murmured. *"Tell me, where have you been hiding?"*

Chester ignored her as the fit passed and the cool air filled his lungs. He placed a shaking palm on the store's glass door. Fresh blood dotted his fingers.

Like before, he focused on his reflection.

And then he was inside.

Shelves and shadowed aisles stretched into the depths of the warehouse. Sections for piping and plumbing. Those new smart lights that could change colors. A forklift sat by the stacked lumber. Chester inhaled the store's aroma, the earthy tang of cut wood mixing with the crispness of rusting metal. It reminded him of those years working on his house, constructing and deconstructing. Making changes and traps. Doing his best to confuse the dark star and deny her fresh souls when she struck again.

"Mmm... but not all of them."

He found a shopping cart and started down aisle 2, Grilling Accessories, plucking a roll of aluminum foil from the shelf. Next came the paint cans in aisle 9. Acrylic latex black with a high gloss. Flat all-purpose white. He didn't care about the brand, the eco-friendly seals stamped on the cans, or the five-year guarantees. He only cared that one was waterproof and the other was not.

With a clatter, he dropped the cans in the squeaking cart.

He was grabbing steel wool from aisle 10 when a whimper drifted through the empty store. Next came the click of nails upon cement. Then the scent of smoke.

He glanced back as a dark form limped past the registers.

A cindering dog.

It turned its smoldering gaze toward him and let out a pained howl. That dog... It wasn't one of his dead, was it?

He pushed the cart onward.

Then a baby cried from the next aisle over.

Wheels clacking, he shoved the cart faster as a woman's raspy voice filled the darkness. "You... didn't save us. You fled... again. You failed us... again."

"No," Chester said. "No, I've made peace with my dead."

He grabbed several rolls of brown builder's paper and blue painter's tape, then pushed the cart around the corner. There he saw her: a woman with skin dotted with still-burning embers, her mouth a charred furnace.

"There is no peace," she hissed, lips splitting with each word. "Not after what she did on your watch."

Chester's eyes fell to the ashen infant cradled in the woman's tarry arms. Tiny lips mewled steam in a cry that rose louder and louder.

Chester said, "My watch is ending."

"But your failure... is eternal."

There were others now. A young boy, tottering on dry legs that went *crickity-crick, crickity-crick*. An elderly *thing* in a red-hot wheelchair, heat-blistered skin oozing grease. And a moaning man wearing jogging shorts and a hoodie half-melted to his skin.

"You're not my burden," Chester said. "Not anymore."

He pushed the rattling cart faster, turning right at the toilets and sinks. He raced past showers and tubs. Deeper into the warehouse. Deeper.

And yet they still came. Walking or shuffling, limping or rolling, the victims closed in from all directions. Some squeezed between wrapped pallets of piping and smeared trails of ash. Others crawled down the shelves. Eleven burned figures neared, their wheezing lungs filling his ears with spiteful madness.

"You... Didn't... SAVE US!"

"You aren't mine... to save," he said. "You were hers!"

It grew in his chest, that familiar hitch. The world narrowed to a pinprick as his heart took on an irregular beat. High above, the warehouse rafters and beams dissolved.

And there it was, a starless sky filled with her black-violet tendrils. J'harr's hungry eyes opening, scouring the cosmos, and now fixating on him.

"Mmm... I've waited for this, old man. I can almost taste it, the tired reek... of your soul."

The knot in his chest tightened and jittered as the air caught in his throat. Had he read the signs wrong yet again? Was he meeting his end here, in the bathroom section of a fucking Home Depot?

Perhaps. Probably. But he still had a few tricks up his sleeve.

Beating his chest like a drum, he toppled the cart and let the contents spill across the floor. He threaded his left arm through the handles of the paint cans, snatching the brushes and paper. With trembling elbows, he dragged it all forward.

One step. Then two.

His back cracked and his shoulder popped. A glance behind him, and there they were: that burned mother cradling her child, that moaning man in joggers, the infant tottering on legs of crumbling coal.

"Why run? My light is nearly upon you..."

"Even your light has its limits."

Stumbling, he found a row of mirrors on display. He hoisted the paints and brushes, the paper and tape. He pressed his palm to the glass and closed his eyes.

In the tired halls of his mind, he visualized his small bathroom at Pacific Manor. That speckled sink with its curved counter. The endless bottles of pills upon it. The toilet with its safety rails, the last toilet his ass would ever know.

He wasn't sure if his plan would work. If his heart could handle the jump.

It turned out that it could.

A whoosh of cool wind and the sulfuric taste of the All. He opened his eyes and found his hand snapping back from a mirror—his own bathroom mirror—as the paint cans and brushes, the rolls of paper and tape, all crashed down around him. Light blooming in his vision, he collapsed onto the tiles.

With trembling fingers, he found his heart medicine and choked down a pill. Rhythm returned to his chest as the All's bitter winds faded. Above, ashen hands silently scratched at the mirror, then faded.

This jaunt had cost him, he sensed. And yes, he still had time, but not very much. J'harr, with her dark plans in motion. Old wounds festering and new wounds opening up. A dozen schemes all intermixed.

No, he couldn't stop them all; he understood this.

But that young girl, well, maybe she had a chance.

15

The Old Mill Shopping Emporium stood at the northeastern edge of Greywood Bay, three blocks from the bus depot and the lumber trains that ran twice a week. A monument to commerce and eighties exuberance, big box stores anchored the outdoor mall, a Bloomingdale's at one end, a Macy's at the other. In between, fountains burbled and heat lamps flickered. A decorative stream wound its way past copper sculptures of friendly seals and raccoons with armfuls of shopping bags. Despite the holiday music, most stores sat half empty.

But for Zelda and her friends, the mall was still a place of infinite wonder. Kiosks hawked prepaid phones and temporary tattoos. The food court promised tastes of the world. Outside Lululemon, sweaty customers stretched for their afternoon run. Inside Good Vibes, teens giggled at discreetly named erotic massagers, knowing they weren't for sore backs.

With three Frappuccinos in a carrier, Zelda paused outside a Game-Stop, the latest best-sellers listed in the window. It pleased her that *Critical Mass* was still holding the top spot.

"Over here, Zelda-bo-belda!" Ali shouted. "Check it out!"

He waved from the entrance of Banana Republic, wearing a hound-stooth blazer as the store's alarm squealed.

"Ali, you can't leave with the merchandise," Maura said.

"Relax, Liam Neeson, I'm bringing it back." He stepped inside and struck a pose. "What do you think? Am I ready for Paris Fashion Week? Yes or yes?"

Zelda wrinkled her nose. "Ready to go over the weather forecast."

"Ow, that bad?"

"Sorry, Ali."

A twirl, a twist, and he slid out of the blazer. He folded it and handed it back to the sales associate with a bow. "Another day, perhaps."

The sales associate rolled her eyes and wandered off.

Sipping Frappuccinos, they roamed the mall. Ali offered the occasional fashion observation that Maura quickly rebutted. She gestured to his long torso, his narrow shoulders, and his tan complexion. Occasionally, her fingers touched him, and Zelda noticed he didn't pull back or recoil.

Maybe things like affection were obvious to everyone but those closest to it. Maybe love formed its own type of blindness.

"If we can't agree on fashion, can we agree on entertainment?" Ali asked. "That party store by the highway is having a sale on fireworks and there's a severe shortage of Roman Candles in my life."

"No way," Maura said. "The last time we went there, you were broke for a month."

"I'm always broke," Ali said. "But at least I had explosives. Please? It's like eighty percent off. We'd be fiscally irresponsible if we didn't."

"Fiscally irresponsible? Do you ever listen to yourself?"

He shrugged. "I'm mostly on autopilot."

Zelda followed them down the escalator, sipping her Frappuccino as her fingers unconsciously traced little symbols on the damp cup. Her thoughts drifted to Uncle Mark.

Perhaps she should tell him about her... *situation*. About the ghosts and Chester. About the All. And about the cruel voice, always taunting, and the visions that crept in at the edge of her sight.

Like that mannequin in the Nike storefront, eyes leaking blood as its lips whispered, *"Mmm... No one will believe you, little thing. You stood in the path of a god. In time, you'll crumble like those before you."*

"Shut up," she whispered.

"Wow, Snappy McSnappersons," Ali said. "Forget I said anything."

Zelda blinked, and the mall resolved itself. They were standing outside Urban Outfitters now. When had she finished her Frappuccino?

"Sorry," she said. "I was thinking of something else."

"I mean, she's not wrong," Maura said and gave Zelda a nod. "They probably invited us just to make fun of us, right? Why are we wasting money on some stupid party?"

"'Cause it's Machiavellian," Ali said. "'Before all else be armed.'"

"Armed?" Maura raised an eyebrow. "You're not gonna, like, shoot up the school, are you?"

"What, 'cause I read some dead Italian's manifesto? Psh." He tossed his Frappuccino at the recycling bin and missed. "My boy Nico dropped a lot of truth bombs, and one of my favs is this: 'Tis a double pleasure to deceive the deceiver.'"

He gave them a proud nod as Zelda picked up the Frappuccino and dumped it in the bin. Maura said, "Okay, so... what then?"

Ali curled an eyebrow. "What do you mean? That's it."

"Ali, that's just a quote you put in an essay when you run out of stuff to say. It's not a plan."

"I never said it was fully formed. But trust me, I'll think of something."

While they bickered, a curious sound drew Zelda's attention toward an otherwise quiet corner of the mall. Past a used record and CD store called Vinyl Countdown stood a thing she had mostly seen in old movies and TV.

A public pay phone.

And it was ringing.

She stared at the box of brushed metal and glass, its aluminum-linked cord and black plastic headset. There was something unsettling about this pay phone that bristled her spine. As she walked closer, it took three rings to realize why.

The pipe that ran up the pay phone's pedestal stand—the pipe that she instinctively knew carried its power and sound—had been cut long ago.

"You hear it, too," said a voice behind her. "The ringing phone."

Zelda spun, coming face to face with a red- and gray-haired woman in her fifties. Despite her clean clothes and presentable appearance, the woman's eyes harbored a nervous gleam. Zelda thought of Annie Paxton, that old neighbor who went crazy and crawled through her window.

Who tried to warn her not to come to Greywood Bay.

"I didn't mean to scare you," the woman said. "It's just... No one else notices when it rings."

"Yeah, 'cause it's not." Ali stepped between the woman and Zelda. "Don't you have a soup kitchen to haunt?"

Then Maura was beside her, too. The red-haired woman's eyes darted from the phone to Zelda, then to her friends like bodyguards on both sides.

"Sometimes it stops for months," she said. "And sometimes it follows me home. But when I answer..."

She reached a shaking finger toward Zelda, then pulled away. Maura moved forward, hands balling into fists.

"Please," the woman said. "Pick it up. Tell me you hear his voice, too."

There was a broken desperation to her, someone trying to hold it together. Zelda wasn't sure what she felt more: pity for this stranger or shame in her own silent voice.

"Folks, is she bothering you?" A security guard slowed his Segway and circled back.

"Yeah, this lady's selling her crazy pretty hard," Maura said.

With a sigh, the security guard stepped off his Segway. He straightened his white shirt and gave the red-haired woman a familiar nudge. "C'mon, Ms. Thorpe, we've been over this. That phone's not bothering anyone."

"But she can hear it," Ms. Thorpe said, her eyes searching Zelda's. "I can tell by her eyes."

It was too much for Zelda. These past weeks and their weirdness. And now this woman, her eyes sheening with need.

"I'm not crazy," Ms. Thorpe said. "Tell them, please... Tell them you can hear it ringing."

Zelda shook her head and looked away. "I don't know what you're talking about."

She didn't stay to watch whatever emotion spread across Ms. Thorpe's face. Perhaps it was confusion or betrayal. Perhaps it was sadness most of all.

No, Zelda didn't want to see any of it.

She wanted to be left alone. To spend a few hours with her friends and talk about boys and school rumors. To buy clothes and make plans for the party. To worry about whatever it was teenagers worried about. Not some woman with her desperate eyes. Not murmuring gods and desperate-eyed strangers and phones that only rang for the wrong kind of people.

AFTER AN HOUR OF RETAIL THERAPY, ZELDA'S ARMS SAGGED and her spirits soared. She carried two bags on her left side and a second Frappuccino in her right hand. She wore a smile fueled by caffeine and an Auntie Anne's cinnamon pretzel.

And now, at the far end of the Old Mill, her feet came to a stop and her eyes rose to a storefront's logo of a bearded man above the words *Anderson Trading Co.*

"Whoa," she said. "Vintage clothes. Nice."

The musty store housed everything from distressed grunge fashion to antique bodices with patterns so intricate they confused Zelda's eyes. Within a moment of entering, Ali, Maura, and Zelda fanned out, wandering among the racks and mannequins.

"Guys, check it out." Maura held up a high school letterman jacket from the fifties. "Wanna grab a soda after the sock hop?"

"Show some respect," Ali said. "That's history you're wearing. Whoever rocked that is probably dead."

Maura stretched and squirmed as she tried on the jacket. "Dead or not, they had super small shoulders back then."

"Sure, it's *their* shoulders that were small." Ali coughed, "Refrigerator."

Zelda meandered through the aisles, taking in the scents and letting her fingertips dance over the fabrics. A corduroy blazer to her left. A flapper dress to her right. Some sort of crushed velvet jumpsuit that zippered in the back and still smelled of smoke. She wondered about the woman who once wore it. Had it been bought for a party? Had the owner gone on a diet and poured romantic hopes into this tight-fitting jumpsuit?

Yes, she could get lost in such a place.

And then she saw it there, in a corner, nearly lost among parasols and top hats and an old jukebox covered in dust.

She wasn't sure whether the dress was authentic Victorian or something altered in steampunk fashion and discarded. It was both tastefully timeless and gleefully contemporary. Her eyes explored every inch. The black leather straps and silver clasps. The burgundy strings that crossed in the sides and tied in the back. The marbled buttons and the cut of the chest. Even the length pleased her, neither too long nor too short, falling just below the knees with a slit down the left side.

And it had a functional toughness as well; it would match her favorite paratrooper boots perfectly. She could even see herself skateboarding in it, and—dare she say it—the whole outfit would look *cute*.

"Whoa," Maura said. "That dress was made for you."

"You don't think it's too much?"

"I think if you're not trying it on in thirty seconds, I'm stuffing you in the changing room. Go, girl. Go."

Zelda nervously carried the dress by its hanger to the register, where a bored goth thumbed through his phone. "Can I try this on?"

Without looking, he asked, "Can you afford it?"

She nodded. It would empty most of her cash card until the next refill.

"Careful with that drink," he said and gestured to the changing room.

Inside, she locked the door and placed the Frappuccino on the stool. It took several minutes to slip into the dress, cinch the belts, and clasp all the buckles. The strings were the hardest to tighten. She found a video on YouTube about corsets and followed along. Hooking her thumbs through the loops, she pulled the strings to her side. It all came together.

And it was good.

Damn, it looked *really* good.

She turned, inspecting herself in the vintage mirrors from several angles. She struck a pose, first playful and then serious. She watched how the dress hung and flattered her shape.

Yes, Zelda knew she was pretty. She'd caught glances from her classmates and the occasional adult. Even that junior Sam, with his beautiful eyes, had held his gaze on her a little long. And no, she wasn't ashamed of her body.

But since the accident, she'd never felt like she truly owned her skin and the bones underneath. It was all a shell, fragile and borrowed. Something to be buried beneath baggy hoodies, unisex T-shirts, and scuffed pants. It took a moment to accept this odd feeling.

Was this what it felt like to be pleased by your reflection? Was this how all the other girls felt? Confident in their skin and comfortable with eyes upon them? It must be nice, she thought. Yes, she could get used to this feeling.

She was turning to tighten the strings when the lights flickered and dimmed. A curious scent danced on her lips: sour smoke and the briny taste of the sea.

The All.

A hand burst from the dusty mirror and seized her wrist. Another hand clamped tight over her lips. She was too startled to scream.

Chester Halgrove leaned out from the mirrored frame where a room of crawling shadows rippled behind him. "Sorry to intrude," he said. "But we've got a problem."

And then he pulled her into the mirror.

16

Zelda clutched her sides as the All unfolded around her, first in misty inkblots and then sharp edges and structures. Old wooden beams and steel girders surged from the earth and intersected each other. Tattered clothes draped crumbling mannequins. A shadow-swept boutique loomed, but only in pieces. The rooms formed a time-twisted amalgamation of shops: a creaking vintage store, a meticulous dressmaker's nook, and the lingering shadows of a trading outpost.

"What the hell?" she sputtered. "You can't... just grab me like that."

Chester grunted. "Sorry."

"What if I was naked or..." She leaned against an old jukebox and fought to keep the Frappuccino from coming back up. "I don't know, using the toilet?"

His bushy eyebrows scrunched, unconcerned. "Lesson four: leap before looking."

He gestured beyond the changing room, where empty glass store-fronts mingled with old brick beneath vine-tangled arches. Dim sunbeams filled the ruins, casting shifting shadows as if unsure of the time.

She held up a hand, still spinning. "Wait, please."

He grumbled. "I forget you're not used to this."

"Yeah. This." She looked back at the changing room and its mirror. "What about Ali and Maura—"

"Your friends will be just where you left 'em."

He took a pen out and drew a shape on her wrist, two circles overlapping and a line between them. Then he let go.

"What's this?" She rubbed her thumb over the ink, but he stopped her. A matching symbol adorned his wrist as well.

"Lesson five: some chains are for protection." He let her hand go and slid open a barn door. Where the hell had that come from?

Outside, the midday sun shared its sky with a dark moon above honeyed shadows oozing across a confused landscape. Most of Bloomingdale's was gone, simply erased. Gutted structures remained. Pylons merged with the metal roofs and fenced stockyards where tired cows chewed dry grass and glanced back.

A chill ran up her spine as one of them blinked.

"I think that cow has four eyes," she said.

"Probably," he said. "We need to hurry."

He followed the cobbled bank of a muddy river. This was no longer the simple stream lazily winding through the old mall, she realized. Instead, a barely tamed torrent bisected tilting streets. Barnacled logs floated and thumped against an old, half-submerged train. A few hundred feet downriver, a waterwheel turned with the water's touch.

The Old Mill, Zelda thought. Now it made sense.

The mall. The mill. The All.

This really was like he said, a place for all things at once.

She caught up to him outside a house of chipped bricks and wood shingles. "So this place," Zelda said, "it's some alternate world, right?"

"A world *between* worlds. Like a gap inside your walls, or... You know how a snail leaves a trail, and you can only see it at the right angle of light?"

Zelda nodded. She remembered camping in elementary school and waking up at sunrise to find the tents speckled in hundreds of snails. Most of the students had screamed and slapped at the fabric. But she found it oddly beautiful, all those glimmering ribbons in the early dawn light.

"This is J'harr's trail through worlds," she said.

"Mmm-hmm. And we've got the light. Well, some of us do. And some of us *did*."

"Can I, like, do what you did with the mirror?"

"Someday, maybe. Now?" He shook his head. "Your mind couldn't take it. The All's not a shortcut; it's a wound. And some wounds are infected."

For a while, she just followed, watching the clouds overhead, some drifting swiftly while others hung frozen and still. The more she turned this place over in her head, the weirder it all felt. Like those impossible shapes in geometry class that Ali loved to talk about. Hypercubes and Penrose steps and—

She slowed as they passed a brick well, where a man in a leather coat and a fur hat drew water from a bucket.

"Chester," she whispered. "Look."

The man's clothes were centuries old, muddy and seasoned. For a moment he held up his hand, as if blocking the sun and squinting.

Zelda froze. "Can he see me?"

"Let's hope not."

"Why?"

"Because if they can see you, they won't ever forget. C'mon."

The cobbled embankment gave way to a reedy path marked by moss-covered totems, rusty lamps, and forgotten sconces. A hill loomed before them. She followed him up the trail, watching his movements with curiosity. Some were youthful and quick, a boy chasing butterflies in the summer. Others were slow and labored, a tired bear at the end of winter. Every now and then, he paused to catch his breath as a worn shadow flickered across his skin.

He was sick, she realized. Probably dying.

She asked, "So, what are we doing here?"

"Lesson six: sometimes we need to chase down our own ghosts."

She scoffed. "Ghosts?"

"Mmm-hmm." He gave her an ominous look and continued on up the trail.

Ghosts.

The word always felt lumpy and absurd. She wanted to believe that ghosts didn't exist. That the murmurs worming through her mind were some form of PTSD. That it was just all in her head, something Dr. Rhonda could fix if Zelda gathered the courage to tell her.

And yet she remembered Sophie Saperstein and what that dead woman had said that summer night in her bedroom. *"No, not a ghost. A memory that once burned with life. And now just an echo."*

Maybe this was what she had meant. Maybe Zelda's ears were attuning to the echoes. If so, she wasn't sure that she liked it. She wished it would all go away.

When they reached the top of the trail, Zelda glanced backward and gasped. It didn't make sense. They'd been walking for ten or fifteen minutes at most. Yet the mall and the river were miles away, just one of dozens of conflicting structures in a schizophrenic maze beneath an odd sky.

She asked, "How are we moving so fast?"

He paused at a fork in the trail. "Who said we're doing the moving?"

"Uh, our legs?" She tapped her dress.

"The record turns. The needle stays in the same spot. We don't move through the All; the All moves through us." After a moment of deliberation, he took the left trail, passing between a pair of rotten redwoods.

"I'm not supposed to see you," she said. "My uncle, he thinks you're, like, a bad influence or dangerous."

"He's got good instincts." Chester bent down, inspecting an odd mound a few feet off the trail. He brushed away twigs and dirt.

"Are you?" she asked. "Dangerous, I mean?"

"Yeah, probably. But there's worse things than me in this town."

"Like J'harr," Zelda said.

"Her allies. Her emissaries. And her echoes."

He brushed the final twigs off the mound. And then she saw the plastic drum, half-melted and obscured by the dirt. A faded warning read *FLAMMABLE*.

This was it, she realized. Holy shit, how hadn't she noticed? This was one of the places Lloyd Betancourt started the fire that swallowed Raven's Valley.

"Lesson seven," Chester said. "You carry the light now. Your dead need peace or they'll feast on your madness."

She didn't like the sorrow creasing his forehead. "I thought you already did," she said. "Those sculptures and—"

"Not my ghosts, Zelda. Yours." His hand shot out and seized her by the wrist.

"What is this?" She tried to jerk away, but he held tight.

"I've seen your demons infecting the All. They're strong. They're ripping wounds open, festering, and calling others and—"

"Chester, please." She tried to pull away again, but his grip was unbreakable. "That hurts."

"I wasn't always like this, you know." His eyes sparkled with sorrow. "Lesson eight: to bring peace to the dead, a part of you has to die."

With his free hand, he traced a symbol in the dust of the melted barrel, something like two fives, mirrored and connected. He smudged three dots at the top with his thumb. Then he pressed his thumb to her forehead.

Zelda screamed.

Because the hillside shattered all around her.

Brown dirt and parched reeds sprouted from the dust. Daylight became dusk. And her hands—the hands that had been slapping at Chester's impossible grip—were different now. Older and larger and... *masculine*.

She looked down, shocked to see dark curls of hair on her legs and muscular thighs moving beneath a pair of shorts. A bare, sweaty chest heaved, up and down, up and down. The trail passed beneath them.

Running, she realized. *We're running. We're—*

That masculine hand rose up until a smart watch filled her vision.

Mile 4

Average Pace: 8:21

Total Time: 33:21

Heart Rate: 139

The world pivoted, and now they were looking back on Raven's Valley, all the houses glimmering on a warm August evening. The distant crack of a baseball bat. The laughter of kids playing in the park. It seemed impossibly beautiful, impossibly peaceful.

Because it was.

The smoke arrived in hazy swells that darkened the fog and thickened the air. Those hairy arms waved it off.

"Go," Zelda said. "Turn around and get out of here."

The jogger did not turn around. Instead, he carried on running. Around a bend in the trail. Past boulders and a pair of redwoods. Further into these hills that she sensed he knew and loved.

He checked his watch again, and Zelda felt his pleasure. This was his best run in months. It cleared his head and calmed his thoughts. No arguments with his wife. No worries. Just the trails and—

The brushfire came fast, impossibly so. A worming torrent of cinders that crawled between rocks and poured through gulleys. The jogger slowed, watching the flames and smoke. First, with curiosity. Then, fear.

Because no fire could ever move with such *intention*. Like it was living and guided.

"Please," Zelda begged. "Get out of here. Go!"

It happened like everything else that evening: first a little and then all at once. By the time the jogger retreated, the path back was a whirling wall of sparks and ash. The heat embraced him, singeing the hairs on his arm and blistering his skin.

Zelda screamed, helpless within this borrowed skin as confusion and fear drove the man further into the smoke. Flames swirled around him, growing, growing.

And dark shapes, too. Things that crawled on six legs and grinned with jagged teeth. Things that hungered.

The pups of J'harr.

The flames consumed him, and Zelda felt it all. The caustic air with each panicked gasp. The rending tear of the pups, jaws pulling her sanity apart, piece by blistering piece.

It was too much to endure.

Then she was pulling away from Chester. Away from his grip and the now-dusty hillside. Away from the All with its fractured landscape and time-twisted ruins.

"I don't want to see it!" she screamed. "I don't want to see any of it! Why are you doing this?"

Chester's eyes glistened. "I'm sorry," he said. "I know how much it hurts. I know that—"

"No, you don't know anything." She wiped her wet eyes with trembling hands. Her skin, it was youthful and unburnt. "You're just a... sick old man. I don't want this. I don't want any of it."

"None of us did."

A small part of her knew what it meant, this burden. And yet the fire, that vicarious pain, it screamed inside her. She pushed him away again, the hillside teetering and the world spinning. She needed to get out.

"Zelda, wait—"

She licked her thumb, wiped the symbol from her wrist.

Then she ran.

Down the hillside and between the towering redwoods. Past the mossy totems with their twisted faces. Each step doubled her speed, and suddenly the All was accelerating past her, faster and faster as Chester's voice died in the breeze.

Zelda wasn't sure where the glass of the mirror began or the All ended. Perhaps at the log-filled river. Perhaps deep in that decaying mall. Or perhaps its edges were nebulous, like the structures that made up this world between worlds.

She hit *something*, and then the All shattered.

She rolled and crashed forward, her clothes catching on shards of glass and her shoulders smacking against the changing room's wall. The stool tumbled. The Frappuccino spilled. For a moment she could only lie there, trying to remember which world she was in as ice dimpled her skin and sticky coffee ran down her sleeve.

The door nudged against her as the goth unlocked it. "Holy shit," he sputtered. "What did you do?"

Two teenagers appeared behind him, a girl and a boy. Yes, Zelda remembered her friends. The boy who usually had something to say, some funny quip.

Now, his mouth failed him.

17

Reading between the cryptic text messages and his lawyer's waffling predictions, Mark estimated that the Ruizes would be arriving in Greywood Bay sometime between noon tomorrow and next year. He had called and left voicemails extending a holiday invitation. He had texted them a list of hotels and vacation rentals. Against the advice of his lawyers, he had even sent them a gift set of almonds, meats, and cheeses from the Lost Coast, tracking it all the way to Texas, where it was signed for and delivered.

Their response was deafening silence.

So here he was, stepping out for fresh air on the apartment's shared terrace after three back-to-back tutoring sessions. He waved as his student ran off, then re-read his text message.

> I know we don't agree on Zelda's guardianship, but we can agree that we all love her? I'm trying to schedule our Christmas plans. Perhaps we could go out to dinner and open presents together? I'm sure Zelda would like that.

He was pleased with the tone. One more olive branch among the forest. He sent the text message off, where it joined the others in a wall of unanswered blue bubbles.

And yeah, if he was being honest, some of his words weren't very truthful. He was fairly certain Zelda wouldn't care to see the Ruizes.

Grandma Ruiz, with her judgmental questions.

Grandpa Ruiz, with his meek stare that had settled in after the stroke.

Alejandro, walking some diplomatic tightrope between them, playing nice with Mark while groping around for information.

"How's Zelda taking to such a small apartment?"

"What subject is she struggling with most?"

"That fire must have been a nightmare. I'm so glad you're both safe. Tell me again how she got out of your sight?"

Up the coast, a flash of the lighthouse. Mark blinked and checked his watch: 6:28. Zelda had agreed to be home at 6:30.

Across the courtyard, Middle Eastern music echoed out over the sizzle of meat in a skillet. The salty tang of spiced lamb tickled his nose. He could see Ali's mom, Yanar, there in the kitchen, the glow of the Hadids' apartment warm against the night.

Last month, Yanar had proudly shown Mark how she tracked her kids with three different apps. She had given him a referral code for a month of free service. Mark had smiled and said he'd consider it.

But he never had.

Because he wanted Zelda to feel responsible. They had agreed to only use location services built into the phones. He promised he would rarely check it. The few times he had, it felt uncomfortable, her every move there on the screen.

Six thirty. Another flash from that distant lighthouse. He put his phone away, wondering why he was nervous. Had he forgotten something important?

Zelda wasn't known for being punctual and on—

"Time," Maya had said, "is all the same... from this side of the sea."

He paced the balcony walkway. Was this what it meant to be a teenager's guardian? To live in that constant pull between trust and fear? And soon the Ruizes...

Christ, he should be spending the holidays in Spain. Watching a rare winter snow dusting Madrid's statues and chapels. He should be enjoying the Mediterranean winds. Walking the streets of Malaga or letting his toes sink into the sand of Marbella on Costa del Sol.

But here he was, in charge of a girl who couldn't leave the country.

Six thirty-two. Flash. Mark shivered as that beam of light swept over him.

Then something warm slapped his back. "There he is, the local hero."

Roman Taumalolo was an imposing Tongan with a sleeve of tattoos and a courtroom voice that always put Mark at ease. He was a few years older, a lawyer, and a Raven's Valley homeowner. His family, including several relatives, were packed in on the third floor, six to a three-bedroom apartment.

"You really dove on that grenade for us at the meeting," Roman said, hoisting a basket of clothes fresh from the laundry room. "Sure you weren't a soldier in a past life?"

"If so, I was the FNG that got fragged right off the chopper."

"Well, the residents of the Heartwood Apartments thank you for your service. That Bibi, she's a piece of work, eh?"

Mark smiled. "She's a piece of something."

"That whole family owns half the council. Whenever they want something, it's all about what the Larchmonts have done for the town. But when the town comes knocking, those Larchmont gates close up fast."

"Handouts for me but not for thee."

Roman winked. "Yeah, we speak the same language." He headed off, then paused at the stairs. "You know, there's another angle we could try. More of a moonshot, but I'm getting tired of hearing my father-in-law fart through the night."

"Want to trade? My fourteen-year-old is about to go feral."

Mark realized he'd called Zelda *his* fourteen-year-old. He felt unworthy.

"Been there, done that, got the wrinkles to prove it." Roman chuckled. "Anyway, this thing, it's a fundraiser. One of those shindigs the Historical Society puts on and I trawl for clients. Maybe we can buy Bibi's ear? Like my daughter says, I'll text you the deets."

Roman ambled off and up the stairs, leaving Mark to the shadows and the occasional flash of light up the coast. Six thirty-seven.

And then came the squeak of a bike's wheel and the familiar clatter of a skateboard in the courtyard below. Young voices followed. Mark watched Ali and Zelda as they said their nighttime goodbyes, bumped fists, and went separate ways.

"And don't you worry, Zeldalicious," Ali called out. "One part dish soap, one part white vinegar, and bam! You'll be the belle of the beach ball."

Her skateboard over her shoulder and a bundle of shopping bags in arm, Zelda bounded up the steps and followed the terrace.

"Hey, Zelda." It was only when he spoke that Mark realized he was lurking in the darkness.

Her scream came out as a single high note and ended just as quickly. "What the hell?"

"Sorry, I was... Well, I guess I was just standing in the shadows like a creep."

"Mission accomplished."

He glanced at her bags. Sephora. Urban Outfitters. That vintage store at the end of the mall. It occurred to him he knew little about her fashion interests. Even after the fire, she'd acquired her new wardrobe in silence, a mix of skatewear and second-hand clothes.

"You know, there's an outlet mall in West Pine," he said. "If you ever feel like raiding the sale racks, we could go together."

She nodded, but her flat expression said it all: she'd rather chew glass. Why was it so hard to connect with her lately?

"Anyway, I made some calzones and a caprese."

They walked toward the apartment, his eyes drifting to her bags. "I ate at the mall."

"I'm not sure a churro and five boba teas count as dinner."

He caught a flash of her smile, there and gone in a blink. "I didn't have bobas."

"You're jittering like you mainlined caffeine." He pointed to her hand, which had been shaking the whole time. "Your uncle's an idiot, but not a total idiot. Go on, tell me I'm wrong."

She tucked her hand in her pocket. "Not exactly."

"Plus, I'm trying a new marinara. A few bites, then you can tell me it's awful. That's all I ask."

"Can we just skip to that part?"

"Not unless you want to fill me in on that fancy dress, Cinderella." He turned the knob, giving the creaky apartment door a shove. "Or why Ali called you the belle of the ball."

"I'll grab a plate."

With a whirl of bags, she tossed her skateboard by the sofa and disappeared into her bedroom. Mark stood there, studying the cramped mess of their two-bedroom apartment. It felt like yesterday he'd spent the whole afternoon cleaning.

Now, backpacks lay by the small dining table, books and assignments spilled out. The once-straight row of shoes Zelda kept by the door had returned to its snaking chaos. Even a few cups and glasses lingered on shelves, remnants of this afternoon's tutoring sessions.

For a moment, light filled the apartment, silver and as cold as the winter clouds. Then that odd feeling returned and wormed its way up his spine. He stepped outside, searching for a flicker of light along the dark coast. He waited several minutes and saw nothing.

Yes, he sensed it now, the shape of that cold itch in his mind. It was something Stacey had said weeks ago as they'd jogged along the pier in the morning. A little town fact, half-forgotten until now.

That lighthouse...

Hadn't it stopped working decades ago?

18

Security Guard Justin Boote didn't care for the detective lady. No, he didn't. Not her clever attitude or that cheerful banter with the staff. He didn't like how the nurses all snapped to attention in her presence. How they offered her coffee from that new machine, the shiny one for the doctors, and not the old plastic one with them pods. Hell, he'd been working security at Greywood General for nearly two years and no one had ever asked if he wanted a cup.

But if something heavy needed moving? Sure, they asked for his muscle.

Or when a patient slipped and busted a hip? They called in his strength.

And whenever some junkie got rowdy—shitting his britches and trying to wrestle the staff—yeah, that's when he got to ring their bells. Which, if he was being honest, he kind of enjoyed.

At least almost as much as his mobile games.

"Mr. Boote, sir, are you listening?" Detective Brown snapped her fingers. "The patient? Has he done anything or said anything or—"

"Naw, he's just sat there mostly, like how y'all brought him in." He nodded down the hall to room 244, where that empty-headed tweaker was spending his third night under observation. Justin wasn't a doctor, but he'd clocked in enough hours around them to recognize the signs.

Akinetic catatonics—what they called retarded catatonics before the word police got to it—often presented with blank stares and minimal responses. Sometimes they parroted what they heard. Sometimes they just took to unusual positions and didn't move. Gabe Garcia—G-dog, according to the neck tattoo—fit that bill to a tee.

"If all he's done is sit there," Detective Brown said, in that tone laced with frustration, "then why was he facing the wall when I entered the room?"

Justin's phone vibrated in his pocket, a custom alert he'd programmed and knew all too well. He fought the urge to check it.

"Oh, that," he said. "Sometimes he gets up and goes to the wall. Got a favorite spot that he looks at."

"His favorite spot?" Detective Brown glanced at Dr. Ranall and Harrison, the night nurse. The pair, so quick to ask him for help this past couple of days, now sat in silence. Funny how cops sucked the air out of a room. "Okay, so he has moved," the detective continued. "And if he's got a favorite spot, that suggests he's moved more than once?"

It took a beat for Justin to understand she was asking another question. "Yeah, I guess you could say that."

"I didn't say that, Mr. Boote. You implied it." She gave him a frustrated smile. "Sir, has the patient moved more than once under your supervision? Yes or no?"

Justin took a moment to consider his answers. He didn't like where this line of questioning was headed. Nor what it revealed.

Like, maybe he hadn't really been watching the patient as he'd been tasked with.

Like, perhaps he'd been roaming the hospital grounds, playing that damn game on his phone that everyone was hooked on.

Like, how he'd killed a few monsters and leveled up twice just tonight.

He knew the detective lady was onto him. That was her specialty, detecting. Shit, *Critical Mass* might really cost him his job.

He said, "I think so."

She asked, "But you were stationed here, correct?"

"Mr. Boote usually handles security in the ER," Dr. Ranall said. "We're short-staffed so we've been spread a bit thin."

Justin scratched at his pocket. "I should probably have my union rep present if we're talking discipline."

Detective Brown's face softened. "Mr. Boote, back up. You're not in any trouble, I promise you. What I'm just trying to figure out is whether Mr. Garcia's fit to be questioned, or—"

"Oh," he said. "Or if he's nuttier than a squirrel turd."

A beat of silence as Justin's phone vibrated again, this time with an emergency alert. A battle underway. Damn, he was definitely missing out on some good loot.

"Yes. Or more specifically," the detective said patiently, "if he said anything that explains what happened at the dump. Mr. Garcia's sanity isn't my area of expertise."

The dead bodies, Justin thought. And how the tweaker had pulled out his own teeth. Yeah, he'd heard what they'd found. Word traveled fast as the wind in this town.

"Nah, he hasn't said a thing," he said. "Least not anything that makes sense."

She took a deep breath. "So he has said something?"

Justin nodded.

"Was it a word or a phrase, anything?"

He searched his memories for what the tweaker had been mumbling. In truth, he almost never listened to patients, especially when he pulled psych watch. He harbored a deep fear of viruses, and the worst kind were the viruses of the mind. Some broken thoughts were contagious.

Down the hall, a lamp flickered at the nurses' station. And just like that, it came back.

"Oh, I remember," Justin said. "Yeah, something about 'night-lights.'"

The detective lady scowled. "Night-lights?"

Justin nodded, but he wasn't so sure now. "He just said it over and over while he was standing against the wall."

"Was he looking out the window or at the TV or—"

"No, it was between them. Sort of a blank spot. Had his nose right up against it." He placed his hand within an inch of his own nose. "His favorite spot, like I said."

"And then what?"

"Well, then I helped him back to bed." Justin left out the part how he'd been a little rough after the third time, maybe squeezed the young Mr. Garcia's stringy arms too hard. Sure, tweakers could be unpredictable, but they bruised easily. Most people did when you were two eighty and built like a door.

"And that's it," he added.

The detective lady jotted it down on her pad. All these questions just for some tweaker's nonsense. No wonder the cops were always holding fundraisers and asking for more.

Then his phone vibrated again, and he knew he could still make the fight if he hustled. He took it out, pretending to check the time as he stood. "Anyway, I should take my break," he said. "Yep. Regulations and all."

THE LOOT TURNED OUT TO BE CRAP. BY THE TIME JUSTIN GOT to the park across from the hospital, the fight was nearly over. A level one hundred Battle Boar, a muscled thing of iron armor and tusks seen only when he raised his phone to eye level. A dozen players were already engaged. Justin spotted a few wearing patient bracelets from the hospital, and one of the janitorial staff. The rest were probably med students and undergrads.

He swiped and got a few decent hits in with his throwing axes. But the Battle Boar was mostly tapped out. His share of the loot didn't cover the cost of his weapons.

What a waste.

With the monster gone, he closed out *Critical Mass* and started the walk back. The hospital fountain burbled, pastel waters shimmering from the lights as a bird splashed about. For a moment, he swore he saw eyes blinking beneath feathered wings.

In a misty spray, the creature took flight, squawking into the fog.

Silly thought.

He slowed his pace at the lawn, watching that detective lady get into her car and drive off. Yeah, he'd been a pain in her ass. And yeah, he could've been nicer. What was it about authority that rubbed him wrong?

Because he'd been distracted lately, he thought, and everyone knew it. One more write-up and there'd be a disciplinary hearing. Then the union couldn't do shit to shield him. And as much as he complained, he knew the truth: this job wasn't that awful. How many gigs could you play games on the sly?

He took the elevator back up to the third floor. A few more hours, quiet as usual, unless that night doctor told him to move boxes. He could probably get some crafting done in *Critical Mass*. That sure sounded nice.

He heard the muttering from room 244 at the same time that he saw the empty chair outside it. Wasn't the nurse supposed to be standing watch? Or had that detective lady given new instructions? Shit, he'd been so distracted by the game he couldn't remember.

A low moan from the room. No. Something wasn't right.

The tweaker's door was ajar.

Pushing it open, Justin spotted Nurse Harrison sprawled on the floor, legs askew. A dinner roll lay to his left and a spilled plate of lasagna to his right. The red wetness crowning his head and spattering the floor wasn't tomato sauce. Justin checked him immediately, pleased to feel him breathing.

"You okay?"

Harrison moaned.

Justin gave him a reassuring pat. "Yeah, you're okay."

At the far side of the room, where nothing but creme paint decorated the wall, stood the tweaker patient, Gabe "G-dog" Garcia. His back was straight and his arms hung loose. His right hand clutched a dented dinner tray.

Rising, Justin eyed the thin man. "Okay, fella, fun time's over."

G-dog made a dry gurgle. "That one was... too weak."

So, the tweaker was back online, Justin thought. Maybe he was hoping to make a break for it. Or maybe just causing some trouble.

Whatever the reason, it ended now. G-dog, a lean one forty, one fifty max. Justin, a solid two eighty. His body quivered at the thought of painting the room with this guy.

"But this one... strong." Another dry gurgle. "We'll take him... Light of my lights."

"Okay. So here's what's going to happen." Justin took several steps toward the patient. "You're going to drop the tray, and maybe I won't snap both your wrists. Otherwise, get ready to wipe your ass with your feet 'cause—"

When G-dog spun and lunged, Justin saw it coming. This wasn't the movies, and monologues rarely fazed the crazies.

But they did buy him a moment to prepare.

G-dog's fingers were scratching at Justin's uniform when the first punch arrived like a freight train. He felt the tweaker's glass jaw shatter with his near-perfect right cross. He almost smiled. He hadn't thrown a punch like that since he'd boxed in the Army.

But G-dog didn't drop. Nor did he fall into the fencing response— arms extended, legs tight as his brainstem stuttered and concussion took over.

Instead, his head simply rubber-banded and snapped back. His broken jaw dangled as something gleamed black-violet in his eyes.

Light of my lights, Justin thought. That's what G-dog had been mumbling as he stared at the wall. It was the last thought that was fully his own.

Then meth-chewed fingers snatched his uniform's collar, stretching the fabric and tugging him into G-dog's embrace. He smelled mud on the patient's breath.

And G-dog smiled.

Smiled so wide his lips stretched and his cheeks split and his broken jaw fell open like a flappy hatch. Toothless gums glistened crimson. And there, at the back of G-dog's throat, something wet reached its way out.

A hand.

A muddy hand spiked with broken teeth.

Justin jerked and twisted, but the embrace only tightened. Something beyond chemicals gave this thin tweaker strength. Something ancient and alien yet humming all around them.

Light of my lights.

It all burst forth from his ruined mouth: a muddy hand, a tooth-dimpled arm, and so much more that slithered and snatched. It parted Justin's lips and slid down his throat. It filled him so full he could only retreat inward—into himself—into a deep cavern of his own mind where his screams echoed off toothy walls of dripping wet earth.

19

D etective Debra Brown drummed her fingers on the steering wheel, hoping the burger would live up to the fuss. After years of rumors and false starts, Zippy Burger had finally come to Greywood Bay. Half the town's cars idled in the drive-thru. She studied the menu, debating between an Atomic Double or some Plutonium Sliders. She'd heard great things about the Cheesy Shock Fries.

Then the call came in over her radio.

She scoffed at the location; she'd just left the hospital half an hour ago. But when she heard the details, she sighed, flashed the red and blues, and squawked the siren. She instructed the cars in front of her to pull out.

Her burger would have to wait.

Ten minutes later, she pulled up to Greywood General, pleased to see a police cruiser already on scene. Still hungry, she hurried across the courtyard and reviewed the facts in her mind.

Something about an assault, an injured nurse, and that catatonic from the junkyard finally finding his voice. And something else about that security guard with the shifty eyes.

She knew Mr. Boote was hiding something; she was a detective, after all. As big as he was, the man had the poker face of a toddler with paint on his fingers.

But she also sensed it was probably nothing. Just some work fuckup he didn't want to bite him in his ass. People thought cops cared about every lie they uncovered. If they did, they'd never leave the station.

And yet, as she entered the ICU, a recurrent thought fumbled around in her mind: why did it feel like something was *off* these past couple of weeks? Like an odd vibe had rolled in with the winter mists and never quite left.

And like some things in this town, few people noticed.

"We've got to stop meeting like this, Detective." That was Dr. Ranall, the hospitalist, chewing a final bite of a protein bar. "I'd even go so far as to say you're becoming a fixture around here."

"It beats chasing teens playing hooky."

He dropped the wrapper in the trash. "Do they say that anymore? Hooky?"

She shrugged. "Probably not. Shows you how caught up I am. Speaking of which—"

"Yeah, you're not here for the coffee. Follow me." He badged her through the ICU doors, took a right, and led her down a long hallway.

The good thing about being assaulted in a hospital was the response time.

The bad thing was that, like all workplace drama, it attracted a crowd.

The exam room was packed with concerned nurses and physicians, two police officers, even a janitor she'd passed on her way out earlier. In the center, with stitches on his forehead and a glazed look in his eyes, sat the nurse she'd been talking to an hour ago.

"Nurse Harrison, right?"

He blinked at her. "That's what they're telling me my name is." He shifted the cold compress to the right side of his head. "Relax, I'm joking. Or am I? Not sure if I was ever very funny."

"Not at all," one of the other nurses said. "But you owed me a hundred bucks. You remember that much, right?"

A few chuckles and smiles. Harrison gave him the middle finger. "Sit and spin, brother."

"Sorry, wrong ward. Proctology's on five."

At least they were all in good spirits, Debra thought. Still, she had a job to do. She leaned in as the responding officer brought her up to speed.

"From what I've gathered, Harrison here was bringing Mr. Garcia his dinner, and that's when the patient snapped. Shot out of bed, struck him with the tray. After that, things get a little confusing."

"How so?"

The officer's tongue circled his teeth. "You'll, uh... probably want to hear it from him." Then he stood up and cleared his throat. "Folks, we'll need a few minutes with Mr. Harrison. If someone could check in on Mr. Garcia and... What's that security guard's name?"

"Boote," Dr. Ranall said, lingering by the door. "Justin Boote. We're still trying to find him."

Debra blinked. "I'm sorry?"

The officer sighed. "Like I said, confusing."

After the last of the nurses left, Dr. Ranall lowered his voice. "Full disclosure: it looks like Mr. Boote took off around the time of the incident."

"*Around* the time?" She gave him her best *God grant me the strength* stare. "For a physician, that's not very specific. Do we know if he left before, during, or after the altercation? Because one implies something the others do not."

He nodded. "I can see if security has footage."

"That would be helpful."

He hurried out of the exam room, leaving her and the officer alone with the distant-eyed nurse. Debra took a moment to organize her thoughts. Even chaos and vagaries could tell a story. She just needed to listen until a through-line emerged.

"So, Mr. Harrison, how much do you remember?"

IT TURNED OUT NURSE HARRISON DIDN'T RECALL MUCH AT all. Just a fractured conversation, a struggle, and some sort of retching noise.

"Like a cat yacking up a hairball," he said. "Sorry, that doesn't make any sense."

Confusing indeed.

Gabriel "G-dog" Garcia wasn't much help either. She found him a floor down in a fentanyl daze and getting prepped for mandibular surgery. With his stitched cheeks, drooping shattered jaw, and toothless grin, the man looked like a giddy Edvard Munch painting.

He couldn't speak—at least, not in syllables she understood as words—but he managed to write a few things while the anesthesiologist searched for a vein.

Why am I here?

Where are my teeth?

What happened to Tim-Tam and Shawn?

Timothy "Tim-Tam" Tamada was the human pincushion found in the rubble at the dump. She had studied his mugshots over the past several days, something cruel in his eyes.

Shawn, they had deduced, was the charcoal briquette, though they were still waiting on dental confirmation. Odd that they hadn't located the source of the fire.

And that the flames hadn't spread.

G-dog tapped the notepad with his unanswered questions.

She didn't have it in her to lie about his friends, and she figured the opioids would soften the blow. She simply wrote, *Gone.*

He read it again and again, broken jaw and toothless gums sounding the word out until she took the notepad back and they wheeled him off, into the bright lights of the OR.

———

A FIVE-MINUTE WALK ACROSS THE HOSPITAL, AND DEBRA had the answer to one nagging question: when exactly did Mr. Boote decide to get up and leave?

At 8:45 p.m., according to the timestamp on the hallway security video. Three minutes after Nurse Harrison entered G-dog's room and four minutes before he stumbled out, rubbing his bloody scalp and fumbling for the emergency phone. The whole thing had happened in less than seven minutes.

It also turned out the answer raised more questions, like:

"Does Mr. Boote usually walk with a limp?" she asked, tapping the screen.

"No, ma'am," the night security operator said. "Not that I've seen."

Yet there he was from a high angle, Boote's lumbering form, favoring his left leg as he shuffled down the hall.

"Maybe he injured it in the scrap," the security operator added.

"Maybe," Debra said, though she had her doubts. G-dog was at least three days into a meth detox. From what she understood, he'd be hitting fatigue, hard. Plus, Boote was a goliath. According to the surgeon, they'd never seen a jaw so broken.

Like a sock full of shattered glass.

So why was he walking with that odd limp? None of it sat right at all.

"Here we go." The security officer traced an oily finger across the screen where Boote lumbered down another hall. "Is it me, or is he just walking into that elevator like some sort of Roomba?"

Debra leaned in. As she'd crossed into her forties, she found herself squinting more often. Still, she had to agree with the security officer's assessment.

A Roomba indeed.

Onscreen, Mr. Boote bumped against the closed elevator doors, backed off, and tried again. Roombas changed directions. Boote, however, just bounced, paused, and limped forward, again and again.

Finally, the doors opened.

She said, "Track him inside, please."

They followed elevator three, its wide-angle lens looking down on the occupants. A tired nurse and a custodian watched as Mr. Boote shuffled in, bumped against the wall, and stared straight ahead.

Got a favorite spot that he looks at, she thought.

Camera by camera, they tracked his odd shuffle. From the elevator down to the first floor and then past the ER. While he turned and ambled left and right, he always seemed to have a lean that brought him back in one central direction.

"What door is he heading out?" Debra asked.

"That's the med school pavilion."

"And what direction is it facing?"

"Lemme see." He double-tapped the mouse, opening the security feed's info panels. *GG CAM 44 MED PAV N.* "That's north."

She glanced at the time code: 8:48. "Are there any other cameras at the fountain?"

"Nope. That'd be campus PD on the outside. Wait... I've got the pavilion. Here."

With another click, he expanded the screen so they looked down on the courtyard, the stone benches, and that fountain with its pastel lights vibrant in the fog.

Sure enough, on one side of the screen, Boote shuffled along, limping past a pair of med students having coffee, past a cafeteria worker smoking an e-cigarette on the sly.

On the other side, she recognized the shape moving toward the hospital. That was her returning after her failed burger run. The time-stamp read 8:50.

Jesus. She'd missed him by less than a minute.

"Well, I s'pose that's one way to quit," the security officer chuckled. "Never a dull moment around here."

She gave the security officer her card, and he promised to email her a copy of the videos. She took the elevator down, wondering why a man who had seemed nervous about getting in trouble an hour ago would just walk off the job.

What had changed his mind in that room?

Outside, she braced herself against the cool breeze, the fog lit pastel by the fountain. Fifteen years in Greywood Bay and she never got used to the winters. How the salt stuck to the skin and seemed to brine something deep inside.

She passed the med school pavilion, following Boote's odd path until she reached the medical center's northern edge. A tall hedgerow and then a grove of alders and oaks signaled the end of campus. Beyond, trees thickened as the ground grew brambled and thorny. The foothills loomed far off, farms and hollows soaked in the misty gray, the kind that held confusing shadows and put a chill in her bones.

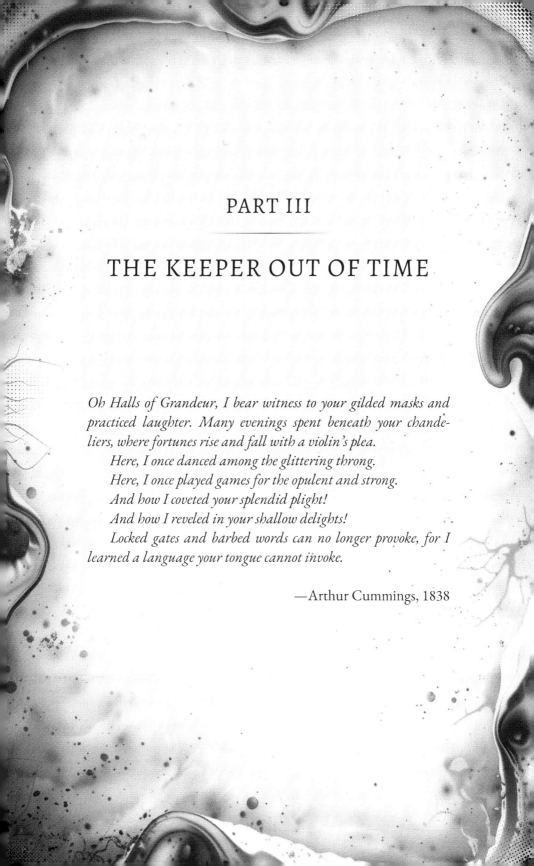

PART III

THE KEEPER OUT OF TIME

Oh Halls of Grandeur, I bear witness to your gilded masks and practiced laughter. Many evenings spent beneath your chandeliers, where fortunes rise and fall with a violin's plea.
Here, I once danced among the glittering throng.
Here, I once played games for the opulent and strong.
And how I coveted your splendid plight!
And how I reveled in your shallow delights!
Locked gates and barbed words can no longer provoke, for I learned a language your tongue cannot invoke.

—Arthur Cummings, 1838

20

For days, Zelda worried she'd mess up and say the wrong thing. Something that would alert Uncle Mark to the beach party. Something that would expose their plans.

But it turned out that on the night of, he was too preoccupied to notice. He had his own party to go to, if that's what adults called it.

A fundraiser of some sort.

"So you'll call if you need anything, right?" He adjusted his salmon-pink tie in the hall mirror of their small apartment.

Zelda swiped a notification off her phone. "Mmm-hmm."

"I'm serious." He removed the pink tie and tried a burgundy one. "Anything at all. That's our deal, right?"

Yeah, that was their agreement, one they both pretended to honor. But she knew there were things they didn't share with each other. He didn't talk about his drinking or his meetings or why he seemed stressed when he opened letters from the bank. And even if the students gossiped, he refused to talk about his status with Stacey.

"It's complicated."

As if things ever weren't.

And there were deeper truths Zelda could never tell him. Things outside the scope of any deal or agreement. Things that would make Uncle Mark think his niece had gone crazy.

Like what she'd seen in the smoky sky over Raven's Valley. That dark star and its infinite eyes.

Or where she had gone with Chester the other day. The All.

And where she was really going tonight: not some girl's night at Maura's, watching scary movies and munching popcorn.

She swiped another notification away. No. She wanted to have a *real* night out, a normal night out, the one kids her age were supposed to have. The kind they could talk about in shared secrets for years. She was tired of being a magnet for the world's madness. This wasn't too much to ask, was it?

"Alright, Zelda, now I need you to be honest with me, okay?"

Her stomach tightened as Uncle Mark turned to her. She shifted her heavy backpack to the other shoulder. Had he seen the change of clothes she was going to wear to the beach?

He smoothed his blazer and sucked in his stomach. "Does this tie go with the jacket?"

A flat smile tugged at her lips. After the lies she'd already spoken, she didn't want to tell him one more.

"Sorry, Uncle Mark. Try the silver one instead."

Two blocks down the street, Zelda's paratrooper boot met concrete as she brought her skateboard to a stop. She popped the tail, caught the nose, and dashed up the steps.

Unlike the Heartwood Apartments, the Monticello Townhomes were built on the newer side of the century divide. Ample paths wound between ferns and sculpted Japanese maples. Its tri-level units and private patios were meant for the university's tenure-track faculty. Maura's dad had to call in every favor the department owed him.

Which was why her parents were out of town for two weeks. Her father, running symposiums on the inequities in the criminal justice system. Her mother, shopping along Rodeo Drive.

"Hey, over here."

Maura hopped down a set of stairs and hurried over. She'd layered her Neumann JV football jacket over a maroon hoodie. A pair of joggers and trainers rounded out a sporty look. Her eyes were done up with smoky accents and her lips sparkled dark plum.

"What?" she asked.

"Nothing," Zelda said. "It's just... you look *great*."

Maura smiled. Sometimes Zelda envied how easy smiles came to her lips. "I just copied this girl on TikTok. Took me like two hours. Besides, I couldn't let you outshine me with that dress. Speaking of which..." She led Zelda up to the townhouse and unlocked the door. "I'll plug your phone in."

Zelda handed her phone over. "You've got the burners?"

"Ali does," Maura said and disappeared into a bedroom with the phones.

Zelda took a moment to admire all the space. A dining room, separate from the living room and the kitchen. They even had a spare room for a study with a Peloton bike. Zelda had been over a few times, but Professor Kerns and his wife never warmed to her presence. She sensed they blamed her for Maura's run-ins with the law over the summer.

They weren't exactly wrong.

"Go change in my bathroom," Maura called out.

My bathroom, Zelda thought. Not *the* bathroom. Did she know how lucky she was not to share it with a middle-aged guy who left the toilet seat up?

With lots of turning and squirming, cinching and tying, Zelda finally got the dress to fit. There were still a few stains, but she hid them with a distressed leather jacket she'd found at Goodwill.

She studied her reflection in the mirror, pleased with the young woman looking back. She looked older, colder, and wise. She wanted to be like a statue, strong and undaunted.

A shimmer ran down the mirror's edge.

"No," she whispered. "Not tonight."

Something bulged in the corner and distorted the glass. Distantly, a baby wailed.

She repeated her command with confidence. "No. Not tonight."
The mirror was still.

WITH A CLATTER, ALI EMPTIED THE SHOPPING BAG ONTO THE
table and slid a burner phone to each of them. "Maura-bo-bara. And
Twilight Princess Zelda. All charged and ready to go. I even gave mine
access to Elrond. I can put him on yours if you like."

"Huge pass," Maura said. "I don't want your creepy GPT crawling
my party photos."

Zelda swiped the phone's screen. No password. And more importantly, no user account that could be location tracked by their parents or
Uncle Mark. For all they knew, Zelda would be here all night.

"Thanks, Ali," she said.

"The guy at the kiosk asked if I wanted to buy shrooms," Ali said. "I
told him, 'No way, Jose. I get high off sports, life, and school; I don't
need drugs to make me cool.'"

Maura opened a cabinet in the kitchen. "Did you tell him that
before or after you showed up for the barbershop quartet?"

Ali gave his clothes a quick glance. Zelda wasn't exactly sure what he
was wearing, but the blazer was a shiny purple with blue stripes down
the sleeve. A pocket square jutted out from a vest with a watch chain
but no watch. The whole thing looked a little too loose.

He said, "Hardy har, Junior Varsity, but it's called regatta casual and
it's all the rage in New England."

"Oh, I've heard of that," Maura said. "I think Ben Franklin started
the trend." She pulled a bottle with a black label from the cabinet, then
gathered three glasses. "So, how'd you manage to sneak out?"

"What else? Subterfuge and chicanery." Ali opened the freezer. "I
spent, like, the last three days acting sick. I mixed some dog food and
curry and let it stew in the toilet for my mom to 'accidentally' find. She
sent me to bed at five thirty and thinks I'm sleeping."

"That's disgusting."

He tapped his temple. "That's Ferris Bueller. Classic. Who wants
some ice?"

While Maura placed the highball glasses on the table and Ali brought the ice over, Zelda unscrewed the bottle and sniffed the neck. It always struck her how vile liquor smelled. Like gasoline and tobacco and old wood.

"Like fire," a cold voice murmured.

"I don't think you drink it with ice," Maura said. "Or do you?"

"Duh. That's why it's called 'on the rocks.' The internet: it's not just for memes." Ali cleared his throat. "But, um, seriously, we should probably ask Elrond."

"Lesson four," Zelda muttered. "Leap before looking."

Then she raised the black-labeled bottle, pressed her lips to its mouth, and took in the burning liquid.

AN HOUR LATER, THEY GIGGLED AS THE RIDESHARE DROPPED them off at the side of the coastal highway. To their right, the distant lights of Greywood Bay winked behind a gauzy curtain. To their left, rolling vineyards and farms sloped to the posh cliffside estates of Sunset Bluffs. Shadowed thickets and wind-sculpted trees loomed straight ahead. Beyond, the dark ocean murmured.

"See, that's the trick when you're fighting nanotech zombies," Ali said, leaning against the driver's window. "Always use acid damage 'cause it slows their regeneration. Oh, and load up on antiviral reagents."

"Ali, come." Maura tugged him away from the car. "Literally no one cares about that stupid game."

"False, millions of users are playing it right now, which is *literally* millions more than no one."

As the rideshare zoomed off, the warmth that had settled in Zelda's stomach and flooded her veins was cooling. They were in the middle of nowhere. The nearest highway light was a distant flicker down the road. Her burner phone only had one bar, which pretty much guaranteed it was useless. And the party was nowhere to be seen.

She said, "I thought you said this was Bottle Beach?"

"So, bad news," Ali said. "Technically, Bottle Beach no longer exists. They renamed it in the eighties, Larchmont Cove, after—"

"The Larchmonts," Maura said. "Wonderful."

"So, you know how people can't own beaches in California?" Ali said, leading them toward a thicket where ice plants blanketed the hills. "Like, they're public land and everyone has to have access?"

Zelda didn't know that. It was one reason she liked having Ali around: even if he talked up a storm, she always learned a few things.

A flash of her father's advice: *If you're the smartest person in the room, you're in the wrong room.*

Dad...

Sometimes she could see his face so clearly it almost hovered before her. But lately, it had started to fade. Damn. Maybe she'd taken one sip too many.

"The Larchmonts own a bunch of the land leading to the beaches," Ali continued. "And they keep buying more, so they've got, like, naming rights or something. Plus, they built walls to keep surfers away. The state has been suing them for decades."

"Great history lesson," Maura said. "So, how do we find this place?"

Ali sighed. "I just told you. Google 'Bottle Beach' and you get nothing. But get my boy Elrond to search for 'Larchmont Cove' and 'party' or 'secret party' or 'secret beach party how do I get there' and... *voila!*"

He came to a stop where the ice plants thinned out and a reed-swallowed fence leaned away from the road. Zelda let her eyes adjust to the darkness. Ali was right. There was some sort of gate and a mailbox covered with stickers and scribbled obscenities. And beyond, a trail led toward that dark thicket.

"In there?" Maura asked.

"In there." With a creak, Ali pushed the old gate open. Zelda noticed the bungee cords wrapped near the hinges. They were new. Some fresh cigarette butts and a vape cartridge lay scattered among the dirt.

"How did anyone find this place before the internet?" Maura asked.

"Oral stories and hieroglyphics." Ali released the chain-link fence, and the bungee cords pulled the creaking gate shut. "C'mon, I can hear music. *Oontz oontz oontz.*"

As he danced a little shuffle, Maura slowed by the gate. A shadow passed over her face as she chewed her lip.

"What's wrong?" Zelda asked.

"I dunno, it's just... We know they're going to fuck with us, right? I mean, it's basically a trap."

Then Zelda understood it. Maura, with her shelf of trophies and her locker bulging with sports equipment. Maura, who cloaked herself in confidence. Zelda recognized the doubt in her friend's eyes.

She was nervous.

Ali said, "It's only a trap if we don't know it's there."

"Stop quoting vermicelli or whatever," Maura said. "I'm serious."

Zelda said, "Hey, if you're not comfortable, we don't have to go."

"What? No, cancel that," Ali said. "With respect, Z-dog, if you're not comfortable, you *should* absolutely go on. It's like... Okay, you know how I said we moved to the States when I was nine?"

Zelda and Maura nodded. They'd heard scattered bits of Ali's early childhood, mostly when he was reciting some fact they quickly forgot. The rest they'd filled in from his mother Yanar and her stories.

The olive farms in Iraq that had been in their family for generations. How the sectarian violence had crept closer and closer. The men in masks, threatening her husband for working with Americans. How they had to flee in the middle of the night as their olive trees burned.

And how she hoped to someday return.

Ali said, "What I never told you was that I had an accent."

Maura squinted. "I've never heard it."

"And you never will. But trust me, kids used to call me the Falafel Ali."

Zelda's shoulders tightened. "That's horrible."

"That's West Virginia. After a coconut, I was the brownest thing those kids ever saw. But you know what I did? I studied everything American, from Mickey Mouse to movies. And I talked. When they made fun of my accent, I talked even more." He clapped his hands, firm and loud. "And I didn't"—*clap*—"stop"—*clap*—"talking." *Clap.* "Because they win when you shut up. Or when you turn around 'cause it's not comfortable. But all of this?" He gestured around, and Zelda knew he meant more than this dark path on the side of the road. "It's just practice."

Maura swallowed. "Practice for what?"

Ali shrugged. "I don't know. Something that matters."

Maura's shoulders rose and her back straightened as the doubt fled her face. She gave Ali a grateful nod that hinted at more. "With all the bullshit you talk, every now and then there's a truth bomb. You're like a skinny little Buddha."

"Racist," he said.

They continued toward the thicket, the beat of distant music growing louder.

Ali shifted his backpack to his other shoulder. "And besides, if they mess with us, I brought enough fireworks to crash the party. Never storm a castle from the outside when you can sack it from within."

"Martinelli," Maura said. "Very cool."

"Eh, close enough." Ali held up his phone. "Elrond, play 'Eye of the Tiger.'"

"Playing 'I'm a Survivor' by Funky Flash."

THE PATH WOUND ITS WAY DEEPER BENEATH A CANOPY OF cypresses, mossy and damp. The music grew. Zelda could hear lyrics first, and then laughter too loud to be masked by the wind or the waves. The glow of headlights came next. Cars sat parked at the edge of the grove. The warm orange of a bonfire danced and sparked in the darkness.

And then they were there, at the fringe of a party. A keg sat in a bucket of ice. Another rested on its side by some coolers. Shadow hands clutched red plastic cups and dark bodies turned, eyes glinting as the three of them entered the grove.

"Holy shit," someone said. "Who called in the anime convention?"

Zelda wasn't sure who they were talking about. Her, with the vintage dress, or Ali, with his suit. Probably not Maura, who actually looked like she fit in. Half the students wore windbreakers and sweatpants, casual and comfortable. Others were dressed in their school hoodies: Bayview Clamdiggers, Middlemarsh Mariners, and a few Neumann Tigers.

What the hell had she been thinking?

Several shapes broke off from the bonfire, and Zelda recognized the slender form of Arianna approaching.

"Wow, amaze-balls," she said. "You guys actually made it. That's so... badass."

There was Finn and several other upperclassmen Zelda had seen in the halls. Cool smiles worn casually on older faces, confident and belonging. And Sam with his beautiful eyes sparkling in the firelight. It seemed like everyone had skin that fit them just right.

"And don't listen to Perry," Arianna said, loud enough so the anime-comment guy turned his head. "He's got the fashion sense of my grandma. I think your outfit is... *bold*. You do you, right?"

Zelda nodded. She wasn't sure whether it was an insult or if Arianna was being sincere. She found it hard to read people lately. Especially girls her own age.

"So, I just want to apologize again," she said. "About the match, the—"

"Forget it." Arianna moved her red cup from one hand to the other and waved it off. "Accidents happen, right? C'mon, this is our night. Slide in and I'll introduce you."

And then she did something that surprised Zelda.

Arianna took her by the hand, leading her toward that great bonfire and those shadowy forms. The juniors and the seniors. The scattered college students, no longer kids but something else, something older and wiser and worldly.

"Whatchya drinking?" Sam asked.

Zelda answered, her voice so small she had to repeat it. "Whatever."

"Cool." He filled a red cup from the keg and passed it to her. "One cup of whatever."

For the briefest moment, their fingers touched among the wet foam, sending a pleasant charge up her spine. She thought of the color olive green.

Like seaweed.

Arianna said, "Hey, y'all, this is Zelda. She's a virgin, so be cool to her, right?" She must have noticed Zelda's discomfort, so she added, "A Bottle Beach noob. Don't worry, we were all newbies once."

Despite the whispering doubt in the back of her mind, Zelda smiled inside. She wondered if this wasn't just the end of one chapter—a long and lonely one—but the beginning of something new, something born in youth and secrets shared here within a grove of music and salty winds warmed by the fire.

21

As the headlights cut the dark coastal highway, a chill swept over Mark's skin and rattled his teeth. Shivering, he turned up the heater. He thought of Zelda, wondering what she was up to. Dark green flashed in his mind. For some reason, he was afraid.

Then the thought vanished.

"That's her estate, the one on the bluff." Roman Taumalolo pointed through the windshield to the rolling hills. "Take a right at the old carriage and follow the driveway."

Sure enough, Mark saw the antique carriages parked at the vineyard's entrance, decorative casks filling its bed. He slowed, turning at a sign.

Larchmont & Cummings, Est. 1851
California Registered Historical Landmark
IN TERRA, VERITAS.
IN CAELO, SCIENTA.

"Something about science and truth," he said.

"'There's truth in the soil,'" Stacey said from the back seat. "'And knowledge in the sky.'"

"And money on the vine." Roman chuckled. "You know the difference between a mansion and an estate? An extra zero."

They followed the driveway, gravel rattling under the car as the shadows of terraced grapevines wound past. Several buildings loomed: a barn, a gazebo, a stable for horses. Atop the ridge, wide windows glimmered against a large stone building, warm and golden.

"Well, here we go," Mark said. "Into the lion's den."

"I don't think lions eat for two fifty a plate," Roman said.

"Two fifty for hor d'oeuvres," Stacey corrected.

Roman grumbled, "I'm in the wrong racket."

The gravel path opened into a courtyard where gas lamps flickered beneath string lights, and decorative pennants swayed in the breeze. Mark brought the car to a stop behind a couple exiting a Bentley.

Hurrying over, a white-gloved valet peeled a ticket from a stack. He jotted the license plate down. "Sir, I'll take your... Hyundai."

"Don't worry, he just cleaned it last year." Stacey winked at the valet and passed him a tip.

Before them towered a weathered three-story mansion built of stone and oak in the style of French chateaus. Steeply pitched roofs and dormers looked down upon spacious patios. The balustrade bordered a terrace, offering a wide view of the gardens and ponds. Guests mixed and mingled, nodding at Mark as he crossed the courtyard.

Stacey gave Mark her elbow. "Let's storm the castle."

As they made their way beneath the lights, Mark could feel himself shrinking. Him, with his sale rack blazer and ten-week-old haircut. Roman, slick in his courtroom suit. And Stacey, all effortless elegance in a gold and green midi skirt with bamboo prints, a creme top, and a linen duster tunic beneath a charcoal gray wool coat. She was the only one who knew what to wear.

"Don't let it all fool you," she whispered. "It's just pageantry designed to make you forget they've got assholes, like the rest of us."

Mark held her hand as she crested the stone steps in her heels. "At least Zelda doesn't have to deal with this crap. I kind of envy her right now."

Stacey glanced at him as if he'd grown a third eye. "As a veteran of our town's teenage trench warfare, I don't envy her one bit."

As they reached the patio, a tuxedoed attendant opened an ornate wooden door, ushering them inside. The hum of soft jazz echoed out from the grand ballroom. And while the music didn't come to a stop as they checked their coats, a few heads turned their way. The partygoers offered polite smiles while measuring them up.

Of course, Mark had sensed these weren't his people and this fundraiser wasn't his place, but the decor and scale confirmed it. His house in Raven's Valley could have fit inside the grand ballroom with room to spare. Ornate chandeliers sparkled amongst ceiling beams as tapestries colored the walls. Paintings and the occasional sculpture added splashes of color and class. To his left, a balcony looked out upon the moonlit bay and a curve of rocky shoal.

And there in the center of the ballroom, resting upon a bed of black velvet cloth, sat a massive ovular glass structure, fifteen feet high and ridged with complex lines and designs.

It was a lens.

And, according to the invitation Roman had forwarded him, it was the reason everyone was here. A fundraiser for that old lighthouse.

"Ron Figueroa, Francis Daniels, Assemblyman Vuong." Roman's eyes scoured the crowd. "Ah, there's that shitbird Strathmore. Looks like tick season's starting early, so excuse me while I make some frenemies."

He plucked a piece of sushi from a tray and headed off into the mix.

Mark and Stacey made their way through the crowd, nodding and smiling. They found some space by a bookshelf display where his gaze drifted to the paperbacks and hardcovers. Some were set spine out and others had their covers facing the viewer. They all featured similar motifs: floral patterns and comfortable rooms, footprints in snow or police tape across white picket fences. Each cover had a cat in a different place, winking at the viewer above the words *A B.B. Mystery*.

"Of course she writes cozies," Mark said. He took a book from the shelf and glanced at the title: *Pies, Poison, and a Purrfect Murder*. "I think I just went into diabetic shock."

"Laugh it up, but they sell like crazy," Stacey said. "She did her first signing in years last spring and half the town showed up."

"I'm sure the senior center was on full alert." He placed the book back on the shelf.

A young woman in a spaghetti strap dress studied a painting of a lumber mill and waterwheel. Her date, silver-haired and sharp-eyed, turned toward Mark and Stacey. A smile crept across his lips.

"Shit," Stacey whispered.

Despite her smile, Mark felt her body tensing. The silver-haired man nudged the young woman, and the two of them approached. He reminded Mark of a jackal emerging from the tall grass.

"Stace, I never pegged you for one of Bibi's soirees," the man said. "And yet here you are. Fifteen years and you're still a surprise."

Stacey said, "Mark, this is—"

"Ryan Jacobs—R.J. to everyone. Or 'that no-good asshole' to a few."

Stacey kept her smile diplomatic. "Your assessment, not my own."

"Yes, you were always the keen judge of human nature. I'm sure tonight is prime hunting."

As R.J.'s gaze shifted, Mark sensed the man sizing him up. He needed to break the tension. "Mark Fitzsimmons," he said. "I teach at Neumann. And you are?"

The woman was barely into her mid-twenties, skin smooth and lips full. "I'm Vanessa." She almost squeaked when she talked. "We met at a yoga retreat, but it's like we've known each other forever."

"Oh, hon, don't be shy," R.J. said. "Tell them your full name."

His arm slid around her waist and he whispered something that put a blush to her cheek. She shook her head.

"She's modest," he said. "You know how it is with these old families and their names all intermixed. Stace, it's like that show you used to watch with those Targaryens and Bannisters."

"I'm not sure that's the compliment you intended," Stacey said. "But I'm happy for you both. Truly."

"Mmm, likewise. It's always nice to upgrade to a newer model."

He plucked a drink from a passing server, raised it, and gave Stacey a nod. With his other hand around Vanessa's tiny waist, the pair meandered off into the crowd.

"Well, isn't he the perfect asshole," Mark said.

"Indeed," Stacey said. "And he knows all my buttons to push."

The server stopped by, offering an assortment of drinks. Mark's eyes lingered over the glasses, and he asked, "What am I looking at?"

"Our estate wines, sir. A '92 vintage Cabernet, one of only eighty-nine to score a perfect hundred from Wine Advocate. It pairs delight-fully with the lamb skewers."

Mark glanced at Stacey, who said, "Hey, my name's Joyce, and that's your choice."

Yet another thing he liked about her. Despite her own steady hand, she never forced his sobriety or judged his relapses. She was there for him, fumbles and all.

And still, there was a distance between them this past month or two. Was he blowing it by bringing her here? Was he screwing up by resetting the clock once again?

"I think I'm good," he said. "But I'll take a sparkling water."

"Sir will find the bar by the drawing room." The server gestured with his chin and sauntered off.

"Ah, yes, the drawing room." Mark gave Stacey a nudge. "Would sir find it in the east wing or the west wing?"

"Over there," she said. "By the Monopoly Man."

Mark didn't need any more description than that. He spotted the bald, dapper octogenarian with a cane and a white mustache and the bar he leaned against.

"Sir will order me a cranberry tonic," Stacey said. "Now, if sir will excuse me, I'm going to powder my nose and fend off a panic attack."

As Mark made his way to the bar, an odd smell tickled his nose and watered his eyes. Some fancy cheese perhaps. Or an imported fish, fermented and reeking of slow rot yet all the rage with the wealthy. For a breath it hit him so hard he almost gagged. Whatever it was—a cheese, a fungus, or some rare morsel fresh from the sea—it was gone just as fast.

Perhaps it was that server with the plate of hors d'oeuvres. Yes, that was it, he told himself.

That had to be it.

22

The Monopoly Man, it turned out, was quite a pleasant old fellow. Mark liked him from the moment he spoke, all piss and vinegar and contempt for the crowd.

"Don't worry, son, I can read that look that you're wearing." The elder gestured to the ballroom with his cane. "If you're wondering who half these people are, you're in an envious position."

As the bartender passed Mark two cranberry tonics, he asked, "How so?"

The Monopoly Man scratched his white mustache with a bent finger. "Ignorance, it really is its own form of bliss."

A scowl creased Mark's face. He wasn't sure if he should be insulted.

The Monopoly Man backpedaled. "My apologies. I didn't mean that as a slight. It's just... If one were to look around this room, they might see success and power personified, yes? Plenty to covet, as it were. But I'll let you in on a secret."

When he leaned in, Mark smelled whiskey on his breath. And something else, yes. That same rot he'd caught a whiff of a moment ago. Whatever the man had eaten, it wafted from his lips, bitter and acrid. Mark shifted back, but the old man drew even closer.

"Slaves," he whispered. "All of them, slaves to their fortunes. Look how they circle and beg." The spittle was really coming from his lips now. Little white crusts in the corner of his mouth as he spoke. He reminded Mark of his own grandfather in his final years, grouchy yet kind, as if time had sanded down his sharp edges and corners. "That's all this really is, just a... a glamour, or a trick. A self-perpetuating circus."

"Ah, there you are, Uncle Harlan." A guy Mark's age placed a hand on the Monopoly Man's shoulder and squeezed. "Aunt Beebs asked me to fetch you."

The man, Mark realized, was Larry Larchmont. He'd seen his face in the paper, one of the sources of the shoddy materials Strathmore and Daniels used to build Raven's Valley. The whole company was mired in more legal problems than the former president.

"Did she now?" Harlan's hooked fingers fumbled with his cane. "Well, it must be time for the suckling. Ever-chaffed is the philanthropic teet." He shot Mark a glance. "Nice talking at you, Mister..."

"Fitzsimmons," Mark said. Then, to Larry, "Nice to finally meet you. My niece and I, we enjoyed our time in Raven's Valley. Big fans."

"Oh." Despite the polite smile on his lips, fear flashed in Larry's eyes. "I'm glad we could help. I... I don't think my lawyers would like me talking."

Then he slinked off, escorting his uncle Harlan across the room by the elbow, a little too fast. The old man gave Larry a frustrated tap with the cane.

Slaves.

Mark looked around, but he didn't see it. What he saw were several city council members, a state assemblyman, and enough gold watches and jewels to be the envy of pirates or dragons.

Or part-time teachers.

As the music and conversations died down, a woman crossed the stage, lithe for her age and elegantly dressed. With a sapphire-studded finger, Bibi took the mic from the singer.

"Thank you, everyone," she said. "And let's have another round of applause for the band, uh..." She glanced at the name stenciled on the drum kit. "Our very own Fog Town Funk. Aren't they a hoot?"

A round of applause filled the ballroom and quickly died. Old

Harlan stood at the stage's edge, leaning on his cane and swaying. There was a resignation in his eyes that struck Mark as lonely and tired.

"The great history of our town mirrors the history of our nation," Bibi said. "Ours is a land of pioneers and builders. Ours is a place of frontiers and a bastion for those who tamed them. The Lost Coast is more than home; it's the foundation of our ideals. A place once beyond the edge of the map, where our dreams can nurture the future and our hearts can honor the past. And that's why we're gathered here tonight, isn't it? To honor the great light that once guided our sailors to safety. To celebrate the installation of a fully restored... I'm sorry, what order?"

Standing by the huge lens, a young man with shaggy hair shouted, "First order!"

"Yes, a first-order Fresnel lens—am I saying that right? Frez-nel?"

"Fruh-nell," the man said in an Irish accent.

"A Fresnel lens that will once again illuminate our coast. Mr. McDermott here is our expert on optics, and he's come all the way from Ireland thanks to your generous donations. All tax-deductible, of course."

"Sláinte!" McDermott raised his wineglass. There was a social awkwardness to the man, Mark recognized. Another outsider, somehow in here with the sharks.

"And speaking of generosity, I've just been informed that the Historical Society is donating one VIP ticket to the private eclipse viewing and mixer, here, next month. Everyone in attendance has now been entered, so please, do keep your calendars open."

Mark wasn't sure what was so special about it, but based on the excited murmurs rolling through the ballroom, it was something.

"A hundred to one, it's rigged," Stacey said, approaching him from behind. "No way the gray Gestapo lets a mudblood into Mar-a-Lago."

Mark chuckled a little too loud at a quiet moment, and Bibi's eyes swept across the ballroom and settled on him and Stacey. Despite the distance and her practiced warm smile, a shiver slithered up his spine.

"Forgive me," Bibi said. "I've chewed your ears off. Allow me to turn the stage over to Dr. McDermott, who will explain the intricacies of restoring a... *first-order* Fresnel lens."

A round of applause before she passed the mic to McDermott. As he started into an introduction of lenses and lighthouses and the history of Ireland's dangerous coasts, Mark spotted Bibi slipping out to the balcony. For the first time tonight, she wasn't surrounded.

"Okay, here's our chance," Mark said.

"Our chance?" Stacey gave him an amused smile. "I've been on Bibi's shitlist ever since I called her out in an op-ed. I believe the phrase I used was 'Jim Crow-era thinking.' You're Han Solo on this one. But hey, no pressure."

She clinked her cranberry tonic against his.

With a few deep breaths and measured paces, Mark cut through the crowd. Cool wind hit him as he opened the balcony door. At the stony edge, a few of the town's gentry stood with Bibi, framed by the sparkling stars and inky-black waters.

Mark pretended to admire the view, waiting for a lull in the conversation. He was back at his middle school dances, teetering and nervous. Sensing there never would be a perfect moment, he made his way over.

"Mrs. Boyle," he said. "We haven't actually met—formally, I mean —but I wanted to thank you. This fundraiser, it's... Well, it's quite something. And the vineyard? Wow, what a treasure."

The gentry studied him, all flat smiles and sharp gazes.

Mark said, "Anyway, I was hoping I could have a moment of your time."

Bibi gave an almost imperceptible flick of her wrist. The others excused themselves, nodding politely to Mark before heading inside. With a sparkling finger, Bibi withdrew a silver case from her clutch, opened it, and plucked out a thin cigarette.

"My one indulgence," she said. "These days, everyone's so up in arms about a little smoke. Meanwhile, they're rotting their brains on the internet and getting recreationally outraged. It's all so... *performative*, is it not?"

Mark sensed he only had as long as the cigarette lasted to plead his case. He surprised himself by taking the woman's silver lighter, cupping his hands, and holding the flame to her cigarette. She exhaled a plume that the breeze quickly swept off.

"Thank you, Mr. Fitzsimmons. It's nice to know that chivalry isn't extinct."

"No, not entirely," he said. "Though I don't think my students would call me chivalrous."

"I wonder if they'd know the word."

"They're full of surprises." As she exhaled, Mark urged himself on, to make the leap and dive right in. "Mrs. Boyle, I came here because—"

"Oh, I know why. I saw your names on the list and it clicked. You, Ms. Layne with her equity crusades, and that ambulance chaser Tamale or... whatever."

"Taumalolo," Mark corrected. Even though the old woman's words dripped with disdain, he forced himself to push on and smile. "As for his driving skills, I can't vouch. And Stacey, well, she's just here to keep me honest. Frankly, I don't think she'd be caught dead at this place. No offense."

"No, I don't suppose that she would." Bibi exhaled again. For a breath, he caught the scent of that same sour reek masked by tobacco.

Then it was gone.

"If you know why I'm here," he continued, "you know that two fifty a plate is a lot to a teacher." He turned to the window and gestured to the warm ballroom. "And you know that all those people inside—Strathmore, Daniels, those councilmen fawning over your art or that lighthouse—they're here for the same reason I am: they want something from you."

"At least you're forthright, Mr. Fitzsimmons." Inhale. Exhale. The cigarette was down to a quarter now. "I respect that."

"I don't have deep pockets or the thick skin to swim with the sharks," he said. "I believe in blunt honesty. For that, I'd like to ask you for a favor—a *personal* favor. See, that fire this summer, it displaced hundreds of families. You draw a lot of water. Your support could get the machinery at city hall moving. You could help those families find homes."

"And that's it? This personal favor?"

"Just hear us out, okay? That's all we're asking. Maybe we can see if there's a way to get you on board."

The cherry glowed, giving her eyes an orange sparkle as she sucked in a final drag. Then she stubbed it out in a crystal tray. She reached out and took Mark's hand in her own, running gem-studded fingers over his wrist. Her soft skin surprised him.

As did the strength of her grip.

She said, "You're a nice man, Mr. Fitzsimmons. But this town isn't your home, and these aren't your people. Whatever it is you think that you're building... I'm afraid you're mistaken."

She let go of his hand and walked back to the door. His throat felt so dry and his stomach so tense that words failed him. This woman, this bitter old woman. She paused, framed by the light of the ballroom and all those adoring shadows beyond.

"I know it doesn't feel like it," she called out. "But I am doing you a favor. A very personal favor."

And then she stepped inside, where the chattering warmth swallowed her up.

———

FIVE MINUTES LATER, ROMAN KNOCKED BACK ANOTHER glass of Champagne. "Ah, you gave it your best," he said, taking his coat from the attendant. "Old Beebs can choke on her crab cakes."

Mark held Stacey's coat out for her. "And as much as I enjoy hearing boomers mansplain the faults in our education system," she said, "I'd rather spend the rest of my night writing grants."

They paused in the foyer, Antônio Carlos Jobim's "Corcovado" filling the room with bossa nova percussion. "Would you get the car?" Mark handed her his parking ticket. "I need to stop by the poor men's room."

"It's down the hall," Roman called out. "Just past the whites-only drinking fountain."

Mark didn't find a water fountain, but he did find the bathroom. He did his business, then washed his hands in a sink so marbled and gilded it seemed conjured from a baroque fever dream. He dried his hands on the softest towel he'd ever felt, the Larchmont crest embroidered on Turkish cotton.

Then he studied his reflection in the mirror. This forty-four-year-old loser, a part-time teacher, part-time tutor, soggy in his off-the-rack suit. His savings shrinking, his assets dwindling.

What the hell was he doing here? Not just in this house, but in Greywood Bay and with his life? Was this really advancement? Or was he just sliding backward, mistaking movement for progress? Christ, he'd probably be couponing soon, like his mother. Telling Zelda to turn down the thermostat and put on a sweater.

He noticed a Glencairn left by the soap. He lifted it, inhaling the scotch's aroma. Caramel and toffee, oak and peat smoke. A warmth that would smooth out the world. *Drink it, yes.*

Instead, he took that hand towel with its gold-threaded crest, placed the Glencairn inside, and rolled it up. Then he dropped it on the floor and stomped. Glass crackled underfoot. He deposited the hand towel and the glass into the toilet, flushed it, and watched as the drain struggled to swallow it all. The water rose... rose...

Spiteful, yes. Immature, absolutely. But Bibi's words had slid under his skin like gravel. He couldn't choke the old bird without getting arrested.

But at least he could choke up her plumbing.

23

By eight, the party was in full swing with high schoolers arriving by the minute. Zelda recognized a few from campus, juniors or seniors mostly, with the scattered underclassmen roaming about. Music, banter, and sporadic cheers filled the windy grove where the bonfire crackled and danced.

Zelda stood at its edge, clutching her red cup and warming her hands. She wondered if Uncle Mark had nights like these. Or if her parents ever did. Nights when they wound up where they didn't belong. Nights when they doubted themselves and their senses.

Like the shapes twisting at the edge of her vision.

Was that a stack of driftwood for the bonfire or a pile of gray bones? Had a dog with fiery eyes just walked through the underbrush?

"Mmm... I warned you, yes I did. One by one by one... they'll leave you alone. Their drift has already begun."

Zelda's gaze drifted, searching for her friends amongst the partygoers. There was Maura near the keg, chatting up a pair of football players from Bayside. She spotted Ali across the grove, using sparklers to draw his name in the darkness while a fellow video geek took pictures in time lapse.

"Alone, with worms in your mind... Alone like that old, broken man. You could have been more. Been my emissary, perhaps."

Something shifted deep in the bonfire, scattering sparks and sending flames crawling up the driftwood and logs. Flames that seemed like spindly fingers. And cindering coals that burned and winked like dozens of furious eyes.

It was warm here, a little too warm. Zelda removed her leather jacket.

She thought of the jogger from the hills in the All and his last desperate seconds. And she thought of the young man who had started it all.

Why was it so hard to remember his name? Why had his face receded into a featureless lump?

A sizzle and a pop from deep in the bonfire. She took a step back as the warmth washed over her and the dancing flames stretched. Even the wind grew suffused with scalding breath.

Lloyd, she thought. Yes, Lloyd and his harvest of sorrow.

Then her fingers made a curious motion. She wasn't entirely sure why, but she followed the instinct and bent down, tracing one of Chester's symbols in the dirt.

"Like a command or an order," he had said. "To lock something of value away."

She wasn't even sure if it would work.

Yet the instant she finished the symbol, the bonfire's heat retreated, replaced by a comforting warmth beneath the ocean's cool breeze. The creeping flames abated.

She copied the symbol in the dirt a few feet away. Then a third, following the circle of the bonfire pit. Another, and then—

"Whoa. What is that?"

Zelda looked up to see Sam, two beer bottles in hand as he eyed the dirt. "It's nothing," she said. "I just... doodle sometimes."

"Cool." He offered her one of the bottles. "Drew's sister works at the brewery, so she hooked us up. It's better than that swill from the keg."

"Oh, thanks." She took the beer, eyeing the open mouth and the missing cap. She'd heard stories about things slipped into drinks and had kept her red cup in hand the past hour.

"Right. Open bottle, creepy dude. My bad." He took it back and offered her the other bottle, cap still on it.

"Not *that* creepy." She tried to twist the cap, but it didn't budge.

"Here." Sam took his lighter and pressed it beneath the bottle cap.

Again, their fingers touched. Again, a color sparked in her mind, mottled amber. What had Chester said about that hue?

With a quick jerk, Sam popped the bottle cap off. "It's all in the wrist."

She took a sip, the bitter, thick foam catching her by surprise. She stifled a cough. "It's... interesting."

"It's called double-chocolate stout." He pushed a strand of brown hair from his eyes and studied the label. "I'm not sure what stout is, but it's probably, like, German. I think most beer comes from there."

"Ali could tell you. He's like a walking ChatGPT."

Sam took another sip, and so did Zelda. Why did conversations with cute boys feel awkward and forced? Why did the silence scream to be filled the longer it stretched on?

Finally, he said, "Anyhoo, so there's a tradition we do. For newbies. Like a Bottle Beach initiation. You down?"

Maybe it was the alcohol softening the world and putting a confident song in her heart. Maybe it was how J'harr's whispers had grown silent. Or maybe it was that, at this moment, Zelda saw a path before her. A chance to be like the others, part of a secret shared among youth.

She took another sip for courage. "Yeah, cool."

"Good. Great. So, follow me." He gestured toward the dark cliffs at the western edge of the grove and started walking.

"Wait." Zelda glanced back at the partygoers, searching for her friends. "We should get Maura and Ali."

"Actually, hold off for a sec. Arianna wants you to go first. Then you get to bring them in. Cool?"

No, she wasn't sure if it was cool. Her doubts murmured, but only for a moment. Then Sam took her hand, and its warmth silenced them.

"Trust me," he said. "You're gonna love it."

He led her past the circle of the cars and through a narrow path at the western edge of the grove. The firelight gave way to shadows, and then moonlight and stars peeked between the clouds. The trail grew rocky. She could feel her heart beating beneath her ribs, a rhythm her body echoed. She wondered if Sam could feel it through her hand.

"So, where are we going?"

"Private beach," he said. "Some old lady owns, like, miles of it. We've gotta go the long way."

"We're going miles?"

"What? No. See that arch and that cave?" He pointed down the beach, where tall cliffs formed a crescent cove of shimmering tide pools. Towering above, rocks merged in a natural arch. Beyond, a shoal stretched into the mist where a lighthouse loomed in the mist like an Ancient Greek column, derelict and forgotten. "It's just down there."

The last of the trees gave way to a slope and then the cliff's edge. He ran a hand on a metal railing, and she realized there were steps here. Old, creaky stairs of concrete and steel clung to the rocky escarpment.

"I should probably get a flashlight," she said. "Ali's got one. He's, like, always prepared."

Sam turned his phone's flashlight on and gave her a wink. "Relax. I've done this in the dark. Just stick to the—*whoa!*"

He stumbled and grabbed the railing. Zelda froze, mid-swipe on her phone's flashlight app. For a moment she saw it all: the concrete and steel breaking free from the cliff and tumbling down to the tide pools and sand. Her body, broken fifty feet below.

Like her parents.

Then Sam turned the flashlight on his grinning face. "Just messing with you."

She sighed. "Seriously, not cool."

"Not even a little?" He started down the stairs.

"Maybe a little."

Step by step, they made their way down until her boots sank into the soft sand and the waves crashed nearby. Even minutes later, her heart drummed in her chest.

Why did everything have to feel so unsteady and raw?

Had the others felt like this? Like a fish swimming through water thickening day by day.

"There we go." Sam pointed to a small cave beneath the arch where graffiti covered the rock walls. "The Wall of Names. Everyone that comes here has to write theirs on it."

"My name?"

"That's how it works. Go for it."

Zelda studied the graffitied rocks. In the moonlight, it was hard to separate the words from the abstract cartoons and images. As she got closer, she could see the white base coat sprayed over the rocks, year after year. And the names stretching back through the decades.

JayDub & Lisa, '13.

Rip Curl Riders, '06.

Breanna, McGreen & King Kush, '98.

There was even a can of spray paint conveniently left on a nearby rock.

Zelda took the can and shook it. She raised her phone's light and found an empty white space. She pressed on the nozzle. With a hiss and a spurt, she started spraying a Z.

Then the paint can died.

She shook it again and again, but nothing came out. "I think it's empty." She turned to Sam, only to discover he had taken a dozen steps back. Something changed on his face.

Why?

No. She knew why. A part of her always had.

She looked back at the graffiti, her flashlight rising, and she noticed that something else was at the edge of the white space. A black arrow pointing to the left, and three words, recently sprayed and still wet.

PSYCHO ZOMBIE ZELDA

The moist shape landed on her shoulder and loosed a scream from her lips. She looked over to see a tendril of seaweed glistening in the moonlight. A hermit crab skittered and fell from the damp tangle.

Don't look up, she told herself.

But that's just what she did.

Thirty or forty feet above, at the edge of the arch, Arianna and Finn and several others peered over, their grins hungry and white. She saw the coolers yawning and tilting.

The seaweed and chum hit her hard, knocking her to the ground and filling her mouth with brine. Next came the sand, battering her eyes and scratching her skin. It dusted her, filling her dress and her bra, creeping into all those places that would take hours to scrape out.

Crawling, stumbling, and spitting out kelp, Zelda heard their laughter receding beyond the high ledge. She plucked a fish bone from her hair.

"What, was pig's blood too expensive?" she shouted. "Try something original for once! God!"

And she sat there, wiping and tugging, peeling seaweed from her ruined dress and digging sand from her pockets. She found another small crab clutching her sleeve. With a sigh, she carefully placed it in the sand, where it scuttled off. She glanced over, but Sam was long gone. Of course he was. Probably laughing and sprinting back to the party.

Sam, with that flash of mottled amber at his touch.

Yeah, she had known this was going to happen. She'd sensed it ever since Arianna had smiled her guileful smile and invited them here.

And yet, a part of her had hoped that she had been wrong. That maybe Arianna was sincere. And that maybe, just maybe, the end of the semester would be better than all the days before it. Zelda had clung to that hope, nurturing it until she'd grown blind to the truth.

She saw how empty it was.

"Stupid," she muttered. "Stupid dumb little girl."

24

Dress dripping, jacket squeaking, Zelda began the long, soggy walk back to the beach party. Perhaps she could duck out on her own without Maura or Ali. Then she remembered they'd used Maura's phone to order the rideshare. She hadn't loaded her cash cards onto the burner, so she typed out a text:

> Guys, I need to go home. Meet by gate?

She hit send.

As she trudged along the dark beach, she scratched and tugged at her ruined clothes. She could feel a few bruises forming. It turned out that sand dropped from up high really hurt.

A moment later, her phone buzzed.

> ✕ Message Not Delivered.

Great. One bar meant no connection, which meant she'd have to make the walk of shame through the party. Unless she could get their attention on the sly. Maybe throwing a rock. Or maybe slipping through the All like Chester had. She felt her fingers beginning to move on their own again.

Then her foot caught on something and she stumbled. For the second time tonight, she found herself horizontal with a face full of sand.

"Fucking... why..."

Wincing, she shined her phone's meager light around. A curious grouping of stones stood on the beach, wine-dark with smooth, glassy edges. It reminded her of a table.

She ran her fingers along it, glad she'd only tripped over a low corner. Head-on, she could have smashed up her knees or broken a bone. There was even a metal loop anchored into the dark stone.

That was when she heard the voice.

"Help!"

It carried with the wind and the waves. She told herself it was just the cry of a nighttime gull over the cove. Or the murmur of a whale. Or a foghorn. Yes, sound behaved funny over water.

She told herself it was anything other than what her instincts whispered. Someone crying for—

"Help!" the voice shouted. "Please! Help me!"

She stood, scanning the tide pools and the waves crashing beyond. Nothing. Just the ocean, and—*there!* For a beat, she caught the sheen of wet hair over a white linen shirt as an arm stretched skyward and waved.

"Help me! Please! There's been an accident!"

The man was a hundred feet out, bobbing just past the breakers, up and down, up and down. Objectively, Zelda knew what to do. She needed to run. To get a signal, call 911, and bring the adults. To do anything other than what her heart was telling her to do.

And yet...

"Shit." She glanced up and down the empty beach. "Arianna, I swear if this is—"

"Help! Please, I can see you! I..."

The man disappeared beyond the crest of a wave. And then... nothing.

"No, no no no." She unbuckled her left boot. Then her right. In five paces, she was shedding her soggy jacket. The water slapped her ankles, frigid and shocking. Next came her waist, and it chased the air from her chest. Yeah, she was a good swimmer, but this was the Pacific in winter. What the hell was she doing?

Her father's voice echoed in her mind, so clear it was right beside her.

She was Zelda.

She was a protector.

She had to do something.

As the wave crashed and the churning waters approached, she jumped up, catching a glimpse of the man in the white shirt.

There was someone else. Another man clutching a barrel and struggling to hold on as it rolled. "Oh God! Oh God! Oh God!" Then the barrel turned, and he slipped into the dark water.

Zelda waded deeper. Eighty feet. Seventy. A wave rose, and she jumped again. As she came down, the sand dropped away beneath her toes.

She was swimming now, riding up to the crest and over. Fifty feet. Forty. If she could time it right, she might make the next wave before it broke.

The current pulled her down the backside of the wave. A shivering breath as she dipped under and came up again.

Then something bumped against her arm.

An empty bottle.

A second bottle thumped off her shoulder. And two more.

She splashed and turned, finding herself surrounded by dozens of bottles. They bobbed and glistened in the moonlight, *tinking* against each other like scattered gems.

Then came the debris.

First the lid of a crate and then several planks. Pieces of barnacled wood poked through the water as splintered barrels tumbled down wave after wave. Something like a doused lantern floated past, its glass muddy and cracked.

It didn't make sense. She hadn't heard any wreck or seen any ship. And yet here it was all around her, pieces of some broken boat crowding the black waters, thicker and thicker.

"Please! Help me!"

Desperate, the man in the linen shirt thrashed about as the waves rolled over and the debris battered him. Ten feet. Five.

"I can't swim... any longer."

Zelda reached across a splintered board. She shivered and twitched, her lungs two ever-tightening knots in her chest. And yet, nothing chilled her body deeper than the man reaching back for her hand.

There was something wrong with him, she realized. It wasn't just the old-fashioned clothes or the odd inflection to his voice.

It was his eyes.

Hollow sockets smoldered black-violet, blinking and mad.

A hand scratched her from behind. Another desperate man fumbled for her. "It's... so.... cold!" His glowing eyes widened. His mouth shivered and stretched. "You're... so... *warm!*"

There were others rising from the depths and breaching now, terrified sailors shrieking and swimming toward her. A choir of howling bodies tangled in nets and torn sails, clasped in chains and crawling over waterlogged debris. Cold violet wafted from empty eyes and past shivering lips.

"Warmth!" they cried, their hands stretching out for her, rancid and gray. "Warmth! Warmth!"

No. This was a mistake, the worst she'd ever made.

Zelda thought of her parents, wondering if she wouldn't be seeing them soon.

She thought of Ali and Maura, wishing she'd stayed back in that warm bonfire grove.

"Warmth! Warmth! Warmth!"

As the debris crushed in and the hands snatched at her skin, most of all she thought of Uncle Mark.

There were so many things she wished she had told him. That she was grateful and thankful, that she should have been better. That he deserved more than a niece who always lied.

"Warmth! Warmth! Warmth!"

Then they were upon her, wormy fingers and black-violet eyes frigid and desperate and endless.

25

Maura was ten minutes into debating the 49ers' best draft picks with Clay when a question percolated through her subconscious and took form in her mind: hadn't Zelda gone off with Sam? And if so, why was he returning to the party alone?

She pushed the worry away. Yes, Zelda was her friend, but she was also her own person, too. She could decide on what boys she wanted to fool around with. It wasn't Maura's business.

Well, not until later when she'd press her for details.

And yet...

"All I'm saying is the Niners are thirsting for a trophy," Clay said. "It's been, what, twenty years since their last Super Bowl?"

"Ninety-five," Maura said. "So closer to thirty. Hold up a second..."

She left Clay by the stereo and crossed through the headlights of a Jeep Wrangler. It was probably nothing, but she didn't like the worried look on Sam's face, like he was angry. Or that Arianna had joined him by the bonfire. Or that Finn and a few others were poking him and laughing. Or that they carried a near-empty cooler with a piece of seaweed stuck to the rim.

"What's the haps, Maur-bar?" Ali intercepted her at the far side of the bonfire. "You're doing your Terminator walk. 'Is your name Sarah Connor?'"

"Nothing, it's... Look, just back me up for a second."

"Roger that. On your six."

For all the shit she gave him, Ali still had the occasional flash of intuition. She was grateful he'd caught on to her discomfort.

As she approached the group, Finn nudged the empty cooler toward a shadow and Sam looked down at his feet. Arianna whispered something, then smiled. It reminded Maura of a billboard, flat and painted. "Heyyyy, we were just talking about you."

"Cool," Maura said. "You guys seen Zelda?"

An odd glance passed among the group, eyes shooting to Sam as he peeled the label from his beer. Arianna blinked. "Yeah, maybe. You know, why don't you try the beach? I heard she was feeling a bit... *salty.*"

A few low chuckles. No, Maura didn't like the rotten undertones, nor Arianna's pearly white grin. "Salty," Maura repeated. "What's that supposed to mean?"

One of the guys muttered something and wandered off. Arianna rolled her eyes. It was like watching a mask fall from her face, one that had grown too heavy to wear. "Wow, dense. Okay, I'll make it super simple for you. It means why don't the two of you, like, go fetch your psycho bitch friend... and head the fuck home."

It was as Maura had suspected. The invitation, the smiles, the introductions all around—it was all just a ruse. Girls like Arianna weren't quick to forgive or forget. Whatever they'd done to Zelda—and Maura had a good idea what it was—she could feel the party's mood shifting around her. Firelit faces turned toward them. Watching. Waiting. Holding their breath.

Maura sighed. "So that's how it is?"

Finn took a swig of his beer, then said, "Seriously, you zeros are killing the vibe."

"Ah, your precious vibe." That was Ali, speaking up and stepping beside Maura. "That's cute coming from Leonardo DiCreepio and Resting Rich Face over there. Finn, bro, I didn't know they made leashes that stretched through three grades." Ali made a whip sound and snapped his hand.

Scattered laughter echoed around them. Someone muttered, "Burned."

Finn scoffed as a nervous flash passed beneath Arianna's smirk. She said, "Yeah, well, at least my family's not squatting at the Heartworm refugee camp. A-gain."

"Wow, really reached for a top-shelf diss," Ali said. "At least I don't have more daddy issues than Miley Cyrus. But no judgment, Arianna, we all fill the void somehow." He gave Finn finger guns.

Arianna's voice squeaked as she tilted her cup. "Fuck you!"

The liquid hit Ali's face and splashed Maura, sour and sticky and reeking of lime. She moved toward Arianna on instinct.

And then Finn was there, between them, one arm holding Arianna back and the other pushing Maura.

Face dripping, Ali shouted, "She doesn't consent!"

Maybe he was joking. Or maybe he really was trying to take Finn on, a guy two years older and six inches taller. Maura wasn't sure.

Because what happened next was a blur. Finn let go of the girls as his left hand found Ali's collar. His right hand pulled back and snapped forward. There was a rip and a few gasps.

Then Ali was on his ass, a swirl of dust around him, collar stretched and buttons popped as the drink dribbled down his jacket.

"What the fuck are you gonna do, cry?" Finn said, his hand still balled in a fist.

For a moment, that's exactly what it looked like Ali was going to do. The bonfire glistened in his eyes. It took him several seconds just to blink.

Say something, Maura told herself. But she didn't know what to say. Until...

"Machiavelli," she said. "This party should lighten up, don't you think?"

Something came back online in his eyes and spread across his face in a smirk. Yeah, he understood. She was so glad she could kiss him.

But they'd have to find Zelda first.

"Finn, I tip my fedora to you," Ali said, wiping his lip as Maura helped him up. "I haven't seen such eager white-knighting since I joined the chess club."

A few chuckles from the upperclassmen. Ali brushed dust from his leg and loosened his backpack strap.

"But it's like Hollywood taught us: never fondle an Iraqi carrying bag of explosives."

And just like that, Ali threw his backpack into the bonfire.

One of the partygoers hit the deck immediately, and a few others scrambled back. But the Nylon just smoldered and the plastic bubbled. Everyone stared, befuddled as the backpack sizzled among the hot logs.

Maura whispered, "Ali? It's not doing anything."

"Sorry. It's my first act of terrorism, so—"

The explosion wasn't as large as she'd imagined or hoped for, not at first. Just a sudden puff and a series of colorful crackling bursts. The noise, however, was deafening.

Dozens of bottle rockets and Roman Candles, Piccolo Petes, and more screamed all at once. Some spun and spat balls of red fire. Others bounced in twisting ribbons of smoke. All the while, a whistling chorus overlapped with staccato pops like battlefield gunfire, rising louder and louder.

One of the cheerleaders dived behind her Jeep as Crackling Balls tossed red and green sparks. A pair of stoners dropped their bong as Sky Rockets boomed in the damp branches above. The partygoers scampered behind trees and rocks or climbed into their cars. Red and green, amber and yellow, the whole grove lit up in a shrieking strobe.

For a few seconds, Maura caught a flip-book glimpse of Arianna, legs askew as she stumbled over the water cooler, taking Finn with her. Someone honked their horn and revved their engine.

Laughing, Maura dragged Ali to the edge of the grove where Sam and Zelda had gone off.

"Dude, that was like the movies," Ali panted. "Badasses never look back at explosions. But seriously, I didn't look back, so how was it?"

"Oh, I think the whole town saw it. C'mon."

As the fireworks fizzled and the cars revved their engines and peeled out, the pair made their way over to the cliffs and down the rickety steps. They called out Zelda's name but heard no answer. A few minutes later, they found something that made their hearts drop.

Zelda's leather jacket and boots lay in the sand near the tide pools and shore. A set of footprints led to the water.

As they scanned the empty dark cove and its waves, Maura said four words that had gotten her in such trouble this summer. Four words she hoped to never utter again.

"I'm calling the cops."

26

Mark was settling into the couch with Stacey, thirty minutes into an episode of *Ted Lasso*, when the edible hit him. It layered a gooey hue over the dark apartment and brought a grin to his lips. It tickled his skin with cozy embers. Yawning, he adjusted the blanket and wiggled his toes.

"Can I ask you something?"

"Uh-oh." Stacey plucked some popcorn from the bowl. "Nothing good comes from asking someone if you can ask them something. Should I brace myself?"

She pressed pause, freezing Ted Lasso's face on the TV. Mark wasn't sure how strong these edibles were, but the guy at the dispensary had promised they'd help him relax. And they had. It was the first time since Zelda's field trip to San Francisco that the apartment was his. Still, a question had been scratching around for weeks, and now Ted's mustache was creeping him out.

"Okay, I'll just say it." He took a deep breath. "Is it just me, or did it feel like we had a thing going for a bit? And then it sort of... fizzled out."

"Fizzled, huh?" Stacey sat up straight and turned to him. "First off, I wouldn't call a Friday night soiree at Condescension Manor a fizzle. A belly flop or a faceplant perhaps, but not a fizzle. And second, how strong were these gummies? 'Cause I haven't been this couch-locked since college."

She stretched a leg across his lap and wiggled her toes.

"The dispensary did make me sign a waiver." He winked at her. And then he thought about how odd winking actually was, and he wondered who invented it first. Damn, his thoughts were going in every direction.

She said, "I mean, I guess we can dig into it now."

"I'll get the shovel."

The world tilted as he adjusted the blanket. Sometimes, it felt like the apartment was so small it would keep shrinking until the walls touched his shoulders and squeezed him to nothing. And then, other times—usually when Zelda was gone—it felt like an empty motel.

But now, with the scent of buttered popcorn in the air and Stacey beside him, the night had an echo of the life he'd left in Madrid. Zelda, off with her friends. His grades were in for the term. And even that fundraiser at the vineyard felt oddly distant, as if it had occurred in a place farther out than the edge of town.

Yes, tonight was the first Friday night he could truly relax.

So why the hell was he stirring the pot? Why couldn't he just enjoy things as they were?

"I like you, Mark," she said. "I mean, obviously, I have pretty strong feelings. I just..."

She swallowed, and he swallowed, too. He wondered how long it had been since he drank his Diet Coke, so he took a sip. Had his gulps always felt like they were on a delay? Shit, he was getting the sativa jitters.

"I just think, maybe we took things a little fast out the gate," she said. "After the fire and the... Well, after *everything*, it was a lot to process all at once."

"To be fair, you were concussed," he said. "Nothing like a head wound to lower standards, right?"

"Right. Me and my history of *amazing* standards." Something sad flashed beneath her smile as a color bloomed in his mind. Gray, like old metal.

Her divorce, he realized. Her creepy ex at the party.

Then he blinked and the color was gone.

"Is it something I said or did?" he asked.

"No, it's not you," she said. "It's... See, there's other factors to consider, you know? Other people."

"Oh." So, there it was. The truth was rarely the first thing past someone's lips. Especially when they were trying to be gentle with your heart. He asked, "Is it my niece?"

He knew the answer before she spoke. "Yeah, it's Zelda."

He sighed. "Thing is, it's sort of a package deal."

"What? No, no no no, I..." Stacey wobbled for a moment and braced herself against the armrest. "Wow, spins. What I mean is, she's great. She's amazing. She's... You're really lucky, you know?"

He nodded. Yeah, he did know. And yet, nine months after arriving at his sister's funeral, he was still uncovering duties he didn't understand. The biweekly therapist. The check-ins with the lawyers and the judge. The parent-teacher meetings and student-family socials. They all stretched muscles he didn't know existed. Parts he sometimes rejected as unworthy.

Shit. Maybe he needed to open up to Dr. Rhonda. Maybe he was the one dampening his own Friday night buzz.

"To lose your parents..." Stacey continued. "I mean, to be there and see that, it's almost unimaginable. My point is, you and me, we don't know if this is going to work out between us. I want it to. But if it doesn't..."

Mark studied her as she searched for the words. With her hair let down and the TV's glow painting her cheeks a cool blue, he realized that he wasn't the only one hitting midlife yet feeling shakier than ever.

He asked, "If it doesn't work out, what?"

Something hardened in her eyes. "I don't want to get attached and have to leave," she said. "Most of all, I don't want to hurt Zelda. She doesn't deserve that."

A little puff of air left his mouth and his whole body lightened. So that was it. Her distancing wasn't because of something he'd done, but something she feared becoming. A friend. A girlfriend. Perhaps, in time, a mother figure to a broken young girl.

He could have kissed her, right here and now. He squeezed her hand, leaned in, and—

Then the doorbell rang.

The apartment snapped back into focus, leaving Mark woozy. He checked his phone: 10:33 p.m. Whoever that was at the door, he had no intention of answering. Not with his heavy eyelids, his black-saucer pupils, and crumbs of popcorn dotting his hoodie.

Then it rang a second time.

"Okay, okay." He wobbled his way over, the carpet like fuzzy grass underfoot. He was too baked to talk to anyone not on his level, and Ted Lasso's mustache was making him itchy. Why couldn't the universe just let him enjoy an evening in peace?

A third ring, and then came the knocking. He practically yanked the door open. "Do you know what time it is?"

He didn't think his mouth could go any drier.

He was wrong.

The last time Mark saw Alejandro Ruiz—Juan Carlos's brother and Zelda's other uncle—the man had been storming out of the house in Alder Glen. Mark had informed the Ruizes he was taking guardianship of Zelda as her parents intended. The Ruizes informed him they were suing for custody. They'd spoken through lawyers ever since.

But here he stood, a man several years older than Mark, always more professional and composed.

"Alejandro. ¿Qué estás haciendo aquí?" Mark said, falling back into the Spanish of half their conversations over the years. "What are you doing—"

"We arrived this afternoon," he said. "My folks, they wanted to get settled at the Airbnb and surprise Zelda tomorrow, but..."

He glanced over his shoulder, where a car idled in the parking lot and two figures looked out from the shadowy back seat.

Mark's thoughts struggled for balance on the edge of an abyss. He was a teenager again, sneaking in after midnight and finding his mom wide awake. He was back at his apartment in Madrid, mealymouthed and confused, struggling to tell Rosalia he'd just seen his sister appear, thousands of miles from her home.

And here he was now, his heart pounding its way up his chest. He dreaded the next words to come from Alejandro's lips.

Because a small part of him knew.

"It's sort of silly," Alejandro said. "But Zelda's grandmother, she's hoping she can see her, just for a moment. It's probably nothing, but she's worried something happened."

27

Chester was listening to K-GRAY's classic countdown, Billy Fox about to play one of his eighties favorites, Dire Straits' "Romeo & Juliet," when something cold dimpled his chest. He lowered the foil origami man he'd been folding and placed it on his desk. He fumbled for the source of the chill, unbuttoning his shirt in two quick jerks.

His necklace. The glass was as frigid as ice.

Zelda, shit...

With shaking fingers, he traced spiral gestures and the clasp released. He hoisted the blue pendant up to his eye.

The suites of Pacific Manor—like the residents themselves, Chester often mused—were a study in slow decay and neglect. He'd complained about the dim bulbs and the flickering lamps. But tonight, the light from the courtyard and its gardens was enough to see what he needed.

Peering through the bottle glass, Chester wasn't sure what he was looking at. Nothing at first. Or, rather, nothing his tired eyes could assemble.

Then a ribbon of black-violet swam through the glassy luminance.

No, not her, he thought. *Not now. Dammit, she isn't ready.*

A shape emerged beyond the glass: a girl engulfed in smoldering waters and fighting for air. Spectral hands stretched out for her, desperate and mad.

And the lights. Lights in the sky. Lights in their eyes.

Sailors.

Squinting and pressing the glass so close his eyelids twitched, Chester saw it all.

Zelda. Somehow she'd drawn out the dead. They were cold and confused and seeking her warmth. Where the hell was she? Some new wound in the All.

It didn't matter. His left hand moved on its own, tracing words his tongue could never pronounce. Ideas and concepts, alien and arcane yet infinitely human. Like the warmth of a fire after a cold, stormy night.

There was a flicker in the bottle glass—an amber ribbon of warmth —and the sailors snapped their faces toward Chester.

Lifeless, glowing eyes. Waterlogged cheeks. Lips as blue as the very waves they fought, so desperate to escape.

"Warmth... Warmth... Warmth..."

The sailors stretched out slimy hands, skin so viscous it slid off in patches. Barnacles spotted their sea-tortured bones. Chester pitied these wayward souls. He might have helped them once, if he was younger, stronger.

If he had room left in his heart.

But they were many, and he was old and alone. At least he could distract them.

"Warmth... Warmth... Warmth..."

Then Zelda's form drifted away. Satisfied that she was safe, he lowered the bottle glass. Only the quiet courtyard lay before him. Ms. Tan, standing near the back door and sneaking a drag on her vape. He inhaled, hoping to catch a whiff of whatever she was toking. Sometimes, it quieted the ghosts.

Instead, something salty and rotten burned his nostrils. Decay, the kind that came from the dark depths of the ocean.

"Warmth..."

The sailor moaned and stepped out of Chester's bathroom. With each lumbering jerk, a new detail emerged: rusty chains wrapped around his left leg, netting fused with mottled flesh, an old wine bottle half-buried within the muddy cave of his stomach.

"Warmth," the sailor burbled. "Give me... your warmth."

Bleed-through, shit.

Then the dead sailor was upon Chester, so fast he couldn't draw a symbol of protection. Cold, clammy fingers seized Chester's right wrist.

"You've stood in her way for so long." With a soggy twist, the sailor pulled Chester's hand.

There was a series of crackling pops and a flash of searing heat. Chester screamed, but a second wet hand clamped over his mouth.

"If I bring her... your eyes... mayhaps she'll let me... move on."

The sailor's mouth opened wide, wider, so wide his head fell back and something like a crab squirmed forth from the ruined depths of his neck.

A crab with a human face on its shell.

With his weak, unbroken hand, Chester clenched the dead sailor's chain. His shaky finger traced a shape on the cold metal links. He thought of a word in the All Tongue, one he hadn't written in decades.

Constriction.

The chain slid from his fingers, faster and faster. In a wet pop, it cinched through soggy fabric, sallow skin, and brittle bone, cleaving the sailor at the hips.

The dead man's torso toppled to the left. His legs stumbled to the right. It was just enough for Chester to break free of his grasp.

Limping, he crossed his suite in five paces. His broken wrist burned as he turned the doorknob. Then he was out in the hall, the calm walls of Pacific Manor greeting him, safe and secure.

Until a honeyed voice called out from a painting.

That familiar shipwreck, it was moving. A painted storm playing out forever upon dusty canvas.

"Mmm... Where are you, old one? I can feel you sticking fingers in too many holes."

Chester froze mid-step, telling himself not to turn around. *Run. Run, you old fool!*

"Run? We both know you won't do that, will you? You ran once, yes

you did. And you've spent every day since living with their screams. Thirty-nine souls for my forge."

The halls tilted. Chester pressed his shoulder against the wall, steadying his shaking legs. He closed his eyes. Then the walls of Pacific Manor merged with the walls of West Pine Psychiatric. He tasted rain seeping down, bulging the paint and softening the foundation beneath him.

Turning a mountain into mud.

No. He wouldn't run. He opened his eyes.

"I made my peace," Chester said. "My dead are no longer yours to torment."

Then he turned back to his suite.

There was no gooey sailor upon the floor in two pieces. Instead, there sat a young boy, his hair blond and curly, skin so smooth it looked painted. Chester knew that child.

That was him.

"Mmm... You made your peace indeed, but not with me. Wherever you're hiding, time will find you."

The boy looked up at Chester with eyes leaking black-violet. He giggled as his fingers twisted a dial on some sort of toy.

Yes, Chester remembered that little figurine. A wind-up drummer his sister Mabel had given him so many decades ago. One of their last happy memories. One he revisited often.

Now, the boy met Chester's nervous stare, a corrupted reflection of youth.

"A gift for the so-called guardian, Greywood Bay's withered old fool. Some knowledge in numbers for what remains of your time."

"Thirteen," the boy said. "Six hundred and thirty-three thousand, five hundred and twelve."

Chester blinked. Between the searing pain in his wrist and his own beating heart, he wasn't sure what he'd heard.

"Six hundred and thirty-three thousand, five hundred and eleven." The boy gave the little drummer a final twist. He placed it on the floor. "Ten. Six hundred and thirty-three thousand, five hundred and ten."

With gentle, precise fingers, the boy released the toy drummer. A wobble, a click, and then it marched forward. Each step brought the hammer down on the drum. *Thumpity thump. Thumpity thump.*

"Eight." The grin that split the boy's face knotted Chester's gut. He'd never smiled with such latent cruelty. "Six hundred and thirty-three thousand, five hundred and eight."

Thumpity thump. Lubbity dub.

Chester felt the tightness in his own chest, beating in time with the drum. And at this, the boy giggled, his eyes a little too small, a little too wide.

"Five!" he called out as Chester turned and rushed from the suite. "Six hundred and thirty-three thousand, five hundred and five."

The boy's laughter and the drumming followed Chester down the hall. He needed someone to help him. To fix his wrist and repair his tired mind. But most of all, his heart. It burned in his chest and drove a blade through each breath. It beat at the same tempo as that drum.

Lub dub. Lub dub.

"One! Six hundred and thirty-three thousand, five hundred and one!"

28

Ben Thomas woke to the same instinctual panic that had gripped him recently: a miasma of fear without reason. Something was wrong, something was gone, something had been taken that he couldn't recall. He pulled the sheets off as his tired mind scoured itself for clues that led him to this room.

Remember.

Old bottles lined a wooden bedside table. Had he been drinking? No. The bottles were dusty and hadn't held liquid in years. Like the ashen walls, his past was blank, a few cracks giving vague hints of something beneath.

Remember...

A pier where a woman stood and held out her camera. "Would you mind taking our picture?"

Dark waters smoothing to mirrored black glass. "There's no better place to study the light."

The starry sky exploding with colors so vibrant he wasn't sure what to call them. "—*sky'une vok'arr zathule n'gä vey'eel.*"

Remember, yes. It was on the tip of his tongue now: how he'd gotten here and what he was meant to be doing. The light bands and the stars and something *beyond*.

"C'mon. Remember. C'mon!"

Then it all receded. Slipped away like errant smoke in the wind. Gone.

Sighing, he climbed out of bed. He scratched himself and took inventory of the small room. A door to his left. A wood-burning stove straight ahead. An odd texture imbued the curved wall, rough yet intentional. Pressing his face close, he saw the faint shape of letters chiseled in and painted over.

I CAN

Knees wobbling, he followed the wall to the window, where moonlight streamed through. His stomach dropped as the dark horizon came into view.

Damn, he was high up. Fifty or sixty feet at least. The ocean lay spread out before him, mirrored stars sparkling above and below.

Where the hell was this place? Some sort of tower?

He edged his way back to the window, stealing another glance down. Wave-battered rocks glistened and lined a flat patch of earth. Scattered debris dotted the shore, splintered wood and barrels all bobbing and clattering. And something else.

At the edge of the tide pools, where algae-encrusted rocks met a damp berm, lay a form entangled in netting, one arm draped over a barrel.

It was a woman.

"Hey! Down there! Hellooooo!"

Only the wind and murmuring waves replied. He called out again. The woman stirred but didn't rise. She was wounded, or maybe worse. He'd have to go down there himself.

Down...

Why did that direction tighten his legs?

He pushed the door open to find a long, circular shaft where stairs spiraled both upward and down. An old metal railing lined the edge. Yes, he was right, he realized; this was some sort of tower or house.

Lighthouse, of course. He *must have* been here before.

Descending, his feet knew the subtle curve of the stairs. His legs knew the width of each step and the flatness of the landing. Even his hands understood how to undo the heavy latches on the door at the bottom. He steadied himself against the wind, then stepped out into the foggy dark night.

Ten steps, and he turned around. The lighthouse base was brick and concrete, some forty feet in diameter. Jagged boulders and stones scratched the soggy land around it—only a dozen acres at most. Thirsty shrubs and malformed bushes rustled in scraggy piles.

But the woman, right.

He hurried down the embankment, stepping around driftwood clogged with tattered sacks. His foot hit a bottle, sending it spinning and shattering among the tide pools. Then he was at the netting, the barrel, and the tangled woman upon it.

She was just a girl, he realized. Some teenager in a torn dress, arms caught up in the rope. Dead? No, she moaned when he nudged her.

"Oh thank goodness."

He wasn't sure who he was thanking.

Brushing a crab from her dress, he recoiled at its grotesque movements. Moonlight revealed its legs as slender fingers. And on the back of its shell, pearl-like eyes glimmered upon a chitinous bulge.

A face.

That was a human.

Mewling, the crab skittered and squeezed into a hole where it glared from the darkness.

Christ, he needed to get off this rock.

"Hey." He nudged her again. "Were you in an accident or... something?"

Her eyes fluttered beneath her lids as her right-hand finger traced little shapes in the sand. Ben scanned the foggy waters, expecting to see a ship or a boat, something sinking into the...

Bay.

Yes, he remembered something now. He was along some sort of bay. He had come here—to this *gray* bay—because...

Remember. *Remember.*

"Dammit!" Then it slipped away. Another tortuous question scurrying inside the walls of his mind.

For now, he needed to get the girl warmed up. Despite the wet clothes, she was skinny and easily lifted. Shivering, he hoisted her into a fireman's carry and brought her inside.

He found another wood-burning stove in the foyer and gently placed her in a chair. It took him a moment to find wood and kindling, matches and oil, all stored in a nearby closet. He noticed a faded black handprint marring the door's inner white paint, charcoal words asking, *How many fires have you made?*

He didn't have an answer.

With the scratch of a match and the crack of some wood, he soon had a fire glowing in the stove. He closed the firebox door and tested the warming metal. Good.

He found blankets in a chest and draped them around her. Then he noticed the black ash on his fingers from the stove.

Interesting.

As the fire grew, he returned to the closet. He held up his right hand, comparing the size to the faded print. It was a fit. But what did any of this mean? He'd have to ask somebody and—

A flash as another word sparked in his mind.

Radio.

Yes, there was a radio transmitter here. Had he caught a glimpse of the room on his rush down the stairs? He must have.

"Just stay here," he told the unconscious girl. "And stay warm."

He hurried up the stairs, two and three at a time. His body instinctually remembered the steps, like they were part of some childhood street. The number fifteen flashed in his mind.

Had he wounded his head and washed up here, just like the girl? If so, how long had he been here?

Another flash, and a name emerged in his mind: Janice.

Her fingers unfolding a piece of saltwater taffy. Blackberry, her favorite

Her lips rising to a smile as she chewed. A smile he wanted to spend the rest of his life waking up to.

And her palm, soft and warm as she took his hand, fingers interlocking among the cool wind of the pier where they walked and they talked and made plans for the future and—

Plans, yes. And a date, not on the calendar, but a promise he'd once made. Dammit, had he forgotten that, too?

Panting, he stopped at the fourth floor before a door marked *RADIO ROOM*. Inside sat a desk crowded with electronics and a window with that same moonlit view. He studied the devices, names popping into his mind. High-frequency and very high-frequency radio transmitter and receiver. Barometers, thermometers, anemometers, and more. There was even a logbook and a cup full of stubby pencils.

With a click, he switched the mic on, needles swinging and diodes glowing. He glanced at the monitor's power level and signal quality, instinctively sensing that he knew what these meant.

There it was, the frequency for the mainland already tuned in. He had a perfectly clean signal. He thumbed the mic.

"Uh... base, this is Point Greywood. Do you copy?"

He lingered in the silence, coiled in anticipation for the crackling response: "Base to Point Greywood. We read you loud and clear. Over."

But it never came.

His nervous fingers pulled a stubby pencil from the cup and traced the tooth marks and grooves. He repeated, "Base, this is Point Greywood. Do you copy? Point Greywood to base. Over."

His words vanished, unanswered, leaving him to wonder how long he'd been calling out, and if he'd ever find an answer beyond the endless dark void.

29

Zelda dreamed she was back at 33 Manzanita Way, shivering and wrapped in a blanket and calling out for Uncle Mark. She was alone, walking room to room, the walls as unburnt and bare as the day of the home showing. Diana Betancourt—the nervous real estate agent—slid her damp hand along a newel post.

"And the accents are oak reclaimed from centuries of shipwrecks. Can you imagine how much suffering they've seen? Yes, we've built a beautiful thing here. Now, if you'll follow me into the stockade..." Diana's voice drifted and echoed off the white walls.

Zelda did not follow.

Because Diana was dead; she died in the fire. And because these stairs weren't part of her home. She lingered, taking a deep breath. Salty and damp, with the hint of sea breeze and kelp. Far off, something like waves crashed in the distance.

She slid her hand over the railing. It was cold and industrial, built not for tasteful style but for utility and strength. The stairs at 33 Manzanita Way never spiraled up, floor after floor. Even the paint was off, the warm whites and cream accents replaced with an off-slate gray, cracked and weathered. And like the stairs, these walls curved.

Leaning out over the balcony, Zelda studied the central column leading down. There was some sort of entry area a few floors below, sparse and utilitarian. An old wood-burning stove glowed cozy and orange near a pile of moth-eaten blankets, like the one she was wearing.

Blanket? When had she draped herself in this fabric?

She pulled at her damp clothes underneath. Her skin shivered and her senses tingled. No, no, this was all wrong. This wasn't a dream. She *remembered*.

Sam's hesitation as he stepped back from the Wall of Names.

Arianna's cruel laughter and her giggling friends.

The chill of waves and the wreckage and the sailors.

"Warmth... Warmth... Warmth..."

Where the hell was she?

A baritone voice came from behind her, low and nervous. "You're awake?"

Zelda spun, finding herself staring into a dusty room crowded with old electronics and lichen-spotted walls. There, by the ruins of long-defunct radio equipment, stood a man. Messy brown hair crowned a head held at a quizzical tilt. Tattered clothes hung from a skinny frame, one that spoke of sickness and malnutrition.

But it was the sharp object in his hand that made her back away.

"I wasn't sure you'd be up." He took a step toward her. "Whoa, careful now."

She thought of the sailors and their screams. Their fingers clawing at her skin until their cold desperation was all that she knew.

She took another step back. The man glanced at his hand and lowered the screwdriver.

"Hey," he said, then: "Hey! Careful!"

She felt it: the railing against the small of her back. Decades of rusted brackets and chalky stone, too tired to hold on any longer. With a moan, it buckled and broke free. First, in a snap that wobbled her knees and loosened her legs. Then, in a weightless sway as the bolts popped off —*tinkity, tinkity, tink*. She fell backward with the railing. For one breathless second, her eyes rose and saw the long spiral stairs leading up to a room pulsing with light.

A lighthouse, she realized.

Of all the stupid places, she was going to die in a lighthouse.

Instead, she hung there, teetering at an odd angle.

Arms outstretched, the man clutched a loose cord from her dress, just enough to stop her lean from becoming a fall. With a rip and a tear, the metal hooks bent. The cord whipped through the holes and slid free.

But not before he pulled her back onto the stairs.

"Whoa there. I've got you. Just take it nice... and slow."

They pivoted around each other until she had space to back away from the ruined railing and the stairs. Loose pieces of concrete peppered the entryway below and echoed up the tower.

"Thanks." They stood there, staring at each other. Zelda, in her torn, soggy dress. This man in his tattered clothes. "So are you, like, the lighthouse keeper, or what?"

"No, no, I'm..." He gestured around the room with a sad sort of exhaustion. "I'm not really sure."

"You're not sure of what?"

He shook his head. "I'm not really sure what I am. I mean, my memory, it's all... foggy. I was up there. Then I saw you down on the rocks, brought you in and tried to call for help, but..." He picked up the screwdriver and pointed to the radio. "No one's answering."

A lifetime of warnings flashed in Zelda's mind. She was alone with a stranger in a lighthouse. A stranger who wasn't making much sense. Her instincts screamed to run away. And yet, she felt a broken kindness to the man. Perhaps an echo of Chester.

She asked, "So what's your name?"

"Ben," he said.

"Ben." She repeated his name, recalling how she'd once read that names personalized things. "You made that fire for me, Ben?"

He nodded. "You were freezing. Kept muttering 'warmth,' so I got it as hot as I could. I just... I promise I'm not a serial killer or anything."

"Thank you, Ben Not a Serial Killer. I'm Zelda."

He placed the screwdriver on a shelf, reached out, and shook her hand. As they touched, an image flickered in her mind. Fireworks over the pier at Coogan's Wharf. A sticky sweetness on her tongue, like salt-water taffy. Then...

Then it was gone.

"Zelda," he repeated. "Like the video game?"

"Something like that." She broke the handshake and stifled her cringe. "So, this is Point Greywood."

"You know it?"

She studied the radio room. "Drove by it with my uncle. Plus, there was an exhibit at the pier. This whole thing is, like, crazy old."

His eyes shimmered at that word. "The pier?"

"You know, greedy seagulls, Ferris wheel, overpriced knickknacks they sell to the tourists?"

He glanced at the floor as his mind wandered through a maze. "It's weird. I can see little flashes of—*wait!* There's a thing with horses and poles—"

"Yeah, the carousel."

"Car-ou-sel," he repeated. "Right. I... I think I was supposed to meet someone there. I made a promise, and then..." His eyes widened. "Damn, I think I'm going to be late." In a quick pivot, he hurried to the radio equipment, where he twisted knobs and smacked the receiver. "Base, this is Point Greywood. Do you copy? Point Greywood to base. Over."

Late? The only thing he was late for was a haircut and a fresh change of clothes. Maybe there was a shelter with his bed.

Zelda paced around the room while Ben repeated his call. She ran a finger over the equipment, rust flaking at her touch. "Ben, I hate to break it to you, but I don't think this is working."

He glanced at the stack of electronics. "No. Probably not with this junk." In a violent swing, he pointed the screwdriver toward her... then beyond. "There's a shelf of spare parts. C'mon, help me switch out the tubes."

"Tubes?"

"Vacuum tubes, y'know? Tall glass with filaments inside. Little pins at the bottom. If they're cloudy, they've gone bad."

"Right, vacuum tubes. Of course."

Inside the closet, tired shelves leaned beneath the weight of fat, brittle boxes. She gave one a poke, something jingling as the cardboard side crumbled. Tubes, a dozen at least. She plucked them out. Cloudy. Cloudy. Cracked.

"Here's one."

With a clunk, Ben unscrewed the final corner and pried the metal top off the radio. "Go ahead and swap 'em out."

"Me? I don't know anything about this." Zelda studied the insides of the radio. It looked like something her dad would have built in his spare time to listen to records. Something delicate and old with rare parts sourced from collectors. "I'll just break it."

"Fine. See if you can find a spare power cord. This one's gone to shit."

While Ben reached into the guts and plucked out vacuum tubes, she returned to the shelving. Higher up, she found a box labeled *Mechanical* that contained knobs and dials, switches and relays. Another box labeled *Electronic* contained capacitors and resistors, diodes and transistors. She moved it aside.

There, near a stack of old books, sat a box labeled *Wiring*.

"Found it."

As she pulled the box down, the rotten shelf collapsed, spilling cables and plugs and spooled wires. She wiped dried, grimy cardboard from her face as a notebook landed open at her feet.

A logbook.

Spooling the power cord, she studied the handwritten page. As words passed before her eyes, her gut soured.

"What's that?" Ben was so close behind her she almost screamed. "Where'd you find it?"

"By the cables."

An uncomfortable thought: it was like the closet had spilled it for her. Like the notebook wanted to be found.

He took both items from her, yet it was the logbook that ensnared his focus, the power cord just an afterthought in his grip. As he thumbed through the pages, Zelda caught a glimpse of an entry.

Date: Unknown. Broadcast for 3 hours w/o response. What is this place & why am I here?

He turned several pages, brow crinkling, lips moving silently as he read.

*High tide w/ distant figures on the far beach. I waved but
they couldn't see me. Tried binoculars, but slipped on the
rocks & they broke.*
I saw them.
*They were standing on the sand across the cove and
chanting.*
It never stops.

Ben's eyes glistened as he turned another page, the handwriting
growing jagged and slanted.

Indians.
Indians, I'm sure of it.
Indians crossing the foggy waters.
*They were beaded and painted, their headdresses rotten and
ruined. Their eyes sparkled like purple gems in the night.*

"Ben?"

His lip quivered as he read and turned the pages, faster and faster.
The inky words gave way to pencil, then to charcoal and something
spattered and brown.

Blood.

"Ben, what is it?"

He didn't answer. Not with words, not at first. But she could read
the fear and confusion in his eyes.

The writing now filled every page of the logbook. Every line and
margin. Every gap.

I can't.
I can't leave.
I cannot leave!

"It's my handwriting," he whispered. "I recognize every word. I just... I don't remember writing it."

With his back against the wall, he slumped to the ground and ran his hands through his oily hair.

"Be honest with me," he said. "Is this some sort of hell?"

Zelda swallowed, struggling to give form to her words. There was a familiar echo to this broken man. Chester, coming after them in his junkyard. Annie Paxton, crawling through a broken window. And yet, something new and distinctly his own. He reminded her of a rabbit chased to exhaustion.

Not chased, she thought. Hunted.

"Is that what this is?" he asked. "Am I dead and this is my hell?"

"I don't know. Maybe we both are, or maybe it's something else." She drew in a salty, stale breath, resolve growing inside. "But whatever this is, we're getting out of here so—"

It began with a low rumble. The structure shook, rattling her bones and sending dust down the wall.

First, a crackling shudder split the gray paint. It peeled in scabby flakes to reveal words underneath.

I can't. I can't leave. I CANNOT LEAVE!

Hundreds. Thousands. Too many words to count lined the wall, chiseled and carved and clawed into the stones of the lighthouse in a ledger of torment.

Then came the sputtering radio, diodes flickering and needles swinging. With a puff, the old speaker murmured to life.

"I can't..." it echoed and mocked. "I cannot leave. I am dead and this is my hell... hell... hell-el-el-ellllllll..."

Shivering, Ben clutched the power cable to his chest. He'd never finished plugging it in.

Yeah, Zelda thought, it was time to get moving. "Let's go."

Outside the radio room's doorway, a rancid glow suffused the stairwell. Shadows fled down the walls, inky and shimmering.

"I remember," Ben said, his eyes drifting up. "That light, I remember... it all."

Unctuous and infected, shadow-laced violet bloomed from the

lantern room. It slithered in tendrils and poured down the stairs. Finger-like, it clawed its way out from splitting cracks in the walls.

"C'mon!" Zelda shouted. "We really need to go."

Feet pounding on the steps, they descended as the hideous light dripped down the shaft and sprouted from widening cracks. Between these gaps—somehow, *beyond*—rotten skin stretched and frayed to reveal a wretched landscape, alien and twisted.

The All.

Zelda raced faster and faster, her bare feet pounding on the spiral steps. She was almost to the foyer when she looked back.

Ben had stopped following. He stood at the landing, his gaze drifting upwards. "Light... of my lights."

"Hey! C'mon!" She turned and hurried back up. "Whatever that is, it's definitely not good."

But his face had taken on an awed softness, slack-jawed and mesmerized. He repeated, "Light... of my lights."

"What? No, no, no." She tugged on his clammy hand. "Hey, Ben, look at me. We need to go, okay?"

"Okay."

As she led him down, each step clung to their feet like a gluey rattrap. Five steps. Ten. Fifteen and a landing. They were almost to the door when his wrist slipped from her hand.

His legs locked and his body stiffened as his face tilted upward, bathed in the sickening glow. "I've stood here," he muttered. "Ten thousand times or more. I remember it all."

"Ben, c'mon!" She tugged his hand, but his body stayed firm as if something anchored him to the floor.

A floor no longer formed of stone but a nest of interwoven bones.

"Ben!"

"Ben... Yes, I think I've been here forever."

The light twinkled in his eyes as tears streamed down his cheeks. Then her gaze rose, too, for only a blink.

She wished it never had.

Because she wasn't looking up anymore but out through an expanding maelstrom. Brick by brick, floor by floor, the glow tore the lighthouse apart. Twitching tendrils wormed through the widening gaps. Chittering forms stalked the void beyond, creatures of shell and spine and tumorous lumps. Twisted mockeries of biology, bearing eyes that shouldn't see and limbs that bent in defiance of nature.

She recognized some as the pups of J'harr. Six-limbed bodies of horns and scales and ring-pierced flesh, slavering and scratching to get in. They howled in delight at the scent of suffering.

There were other beings, too. Misty human forms—wraith-like and tortured—moaning in ecstasy and thrusting violative fingers through the gaps. Mounds of crustaceans tumbling over each other. Crabs with human faces stretching out from their shells.

And there were things beyond any form Zelda's mind could assemble.

Crystalline clusters congealing upon shimmering organs writhing and folding inward in an infinite loop. Glowing kites crowned with teeth that opened like blooming flowers.

But the light most of all...

It scarred a path, burning away the world's sturdy edges. It dissolved the lighthouse until its stairs simply unraveled and the bricks drifted into a hungering abyss.

Zelda might have stood there forever, staring into that maddening fracture. She sensed she had lingered for lifetimes.

Then a hand grabbed her by the shoulder, shaking her free of the paralyzing light.

"Zelda, this isn't for you." Grim epiphany spread across Ben's face. "I remember it now, all of it. This place, it isn't for you."

His hand lashed out. She flinched as it shot past and skimmed her left ear, moving something behind her with a *clunk*. Then a different glow traced the nervous lines of his face.

Daylight.

"Please don't forget me."

He shoved her—hard—and she fell back through the door of the lighthouse, tumbling out onto concrete and scraggy earth. A final glimpse inside: the swirling void closing in behind Ben, a hungry wave teeming with creatures of rending claws and gnashing teeth.

Ben slammed the door just as they reached him.

Then: quiet.

The murmuring ocean.

The distant cry of a gull.

Heart pounding, Zelda limped her way back up the steps, calling out, "Ben! Ben!"

There was no handle or knob on the outside. Only a stark, smooth patch of metal, interrupted by the outline of bolt holes, scars of a former entrance. No matter how hard she pushed or pulled or dug her fingers into the seams, the door remained shut.

"Ben! Please open up! Please!"

Her fists met the door in dense, muffled thuds. Her desperate pleas reverberated and faded beneath the morning breeze.

"Ben..."

Something buzzed overhead, scattering dust and sea spray as it banked into the rising sun's glow. Lifting her hand, Zelda squinted into the sunrise.

Past the edge of the lighthouse, the soggy land formed Point Greywood, a shoal, jagged and glistening with tide pools. It connected to a misty cove beneath towering cliffs, fog burning off in the daybreak.

Zelda watched the humming object circle back now, its windows glinting. With its black nose, orange paint, and distinctive white stripe down the side, she knew exactly what it was; Ali had taught her.

An MH-65 Dolphin search-and-rescue helicopter flown by the Coast Guard.

And it was returning for her.

30

The longest day of Mark's life began the previous night.

It started with the Ruizes' surprise visit, souring the edible's cozy hue and infusing the evening with rising suspicion. It bubbled into a vague fear when Zelda never answered her phone. It congealed into paranoia at the Kerns' townhouse, where he heard Zelda's ringtone, muffled as he pressed an ear to the door. Then Maura's when he dialed her. And Ali's as well.

When he kicked the door in and discovered three phones and no kids, the fear metastasized. This was something wretched and confusing, a cancerous terror that spiked his pulse and clogged his throat. He told himself panic had an upper limit. That his heart couldn't beat any faster.

When the Coast Guard called before midnight, he realized he was wrong.

So very wrong.

They used terms like MISPER for "missing person," PIW for "person in water," and LKP for "last known position." They talked about search grids and drift patterns and survival times. Mark heard it all, acute and precise. And yet this had to be happening to someone else, someone distant. He needed to sit on the couch to focus while Stacey asked everyone to stay calm and speak slowly.

Because the entire Hadid family was in his apartment now, along with the Ruizes and several neighbors. Half the Heartwood residents were awake and helping out, calling friends on the police force, the highway patrol, the National Guard. Pavarti phoned an ex who asked his high school daughter to dig up more of the story. When the response came in, everyone crowded around Pavarti's phone.

A secret bonfire party at the beach. Some sort of altercation that ended with Ali setting off fireworks. The highway patrol stopping by.

And a girl who had gone missing at the beach.

The phrase *probably unalived herself* scrolled past. Grandpa Ruiz squinted and asked in a low voice, "*¿Qué significa esto?* This... unalive?"

When someone answered, Grandma Ruiz gasped and crossed herself.

"Christ, Mark, how could you have let her sneak off?" Alejandro muttered. "And you wonder why the family doesn't trust you?"

No, Mark thought, he never wondered at all. Sometimes he barely trusted himself.

Hours blurred in a chain of phone calls and updates punctuated by cups of coffee and trips to the bathroom. Maura arrived, and then Ali, who filled in more blanks. There were burner phones he'd bought, and the sleepover at Maura's while her parents were away. There were beers and some sort of prank pulled on Zelda.

And then her boots and jacket found at the edge of the beach...

Unalived herself.

No, it wasn't like her, Mark thought. It didn't make sense.

When Yanar learned how Ali had faked being sick, she hauled him off by his ear. It was amazing how strong the little woman was.

Then somehow it was dawn and Mrs. Taumalolo was cooking breakfast in Mark's kitchen while Stacey caught some shuteye on the sofa. Sausages and eggs, beans and hash browns. It all came together as someone passed it to Mark and told him, "Eat, eat. You really should have something in your stomach."

With trembling fingers, he sliced the breakfast sausage so hard he cut through the paper plate. They didn't have enough tableware, he realized, because he'd never bought more than a single set for him and Zelda.

They were supposed to have moved out and would do the real home shopping soon. They had decided it together.

Together...

He muttered an apology that no one seemed to hear.

A phone rang again. First one and then several. Something about a radio broadcast, a Coast Guard helicopter, and a girl spotted from the air.

A girl waving back.

Mark was out the door and at his car so fast he realized he was still holding his plastic fork. Stacey tossed him his keys, saying, "Take Cahto Street to Shoreline Park and then the crosstown—"

"—to Highway 1, got it." He put the car in drive. "Call the Ruizes and give them directions. Please, I mean."

"On it." She took his phone while he peeled out. "It sounds like she's okay. But, Mark, please listen to me: this wasn't your fault."

He nodded, but her words were a thousand miles off. All that mattered was the street before him, then the parkway, and the on-ramp he needed to take. All he heard was the car's engine straining and the creak of his grinding teeth.

"This wasn't your fault," she repeated.

"Thanks, Stace," he said. "I'm sure Judge Fulghum will feel the same way."

WITH THE SUN BARELY UP AND THE WEEKEND TRAFFIC nonexistent, Mark blew through nearly every stop sign on the drive to Point Greywood. In the morning glow, the distant vineyards and estates looked different. A haze and malaise hung about, as if the uplands were fallow and unnoticed. For a moment it struck him as bizarre: they'd been here last night and yet he could hardly remember the shape of the terrain.

Then it slipped from his mind.

A mile down the coastal highway, a helicopter idled on a flat patch of grass at an artichoke farm as lights flashed in the haze. Frustrated surfers and fishermen conferred and gestured to a beach blocked by the cops. A dozen emergency vehicles sat parked every which way. In the turnout, a woman struggled with two excited bloodhounds while a man in a wetsuit loaded his jet ski onto a truck.

"Half the town came out," Stacey said. "Say what you will about Greywooders, but they're helpful in a pinch."

As the cops waved him over to the parking lot, a dark part of Mark's mind stirred. A Coast Guard search and rescue. Ambulances and fire trucks called out. A boat ride or a helicopter trip, or maybe both. His little mental accountant was adding it all up.

He seethed at himself for letting such a thought take form. Because the most important thing wasn't money but the girl who'd been entrusted to his care. The most important thing was that Zelda was alright.

Then two paramedics parted, and there she was—his niece—at the far end of the lot. A thermal blanket wrapped her skinny frame as she sat on the ambulance bumper.

She was gesturing and talking.

She was alive.

He wasn't sure if he fully parked the car or if he simply jumped out. Distantly, he heard Stacey shouting that he'd forgotten his keys. He didn't even have his running shoes on, but she would have been proud of his time.

It was the fastest hundred-yard sprint of his life.

When Zelda saw him, she stepped down from the ambulance, a nervous glimmer in her eyes. "Uncle Mark, I'm so sor—"

She didn't get a chance to finish.

Mark wrapped her in the tightest hug he'd ever given. His arms squeezed her thin body against his. He felt her coldness and dampness, a chill even the thermal blanket couldn't contain. He felt her heart banging as she spoke.

"I'm okay," she said. "I'm—"

"Let me see you." He took her face in his hands, turning her head and searching for wounds. He heard her words but he needed to see for himself. There was a small scratch on her chin and a lump near her eyebrow just starting to bruise. He plucked a strand of seaweed from her hair.

"I'm fine, Uncle Mark. I promise."

A wall of faces and bodies swirled at his periphery. People snapping pictures that would end up in the paper. Paramedics who needed to take her vitals or rescuers who needed a statement. Strangers offering congratulations.

Stacey asked them for a moment while Mark hugged Zelda again.

"Goddammit, Zelda," he whispered. "I thought I'd lost you. What the hell were you thinking?"

"I don't know. I just... Are Ali and Maura—"

"They're fine. They told me everything."

A stunned puff fled her lips. "I'm such an idiot."

"I'm not going to argue with you there. This is... something else."

Her gaze shifted as a group of Coast Guard search-and-rescue personnel returned from the beach.

"One sec." Zelda hurried over to the men as they loaded cables and equipment into a truck, shouting, "Hey! Did you find him?"

Wobbly and suddenly aware he'd barely eaten, Mark followed her. He could taste the adrenaline fading as shivers and shakes spread through his body.

"Did you find him?" Zelda repeated to the coastguardsmen. "Is he okay?"

One of them hoisted something the size of a battering ram with a triangular tip and a motor into the truck bed. The other turned around, a weary scowl on his face.

"No, kid," he said. "We didn't find him."

"Did you check inside? The lighthouse, the door, he locked it so—"

"Yeah, we did. That's what the hydraulic cutter is for." He gave the steel and rubber object a tap and shoved it into the truck bed. "And the ladders. Hell, we checked every damn inch. There's no one else there."

"But..." Zelda hesitated. "You're sure? He was inside. He—"

"Really? C'mere." He took Zelda by her wrist and hauled her over to the edge of the parking lot, where the sandy wash looked out at the bluffs and the arches.

"Hey!" Mark hurried after them. He didn't like the way the man was dragging his niece. "Don't touch her like that."

"That lighthouse? That one?" The coastguardsman pointed out to the bay where the shoal connected to the beach at low tide and a shadow towered in the mist. "You're sure he's inside?"

"Hey." Mark pulled the man's hand from his niece. Now the adrenaline was back and his heart drummed as the world went narrow and metallic. "Don't touch her."

The coastguardsman was younger and in excellent shape. Yet when he sized Mark up, something retreated. "Look, pal, I'm just having trouble understanding how anyone could be inside that lighthouse."

"She said there was." Mark caught a shadow of doubt clouding Zelda's eyes. "Right, Zelda?"

"I don't know... I thought..."

"If there is someone—if anyone was there—you'll need a damn wrecking ball to find 'em," the coastguardsman said. "They decommissioned it decades ago. Filled the first floor with concrete. You know why? 'Cause it keeps dumbass teens from getting stuck there at high tide."

Her jaw tensed as she swallowed. She wanted to say something; Mark could see it. "If she says someone's there, they were."

"Sure, buddy," the coastguardsman said. "I can't imagine a teenager would ever lie." He gave Mark a smirk and headed back to the beach.

For a quiet beat, his eyes searched her face. He could see his sister Maya there, her soft gaze looking back. He could see a spark of Juan Carlos, endlessly inventive and clever. And something else, too. Something that drove a spike of pity through his heart and made him think of old Chester Halgrove.

"Zelda," Mark said, "is there something you want to tell me?"

Then a new worry widened her eyes.

"Uncle Mark, what are my grandparents doing here?"

31

D etective Debra Brown puffed her cheeks and sighed before drowning her frustration in a lukewarm sip of coffee. She closed her eyes and probed the conflicting depths of her mind. None of it made any sense. For the past hour, she'd reviewed everything the hospital had on the assault in room 244 and the missing Mr. Boote.

The video of his departure.

The timecards and badge access logs.

Even his cellphone—which security had found left by the fountain. It had taken the department's sole IT specialist minutes to crack it with Cellebrite. The passcode was 42069247.

Of course it was.

And yet the phone was another dead end. Boote's app usage had mostly focused on some game and little else.

She took one last look at Mr. Boote's employment files, hoping something might jump out. A few complaints of excessive force. A transfer. Instead of connections, all she saw were pixels and her own tired reflection in the screen. Where the hell was he?

Perhaps in a ditch and decomposing. Perhaps dead like the two others at the dump. She didn't like the answers her mind offered back.

She thanked the hospital's head of security and ventured out into the halls of Greywood General. It was noon; the light looked a little funny. She needed something to eat.

First, she stopped by a postoperative care room in the reconstructive surgery unit.

She found Gabriel "G-Dog" Garcia reclining in bed and watching TV. Beneath a mask of gauze, elastic bandages, and Steri-Strips, the man looked like a modern mummy. A few wormy scars threaded with spiky black stitches jutted between loose dressing.

It was G-Dog's eyes, however, that halted her at the doorway. The trauma had turned them into violet starbursts—subconjunctival hemorrhage. They gleamed like burst plums with each blink.

"Oh, you're back," he said. "I remember you from my dreams. Detective... Debra Downer? *Price Is Right*'s almost over, but I'll tell you a secret..." He aimed the remote at the TV, muting a commercial for antacids. "This episode's a rerun."

His lips spread in a giddy, drugged grin. Despite the temporary dentures, his words were clear.

"Come on down."

Debra returned his smile. It was enough to wave her closer. She sat, scanning the bedside mess: half-eaten cups of applesauce and little torn pouches for medication. All things considered, G-dog was having a good time. Hell, he probably thought he was talking to the pope.

"Mr. Garcia—G-dog—is it still okay if I call you that?"

"Call me whatever you want. Wait.... this is crazy... but what's your number? I'll call you, maybe."

Cheeks stretching beneath the bandages, he giggled for a good twenty seconds before moaning in pain. She didn't have the heart to tell him he'd gotten the lyrics wrong. Then he fumbled for a cord with a red button at the end, thumbing it again and again. An indicator lit up, *PCA Pump Active*, and the lockout timer began.

Just her luck, she thought. If this was G-dog at his most clearheaded, she wasn't sure what to expect once the Dilaudid hit his opioid receptors.

"G-dog, I appreciate all your help. Everyone does. It's just... We're still trying to piece together a few things. What happened at the dump? And what happened in your room? Things are... fuzzy."

"Not that fuzzy. Not from where I'm standing. I got kidnapped, assaulted. I saw it all from—*oh!*" He closed his eyes and shivered. "That's really something."

"Mr. Garcia—"

"When you've been sucking tailpipe for years and you get the good stuff—the primo pharma—well, there's just no going back, is there? Dog as my witness, I'm going clean after this."

The machine clicked, indicating the PCA pump had dispensed the dose.

"Mr. Garcia...?"

He smiled and reclined, melting in among the pillows. Dammit, he was probably orbiting Saturn about now.

Sighing, she leaned in to get a close look at the surgeon's work. Mr. Boote had really done a number on him, hadn't he? But it wasn't just Mr. Boote. G-dog had been holding his own teeth when they'd found him. Then swallowed them.

Like a kid caught with a handful of candy.

As she stood, her chair squeaked and G-dog's ruby gaze turned to her, clear and focused.

"I was G-dog at the dump." He spoke slowly, precisely. "Just a junkie on the scent of another score. G-dog. Tim-Tam. Shawn. I saw it all from a muddy prison in my mind. I *was* G-dog, don't you see? My friends are all dead, but for a moment I was more. A passenger, carrying her Ascended. But my flesh, it was too polluted. He needed more strength."

Debra knew better than to interrupt a person of interest when they were talking. Even if the words didn't make sense. Yet G-dog's eyes held such clarity she almost wondered if they'd given him Narcan instead.

"I've had a near-life experience, don't you understand? I've seen... her..."

Then it came, the haze as the opioids dimmed his eyes. With a drooping smile, G-dog slid back into his bed.

"You've seen who, Mr. Garcia?"

"Seen... the light... of my lights."

She spent the next several beats hoping for another ember of clarity in his red eyes, but the curtain was down; the show was over. The day nurse stopped by to check in, smiling as she tucked G-dog into his sheets. At least he was in good hands.

Debra grabbed another coffee from the fancy machine and said hello to Dr. Ranall as his shift ended. They flirted for a few minutes, discussing the upcoming eclipse, the holidays, and how for both of their professions this was the worst time of year. He invited her to go caroling with his church. She told him she'd give it some thought.

But her mind was back in that room, wasn't it? G-dog's gooey words still dribbling through her thoughts.

Why couldn't she just live in the moment?

Why did she let her job keep intruding on her social life?

This wasn't how others lived, was it?

"Well, it's an open invite," Dr. Ranall said. "If you like hot cocoa and snickerdoodle cookies."

"Perhaps I'll take you up on that," she said. "Who doesn't like cookies?"

"Monsters, that's who." He smiled with a mouthful of perfect white teeth.

A few minutes later, she was nearly out of the ICU wing when a familiar man with a phone to his ear hurried past her toward pediatrics.

Mark Fitzsimmons.

She almost said hello but stopped herself. His hushed tone. His tense posture. The way he slowed at an alcove and paced. Most of all it was the words that he used. She had learned to read lips long ago.

Attorney.

Emergency hearing.

Zelda.

Debra flagged down a nurse and asked, "That man over there, I know him and his niece. Is she okay?"

The nurse shot Mark a quick glance and returned an even quicker nod. "Yeah, she's stable. We're checking vitals and running blood work to monitor for hypothermia and—"

"Hypothermia? Wait, what happened?"

The nurse shrugged. "Unclear, but it sounds like the Coast Guard pulled her out of the bay. Girl's lucky to be alive. Excuse me."

As the nurse left, Debra lingered by the station, watching Mark pace and talk into the phone. Whatever this was, she sensed it wasn't going to be over anytime soon.

A few inquiries, and she found Zelda in a room where the ICU joined pediatrics and the walls grew colorful and cute. Like G-dog, Zelda sat in her bed, connected to machines. Unlike G-dog's, Zelda's room was packed.

A couple in their sixties fussed with a nurse and bickered in Spanish. Grandparents, Debra figured. A man in his late forties spoke quickly into a phone. She sensed they were on the same call, but not on the same side.

Then she remembered: that judge, what was her name? Fuller or Fulbright? The court clerk had contacted Debra for details when Zelda was detained and questioned.

But never charged.

As Zelda's gaze swung to Debra, her eyes widened and the words "oh shit" formed on her lips.

"Hey, Zelda." Debra offered her a smile. "This isn't police business, I promise."

As usual, she found such an insistence rarely soothed a teenager.

"I was nearby, and I heard about some incident," she continued. "I just wanted to check in. How are you?"

"Fine. Just, you know... Embarrassed."

"Embarrassed?" Debra approached while the man on the phone beckoned to the grandfather, and they both hurried into the hall.

Zelda's eyes fell to her hospital slippers. "I heard, like, they had the whole town searching for me."

"As they should. Those tides are deadly. You're not the first to get pulled out, so don't be embarrassed, okay?"

Another nod. What was it about teenage girls that made conversations so hard? Debra tried to remember those years of her own—the clumsy kisses, the doubt—yet her mind retreated inward like a nervous turtle. Maybe that *was* the answer.

"So, like, am I gonna get arrested again or...?"

"What? No, of course not." Debra slid a chair over to the bed. "If we booked every kid that went to a beach party, our lockup would be filled through next year."

Zelda's eyes rose as her grandmother hurried over. *"Zelda, no le digas nada a la policía, ¿Entiendes? Ni una palabra."* Then, to Debra, "I think you go."

"Grandma, it's okay."

Debra knew enough Spanish to fill in the blanks. She wasn't sure why, but as she rose, she gave Zelda a pat on her legs. She liked the girl. The world felt a little warmer in her presence, and her cop brain slowed down.

"I'm glad you're safe," she said. "Rest up. And don't scare your uncle like that, okay? If you need anything, you let me know. Cool?"

Another nod. Did kids even say "cool" anymore? For a moment it looked like Zelda wanted to say something, so Debra gave her the space. Unspoken words weighed on her chapped lips.

"You said 'I'm not the first,'" Zelda said. "Has anyone else gone missing over the years?"

"Gone missing? Sure, plenty."

"What about by the lighthouse?"

"You mean Point Greywood?"

Zelda's chin dipped in a tense acknowledgment.

"I don't know off the top of my head. Why?"

Whatever it was, it flittered on Zelda's tongue and then vanished back down her throat. "Nothing," she said. "Forget it."

But it wasn't nothing; she was lying. Every sense in Debra's body lit up. Yet not all lies meant deception. Some were protection. Her instincts whispered that this might be such a case.

"Tell ya what," Debra said. "If you keep your nose clean, I'll look into it for you. Cool?"

This time Zelda repeated, "Cool."

Out in the hall, Debra lingered, hoping to offer Mark a word of support or encouragement. But he still had the phone to his ear, pacing by the stairwell and arguing. Something about sneaking out from a sleepover. She stifled a laugh, not envying the guy. It was hard enough raising a teenager, let alone one that wasn't your own.

She was riding the elevator down when a realization sparked through her mind: wasn't this the same elevator Mr. Boote took? She turned, facing the wall just as he had faced it.

Staring at it.

Night-light.

Light of my lights.

Lighthouse.

Point Greywood?

She scoffed. "Silly."

With a ding, the elevator doors opened and Debra realized she was still standing there like a crazy person and staring at nothing. A young couple—pregnant wife, nervous husband—eyed her with polite suspicion. She excused herself and stepped out.

No. It wasn't anything. Just word salad connecting separate ideas.

Still...

Instead of turning left for the parking lot, she took a right and followed that same path Mr. Boote had wandered. She found her fingers sliding over her phone's keyboard.

A quick web search: *Light of my lights. Lighthouse. Point Greywood.*

She found nothing on the first page or the second. By the time she stepped out into the courtyard and the cold winter sun, she was almost done scrolling. This was a wild goose chase, her mind assigning false meaning where none existed. Hell, she should take some time off. There was more to life than work. More to the world than the weird happenings in a small town.

Then she saw it, one result buried in the bowels of her web search.

Greywood Bay Historical Society: A Treasure of the Lost Coast.

She slowed, letting a group of med students pass her. She clicked the link and skimmed the website. Some history enthusiast describing their visit back when the word "blog" was new. The article featured a photo of a plaque, timeworn and faded. Debra sat on the edge of the fountain and squinted.

Arthur Cummings's poem "Light of My Lights" inaugurated the comple-
tion of Point Greywood Lighthouse in 1857. The original bronze plaque
—both practical and symbolic—withstood over a century of corrosion
before its removal. Despite boasting a lens seen for miles, the coast
remains deadly, having seen countless shipwrecks over the centuries. The
NOAA designates the region as cautionary, with tidal charts featuring
dense warnings...

The rest of the blog contained nautical notes and historical curios:
the sourcing of granite from local quarries, the role of the keepers, the
lens imported from France. One thing at the bottom caught her eye.

The map.

It was a low-resolution scan of an already low-resolution photocopy,
some mid-century illustration popular in small towns. Hand-drawn
trees and coastal bluffs were almost fantastical. Local hotspots highlighted.

A smiling redwood grove in the hills.

A tepee and tobacco-smoking Indian denoted tribal lands.

A happy bunch of grapes in the wine region.

Shark fins circling a nervous surfer beneath the label *Bottle Beach.*

But they didn't call it that anymore, did they? One of those rich
families owned that stretch of land and fenced it off. And there it was,
Point Greywood.

She lowered her phone and studied the edge of the pavilion, the edge
of campus, the thicket... and beyond.

Mr. Boote had walked that direction. Had faced it in the elevator.
Had G-dog faced that in his room?

"Got his favorite spot that he looks at."

She swiped to her map app and waited a few seconds for it to cali-
brate her direction.

332.5 degrees north-northwest.

No...

She pinched and zoomed out until the medical campus became the
edge of the university, then the edge of town. She panned and zoomed,
the state parks and national forests merging into a verdant green as
photographed from space. The coastal highway. The farms and valleys.

And there it was, Point Greywood, just past the vineyards. She stuck a pin in the hospital, then a second at the lighthouse. She swiped south and stuck another in the dump where they found G-dog and his friends.

A little puff left her lips.

Thirty-seven miles.

It wasn't exactly a straight line between the points, but it was pretty damn close.

She closed her eyes and let it all take shape in her thoughts. Somewhere above, a warbler called out. Had G-dog wanted to get taken in to the hospital? Like some sort of pit stop?

A passenger carrying her Ascended.

It didn't make sense. Not unless...

Unless he was passing something off to Mr. Boote.

Something on its way to Point Greywood.

32

Mark squeezed the phone, knuckles white as he paced the hospital corridor. The murmur of nurses and the beeping of distant machinery provided a backdrop to the hushed but fierce words spilling into his ear.

"Your honor, I assure you that Zelda's safety is Mr. Fitzsimmons's foremost concern," said his attorney Ms. Phong, her voice sharp over the crackling line. "We've provided countless character references—"

"Character witnesses," Judge Fulghum cut in, stern and frustrated. "Don't change the fact that he left a child unsupervised. From what I'm hearing, she's lucky to be alive."

Mark paused at the window for a better signal.

"Supervision isn't the sole metric of guardianship," Ms. Phong said. "If it was, every parent would be under scrutiny. Some hourly."

"The Ruizes would like to remind your honor that Mr. Fitzsimmons is not her parent." That was Ms. Chou, their attorney, cutting in. Mark didn't have to strain to hear the Ruizes and Alejandro all talking over each other.

They were just down the hall by the vending machines.

"He's an uncle," Ms. Chou continued. "One who was—until

months ago—eight time zones and six thousand miles away. More importantly, an uncle who has repeatedly failed Zelda in his duties."

Mark pressed his forehead against the cool glass window, shivering. Ten p.m. to six a.m. Eight hours missing, in the ocean, on the shoal, cold and alone. Maybe they were right. Was he really cut out to be a guardian for a teenage girl?

Maggots in her heart.

"Mr. Fitzsimmons, are you still with us?" prodded the judge, the signal clearing momentarily. "Hello?"

He could feel the eyes of the Ruizes on him down the hall, dagger-like glares on his skin. "Yes, your honor," he said. "Zelda is more than just my niece. She's a promise I made to my sister. And nobody takes that promise more serious than I do. I spent the whole night thinking about what I could have done different. Changes will be made, I can guarantee—"

"Mr. Fitzsimmons?" a young doctor called out from the door of Zelda's room. "She's ready now."

"Right, okay." Cupping the phone, Mark hurried over. The frosted glass revealed only a blurry glimpse of a shape by the bed. "How is she?"

"We've run a full panel of tests—lab work, chest X-ray, EKG," the doctor said, scrolling down his tablet. "Everything's within range. There's no sign of hypothermia or water inhalation. A few scrapes and bruises, but she's in good shape considering the... attempt."

Mark sensed the doctor trying to take the word back as soon as it was spoken. "What do you mean 'attempt'?"

The doctor closed his tablet. "I did my residency in San Francisco. The Golden Gate, she's beautiful but a magnet for jumpers, especially during the holidays. I stopped counting corpses around fifty, and I only met one survivor. Know what he said? 'I regretted it the whole way down.'" The doctor locked eyes with Mark, a hint of sorrow in his gaze. "The sea is indifferent, but your niece got lucky. I hope she's not indifferent to the second chance she's been given."

He gave Mark's shoulder a friendly pat, then walked off. A second later, Judge Fulghum's voice buzzed over the phone. "Mr. Fitzsimmons?"

"Sorry, you were saying—"

"I was saying that your relationship with Zelda and her parents' wishes have been taken into account. But her safety comes first. Decision forthcoming." Then Judge Fulghum ended the call.

"Thank you, your honor." Mark's grip on the phone eased, though his chest remained tight. A few hours, Christ. He took a deep breath and pushed the door open.

Zelda's room smelled of antiseptic and lemon cleaner, a stark contrast to the ocean still lingering in his nose. He found her sitting on the edge of the bed, feet swinging above the floor. She looked small, swallowed up by the hospital gown draping her thin frame. Damp clothes lay in a plastic bag.

"Hey, kiddo." He handed her a backpack. "Stacey grabbed what she could. Probably not the most fashionable, but—"

"It's perfect, thanks." She unzipped the bag and pulled out a camouflage hoodie. "I'll change in the bathroom."

Mark turned and gave her privacy. Her hospital slippers whisked the tiled floor. Then the door clicked and locked. He had only a few seconds of quiet before the Ruizes crowded through the doorway, led by Alejandro.

Please, Mark thought. *Just give me one moment to catch my balance.*

"Character witnesses?" Alejandro's voice was like gravel scraping tiles. "I don't care what your attorney says. This is on you, Mark, and you know that."

"Yeah, I know." The bed squeaked as Mark leaned against the plastic guardrail. "You've made that perfectly clear."

"*Esto nunca hubiera pasado en nuestra casa.*" Mrs. Ruiz spat the words, her face flushed with anger. Mr. Ruiz stood behind her, eyes downcast and silent.

"You think this wouldn't have happened in your house?" Mark scoffed. Sometimes it felt like Mrs. Ruiz forgot he spoke Spanish. Or maybe she was just baiting him. He inhaled, fighting to keep his tone controlled. "Yes, Zelda screwed up, but she's not the first teenager to sneak out."

"*¿Un error? Esto es más que un simple error.*"

"Enough." He kept his voice firm and volume low, conscious of Zelda in the bathroom. "She's safe now. That's what matters."

"Ese juez ni siquiera sabe lo que está diciendo. Puro aire caliente."

Mark ignored them and rubbed his tired eyes. Sometimes his niece changed clothes so fast it was like a magic act. But today, the heavy seconds stretched on.

When he opened his eyes, Alejandro was within three feet. "It makes sense. All of it, now it makes sense."

Mark sighed. "What are you on about?"

Alejandro's voice dropped to a whisper. "C'mon, Mark, everyone knows about you. The family, my brother, they all *talked*. What did you cost your investors? Twenty million, right? You're a cautionary tale. Someone who scampers off to the other side of the planet and shows up every few years."

"That's not..." Mark hesitated. Where was the brother-in-law he'd met years ago? What was this venomous thing that had replaced him over these past nine months? "Alejandro, if you think you know anything about me—"

"But I do." Alejandro's nostrils flared. "I just didn't want to believe it. Then it clicked. *If* the trust is paying you. And *if* something should happen to Zelda... *Cui bono*. Who benefits?"

Mark felt his back straighten and his shoulders tensed. A creak of his teeth as his jaw clenched. He hadn't thrown fists since he was a teenager, but he could see what was coming.

Alejandro's smirk as more insinuations flew past his lips.

Mark's lizard brain taking over.

His right hand balling and—

No...

He choked back the rage and spoke slowly. "If you think I'm making money off this, you've got worse financial instincts than I ever had."

Alejandro inched closer. "Or maybe I just know a scammer when I see one."

"Uncle Mark?" a quivering voice interjected. Zelda emerged from the bathroom, wearing a hoodie and one shoe half-laced. "Alejandro. What's going on?"

Alejandro blinked, and it was like watching clouds dissipate in the sun as warmth returned to his eyes. "Nothing. Forget it."

Zelda looked at each of them, her voice breaking as she spoke. "I just want to go home."

"*Zelda, mija.*" Mrs. Ruiz placed a gentle hand on her shoulder. "You will go home soon. With us. Where you belong."

Zelda's eyes glistened as she broke off her grandmother's embrace. It wasn't fair, Mark thought. Seeing her pulled like this, a fraying toy between dogs.

"Keep your phone on," Alejandro warned as Mark and Zelda neared the door. "The judge will be calling soon."

Mark nodded, no need for further words. He was surprised when Zelda's cold fingers tugged the sleeve of his jacket.

Together, they stepped into the hallway, leaving the Ruizes and their bitter glares behind.

"I really fucked up, didn't I?" Zelda whispered.

On most days he might have asked her not to swear. Or to do so with some creativity.

Today, he was tired. So fucking tired. He didn't say anything for thirty paces. He barely noticed the nods and smiles as he passed the nurses' station.

As they turned a corner, her grip tightened on her wrist.

"C'mon," he said. "I parked in a loading zone, so..."

Zelda's eyes stayed locked on a double door, where a nurse had just passed through. With a click, the door closed.

"What is it?" Mark asked.

Her lip trembled, and her eyes glistened with silent dread. A gasp escaped, barely louder than a whisper. Following her gaze, he looked toward the empty hall. Then he saw it—the sign on the glass door: *Burn Unit.*

Poor girl. It seemed like they couldn't escape Raven's Valley, even here. He squeezed her hand. "Hey, you okay?"

She blinked, eyes refocusing. "What? No, it's... nothing," she said quickly, a bit too quickly. "We should really go."

They stopped by the elevator, but her gaze flicked back to that double door. Another nurse walked past, and a shiver racked Zelda as the door swung open and shut.

Does she know about Maya? he wondered. *Should he tell her?*

His mind spat it out. No, of course not.

She needed stability underfoot, not her uncle's crazy thoughts in her head. She needed...

A lighthouse for the storm.

Maya's haunting words from that night long ago.

He needed to be that lighthouse in her storm.

But God how these waves were pulling him under.

33

With a groan of her tired bones, Bibi slid into the Georgian mahogany Gainsborough Chair behind her redwood writing desk. She took a few beats to organize the space. The paper from Japan, so thin and smooth it was like writing on silk. The ink from Germany, near black that glimmered in the right light. With a click, she unlatched an urushi lacquer box and let her fingers caress each of her fountain pens. She had chapters to write, and this ritual put her in a good mood.

Or rather, it had.

Tonight, she found the words gummy and clumsy, each sentence harder than the last. After twenty minutes of scribbling, it displeased her to see she had only a page and a half. And a throbbing hand.

She squeezed the wrinkled base of her thumb, massaging the knot. No, she realized, a lump.

Where her index finger joined her palm's webbing, a bruise had formed. She pressed her left thumb against it, wincing as something firm yet tender slid underneath.

Great. Another cyst or age spot. Like all the other changes about town, it seemed her body wouldn't be spared. Perhaps her money could delay it. She made a note to phone Dr. Mitchell, then resumed her writing. It took her another fifteen minutes, but she found her flow.

Biscuits and Blackmail, her most recent book, had ended on a cliffhanger. She'd left her detective stranded in an old mineshaft rigged with explosives. And the cat—well, she had implied it died in the collapse; she was *so tired* of that damn thing. But her readers were furious. God forbid another mystery end at Reichenbach Falls.

So here she was, an antique chair groaning as she tried to write her way out. Paragraph by paragraph, she found her stride and the story. The detective would swim out through a flooded tunnel, discovering the dumped chemicals the town's mayor had been hiding. The cat would escape in—what else?—a mine cart.

She chuckled to herself. Yes, she was taming the words and getting her story in order. Still, a doubt nagged from the shadows. Just when had she started to despise this whole process?

She wasn't sure, only that at some point the rot had set in.

Perhaps it began with her readers, their gushing, hollow questions. "Where do you get your ideas?"

Perhaps the editors, with their pedantic suggestions. "Keep your sentences short and your words simple; we're competing with TikTok these days."

Perhaps the marketing department, kids with colored hair and vapid schemes. "What if we partnered with Hallmark and made a cookbook for Christmas?"

And the so-called critics, ugh...

She pushed past her cramping hand as her pen slid across page after page. Yes, the words obeyed; the story was coming together. She even saw a title emerging: *Whiskers on Wheels & the Coal Mine Caper*. She snickered and grinned.

Then her phone vibrated.

"Oh, bother." She was certain she'd silenced that wretched device, but here it was, a notification blinking on the display.

Bibi mostly abhorred the internet and the mush it made of people's minds. Attention spans like puppies and distractions on tap. Yet she, too, felt its pull. She wanted to ignore that intrusion, and yet she'd already seen what it was.

With a swipe and tap, she stared into the abyss of social media and a photo of her book staged by a candle-lit bathtub. Someone who self-described as a "mommy blogger" had tagged her in a review.

She had given her two stars.

"Suds & a story. My idea of relaxing. Unfortunately, the latest feline foibles didn't scratch the itch."

Bibi's eyes scoured the review.

"Meandering."

"Hard to follow."

"Lacked the punch of her earlier works."

Oh dear...

Her readers loved to message her, inviting her to groups and proclaiming themselves clever. Yet, without explicit signposts for each twist, they wound up confused. Some struggled to distinguish between the author and her characters. But readers were like cattle, and they all needed prodding—some more than others. So, time to get started.

Despite the ambiguous username, it took Bibi all of five minutes to track the mommy blogger down. Her LinkedIn. Her Facebook profile. Which groups she belonged to. Bibi wasn't psychic—well, not quite—but she was a mystery writer. Everyone left breadcrumbs online.

Here it was, the mommy blogger's story starting to emerge.

Eighteen months at a community college.

A part-time job at the local beauty salon.

A sudden marriage and a baby bump in her photo.

A caption, *God gave us an unexpected surprise. #blessed.*

Bibi found a public wish list: diapers, clothes, a pack 'n play. Another picture of the young mommy and daddy tagged by a grandparent, clothes a few seasons past peak. Youthful eyes sparkled with nervous implication: their whole life was about to change.

Scrolling and tapping, Bibi uncovered more layers to the story. A photo of their baby in an incubator. Scared parents trying to smile above a caption, *Please pray for baby Krystal.* A GoFundMe for medical expenses that raised 966 out of 12,000 dollars.

Meandering...

Ah, here it was. A first birthday photo followed by a second and then... *nothing*. It was amazing how much a void could actually say. By searching the baby's name and a hyphenated version of the parents, Bibi found the ending.

The funeral had been held eleven months ago, January 19. The caption, *The Lord called our little angel back to heaven, but she'll live on in our hearts.* Funny, Bibi thought, how they thanked their god for blessings yet didn't blame him for the hypertrophic cardiomyopathy that weakened baby Krystal's heart until it could no longer beat.

Hard to follow...

Through a series of sock puppet accounts, she registered with a remailing service that would send the so-called critic a recurring care package: a card wishing Krystal a happy birthday, a recording of a heartbeat on CD, and a cake—something expensive and exotic—with a special message: *If only you'd listened to her heart a little closer. #blessed.*

She found a coffin maker and ordered ten child-sized coffins to contain the gifts, arranging delivery on Krystal's birthday every year for a decade. She wondered, *Does this lack the punch of her earlier works?*

Maybe. Probably.

But it still brought a smile to her face.

"Beebs? You coming to bed?"

She looked up to see Harlan in her study doorway. With his white mustache beneath tired eyes and his arms like thin branches, he reminded her of a mossy birch at the end of too many seasons.

"Oh fiddlesticks, look at the time," she said. "I got caught up in correspondence, I'm afraid."

His eyes scoured her desk, coming to a stop on the stack of invitations bearing the Larchmont & Cummings Vineyard crest. "You're not starting those now, are you?"

She straightened the invitations. "Well, they certainly won't write themselves."

Something wounded flashed in his eyes. Goodness, when had they both gotten so old and so tender?

"I'm sorry, dear," she said. "That was unkind of me."

"We don't have to keep doing it, Beebs," he said. "That damned party, all of this. In fact, I'd prefer that we didn't."

She tilted her head. "You've been drinking. You always get sentimental when you drink. It's rather off-putting, I must say. And besides, we have obligations. Or have you forgotten?"

"I've certainly tried," he said. "Good night, Beebs."

"Mmm-hmm."

And like an errant leaf, he drifted out into the hall, gone.

Bibi fumed for several minutes, wondering if she'd recapture her flow. No. Tonight's writing was finished.

She tucked the manuscript pages into a drawer and centered the invitations before her. She switched fountain pens to a vintage Montegrappa with a flexible nib that gave her letters wide downstrokes and hair-thin cross-strokes. With her Spencerian script upon the Bella Figura card's cotton and deckle edges, the invitation burst to life.

> As the stars align and the veiled heavens take pause,
> Let us celebrate good fortunes and futures.
> Let us stand together as the universe offers hints of its mysteries.
> Join us for a private afternoon of reflection and renewal at Larchmont Cove.
> Next Monday, 11:21 AM
> Sincerely,
> Bibi

Satisfied, she licked the envelope and affixed an adhesive seal.

Ten envelopes later, and the discomfort returned to her hand. She squeezed that lump with her thumb and winced. Goodness, it really was no fun feeling the march of the seasons.

Then something bristled her spine.

It began as a feeling: a voyeur's gaze sliding down her neck and caressing her shoulder. A cryptic notion: was she truly alone?

She turned to the window, where Bay Laurels offered a dappled glimpse of the dark vineyard and its terraces. The night was still, windless.

And yet, one of the branches was bent.

She capped her pen and rose. The invitations would have to wait.

Outside, a starless haze hung over mist-swaddled hills. A coyote's howl crossed the valley. Down the road, the laborers' bungalows glowed citrine in the shadows. Had one of them wandered up the estate? If so, she'd put a word in with Manuel.

She braced her robe against her chest as that icy caress swept over her again. No. That wasn't a laborer, nor a coyote.

Someone was watching her.

The pop of snapping twigs sent a gasp from her lungs that shamed her. Whoever was here, they had no idea who they were provoking.

"You're trespassing," she announced. "If you possess an ounce of self-preservation, you've got ten seconds to leave. That means run, now. Ten... Nine... Eight..."

There, she sensed it: movement by the rows of dormant vines. Another crack of a branch.

"And now you're destroying property. Those vines are priceless, so I hope you've brought your attorney. Five... Four... Three..."

She knew better than to let the countdown finish. With a brisk shuffle, she hurried down the stone steps. Even in her slippers, her toes knew the soil; this was her land. How dare someone set foot on it without invitation?

"You think I'm afraid?" she asked. "Very well, let's do this."

In twenty quick paces, she found the source of the noise. Whoever had been standing here was enormous. Shoe prints created a circle of compressed earth. Two holes of soil had been scooped out by massive hands. And the cracking of vines, here they were, bent and broken and pulled clean from the ground.

"Oh, you are going to rue this day, mister." Bibi followed the tracks in the soil, privately amused. It had been a while since she'd got her blood pumping. "I can smell you, and you reek of..."

Of what? she wondered. Earth and iron, sweat and decay—these scents filled her nostrils. And something else, too: something half-remembered, as if from a dream.

"There you are."

The man's form remained still as she drew closer, a skinny effigy resting beneath the vines. She studied the mist-dampened flannel, the lumpy dungarees. A burlap sack that once held grape pomace and was painted with two X's for eyes.

A scarecrow.

One of the many scattered about the vineyard during the Halloween hayride and fundraiser. The kids loved them and ran screaming. Bibi couldn't stand all that shrill yattering.

This scarecrow, it shouldn't be here. Someone had taken it from the storage shed, propped it at the base of a vine stalk, and left a present at its feet.

A circle of torn vines lay in the moist earth, forming a head with two huge handprints for eyes. Beneath them, a curve of white and yellow pebbles depicted a smile. She winced at their stench, an amalgam of rot and decay that crept into her nostrils and down her throat. Something once fed with blood, now fouled and redolent of the earth's deepest mud.

Not pebbles but teeth, Bibi realized. Those were teeth in the soil.

The man emerged from the vines behind her, gaze bristling her spine and dimpling her skin. She spun yet held her ground as he rose, erect and enormous. A hulking thing of sagging skin and tattered uniform. Brambles and twigs were caught in his jacket, like a feral creature at the end of a desperate run.

And his lips...

Bibi swallowed as his dry lips stretched into a toothless smile and something burbled at the back of his throat.

Oh dear, she thought, numbly.

The man stretched out a hand toward her, mouth opening wide, wider, until a familiar voice groaned from deep inside.

"Hello... Mother."

34

Zelda could feel the eyes of the Heartwood Apartments residents upon her. It began the moment she stepped out of the car. It followed as Uncle Mark escorted her through the courtyard. Even the bouncing basketball slowed, the game grinding to a halt and the players whispering as she passed. A door flying open and the shout of a friendly voice only broke the silence.

"Oh-Em-Gee, it's sea legs McGee!" Ali slid down the banister and hurried over. "I wanted to get you shrimp tacos as a welcome home, but Maur-dog said it was distasteful."

"No, I said it was idiotic," Maura said and shoved Ali aside. "You okay?"

Zelda offered a weak nod, but Maura surprised her by wrapping her up in a hug. In that moment, Zelda realized it was the first time the two girls had really touched off the wrestling mat.

"Zelda, we'll be inside." Uncle Mark gave Ali and Maura an uncertain glance. "Ten minutes. Then you're helping with dinner. Got it?"

While Uncle Mark and Stacey went up the stairs, Ali and Maura dragged her to the gazebo. Beneath its roof and pillars, she could still feel the eyes upon her. Faces peered out from windows, between blinds.

Even Pavarti lingered by the parking garage, waiting to take Stacey home and catch up on the gossip.

"So this is what it feels like to be on a microscope slide." Zelda sighed. "How many people know?"

"Well, it was a trending topic in the class chat groups." Ali swiped his phone open and checked the screen. "But Elliot's an admin, so I had him enable slow mode. Now it's just pics of Mandy barfing on Yumi's jacket. Someone turned it into a meme, see?"

Zelda studied the screen where a sick sophomore's pale cheeks and crossed fingers fought to contain a spray of pink vomit. Ali swiped, showing how someone had edited her into scenes from *The Exorcist*, *Pitch Perfect*, and *Harry Potter*, when Ron Weasley spat up slugs.

"She chain-chugged wine coolers, then tried to give Yumi a lap dance," Maura said. "The whole thing was mega awkward."

"Which is good because you weren't the only one with a bad night," Ali said. "Bummer you missed the fireworks."

As he lowered the screen, something caught Zelda's eyes. She took his phone and swiped back up. "What's this?"

Words like *suicide* and *cry for attention* had several likes and laughs. Another one read, *Maybe she just tried to end it all & failed. So dramatic!*

Zelda asked, "Wait, do people think I tried to kill myself?"

"No way." Ali took his phone back and closed the chat app. "They're just goofing."

Maura's eyes said otherwise. "But I mean... didn't you?"

Zelda's mouth went dry, and the words gummed up in her throat. Like many her age, her mind drifted to dark places. Sometimes she wondered if the world would be better off without her.

But acting on it? No, she would never. In some ways, life had become even more precious after her parents' death. Every minute delicate and valuable.

"Of course not," she snapped with a surprising firmness. "Why would I..."

Then she remembered: the boots and clothes left on the beach—that stupid prank. The optics weren't on her side.

"There was, like, this really old man in the water. That's why I went out. I thought he was drowning."

"Hold up," Ali said. "So you saved a drowning old man?"

"Badass," Maura added.

"He wasn't *old* old, but like old-fashioned. He had these clothes from way back, but not vintage. Like..."

They waited, brows crinkled and eyes wide. She knew the next words were going to be clumsy. Not because Ali and Maura wouldn't believe her, but because an unspoken hush had fallen over the topic since the school year started. Maybe they had hoped—much as she had —that if they never said those tainted words again, the memory might fade.

But it was Maura who spoke first. "What, like a ghost?"

"Ah, trigger warning," Ali said. "Not the G-word. I thought we agreed to forget, like that time Elliot ate too many eggs and sharted in choir."

"Serious mode, Ali," Maura said. "I want to hear this."

"Yeah, and then the next thing we know some demon-thing's burning down another neighborhood. No thank you. And no offense, Zelda, but whenever you say you saw a ghost, it's me who ends up in trouble. They always go for the hero first."

Maura elbowed him, almost knocking him off the bench. "Motor-mouth, give it a rest." She leaned in, eyes alight with intrigue. "So, what'd you see?"

Zelda took a deep breath.

Then she told them.

About the sailors. About the lighthouse. About the man—Ben— and what he'd said.

"I think I've been here forever."

Maura listened intently while Ali's legs dangled and swung. No matter how he sat, it never looked comfortable.

She was about to tell them about the light from the top of the tower when Ali's eyes rose and Maura shot Zelda a look: *Someone's coming.*

That someone was Stacey.

"Whelp, look at the time," Ali announced and slapped his knees.

"Since I'm grounded until the New Year, I'm gonna bank some good karma and help with the chores. Toodles."

Then he was off, running across the courtyard and up the stairs, all swinging arms and gangly legs.

"I should bounce," Maura said. "My brother's coming down and he's going to watch me closer than the last nacho on the plate."

Stacey smiled as Maura shuffled off. "Teachers can really kill a party, can't we?"

Zelda sighed quietly. She liked Stacey, and she never forgot how she'd walked her through all the feminine products this past summer. It even amused her to see Uncle Mark nervous in Stacey's presence, just a big kid with a crush.

But she was tired now, the last eighteen hours catching up. She didn't have the energy for a multigenerational heart-to-heart.

"Hey." Stacey brushed her hand on Zelda's arm. Just a brief touch yet it grounded her. "I have no idea what you're going through, and I'm not going to pretend that I do, okay?"

Zelda studied her shoes and nodded. "Okay."

"What I am going to say is that if you need to talk, I'm here to listen. No judgment, deal?" She held out her fist and Zelda gave it a bump. "Now be good to your uncle. He was up all night and he's running on Red Bull and fumes."

As Stacey headed off to catch a ride with Pavarti, Zelda took a moment to compose herself. Walking up the stairs, she caught a glimpse of someone peeking out a window.

Suicide.

A cry for attention.

Maybe she just tried to end it and failed.

This was going to stick; she knew it. No matter what else happened at school—the fights, the hookups, the gross party pics—she would always be the girl who got seaweed and sand dumped on her. The girl who got too emotional, too dramatic. The girl who walked into the water.

The warmth of the apartment caressed her cheeks and the scent of spiced meats soothed her worries. Uncle Mark was in the kitchenette, sautéing vegetables. His hand holding the olive oil still trembled.

"Uncle Mark—"

"Hey, kiddo. We've got your favorite fajitas coming up in a few."

She wasn't sure why, but seeing a stack of homemade tortillas resting on a damp cloth by the skillet broke something deep inside. She leaned in and hugged him.

"Sorry I'm such a fuck-up."

He didn't say anything, just let the vegetables sizzle.

Uncle Mark, who had moved here from Madrid to raise his dead sister's kid.

Uncle Mark, who taught part-time at Neumann Prep so she could get in on a discount.

Uncle Mark, who tutored kids in Spanish on nights and weekends and made tortillas by hand.

She didn't deserve any of this.

With the vegetables blackening, he broke off the hug. She asked, "I'm in pretty big trouble, aren't I?"

He dropped chicken in with the vegetables and placed a tortilla on a separate skillet. He studied the bubbles forming on its surface. "I think we're both in big trouble. Go wash up. You smell like a hospital."

Zelda found her phone plugged in by her bedside desk. She gasped when she saw the screen: 246 missed calls.

She scrolled past Uncle Mark's frantic calls—dozens upon dozens. Past others, including the 915 area code for El Paso. Her grandparents, shit. There were the Greywood Bay Police and the Greywood Bay Rescue Services. Even a call from Neumann Prep Student Health.

She never realized so many people knew she existed.

There, for the last several dozen missed calls, was an unlisted number.

As she reached that final notification, her phone vibrated. *Unknown Caller.* She answered on the third ring.

At first, she wasn't sure what she was hearing. Static perhaps. Or the whistling of the wind and the waves.

"Hello?"

Then came the voice, nervous and distant from beyond a wall of crackling veil.

"—this is Point Greywood. Do you copy? Point Greywood to base. Over."

That voice...

She knew who it was. She pushed past her fear and answered. "I can hear you, Point Greywood."

A pop and a click as Ben's voice repeated, "Base, this is Point Greywood. Do you copy? Point Greywood to base. Over."

She waited and listened as it cycled, a desperate echo repeating again and again and again.

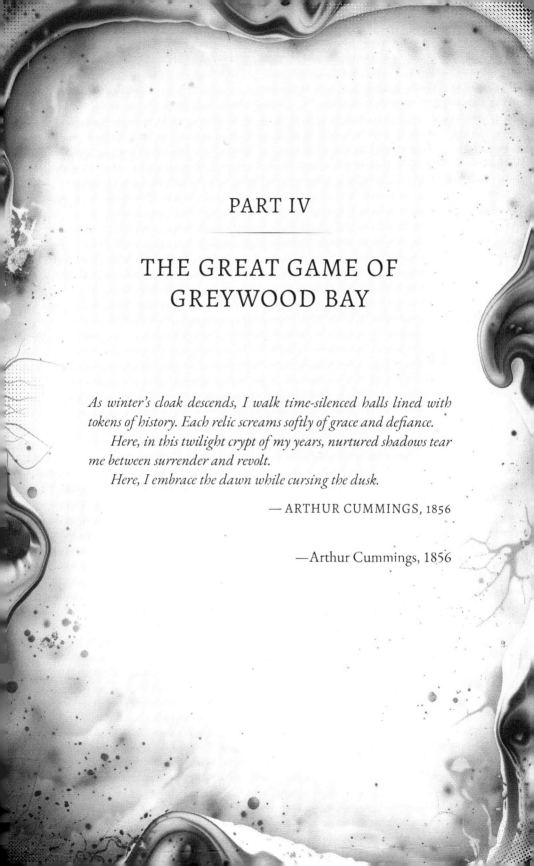

PART IV

THE GREAT GAME OF GREYWOOD BAY

As winter's cloak descends, I walk time-silenced halls lined with tokens of history. Each relic screams softly of grace and defiance.

Here, in this twilight crypt of my years, nurtured shadows tear me between surrender and revolt.

Here, I embrace the dawn while cursing the dusk.

— ARTHUR CUMMINGS, 1856

—Arthur Cummings, 1856

35

D r. Rhonda studied her office in the silence between patients, deciding she needed to rearrange a few things. She had the girl up next—Zelda—and they'd yet to break through. Fortunately, she had a few tricks up her sleeves.

Most who entered her office gave little thought to its layout and decor: the Knoll seats and sofa, simple and calming; the textbooks on the shelf, conveying confidence and knowledge; the trinkets scattered about—fidget spinners for her patients who couldn't sit still and kawaii plushies for those who wanted something to squeeze. They told a quiet story and served a purpose. They communicated.

Today, they needed to work with a fourteen-year-old girl.

Because the judge in the custody dispute was awaiting Dr. Rhonda's assessment and she wasn't sure what to believe. There were plenty of rumors.

She cleared the eye-level shelf of the old Khmer buddha from Siem Reap. She moved a crystal bird that sparkled in the light. And the antique cuckoo clock from Monterey, she put that away, too. She studied the empty space.

Yes, she had a few ideas.

From the closet she dug out a dusty Sega Genesis found at Goodwill. Digging deeper, she withdrew a Polaroid SX-70 camera, its vintage design offering a friendly reminder of simpler times. Zelda once talked about camping with her parents, so Rhonda slid out an empty gear box covered in national park stickers.

She arranged these on the shelves behind her chair. When Zelda was sitting on the couch, they'd be at her eye level. If she noticed, it might give them something to discuss.

Goodness, had it always been this hard to connect with the youth? Or was she drifting out of touch? Either way, the implications unsettled her.

She took one last look at the judge's questions, twenty-five in total.

Does child appear well-nourished and properly groomed/clothed?

Does child appear emotionally fulfilled with interests, hobbies, and a sense of purpose?

Are child's statements about events/home life truthful and consistent?

This final one worried her most of all.

With the chime of a Zen garden gong, the bell signaled her patient's arrival in the waiting room. She folded the form, placed it on her desk, and paused at the door.

There was more than one person on the other side.

"... you know how much we care about you, right?" Though hushed, the deep murmur of a man's voice carried the undercurrent of persuasion.

Someone else spoke, feminine and Spanish.

The man continued. "What she means is, you know how important *her* opinion is, don't you? Maybe help her understand how different things would be. More stable, yes?"

Dr. Rhonda opened the door, finding Zelda at the eye of a fast-flowing conversation that screeched to a pause. Face flushed, her eyes fell to her mismatched Converse. A squat woman—her grandmother—and a sharp-chinned man leaned in from either side of the girl. In the corner, her grandfather sat, thumbing through a magazine and trying to make himself shrink.

"Zelda," Rhonda said. "Please, come on in."

For the first time in their months of sessions, the young girl hurried into the office. Dr. Rhonda smiled at the visitors, and they returned it, but the insinuation was clear.

"*Nosotros esperaremos aquí afuera por ti, mija,*" the grandmother said, speaking past Rhonda and into the office. "Uh, we wait... here."

"I'm afraid this room is for patients," Rhonda said, her professional instincts flaring. "You can wait in the lobby."

It wasn't the first time adults had bristled at her commands, not even the first time this month. But she stood firm, closing enough of the door behind her to break any sightline.

Nodding, the grandmother and the uncle filed out. The grandfather sighed and closed the magazine.

Family. They put the work in family therapy.

Inside the office, Zelda settled in the Knoll Womb Chair, a choice she'd never made once in five months. Dr. Rhonda sighed inwardly; the shelf was out of view.

They spent the first ten minutes as they always did, warming up. Rhonda asked gentle probing questions and Zelda answered with as few words as possible. Still, her body communicated. Downcast eyes. Hesitation.

And her fingers most of all. They traced little patterns in the chair's fabric. Odd. Had Zelda previously displayed motor stereotypic compulsions?

As soon as the thought formed in Rhonda's mind, Zelda tucked her hands into her pocket. Goodness, she really was a sharp girl.

"So, elephant in the room," Rhonda said. "But we need to address it. I'd like to talk about what happened."

Zelda swallowed. "Could we, like, park that elephant for a while?"

Rhonda smiled. "My policy has always been transparency; you know that." She waited for Zelda to nod, but she never did. "And being transparent, you should also know that questions have been raised about your safety."

"I'm safe."

"Yes, you are now. But a few days ago?" A flash of question 17: *Does child comply with household rules, curfews, and demonstrate responsible judgment?* Rhonda leaned in. "Why don't you tell me what happened the night of the party?"

"Everyone knows what happened, right? It was, like, front page of the newspaper."

"So was the raccoon problem. And I believe today's top story had the mayor warning people not to look straight into the eclipse, so..." She shrugged. "People don't remember as much as we think."

Something about that statement narrowed Zelda's eyes. "What do you mean?"

"Beach town drama: all foam and no storm. It'll pass. But for a while it might feel like you're drowning. Sorry for all the sea metaphors."

Something in her words pushed Zelda inward. Rhonda was losing her again; she could see it.

She continued. "What I mean is, why don't you tell me *your* story? Not the one in the paper. Tell me about the girl who went night swimming. Were you skinny dipping or—"

"What? No, ew. No, definitely not."

Rhonda almost laughed. "It wouldn't be the first time it happened. When I was your age, they called it Kissing Cove. They even had this rock with graffiti—"

"The Wall of Names," Zelda said. "It's still there."

"I'm glad to hear that." It struck Rhonda just how long it had been since she'd felt the sand between her toes. "So, you're not skinny dipping or surfing. Midnight isn't the best hour for whale watching, so...?" She spread her hands out as if to say, *What was it?*

For a moment, Zelda sat in silence. Another question from the form flashed in Rhonda's thoughts. *Child does not exhibit high-risk behaviors like substance abuse, self-harm, unprotected sexual activity, etc.*

Finally, Zelda whispered, "You wouldn't believe me."

"Why do you say that?"

"Because you wouldn't."

She waited for Zelda to elaborate, but she never did. Another flash: *Child communicates needs, seeking out support or comfort when emotionally required.* She didn't like how the judge's checklist was shaping up.

"Zelda, in five months you've never given me reason to doubt your words. But with respect, you also haven't given me many words, either. So, why not roll the dice and see?"

Zelda let out a little scoff. "Why roll any dice when the game is, like, pretty much rigged?"

"Rigged? How so?"

The girl stood up and paced, first to the window and then past the shelf. She came to a stop at the tabletop Zen garden, her finger tracing its way across the sand.

"It's like the house always wins. I talk, people will say I'm just crazy. If I don't, everyone just assumes I'm all depressed or whatever."

"You mean a paradox?"

"Everything's a paradox." For a long time, Zelda just stood there, finger tracing little lines around the Zen garden's rocks and tiny bonsai. She said, "If I go with my grandparents, I'll be super miserable. But if I stay with Uncle Mark, I might put him in..."

Rhonda sensed her young patient trying to take back her words. She asked, "In what?"

"Get him in trouble," Zelda said. "Like, stressed about money and stuff, you know?"

Rhonda nodded. More than once Mr. Fitzsimmons had asked to defer payment until his insurance came through, and she'd always agreed. But she sensed that wasn't quite it, was it? The girl was trying to conceal something almost revealed.

Might put him in danger? she wondered.

Frustrated, Rhonda sighed. "Zelda, you care about your uncle; that much is clear. But the question is, do you communicate? Do you let him into your life—your *real* life? Do you share enough so others can make informed decisions about your well-being? You say it's rigged. But from where I'm sitting, you're barely playing. Meanwhile, decisions have to be made."

"Like that form you have to fill out?"

Rhonda's back stiffened as her eyes flicked to the desk. Had she left it out?

"Transparency, right?" Zelda smirked and paced over to the shelf, pausing to admire the old Sega Genesis. "My uncle left his phone unlocked, and I saw it. Uncle Alejandro, I mean. He was translating it for my grandma."

"Yes, Zelda, like that form." Rhonda let out a quiet breath. It wasn't every day that a patient kept her on her toes. She fell back on a question so basic she almost winced. "So, how does that make you feel?"

"Feel?" Zelda traced a finger across the old Sega Genesis, checking it for dust. "Like everyone's talking around me, but no one's asking what I actually want."

"Sometimes people have to talk around the truth, hence..." She gestured around the office as if to say, *Exhibit A*. "So why don't you tell me what you actually want?"

"The impossible." Her voice cracked as she spoke. "I just want for things to go back to the way they once were."

36

Debra rolled down the window and took a deep breath of the vineyard's sylvan air. These were beautiful lands, hills and hollows rich and fertile and bursting with life, even in winter.

And yet this part of town always put her on edge. Perhaps it was the decade-old city-issued sedan she was driving. Perhaps it was her outsider status, felt most among these monied estates. Or perhaps it was the knowledge that no matter how hard she worked, no matter how high she rose through the ranks, the only time cops visited such a place was in search of donations.

For now, she pushed those thoughts aside, pulling into the court-yard and parking near a fountain. In its shadow, the Larchmont estate was more of a castle than a home. Pennants whipped in the breeze. Far off down the hills, field hands pruned dormant vines. In the afternoon light, it could almost pass for a renaissance painting.

The front door creaked open as she neared, and a well-groomed man in his fifties emerged. He wore a subtle blazer bearing the vineyard's crest. A butler, Christ. What year was she in?

He asked, "Can I help you?"

"Afternoon." She put on her best business smile, polite but firm. "I was wondering if I could speak with Mrs. Boyle."

With an imperious flick of his eyes, the butler sized her up. "She's not expecting anyone this afternoon. Nor is she taking callers or... whatever this is."

"No? How about friendly detectives?"

There were few things she abhorred more than being an investigatory cliché, but the old bi-fold snap and flash of the badge had its charms. The butler tensed.

"Relax, Pennyworth, I'm not serving warrants. Actually, I was hoping Mrs. Boyle could offer us some insight on—"

"Please, Mr. Osmond," said a calm voice just beyond the door. "Let the detective in."

Without missing a beat, the butler opened the door wide and held it with his back. With a nod, he gestured inside, where Mrs. Boyle stood clutching a clipboard and a fountain pen.

"You caught me between lunch and my afternoon revisions." She wiped something from her lips and smiled. "And I will never pass up a chance to chat with the law. Walk with me, Detective Brown."

As the door closed behind her, Debra's eyes swept through the foyer, cataloging it all. Paintings and statues, vases and sculptures. Antique books strategically placed about, not for reading but as stylistic accents. The whole thing reminded her of a soulless museum.

"I'm surprised you know who I am," Debra said. "I don't think we've formally met."

"Formally, no, not yet. But I can't scribble my little yarns without help from your department. I'm blessed to consider Dave a close friend. He's said good things about you."

It took Debra a moment to realize she meant David Coleman, the chief of police. In over a decade, she'd never heard him called by his first name. Certainly not in the boys' club that made up her department.

"Chief's got a lot of experience," Debra said. "I can't think of anyone better to offer you insight."

"It's a balancing act," Mrs. Boyle continued. "These little mysteries, that is. Readers clamor for authenticity, but when you give them details, they call you long-winded. Go light on procedure, well, they'll say you didn't research."

"That's the public for you. People are disappointed to find out my job's mostly knocking on doors and filling out forms."

A right turn down a hallway, and then the butler stopped before a study and gestured in. Towering bookshelves lined the walls, ending at a gorgeous redwood desk. Dusty curtains framed a view of the coastal cliffs and the vineyard. Nearby, a mirrored chessboard sat atop a gorgeous slab of black stone. Curiously, there was only one chair.

"It's a wonder you get any work done with this view," Debra said.

"I'm quite fortunate to have a flexible timeline. Have you read any of my books?"

"Read? No, but I listened to a few. *Muffin but Murders*, I think. Oh, and *Pie or Die* with the—"

"The Tart and Tabby twins. Yes, that was a fun one." Her eyes flashed as she smiled. It struck Debra that this old, wealthy woman— this community magnate—enjoyed the same flattery everyone else did. She ran a hand along a shelf full of colorful books. "I keep meaning to write more in that series, but at my age the hours escape me. Here, I'll send you off with a signed copy."

"That's kind of you, but there's no need—"

"I insist. There's nothing like the smell of a book." She removed a hardcover from the shelf. "Let me fetch a better pen. This one feathers on offset paper."

"Thank you." As Mrs. Boyle fished around in her desk, Debra studied the cover where a pie sat cooling on an open window, a jam jar lay broken hinting at blood, and a wise calico licked its paw and smirked at the viewer. "To be honest, I'm surprised I'm not tripping over cats."

Mrs. Boyle laughed and opened her desk drawer. "Truth be told, I can't stand the things. Terribly allergic, I'm afraid."

Debra turned the book over to the author's photo. Like Dean Koontz and his beloved golden retrievers, there Bibi sat in a high-back chair, surrounded by more cats than Hemingway.

"Guilty, I'm afraid," Mrs. Boyle said. "One must project a certain persona. Please, have a seat."

She gestured to a pair of leather couches flanking a glass coffee table. A stack of invitations rested there, each bearing the Historical Society's distinctive lantern and scroll emblem at the top.

As Debra settled in, Mrs. Boyle flipped a brass switch on her desk and an old intercom clicked to life. "Mr. Osmond, would you bring us some refreshments? Something from the tidal cellar, perhaps."

A gruff voice replied, "Of course," and for a moment Debra had the strangest sense that she'd heard it before.

Silly thought.

"So," Mrs. Boyle said, "what brings you to our fair corner of town?"

Debra found her tongue circling her teeth. Teeth. That was part of it, yes, but now that she sat in this palatial study, her thoughts felt discordant and absurd. This was a mistake, most likely. And if not, it was the oddest line of questions she'd followed.

She said, "Your son, Grant Larchmont, he—"

"Oh, dear." Mrs. Boyle bowed her head as her eyes searched the Persian rug. "That stain never washes out, does it?"

"I'm sorry to open old wounds." Even though it had been decades, there was no easy way to broach the topic. Not when someone's child was posthumously accused of murdering thirty-nine residents of a psychiatric hospital. "It's just that I'm working a case that shares a few details with Grant. There was this man found in a dump—"

"That business in Fort Darrow, with the bodies? Yes, my nephew filled me in. He owns it. Or rather, some court does now, I suppose."

"Larry's been helpful," Debra said. "The thing is, one of the men involved removed his own teeth. And then another man, well, he said something rather odd. 'Light of my lights.' You remember that, don't you? It was something they found in Grant's diary."

"Of course I remember that." Another sad flicker in Mrs. Boyle's face. It was just what Debra needed to push on. Because what came next was the strangest thing of all.

"Coincidences come in pairs, but in my experience, they're never triplets." She took out her phone and turned a screenshot of the map to Mrs. Boyle. "See, if I plot out these instances, from the dump to the hospital and on, it forms a line headed north, towards this lighthouse. And that phrase, it comes from a poem—"

"Arthur Cummings, 1857." Mrs. Boyle swiped and followed the line on the map. "I'm sorry, Detective, but it sounds like you're saying I'm in danger."

Debra sat back. "I'm not sure. But, Mrs. Boyle, what I am asking is for you to be as forthcoming as possible. These similarities... Was there anyone your son might have worked with or confided in? Anyone who had access to information he shared?"

"Like an accomplice?"

"Or a copycat, perhaps. Someone who knew his... proclivities and eccentricities."

Mrs. Boyle clicked her tongue and stood up, pacing the coffee table. Her left hand kneaded the webbing of her right hand.

This whole idea was foolish, Debra thought. Here she was, stoking an old woman's fears. Asking her to dig up something that happened decades ago. She'd get it both barrels from the chief in a few hours. Hell, she'd probably get put on leave.

"'Light of my lights.'" Mrs. Boyle clasped her hands. "Now that you mention it, there was someone. It's a bit odd, but... Would you pass me that pen?"

And like that, Debra's heart raced and her thoughts swirled. Maybe she hadn't been chasing phantoms, after all. Maybe there was a connection. She reached across the coffee table, past the stack of invitations.

Her fingers never touched the fancy pen.

A glint of metal from the corner of her eye. Mrs. Boyle lashed out, a whip-like snap to her hand, so quick it stole the air from Debra's chest.

No, she realized. It was the knife.

A pearl-handled dagger jutted from her chest, buried beneath her left breast to its opulent hilt. The pommel pulsed arrhythmically with her gasp. Then Mrs. Boyle slid it in deeper.

"Hush now," she whispered. "It's almost over. The blade's in your heart, so just—"

Panicking, Debra reached for her side-holstered Glock 17. Like with the pen on the table, her fingers never made it.

Mrs. Boyle's other hand seized Debra's wrist and twisted. A crack, then a flash. Debra let out a tiny shriek as something popped deep inside her chest.

"There we go, sweetie," Mrs. Boyle said. "We've got this. Just relax..."

But Debra couldn't relax. Her broken hand was bent at a sharp angle and her senses flared. How could this old woman move so terribly fast? What gave her such brutal strength? And most of all, how had everything gone sideways in less than a second?

"I know this feels like cruelty," Mrs. Boyle said. "But you've been given a great honor. Her servants will eat well."

Something flashed in her eyes, black-violet tendrils tracing the edges of her pupils. Debra thought of a cold star swallowing a dark moon. Had Bibi always had a second row of teeth?

Debra's body shivered and spasmed as the world faded. "They'll... find out."

"Shh. They won't even notice." With her left palm, Mrs. Boyle pressed Debra against the couch, the weight of a hundred boulders beneath her wrinkled skin. With her right hand, she twisted the hilt until a crimson rose blossomed around the blade.

She felt cold inside. So frigid and desperate for warmth.

"Why?" she coughed.

"Because you were on the right scent but your pathing was off," Mrs. Boyle whispered. "He wasn't heading to the lighthouse. My son, he finally made his way home."

And then it came, the dying darkness.

It crawled in from the edges, a dozen impossible windows tearing open and spilling shadows across the study. As Debra's world receded, someone else appeared.

There, at the study door, loomed a baleful form she'd seen several days back.

That voice on the intercom...

Mr. Boote's skin hung loose and sallow, his smile a moldering hole around empty gums. And his eyes... Like Mrs. Boyle's, they flickered with black-violet—

Light of my lights, Debra thought, with her last thought. It finally made sense. *Light... of my lights.*

37

It was an exquisite pleasure, watching the dimming light of the eyes. First, the denial and shock. Then the instinct to fight back. The mind was a fortress of infinite defenses, and in those last seconds it deployed every one. Bibi savored the fight.

The body, however, was a simple machine, one that knew the truth of its wounds: a spiked heart would never heal. With a sigh, the detective slouched in this knowledge. Her eyelids relaxed.

For one beautiful second, Bibi marveled as her guest's conflicting systems found harmony, body and mind. Part of her envied the young woman. What shores she would soon behold.

She withdrew the blade. "Look at the mess you've caused," she said. "Well, come on now and clean it up."

The lumbering form of that security guard—Boote, his uniform had read—took the knife and wiped it on his leg. "Here," he grunted. "Clean."

"Not that," she snapped. "This poor woman you led here. Or did you think no one would notice you stomping your way across the county wearing that... *suit?*"

Boote shuffled closer, a herky-jerky trot until his shoe caught on the carpet. He regarded his foot like it was some foreign object, a piece of toilet paper stuck to his heel. She wasn't sure how it all worked, this body that her son was borrowing, but she imagined it like a bulldozer with a child fumbling at the levers and stretching to see over the wheel.

Her messy, muddy child.

She said, "Go on. Take her to the tidal cellar." With the way his face scrunched, it was hard to tell confusion from loose skin. "In the basement."

"Base-ment," he grunted. "West wing."

"No, *east* wing. Heavens, follow me." With a grunt, he hoisted the dead detective, draping her over his shoulder and spilling wet ribbons. "And don't get any more filth on the rug, goodness."

Exasperated, Bibi led him through the hall of portraits, where her ancestors stared back with their painted gazes and chipped frames. She could hear their murmuring disappointment. What did they know of ambition or patience? They had squandered their good fortunes, nearly costing the Larchmonts their legacy. Their reach had been measured in mere decades.

Hers, however...

Patience, yes. She told herself not every plan unfolded to her liking.

"Watch the curtains!" She winced as Boote's bumbling painted a red smear on the Italian silk. "Left. Left at the reading room."

"Left-uh," he croaked.

Yes, it was nice to have him home again, she supposed, in whatever form he had commandeered. But couldn't he be more discrete? Grant Larchmont. Even if no one else could sense it, she smelled the rot upon him since he spilled from her womb. No wonder their benefactor had found a willing slave.

"Emissary." He paused in the middle of the reading room.

"What?"

"Not slave. Em-i-ssa-ry." He grinned that toothless grin while his muddy tongue circled the inside his mouth. "And don't forget, you owe her a debt."

She shivered, drawing her jacket tight across her chest. Was her son now fumbling around inside her mind? Was this some new gift?

"No, I haven't forgotten," she said. "Carry on. That way."

His grin widened. "*Mmm... Good.*"

He continued through the reading room, the detective's legs bouncing with each step while his own head lolled to the right. He stopped at a large door in the hall, pulled it open, then hissed as he spun.

With a newspaper under his arm, her husband Harlan entered from the garden deck. He paused, hand brushing crumbs from his mustache. His eyes bounced between his wife, the guard with his sagging skin, and the dead body draped over his shoulders.

"Beebs, what is this?"

"Just a mess that needed cleaning." She put on her sweetest smile and walked over. "You know that recurring dream that I've been having? The one with the rats in the lighthouse?"

"I thought you were being metaphorical."

"One of them showed up on our door."

She gestured to Boote, who gave an odd tilt of his shoulder. The corpse's arm swayed, limp and lifeless. "Rat," he said. "Raaaaat."

Harlan asked, "Who is she?"

"Just a detective. Nothing to worry about."

"A *detective*? Beebs, someone will come asking. She'll be missed. She'll—"

Bibi waved it off. "*She* takes care of us. Always."

"That's not..." He swallowed, chin shaking and eyes dampening. Her Harlan. Her sweet Harlan, who never asked for much and always treated her well. Who gave her his family name after hers was sullied and soured. "We can't keep going on like this, Beebs. I'm tired of it all."

She took his frail, wrinkled hands and raised them to her cheeks. "We're safe. She was no one, I assure you."

"She's someone. They're *all* someone."

He pulled away from her touch and tucked the newspaper under his arm. His cane clomped on the floor as he shuffled off for his afternoon nap.

It always broke her heart to darken her dear husband's mood. He'd never understood what he was marrying into. When he finally had, it was too late. Vows had been made. Yet he'd always been supportive of her... *obligation*.

But he was right, too; she knew it in her bones. Lately, they'd both become so very tired.

Soon, that would be fixed.

She returned to the cellar door, where Boote waited with the corpse. She turned the light on and gestured into the depths. "In we go."

"Father." Boote gave a loose nod toward the hall Harlan had shuffled down. "Will he renew his vows, too? Or does he need... incentive?" His toothless mouth yawned, and a muddy hand spotted with rotten teeth wriggled its fingers.

Bibi slapped him so hard his head snapped to the right and the arm slithered back down his throat. "Don't be rude."

She could see her son in there, behind those dim, borrowed eyes. And something else. He opened his mouth, but no hand wriggled out. Only a blink of her *benefactor's* radiant dark light from the depths of his throat.

"Mmm... a pact is a pact," J'harr murmured. *"Remember your side of the bargain."*

Bibi wagged a finger in that big, droopy face. "And don't forget who opened the door from this side."

"Opened... but only a crack."

"A crack can always be widened. Or closed. Now come. Your servants must be hungry."

For a moment, Boote just stood there, mouth open and eyes blank. A puppet within a puppet. What was it that fueled her son's compulsions all those years ago? Was Ascension worth forfeiting his body?

No. Of course not. This world was rich with delights, and she had so much more to discover.

But for now, they still had the corpse.

The luster returned to Boote's eyes as his body shuddered. It was only Grant in there now, and for that she was thankful. J'harr's murmurs had left her with a migraine.

She led him through the wine cellar to a second set of stairs few knew existed. With an old flashlight, she illuminated the salty depths. She could hear it, the low hum of the waves. The walls glistened, damp and earthy, basking in the breath of the bay.

And then her flashlight came to it: the natural well descending into the rumbling depths. "Well, go on, then."

Boote twisted his large shoulders, shrugging off the dead weight like an old jacket. The detective slid over the edge and tumbled into the depths.

But not all the way.

Her corpse struck an outcropping, wedging between rocks. Bibi widened her flashlight beam, and there the detective lay, staring up at them with that sorrowful mask.

"Goodness, what a mess," Bibi said. "Fetch a pruning stick and—"

"No. Wait." Boote's big hand pawed at her back and she almost gasped again. She didn't like being touched, not by strangers and never by her son. "Her servants... already here."

Squinting, she scoured the black depths with her beam. The walls seemed to be moving.

No, something skittered and crawled out from *between* the walls. Creatures of prehistoric shell, born from the lightless depths of ancient tidal caves.

Crabs, she realized. The malformed servants of J'harr. Lumpy carapaces with twisted human faces bursting between scabrous cracks. With each skitter and shuffle, the shells split and lips mewled in wet torment.

Then they were upon the dead detective and—

No. Bibi turned as their chitinous clatter gave way to the tearing of fabric and flesh. The howling wind dampened their feeding, but not entirely.

"There is another matter," Bibi said. "Other pests in the vines, so to speak. You've felt them, too, haven't you? *Things* in your blind spots. I believe it's time to take care of your debts, too."

Boote's dim eyes stared into the depths, entranced by the feeding. His slouching posture, his drooped skin. Her son, as much an abomination before his Ascension as he was after.

"I said it's time to—"

"We heard you." He smiled his toothless smile. From the back of his throat, she swore an eye rimmed with toothy shards winked back. "We'll find where the rats are hiding; we'll settle our debts. Why else do you think I came back?"

38

Mark cursed when thunder rumbled and the cuff link slipped from his fingers. In the flickering lights, he searched the old carpet, rain playing a low drumroll on the roof.

"Found you."

He wasn't looking forward to driving in this weather, but the council had him by the balls. According to Stacey, they'd scheduled the hearing last minute, hoping he wouldn't show up.

Small-town government. It moved at whatever speed suited its needs.

"Okay, Greywood Bay Housing Ordinance 8.5.2." Zelda crossed her legs on the couch and flipped through a stack of highlighted pages.

"Eight five, huh?" Mark fastened the cuff link and smoothed his dress shirt. "Oh! 'The city council is empowered to expedite housing projects for disaster relief, on the condition that such projects comply with environmental and community welfare guidelines set forth in the Greywood Bay Millennium Housing Plan.'"

"Nice." Zelda turned the page. "CWC-17A. What's that?"

"C-W-C. That's the Community Welfare Clause, so 17A reads..."

He closed his eyes. "'The city pledges to maintain and improve quality of life for its residents through sustainable development...'"

Zelda tapped the printout. "'In particular...'"

"'In particular... by providing adequate housing and essential services in response to unforeseen calamities.'"

"Wow, that's perfect."

"Never mess with a teacher who spent a decade fighting Spanish bureaucracy."

He gathered the rest of his supplies: the laptop, with a dozen different connectors for the presentation, and the legal documents Roman had helped them review; the only thing that wasn't coming with him was Zelda.

"Sure I can't tempt you with a peek at the inner workings of civic duties?"

Zelda's expression said it all: she'd rather eat glue. "Please don't say 'tempting peek' and 'civic duty' in the same sentence. I've got some work to do."

"Fair enough. But farming elites in *Critical Mass* doesn't count." He cleared his throat. This next part was hard, always. "You know you're still grounded, right?"

She nodded. "I know."

"No sneaking off, Bueller. Pre-approved places only."

"You and Ali should have movie night. He loves ancient cinema, too."

"Ancient? Ouch. Tell me you've seen it."

"It's the one where the boomer from *Mission: Impossible* turns his parents' house into a bordello."

Mark couldn't help but laugh. "Okay, first off, there are so many things wrong with that statement. Second, I can't believe you know the word 'bordello.' Extra credit: take the afternoon and culture yourself. *Ferris Bueller's Day Off*. Consider it restitution."

Zelda's phone buzzed and she quickly silenced it. She'd been doing that a lot lately. Still, he tried to respect her privacy. For a teenage girl, sharing a small apartment and a bathroom with her uncle was its own kind of hell.

"And hey, pop quiz for the know-it-all," he said. "When are your grandparents picking you up?"

Zelda held up five fingers.

"And how will you be dressed for them?"

"A trash bag and a tutu."

"Nicely. You'll be dressed nicely, which means something other than a hoodie and a pair of jeans that went through a wood chipper."

She shot him a tired look from the couch and picked up her phone.

He despised being an authority figure instead of the fun uncle who visited from Spain and brought weird presents. Sighing, he checked the traffic on his phone, sensing the crosstown expressway would be a mess. It seemed the whole town forgot how to drive when it rained.

Still, he couldn't send her off with her grandparents on a low note. Not after Dr. Rhonda bought them some time.

"Look, we've had a rough patch." He sat on the couch beside her. "And your grandparents, they show their love in different ways. But they do love you. We can disagree but still see some good in each other. Family most of all. Cool?"

"I guess."

The old couch squeaked as he stood. "I'll take an 'I guess' over an eye roll any day." She rolled her eyes and smirked. "There we go."

TWENTY MINUTES LATER, MARK PARKED IN THE GARAGE beneath city hall and fixed his damp hair in the mirror. There was a lot riding on this afternoon; Stacey had told him as much. It wasn't often the city council called them into a closed-door session, even if it was a stonewalling tactic.

Which was why he'd spent the past day learning how to swing a procedural sledgehammer.

As he walked through the parking lot, his pulse spiked and sweat glazed his back. He passed several parked cop cars by the police station elevators.

Why was he suddenly so nervous? Had he left something at home?

He double-checked his folders and laptop, his dongles and handouts. Everything was as it should be.

And yet...

With a ding, the police elevator opened up, revealing a tall man with silver hair and a stern face straight out of *American Gothic*. He gave Mark a nod and walked past him, carrying a cardboard box of office supplies.

Had he seen that man at Bibi's fundraiser? Yes, he thought that he did.

And still, the doubt persisted. What the hell had he forgotten?

"Mark, over here!" Roman shouted from across the garage.

Stacey waved and held the elevator to city hall. "We're starting in five."

Roman slapped him on the shoulder as he stepped in. "Hope you two brought your boxing gloves, 'cause we're going toe to toe with gentry."

"You kidding?" Stacey said. "With the three of us, they won't make it to round two."

39

Zelda spent the morning gathering the items she had discreetly shipped to Ali: the coins—twenty-five- and fifty-pesetas from before Spain joined the EU, the jewelry glue, the fine-grit sandpaper and toothpicks, and the polishing cloths. Ali had helped her order most of the craft supplies from the Last Castle. The final piece—the empty cuff link bases from Etsy—had arrived last night. More than the objects themselves, she needed Uncle Mark out of her hair for a few hours.

The present wasn't going to assemble itself.

For an hour she followed YouTube instructions, sanding down one side of each coin to give the glue friction. She applied a thin layer of adhesive. Now, carefully lowering the first coin into the empty cuff link base, she held her breath.

Almost...

Almost...

There.

She let out a slow exhale and smiled. The measurements were right; this fit was perfect. The old coin sat snug, its central hole flanked by two ancient towers and the words *Espana 1997*.

A custom cuff link for Uncle Mark.

She let it sit while she double-checked the instructions Ali had texted.

Wipe away excess glue.

Let it dry.

Apply resin sealant.

She was balancing the resin bottle in one hand and her phone in the other when the call shook her grip.

"No, no, no." The bottle tipped and the glue splashed out, a glistening streak across the old carpet. In less than a second it was already sinking into the fibers. The cuff link clattered and rolled behind a stack of books.

It was the third time that unknown number had called this morning, always with the same garbled message. "Point Greywood to base... Point Greywood to base..."

She did what she'd done every time: she sent it to voicemail. Not today.

The more she blotted the mess with paper towels, the more it stuck to the carpet.

She spent a few minutes searching through drawers and cabinets for something to remove the smeared puddle of resin. Their grouchy landlord, Mr. Glendale, always yelling at the kids not to run and berating the residents to turn down the heat. He'd ding them on the damage deposit when they moved out.

If they ever moved out.

She sent Ali a text asking for help.

And that's when she smelled it.

The odor was sickly yet sweet, a biting mix of rot and... something else? A floral aroma of grapes with a hint of old wood that reminded her of a deep cellar. Where had it come from?

She checked the cabinet for a dead animal yet found nothing. She sniffed the glue, but it only burned her nose and turned the world blurry. She checked the bathroom, the shower, then the toilet. She was about to check the sink when a *boom* echoed through the apartment.

Someone was banging on the door, *thumpity thump. Thumpity thump.*

Maybe Ali was outside with some glue-dissolving solution. Maybe

Uncle Mark had finished the meeting. Maybe her grandparents were early.

And yet...

Another knock. *Thumpity thump. Thumpity thump.*

The smell... Was it coming from the door?

Zelda pressed an eye to the peephole. Stretched by the dusty lens into a fish-eyed shadow, a woman stood outside. Hair dampened, blazer loose around the neckline, the woman had a confused lean, as if she was catching her breath after a long run.

But her face...

As the woman turned her gaze upon Zelda, she recognized it at once.

Why was Detective Brown on her doorstep?

"Great." Zelda searched her memory. Was she in trouble for the party or the rescue operation? Had the Ruizes won some sort of emergency injunction and Detective Brown was here to whisk her off? She summoned her courage, undid the latch, and turned the knob.

The doorway was empty.

Stepping out onto the terrace, Zelda scanned the nearby apartments for any sign of the detective. The groundskeeper trimmed the hedges in the drizzle. A few neighbors clutched umbrellas and packed skis into a van. A glance over the rail revealed nothing. But what was she expecting? A crouching detective? Some middle-aged woman playing doorbell ditch and giggling in the shadows?

No. This was something else. Her instincts flared.

And that smell...

What had started as the sweet odor of rot had become a salty tang, redolent of briny caverns. It stung her nostrils and moistened her eyes, now sweeping through the apartment.

Closing the door, she heard the bathroom faucet burbling. Strands of seaweed and sand dripped into the sink as warm water steamed the mirror. Had she left it on? Of course not, yet the handle was damp to her touch.

With a nervous twist, Zelda shut the water off.

Then she saw the woman in the mirror.

With a swipe of her hand, Detective Brown rubbed the steam from inside the mirror. Zelda screamed and spun, expecting to find the detective in the shower. She found only an empty tub.

Because she wasn't behind her, Zelda realized. She was on the other side of the mirror.

"Zelda Ruiz," the detective said. "Funny. Somehow it makes sense."

That voice... Zelda didn't like its dry tenor and stiff words. And the smell most of all. A voice formed by lungs, dead and rotting.

"I always thought there was something unique about you."

From a pit of deep fear, Zelda forced herself to turn, to meet Detective Brown's milky gaze. To see her. Zelda swallowed to moisten her throat and give her own voice an echo of strength. No matter how many times she looked at the dead, it never got easier.

Maybe it never would.

"Detective Brown. What happened?"

For the first time since she'd met her, uncertainty wrinkled the detective's face. She was confused, unbalanced, turgid eyes blinking out of sync above quivering lips.

"I don't know... Don't quite *remember*. There was a question, and then a blade. I spent weeks walking the beach, searching for a way up the cliff. When I found a path, the town was empty. I looked in a thousand mirrors, yet no one looked back." She placed her hand on the glass, the moisture dripping down Zelda's side and frosting the edge. "Your warmth drew me here."

"My warmth?"

The dead detective nodded, something wistful in her eyes. This woman, she had been nothing but the face of bad news, a role Zelda had consigned her to. Yet now, Zelda realized she was more than just an authority figure. A human. A soul lost in confusion. And a part of Zelda's heart broke.

"Your warmth," the dead detective said. "It's the only light we can find. Everything else is infinitely dim."

Only one word, but Zelda hesitated to repeat it. "We?"

Her phone vibrated on the coffee table, yet she was certain she had turned it off. Somewhere, through the apartment's thin walls, another phone rang. And from the courtyard, another. Then another...

"There are others," Detective Brown said. "I see them in the mist. And they see you, Zelda Ruiz. Oh, how they crave to be heard."

Another phone echoed out from the alley behind the apartment. And then another.

"Stop it." Zelda closed her eyes. "Stop it, please. I don't want any of this."

"It won't end. Not until light extinguishes light."

Phones rang out everywhere now, a shrill song enveloping the apartment and slicing into the soft layers of Zelda's mind. This was madness and isolation, a storm only for her. The insanity that had haunted Chester for decades and—

And then a knock at the apartment door—*they've found me*—and Zelda was running to it, because she knew she hadn't locked it. They would pour in, all the dead screaming to be seen and heard and—

"Stay out!" she shouted, just a little too late.

The door swung inward, and Ali entered, backlit by a swirling wall of daylight and shadows. "Dude, you see all those birds? There's got to be hundreds! It's like an avian convention."

With a bottle of acetone and his modeling kit in hand, he studied Zelda's confusion. The spilled resin. The smell. The bathroom mirror, still steamed and dripping.

"So... did I catch you at a bad time?"

"It's just..." The ringing, squawking chorus petered off, and dozens of black-feathered birds took flight from the courtyard.

"Just what, Zelda-rooni?"

She hesitated, knowing Ali would struggle with what she'd seen. But if she couldn't talk to her friends, she was truly alone. "I need you to keep an open mind."

He let out a nervous laugh. "Okay, we're doing some *Ghostbusters* stuff, aren't we? I got you, boo... I think."

She led him into the bathroom, but there was no ghost in the mirror, and the sickening death scent was fading. The only remnant of the detective's presence was the steam on the glass, the cool frost in the corners.

And something drawn in the fading moisture.

A rectangle with a circle in the center, and two wavy lines bisecting its sides.

Ali tried to wipe the moisture off, but it didn't go away. "That's... on the other side."

"It is," Zelda said. "And you won't believe who made it."

He raised his phone and snapped a picture. "So, what ancient horror was dropping DMs on your mirror?"

"She's not ancient," Zelda said. "But yeah, spoiler, she's definitely dead."

Then she told Ali.

He blinked twice and furrowed his brow. For a moment, she thought he might not have heard her, so she repeated the name.

"Right, Detective Brown," Ali said. "No, I heard you, Z-dog. It's just... I don't know who the heck that is."

40

Ali wasn't sure why Zelda was looking at him like his head fell off, but he didn't like it. Nor did he like the things that were locked in her orbit. Things his rational mind shoved back, stored away, and preferred not to revisit.

That anomaly he chased into old Chester's junkyard this summer.

That night in the shipping container, and how it lasted for weeks.

The *ifrit* his drone tracked through the smoke and flames of Raven's Valley, and how it wore the face of that incel who started the fire.

That guy... what the hell was his name?

"Ali, tell me you're kidding," Zelda said. "Brown. *Detective* Debra Brown."

"What, does she show up like Candyman if you keep saying her name?" He stepped out into the living room and instantly spotted the mess of resin and paper towels. "Oh damn, that gunk is gonna set. Elrond, how much time do I have to get epoxy resin out of a carpet from, like, the Gold Rush?"

As his phone flashed an answer, Zelda poked him. "I'm serious. Detective Brown, from the police station."

"That's where they keep them." He glanced at the instructions on the screen. "Step one: apply a small amount of acetone. Grab me like twenty cotton balls."

"Ali, hold up." Zelda was really staring at him now, that intense look that made him feel like the world had gone out of sync. "We got arrested at the hospital. You distracted the nurse while I talked to Chester. They hauled us in, together."

"Okay, technically, we just got detained." They needed to hurry with the resin, so he blotted the mess with a paper towel and gently wiped. "And the detective wasn't named Brown, I remember. It was..."

He stopped scrubbing. Maybe the fumes were making him light-headed. Maybe seeing all those warblers circling had put him on edge.

Maybe...

"Ali, look at me."

In the cool light and the dim, crummy apartment, he thought Zelda resembled something of a ghost herself. He'd never seen her truly happy, truly carefree, like some of the other students. Now, a latent mania burned in her eyes. Maybe she really was haunted. Maybe she was unheard and unhealthy. Maybe the two weren't that far apart.

"Yeah," he said. "I hear you."

"Detective Brown," Zelda said. "She's got, like, big shoulders, dark hair, and that little spot by her lip. She's always wearing blazers and suit jackets and—"

Then it came to him in a few grayscale details: the cold hue of the walls, the filing cabinet in the corner of her office, the coffee on her breath. He had always thought a detective would have charts and strings and boards filled with mugshots. Instead, it was more depressing than Mrs. Saperstein's classroom.

"Wait," he said. "Wait, just... give me a second."

Another detail emerged. His own heart pounding in his chest. Zelda's shoulders to his left, and Maura's to his right. They were seated before that metal desk, the detective calling each of their parents, one by one by one.

"This is Detective Debra Brown of the Greywood Bay Police. Am I speaking with Yanar Hadid?"

"Weird," Ali muttered. "It's like I totally blanked."

As he tried to keep her image in his mind, he felt a beam sweeping over it, softening the edges and blurring her details.

"She had one of those plastic flowers," Zelda said. "You know, that dance when the light hits it."

Yes, he could see it pushing through the hazy curtain. It was orange and purple and said something like—

"'Sunshine or rain, don't ever stop dancing,'" Ali muttered.

He squeezed his pounding temples and stood up. He needed some fresh air. He wasn't sure if this was a migraine, but it was one of the worst headaches he'd ever had.

"You remember her, right?" Zelda asked.

"Yeah, I remember her."

He opened the door and steadied himself against the frame in the overcast glow. The storm was abating, and the winds had died down. Yet even in the light, an uncomfortable thought took shape.

If he didn't remember Detective Brown, what else might he have forgotten?

"We need to A/B test this," he said. "I'm calling Maura."

It turned out Maura didn't remember the detective either. Not until she sat on Zelda's sofa, closed her eyes, and pinched her forehead. Not until Zelda and Ali described enough details. And not until she leaned forward, muttering, "Wait... wait..."

Then it came, that same wide-eyed epiphany.

"What the hell?" Maura said. "It's like there's nothing. Then she's suddenly there."

"Like remembering homework a minute before it's due," he said.

"Is this, like, gaslighting or something?"

"Or something," Zelda said. "Detective Brown, I saw her in my mirror. And she left something. I don't know what, but... Ali?"

He swiped his phone, opening the photo of that symbol in the mirror's moisture. He didn't like it. There was something familiar, too, yet he couldn't remember where. He thought of Chester's mad scribblings on the junkyard sculptures.

The very sculptures Ali saw running through the fire of Raven's Valley.

No, a little part of his mind whispered. *Put it out of your thoughts.*

"I'm not sure what it means," he said. "And I ran out of credits for Elrond, so we'll need to wait until three."

"Wow, finally something I can do that your boyfriend can't." Maura took the phone.

"Elrond is not my boyfriend. We're in an open relationship and you're always my home base—"

"Gross."

"Plus, my ancient Sumerian is a bit rusty."

"It's not Sumerian. It's flipped, 'cause it was in a mirror, right?" She tapped the screen and adjusted the image. "Ali, we've been there. Sixth grade, Ms. Parker's history class. We had to listen to some dude talk about using whale blubber for lighthouse oil. You almost knocked over an old totem." A few taps on the web browser, and Maura turned the phone toward them again.

"Lighthouse," Zelda muttered and leaned in. Ali couldn't help but notice her fingers tracing little swirls on her jeans.

"It's a lantern and a scroll, see?" Maura said. "That's the emblem of the Historical Society."

41

After two hours of procedural sparring, three presentations on subcommittee findings, and motions to solicit public feedback and input, Mark's headache was in full force. Even with Stacey and Roman, the gears of local politics turned slow.

"It's how they break your spirit," Roman whispered as yet another PowerPoint presentation was deployed. "It makes the DMV look like NASCAR, doesn't it?"

Now, with Councilman Brand closing his laptop, Mark and Stacey had an opening. The councilman said, "Let's break for a moment while Ms. Layne and her colleagues set up."

As she connected the computer, Mark passed out copies of the slides, highlighted action plans, and takeaways in bright, bold text. He left a stack before each member.

There was Mr. Beyer, the assistant director of emergency services, and Mrs. Adams, the public works director, both leaning in and talking quietly. Beside them, the finance director, Mr. Goff, a man with a perpetual cough. One of the heads of building inspection, Mrs. Lopez-O'Donnell, offered Mark a friendly nod and flipped through the handout. At the end of the table, the planning commissioner yawned before digging into a package of peanuts.

Mark had two minutes to spare when a notification chirped on his screen. Zelda had left the apartment.

Shit...

He had activated the tracking app at Judge Fulghum's insistence. Still, it felt creepy to set a geo-fence around the apartment. Like he was stalking a wild animal.

Or a teenager.

And yet here it was, proof that Zelda was leaving when she said she wouldn't.

"Goddammit, kiddo," he muttered, ducking out into the hall. He was about to call her when a text message arrived.

> Heading to the library & historical society for a bit.

> Zelda WTF?

> Thought it was OK. You said only school-related places.

He clicked his tongue. Yeah, he had said those exact words. Now here they were, coming back in little pixels and an emoji with a stack of books.

> Is this school related?

> Extra credit!

She added a few more emojis: a student, a pen, and a line going upward that Mark took to mean her grades. It was amazing how much kids could say with a few symbols.

"Mr. Fitzsimmons?" That was Vice-Mayor Lydia Barton, holding the conference room door as the committee filtered back in. "The table is yours, if you're ready."

Mark collected his thoughts and smiled. Damn right he was ready.

NEARLY FORTY MINUTES LATER AND THE COMMITTEE WAS reeling. Whatever tired, bureaucratic expressions they had worn at the presentation's beginning gave way to nervous murmurs and the scratching of pens. Notes were passed between members. Even the assistant director of emergency services leaned in to confer with the vice-mayor. Mark and Stacey never gave them a moment to rest.

While one handled the presentation, the other paced the table, directing the members to the local, state, and federal laws they were citing. Stacey even had a grants packet detailing potential tax advantages if they moved fast.

And where she was the carrot, Mark was the stick.

There were court cases citing precedent for overruling local review boards. There was a new bill making its way through the state legislature that would claw back power from onerous committees. With a statewide housing crisis, the governor was looking to make examples. Wouldn't it be a shame if Greywood Bay caught his eye?

This town, with its love for seasonal tourists, eclipse parties, and wine festivals. Yet beneath it, the motto might as well be "Welcome to Greywood Bay: When are you leaving?"

"Okay, Mr. Fitzsimmons," the vice-mayor said. "I think you've made your point."

"If we did," Mark said, "permits would be signed and shovels would be breaking ground."

Someone cleared their throat as Stacey shot him a look: *Pump the brakes.*

But Mark didn't want to slow down or stop. As Rosalia had taught him, one way to win a fight was to exhaust the other side.

"If I could, Mr. Fitzsimmons, Ms. Layne, Mr. Tam..." The assistant finance director tried to read Mr. Taumalolo's name off the card but struggled.

"Roman is fine," the big man said.

"Right, Roman. See, the thing is, all of us here, we're sympathetic, truly. I wasn't supposed to say anything, but..." He shot a glance toward Councilman Brand, who returned a subtle nod. "The subcommittee would be willing to share a surprise, long as it doesn't leave the room."

"As long as what doesn't leave?" Mark asked.

"Well, it's the holidays, and we all need a bit of good cheer. I think you'll be happy."

With a wave to some aides and the squeaking of chairs, several subcommittee members scooted back from the table. A moment later, the aides returned, carrying a large, cloth-draped board. They placed it in the center of the table, and when the vice-mayor nodded, they removed the cloth.

Stacey leaned forward and squinted. Roman paced to get a better angle. After a half dozen blinks and tilts of his head, Mark still wasn't sure what he was looking at.

There were little blocks on wheels with porches around them. There was something like a playground, unpainted and haphazardly glued together. There was a little area that looked like a leasing office with a parking lot made of pasted black felt. It all resembled something his students might have 3D-printed and tossed together the day it was due.

"So... it's a trailer park?" Roman asked.

"No, goodness, no," the planning commissioner scoffed. "These are 'compact estates.' Each of them optimized for maximum-efficiency floor plans."

"Tiny houses," Stacey said.

"Two hundred and twenty-two families lost their homes in the fire," Mark said. "Corners were cut. People died. Lawsuits are flying like bees to a hive, and the committee's solution is... tiny homes?"

"These are high-quality dwellings," the commissioner added, "built around the Japanese principle of *kanso*, which means—"

"Simplicity and the elimination of clutter," Stacey said. "Yeah, I've watched *Sparking Joy*."

Mark sat just to stop the room from spinning.

"What's this number here?" Roman tapped a little QR code with some digits on the side of a house. "Two fifty. Don't tell me that's the square footage. Most of the homes in Raven's Valley had another zero at the end."

The vice-mayor smiled. "The units come in a variety of sizes."

"Oh good," Stacey said. "Because for a moment I thought the committee might be suggesting a family of five live in one of these."

"My cousin wouldn't even fit through the door," Roman grumbled.

A few nervous glances passed between committee members as they side-eyed each other. "I'm afraid our hands are tied," the director of building inspection said. "The county defines anything larger than six hundred square feet as an accessory dwelling unit—ADU—and the permits get onerous at scale. But these? We can move much quicker. We could have the first fifty under production contract in, say, eighteen to twenty-four months. Pending committee approval, of course."

"So they are tiny houses," Stacey said. "Not 'quaint estates' or 'portable palaces' or—"

"What they are," Councilman Brand said and tapped the model community, "is a solution to a problem that could take years of litigation and might pay pennies. This is a good offer. Frankly, it's probably the best and final offer—"

Mark had enough. The months of hearing after hearing. The platitudes and false promises. The fall benefit concert in the park and the confident statements made to the press about fast-tracked solutions. His forehead throbbed and his shoulders tightened. Hell, he'd fractured his collarbone saving lives during that fire. He'd never asked for a medal, a commendation, or even a thank-you. But he was tired of begging for handouts on behalf of others. It was too fucking much.

He didn't even realize what he was doing until it happened. In one quick motion, he took the board—and the half-assed model upon it—and flipped it all over.

Tiny homes snapped and scattered. Little fuzzy trees collapsed against the table. In a clatter of cheap plastics and glue, the board wobbled and slid from the table. Christ, he could even see a Home Depot sticker on the bottom.

The subcommittee members, frozen. Their eyes, stunned. Even Roman and Stacey held their breath. In this chamber of silence, Mark knew he'd probably lost them and blown this whole thing. All the trust put in him and Stacey and Roman, gone. Maybe he'd hit rock bottom.

But he could still bring the committee down with him.

"Your best and final," he said, "isn't even an acceptable beginning. We've spent months being nice and polite. Perhaps you've mistaken patience for weakness. But don't mistake our resolve, or the dynamics of this situation: we're not here asking for favors. These are demands for what the community is owed. And soon, they're going to stop coming from our friendly faces and start coming via certified mail and subpoenas. Now, I'm no lawyer, but I bet Roman could give you a rundown on what 'discovery' might entail. What all the emails and hours on the golf course added up to. Why some families got homes in Raven's Valley below market rate. And how it might be perceived the city council is steering things in a certain direction."

With the model destroyed and the table scratched, the silence pervading the room was even thicker now. He had their attention. He could see his insinuations stiffening postures and pursing lips. Even the vice-mayor's jaw was moving like she'd bitten into a lemon.

"Mr. Fitzsimmons," Councilman Brand said. "We respect your passion, truly. It must be frustrating for someone like you—someone who didn't grow up here and maybe isn't used to our way of life. Things move at a different cadence. But this subcommittee, this council, heck, this community—it's doing as much as it can. Lots of folks with fast ideas come and go, but Greywood Bay, well, she weathers her storms. I'd think long and hard about what rejecting this proposal means. One might not be aware of what they're going up against."

Mark could feel Stacey squeezing his hand beneath the table. He wasn't sure if she was asking for calm or offering her approval. Whatever it was, it filled him with strength.

He said, "With respect to you, Councilman, and to this committee, that blade cuts both ways."

42

While Ali biked ahead and Zelda skateboarded down the damp sidewalk, Maura spent the ride collecting her thoughts. Something skittered around at the edge of her memories. A discomforting question itched, like the skin beneath her broken arm's cast, waiting all summer to be scratched.

If she had forgotten about someone—a detective she'd met twice—what else was she missing?

Were there moments locked away? Moments she didn't want to remember, like Ali and his fear of that muddy thing that dragged him into the container?

Like Zelda, and what she said was in the sky over the fire?

A dark star, seething and covetous.

They took a right at Bancroft Boulevard and followed it through midtown, the little shops and boutiques glowing in the misty spittle. At the end of the road between a playground and the south side children's library, she saw it: a scroll and a fancy wooden sign.

Greywood Bay Historical Society
Illuminating Our Legacy & Guiding Tomorrow

"Up there! That's the symbol she wrote." Ali hopped off his bike and let it cruise into a bush. "Yo, Z-geist, is your ghost sensor lighting up?"

With a clack, Zelda brought her skateboard to a stop before an old Queen Anne Victorian, two floors of deep auburn and gold featuring intricately carved woodwork. The roof comprised an assemblage of turrets, gables, and bay windows. The wraparound porch felt both elegant and foreboding. Maura lingered while Zelda hurried up the stairs.

"Ali, fall back," Maura said.

"What? I thought you were down with this?"

"Just chill. Quit provoking... whatever this is."

They watched as Zelda tried the door, then cupped her face to the dark windows. The *pitter-pat* of the light rain competed with Maura's heart, and she realized she was holding her breath.

Then Zelda jumped back from the door.

"That better not be an Annabelle doll," Ali muttered. "Or a nun."

Whatever had scared Zelda faded, and she peered back through the window once again. Another thirty seconds passed, and she hurried back down the steps, shaking her head. "Sign says it's not open 'til the New Year."

"Whelp, it was a nice try," Ali said. "Let's go raid the library's Blu-Rays."

But Maura wasn't so sure. Something kept Zelda's feet glued to the sidewalk. "You saw something in there, didn't you?"

Zelda nodded, her eyes nervous and uncertain.

"What was it?"

"I'm not really sure," Zelda said. "It was probably nothing, but... I think it was an old woman."

"Wow, can't imagine we'd find an old woman inside there," Ali said. "I think you've gotta be, like, friends with Lincoln just to get in."

"I think she was gliding."

Maura felt every hair on the back of her neck stand at attention. The light drizzle was no longer pleasant, but like a warning.

"Gliding?" she repeated.

Zelda nodded. "She went right past me and didn't notice. But, like, I'm sixty percent sure her legs didn't move."

Ali said, "Well then, we agree: it's time to head home."

Brakes squeaked on the other side of the building, drawing their attention to a pathway between the park and the old Victorian. Hedges and a low fence ran the property's length.

"Follow me," Zelda whispered. "And hide the bikes."

Maura tucked her bike behind the bush where Ali's was already resting. She hurried after Zelda, staying low and silent. Behind them, Ali slipped on a patch of wet grass as Maura shot him a look. *Quiet!*

On the far side of the building, a stern-faced man walked to the rear of a Greywood Bay police cruiser. Maura gulped. She saw their afternoon: yet another trip to the station, another lecture from her parents, asking why she couldn't stay out of trouble like her perfect older brother.

But the silver-haired man wasn't here for them, she realized. He popped the trunk of the cruiser and removed a cardboard box, loose objects rattling about.

She saw framed photos and certificates. Stacks of books and mementos. A coffee mug and some folders.

The man carried it past the hedge and disappeared for a moment, then emerged empty-handed. He pulled a second box out, and this time, Ali raised his camera.

WTF? Maura mouthed.

Ali tapped his eyes, and she understood his meaning: *surveillance.*

Whatever he saw on the screen sent a little gasp from his mouth.

For a beat, the silver-haired man's head swung in their direction, and it was Maura's turn to nearly lose it.

She knew him. Her mom had written an op-ed in the newspaper last year, criticizing the town's purchase of a surplus military truck. She'd seen his photo at the police station, too, both times they'd been detained. He'd been smiling from inside a frame above the words *David Coleman, Chief of Police.*

Now he stared at the bushes, the rain dripping down his hood and the sharp lines of his face.

No one moved.

Then he tightened his jacket and hurried back to the car. With the moan of a tired engine, the old cruiser pulled away.

Maura didn't like this. There was something off about this whole afternoon. Even if Ali always spooked at his shadow, she was starting to agree: they should probably leave.

Then Zelda vaulted over the bush and raced down the alley.

As Maura hurried after her, Ali tugged her sleeve. "Not now," Maura whispered.

The boxes sat on a loading dock at the back of the Historical Society, under a sign reading *DELIVERIES*. A large door loomed atop metal stairs. Maura was already halfway up when Ali finally pinched her.

"Box... Brown... flower!" He gestured to his phone, and she realized what had made him gasp. It was the same thing Zelda now lifted from the box.

An orange and purple flower, plastic and damp. There was a tiny solar chip on the pot that made the stem wiggle and the leaves dance. And here it was, another memory bursting from the mental fog. That stupid flower had been dancing both times they'd been busted.

"This is Detective Brown's stuff," Zelda said. "See?"

When it came to the discomforting, the supernatural, the occult, Maura considered herself open-minded. Yet every time Zelda delved into the otherworldly, Maura felt herself trying to reject it, spitting it out like bitter soup. She forced herself to swallow.

"So what does it mean?" Maura asked.

"I don't know," Zelda said. "But she led us here, so it has to be something."

They rummaged through the box, but there was no order or story to the contents: a framed diploma, Master's of Criminal Justice; a citation for ten years of service in the Greywood PD; a coffee cup that read *Mugshot Ready*. It was just stuff, like her office had been cleared out in a hurry.

"Uh, guys," Ali said. "I think we should get away from the door."

It took Maura a second to assemble it all. The doorbell, where a little light blinked. Beneath the delivery sign, a note written in cursive: *Ring bell for signature confirmation.* A shadow passed the window, not five feet away.

There was no way they'd make it back to the bushes in time.

"Get underneath," Maura whispered and grabbed Zelda's sleeve. She pulled her down the metal stairs and into a cubby beneath the door. Seconds later, the bell buzzed and the door swung open above them.

Huddling together, the three held their breath as the metal landing rattled above. Maura stole a glance upward at the gap between the stairs and the building.

A pink blazer.

Tan boots.

A shadowed arm, bracelet glinting in the light as it reached for the first box.

Then came the stench, reeking of fermentation and foam. Maura stifled a gag as the shadow above picked up the box and brought it inside.

The door creaked shut.

Silence. They waited.

The door opened again, and the second box was hoisted up. Whoever stood above paused long enough to make a nasally grunt. "Hmmph." Then the door swung inward, groaning. In another second, it would slam shut, locking them out.

But not if Maura could help it.

She surprised herself as much as the others. With a silent gesture, she reached up through the gap. Her arm shuddered, and she winced as something cracked.

The door hadn't closed, not entirely.

They waited, the rain drizzling down and the three of them huddling so close their skin grew sticky against each other. When it felt like they might just start shivering, Zelda whispered, "Okay."

Slowly, silently, they each squirmed out of the cubby. It was only when their bodies had space that Maura realized Ali was squeezing her left hand. "Man, your palm's damper than a swamp."

"I'm a profuse sweater," he said, tiptoeing up the stairs. "Bummer we're locked out. I kind of wanted to tour the granny castle."

"Who said we're locked out?" Maura dug her fingers between the landing and the cubby below. Wiggling the door, she pried it a quarter inch open, removing a glass and plastic rectangle wedged in the gap.

Her phone.

It wasn't broken, but the screen was now cracked. "Good thing I have Apple Care."

Then she opened the door.

43

They were trespassing; Zelda knew this. Breaking and entering, and probably violating some antiquities law. But she didn't care. Detective Brown had given her enough signs to push through the doubt. There was something inside the Historical Society screaming to be found.

She just wasn't sure where to begin.

As Maura gently closed the door behind them, the shadows took form.

To their right, industrial fridges and coolers lined the wall. To the left stood a metal cabinet filled with enough fancy plates to feed fifty guests. Prep stations and stoves sat, polished and bare. This was some sort of kitchen.

"Shoes," Ali whispered. "What is this, amateur hour?"

Maura wiped her muddy soles on a mat. "Sorry, it's only my second break-in."

Zelda held up her hand at the door to a dark hallway. Silence, then...

Something moved down the hall to her left. Zelda waved them back into the kitchen. Crouching between the industrial fridge and a prep table, the three held their breath as footsteps drew closer and closer.

A shadow passed by, that same salmon-pink blazer. The woman was old yet confident in her stride, that obnoxious lady from the council meeting.

Bibi.

With a whistle of amusement, she opened the back door and studied the rain. "Goodness," Bibi announced and clicked open her umbrella.

And then she left.

They waited several beats before regrouping by the hall. "Lucky her hearing aid sucks," Ali said. "You think she's the only one here?"

"Probably," Zelda said. "Otherwise she wouldn't have turned off the lights."

"Unless the guard dogs see in the dark." Maura gave them a wink.

The Historical Society's halls meandered this way and that, between dim parlors and lounges rich with old books and antique couches. Then it opened up into a room filled with curious shapes. A whale jaw loomed, taking up half a wall. Old oars crossed a dugout canoe. Twin totems stood in the center, open-mouthed animals staring back from the shadows. Bears and birds, and something near the top wreathed in tentacles. It had far too many eyes for an octopus.

Yeah, they were on the right trail.

"Told you we've been here," Maura said. "You left your lunch at school, so we shared my pretzels."

"I can't believe you remember that," Ali said.

Zelda noticed a flicker of sadness in Maura's eyes. "Yeah," Maura said. "Well, it wasn't anything."

Dusty paintings and old tintype photos of miners and fur traders stared down from the high walls. Bows and arrows gathered dust on shelves beside long rifles and flintlocks. They tiptoed around the museum curios, Ali occasionally snapping a picture. The place was enormous, a labyrinth of artifacts going back hundreds of years. On a field trip, it would have bored Zelda. But now, in the dim light, she could feel something connecting all these objects.

The touch of J'harr.

"So, where's the detective's stuff?" Maura whispered.

"I don't know," Zelda said. Then she noticed the trail of water. "Hey, stop walking. Everyone just... freeze."

Ali and Maura paused on opposite sides of the room. Zelda bent down, angling her phone's flashlight along the floor.

Sure enough, little droplets of water glistened on the museum's hardwood floor and ran down a long hall. She followed it past an antique sign where a purple turban-wrapped head floated over text for a fair nearly a century ago. Some weird mystic named Armando the Great.

The wet trail came to an end at a set of stairs descending into darkness. A sign read *Historical Society Archives by Appointment Only.* Ali groaned. "We're doing a stealth mission into Dracula's basement?"

"It's not stealthy if you keep jabbering," Maura said. "C'mon."

"This calls for a research montage," he said. "Elrond, play 'Circles' by Post Malone."

"Playing 'Signals' by Ross Mulrone."

"Ali, mute."

Discomfort slowed Zelda's descent. It felt like years since she'd had one normal day. A morning without some new nickname online: *Psycho Zombie Zelda.* An afternoon without J'harr's taunting murmurs. An evening without a ringing phone. If she could just find out what the dead detective wanted, then maybe, just maybe, she'd be closer to bringing balance back into her life.

At the bottom of the stairs, the archives stretched off into a shrouded basement. Shelves and nooks created a maze of odd shapes. Their phones cast weak, cool light upon racks of magazines and clippings, old trinkets for exhibits long past.

As they found a row of model ships, Ali murmured his approval. "These are classics. Boucher, SS California. She was one of the first steamships of the Pacific. Ran the gold rush, Panama to San Francisco."

"Cool facts," Maura said. "You and Elrond can talk about it on your trip to Skull Mountain."

"First off, it's Mount Doom. Second, Elrond never went east of Rivendell after Isildur's betrayal—"

"Guys," Zelda whispered.

"And third," Ali continued, "this model is probably worth a few grand at least."

"Guys, look." Zelda pointed to the end of the row, where two wet cardboard boxes sat on a table. There were other items, too: a duffel bag, manilla folders, shopping bags, and more, all hastily placed together.

They each took a bag and opened it. "Clothes," Maura said. "Like they were just stuffed in."

Ali pulled several pages from the folder. "Rental agreement. Payroll. A parking pass for city hall: D. Brown."

"They're gathering up her whole life," Maura said. "This is insane."

"No, it's methodical," Zelda said. "Which means there are probably others. See what you can find."

"Take photos of everything," Ali said. "Hoover it up and Elrond will sort it all out."

They each went in a different direction, searching the rows of artifacts. Zelda's eyes swept over old bells and gavels and charters dating back to the town's founding. Some were even older. A row down, Maura tapped an old drum. In the next aisle, Ali blew dust from a diorama of a drive-in movie theater. Zelda found herself coming under the nostalgic spell of the town's glory days. A parade for veterans of the Great War, painted in bold, patriotic strokes. An invitation to a New Year's party at Larchmont Vineyards, 1901. Everything perfect and precise, with a clear message: simpler times.

But Zelda knew things weren't always simple.

Not for the migrants who picked the grapes or the artichokes the region was known for. Not for the seasonal workers who came in the summer but couldn't afford to put roots down. Nor the timber workers or longshoreman, many staring out from old photos now, their legs or arms missing. Or the miners, faces stained oil black. And not the fur traders or the indigenous people they displaced.

Her light played over a hand-painted placard depicting a frontiersman in a coonskin cap facing off with a Native American, their weapons drawn on each other.

Destiny's star beckons us west! Let not the savage reclaim what progress has tamed! To the bountiful shores of California—lands rich with promise. Strike your claim!

She took a picture and added it to the list.

"Oh snap!" Ali whispered. "Zelda, it's your lighthouse. C'mere!"

Deep in a shelf of maritime memorabilia, Ali withdrew a model. Indeed, it was Point Greywood lighthouse in miniature form.

She studied the shelf, snapping pictures of newspaper clippings and old nautical maps. Something like a chart of moon phases. Tidal patterns that swirled around the lighthouse and the shoal.

Like some sort of whirlpool.

Ali handed her a pile of documents. "My boy Elrond is gonna be trained better than the CIA. Turn the page."

As the old paper slid between her fingers, Zelda's stomach dropped. "It's him. Ben, from the lighthouse."

Staring back from a photo yellowed by decades was the man she'd met on the night that now felt like a dream. He stood smiling and shaking hands with another man, someone older. They both wore blazers, but Ben seemed to be the junior , his stance one of nervous excitement.

The headline read *Visiting Postdoc to Assist University in Rare Optics Research*.

"What's a postdoc?" Zelda asked.

"It's a researcher," Ali said. "Like, after they finish doctor school, but not totally."

Maura poked her head over. "Now I'm even more confused."

"You're not ready for the NFL but you're done with college."

"Got it."

Ali snapped photo after photo while Zelda scanned the clipping's text.

On a cool August afternoon, the university physics department welcomed Dr. Ben Thomas, 30, to campus to begin his year-long fellowship.

"From the stunning landscape to the unique interplay of liquid and light found nowhere else, the Lost Coast has fascinated me for years," Dr. Thomas said. "This generous funding makes my research possible. I'm truly grateful."

A recent graduate of Caltech, Dr. Thomas will lead a fall seminar series. The first, Wavefronts and Wavelengths: A Deep Dive into Optical

Physics, is on September 3rd. Thanks to the sponsorship of the Historical Society, these seminars are free and open to the public.

Aside from his research, Dr. Thomas is an avid hiker and bird watcher. He hopes to witness the famous Pacific Flyway migration during his stay.

"C'mon, more data," Ali said. "Elrond hungry. Zelda, dig in by the water cooler. Maura, take the next row. We'll meet up in the middle."

"Copy that," Maura said.

An icy finger slid down Zelda's spine. Ben—Dr. Ben Thomas—and his words echoing out of time.

While Maura searched among the oversized shelves, Zelda took in the photos and articles detailing the town's social events.

2015, Raffle Nets a Cool Million for New Children's Zoo.
2007, Veterans Benefit & Black Tie Banquet: What a Ball!
1999, Citizens Group Holds Hearing on Dangers of New Skate Park.

She wiped dust from the glass and almost laughed. There was Mr. Fitch, her science teacher, arguing on behalf of the town's skaters to build a half pipe.

And here, in 1998, another page: *Historical Society Fundraiser Fills Foundation Coffers.*

Zelda took in the Kodak moment: the kind of university event Maura's parents often attended. Gray-haired deans and donors all smiling for the camera.

Wait...

A man in the photo drew her attention. His flat smile. The lines of his face. Those hawkish eyes. She had seen them staring back not thirty minutes ago. That was the chief of police.

He'd barely aged a few years, let alone thirty.

"What the..." she muttered.

Another photo: *Coastal Cleanup Saves Birds From Oil Spill.* And there was the chief of police on the beach in 1998, a gooey bird in his hands. Yeah, he looked younger, but not by three decades.

"Guys, this really is Dracula's basement," Zelda said.

She snapped photo after photo, finally seeing the faces for the first time—and what was missing. Age lines, hairlines, crow's feet and more. All these markers of time that should have sprouted were conflicting suggestions down through the decades. Even a few job titles shifted.

Ellison Mitchell, head butcher at Kelan's Meats, shows students how to section a rib roast.
Chancellor Brand Taps Donors to Direct University Board.
Grape Expectations: Local Vintner's Wine Wins Coveted State Cup.

The woman in the magazine article was a healthy middle age, roller-set hair and wavy curls hung over cheeks full of blush and a flat, powerful smile. Zelda recognized her eyes most of all. She had turned that entitled gaze upon Uncle Mark at city council. She had been inside this building not twenty minutes ago.

Now, Barbara Boyle looked back from seven decades ago.

"Hey, check this out," Maura said, from one row over. "I think that old lady left her jacket."

But she's not an old lady, Zelda thought. She's something else.

Maura rounded the corner, carrying that salmon-pink blazer. At some point, the scent of rot had crept back, tingling Zelda's nose and watering her eyes. "Maura," she whispered. "Where's Ali?"

Then a hand reached out from beneath the shelf and grabbed Maura's foot.

She screamed—because of course she screamed—only to find Ali crawling out of the gap and pressing a finger to his mouth. Zelda read his lips, and she knew. *Someone's here.*

"Ah, the squeak of young lungs." The voice spoke from several aisles over, wet and sonorous. "I was wondering what kind of rats were hiding under my porch. Only children would be so naïve to think they were unnoticed. Come, so I can see you. You've touched far too many trophies to leave."

Zelda felt Ali's and Maura's hands clutching hers, their bodies trembling. The presence glided down an adjacent aisle, a twisting confusion of fabrics and limbs. Something like a lumpy wet arm stretched and freed itself from a white blouse. Tan pants tumbled past a squirming leg, dimpled with warts. And a nail—pink and polished—split along the quick as wormy tendrils bulged out and probed the shadows.

And that smell...

Zelda squeezed her sides to keep her stomach from twisting and emptying.

"Yes, I can sense each of you stifling your screams. But your bodies betray you, breath by breath. Come, little rats. Make this easier and show me your faces."

As an old chain fell from a shelf in an adjacent row, Zelda eyed her two friends locked in fear and confusion. There were worse things than death. There were the pups of J'harr. There was her maddening black-violet light. And now, glimpses of this abomination of tendrils and teeth. Whatever was coming for them, it would soon round the corner.

She had gotten them into this mess, Zelda thought. She had to get them out.

She grabbed an old trophy and threw it as far as she could. Through a gap in the shelf, the drifting thing quivered as milky eyes tracked movement. In a crash of wood and metal, the trophy bounced off a table and rolled to the copy machine. Brass glistened and spun.

Whatever Zelda thought of the creature, it was its speed most of all that chipped away at rational thoughts. It wore the skin of an old woman—vestigial arms and gray hair—yet it moved with lashing quickness. A blur of teeth and whipping tendrils, eel-like and writhing. It burst past the end of the aisle and scrambled over a table, sending a chair spinning.

Run, Zelda mouthed, pushing Ali and Maura away down the aisle.

They made it ten paces before the voice shouted, "Oh, you think yourself clever? But clever rats run so much faster."

Zelda glanced back and a little part of her mind locked up. There, turning to face them, the remnants of Bibi Boyle's nude body unfurled, a veneer of frail flesh sliding away to reveal a misshapen frame somehow larger within. Eyes, Zelda thought. So many milky eyes blinking among tumorous skin. Where palms once joined fingers, skin uncoiled like ropes, latching onto the shelves and the nooks.

"Why can't I see you, little rat? Who's hiding your face from our sight?"

Zelda realized what was happening almost too late.

With a shuddering jerk, the Bibi-thing tugged the row of artifacts. Pictures toppled and vases wobbled. A glass bottle boat struck Ali on the head and—unlike what movies had taught them—the glass didn't break.

But Ali's legs buckled.

Then the shelf teetered, tipped, and smashed into the next row over. They were trapped in a narrow, triangular passage. Zelda and Maura protected their heads as the shelves emptied and inched closer, closer.

And that wormy, squirming Bibi-thing...

Her bulbous shoulders bent and her neck elongated. Crouching, she poured herself between the tilting shelves. First a long, spindly arm. Then her puckering face. Zelda thought of the hagfish she'd once seen at the aquarium, a twisting frenzy as it dug into the seafloor.

The Bibi-thing stretched out a hand for Ali. Close. Closer...

"Whatever light you're hiding inside, we'll peel it apart. You shouldn't have come here—"

A glint to Zelda's left, then something *whooshed* past her ear. She wasn't sure where Maura had found the antique whaling harpoon, but her form was flawless. With a scream, Maura drove the metal tip through the gap, meeting the wormy arm mid-stretch.

Then it was the creature's turn to shriek.

A raw seam opened up the length of the Bibi-thing's forearm. Black-violet light sizzled and shimmered. Hissing and groaning, the creature retreated, just enough for Ali to crawl out. With its other hand, it shielded its eyes.

Oddly, Zelda sensed there was someone else here in this basement of writhing terror. Her hand went to her pendant, which was tight on her throat.

"Why?" the Bibi-thing hissed. "Why can't I see you?"

Zelda didn't wait for an answer. Pulling Ali with Maura, they raced for the stairs as the wormy creature thrashed and fumbled through the shadows.

"Wait." Zelda stopped at the top of the stairs. "Help me close these."

"That's one pissed-off Squidward," Ali said, while Maura shoved the basement door shut. "That door isn't going to stop it."

"Maybe not. But this might slow her down."

With a click, the latch slid into place. Then the door shuddered, curls of dust falling from the rattling frame. Chester's voice echoed in her mind.

"This one means 'to lock or unlock something of value.'"

And nothing was more valuable than her friends.

Her fingers moved on their own as something warmed in her heart. Detective Brown, and her words in the hospital. *"If you need anything, you let me know. Cool?"*

Yeah, Zelda thought. *We need some help.*

She reflexively traced the locking symbol on the door, and it stopped shaking. Just like that.

"Nice move, Dumbledore," Ali said. "What was that hand thingy?"

"I'm not sure I even know," Zelda said. "Now, let's run."

It took them less than twenty seconds to sprint through the museum, the halls, and then the kitchen. In a clang of metal and hinges, Maura kicked the loading door open. The rain hit their faces, heavy and cold. Zelda had never been happier to see the clouds and gray afternoon glow.

They found their bikes and her skateboard. Then their wheels hit the pavement. As they pedaled off—Zelda holding on to the back of Maura's bike and the street rattling beneath—the past hour and its horrors began to take on an odd hue. She felt mist rising in her mind, blurring monstrous shapes and softening sharp edges.

She told herself not to forget it; she fought to hold on.

But when they arrived back at the Heartwood Apartments, soaked and shivering, she realized she had forgotten something else.

The Ruizes were here.

They'd been waiting for twenty minutes.

44

With a wet gasp and a backward snap, Chester pulled his face from the birdbath. It took several beats of his tired heart to reorient himself. The throbbing wrist and the brace that encased it. The sparse bushes and droopy trees. Distant waves murmuring beyond damp bushes and sculptures.

Yeah, he was back at Pacific Gardens. He suspected he'd taken his last adventure past its gates.

J'harr's taunting countdown played in his head.

Three.

Twenty-three.

Eighty-one thousand four hundred and twenty-three.

At least that girl and her friends were safe...

For the moment.

He plucked wet shards of bottle glass from the birdbath and scattered them back among the sculptures. He wasn't even sure what it was. Just driftwood and glass and aged nautical knickknacks, some soothing amalgamation meant to keep the residents placid and numb.

Shivering, he wandered across the rainy grounds, a hitch in his throat and numbness to his step. He slowed just to make sure his feet were touching the bricks.

Seven.

Seventy-seven.

Eighty-one thousand three hundred and seventy-seven.

He spotted Ms. Tan long before she noticed him. In the dusky shadows and drizzle, she looked like a raccoon tucked in a storm drain. She brought that vape pen to her lips. The end glowed, a spark as artificial as the oils it atomized. Chester caught a whiff as she exhaled a cloud of earthy terpenes, probably some new strain engineered to send you to space.

She snuck a second hit, glancing back at the rec room, where Freddy was setting up for the evening's movies. A few residents snoozed, unfinished dinners before them. For a while, Chester had wondered if they were drugging him. But after a few weeks, he realized institutional-grade mashed potatoes and beef stroganoff had a tranquilizing effect.

"So, what's for dinner?" he asked.

Ms. Tan coughed, shoving the vape pen into her raincoat pocket.

"Mr. Halgrove," she said. "You shouldn't be out in this weather. Not after that tumble you took."

Chester grunted and squeezed his wrist brace.

"Come. Let's get you inside."

Taking him by the elbow, she led him toward the warm glow of the hallways and the promise of muzak. They'd been on a sixties kick lately. He wasn't sure he could listen to another Dramamine cover of Buffalo Springfield's "For What It's Worth."

The door opened, and Freddy poked his head out. "I heard a scream."

Chester liked Freddy. He was the only caregiver that insisted the residents call him by his first name. He was patient and gentle, unlike Mr. Comerford, who occasionally left a bruise.

"Oh, just Mr. Halgrove, giving me a mild heart attack," Ms. Tan said.

As she passed him off to Freddy, Chester coughed and clutched his chest. He keeled over, wobbling at his knees and reaching out for support. His fingers fumbled at Ms. Tan's raincoat.

"Whoa, buddy," Freddy said. "Just take her nice and slow. I got you, okay?"

Another retching cough, then another. He gave the caregivers the full weight of his thin frame and leaned between them.

Then, as fast as it started, it was over.

"Hey, what's our deal, old-timer?" Freddy gave him a gentle pat on the back. "Your ship ain't ready to sail. So why don't you tell me 'bout them little figures you've been folding? They look like origami."

"Yeah," Chester coughed. "Origami."

"And didn't you say you was an artist?" Freddy closed the door behind them. "I bet you made all kinds of wild stuff. Let's go see 'em."

With a gentle hand, he led Chester down the hall. Yes, Chester had made all kinds of things over the years. A few that would make even Freddy check his closets and keep the lights on at night. But for now Chester smiled inwardly. Not at the memory of his creations, but something he'd just taken. His trembling fingers pushed the stolen vape pen deeper into his pocket.

45

Cupping her bleeding forearm, Bibi shouldered the study door open and stumbled to her desk. With a trembling hand, she tugged the bottom drawer open. There were antacids and mood stabilizers, capsules for anxiety and focus. There were ancient tonics for digestion and cutting-edge pills for fat loss and libido. Remedies she knew well as the debt of time added up.

But the painkillers, damn. She had to stretch her memory back to recall the last time she'd felt such discomfort. Grant's birth, perhaps. The boy had nearly split her in two.

She choked four Percocets down and ground her jaw. Those rats in her basement—those faceless kids—how the hell had they managed to wound her? And who was shrouding them from her sight?

No matter. Soon, all would be renewed. For now, she had appearances to keep up.

She clicked the intercom. "Mr. Osmond, fetch the doctor. Have him come at once."

"Of course, ma'am." There was a pause from the other side. "Forgive me, but... I saw some blood in the east wing. Is everything okay?"

"If the doctor isn't on his way in sixty seconds, he'll be stitching two of us up. Consider how many words you wish to waste."

"Yes, ma'am." The intercom clicked off.

Bibi collected her thoughts, swaying as the festering gash leaked onto her antique desk. How many kings had signed proclamations on this wood? How many nations' fates had been decided?

With a swipe of her good arm, she sent a fresh stack of manuscript pages fluttering. Gold nibs and lacquered pens scattered and rolled. She admired the mess; she'd forgotten how good destruction felt.

Time to assess the damage.

Rolling up the bloody sleeve of her blouse, she knew the wound was going to be bad. And yet, when she saw it, she cried out.

The harpoon—a trophy from the whale hunts of her youth—had torn her from wrist to elbow. Of course, it hadn't exactly been *her* arm. But a limb was a limb, and a wound was a wound. This one bit deep. Writhing veins and knotty tumors squirmed in a thin crimson bath. From deep inside, ribbons of black-violet pulsed. Her dark blessing was seeping out.

Bibi found a roll of tape in the top drawer and a stapler beside it. In five quick circles, she sealed the wound. She pressed the stapler against the seam and bit her lips.

Clickity-clack. Clickity-clack.

"Beebs, you okay?" Harlan stood at the study door, his tired eyes scouring the mess of papers, her ruined blazer, the bloody blouse. "Dare I ask how you got that?"

"Not if you want to see the New Year," she said. "Or any decades beyond."

He took a few slow steps into the study, his robe long and dangling, silk pants hanging loose. For a moment it stunned her, this once noble man she had seen the centuries with. Now here he stood, a withered reflection, too tired to ignore.

"If you're getting wounded, you're drawing attention. We've always flown low; you know that."

She ignored him and crossed the study, stopping before the great chessboard in the far corner. "It's just a nuisance," she said. "We've had our fair share of rats over the years."

"Few that bite back." His eyes fell to the chessboard. "Fewer that require making direct contact."

"Sometimes we need another perspective."

"Or sometimes we don't know when enough is enough." His wrinkled hands touched her own, tenderly pulling her fingers from the chessboard's cool edge. "Don't you think it's time, Beebs? Rest on your laurels and let a new generation take over."

The thought was so appalling her stomach twisted. "Oh please. You haven't left the manor in years. Have you seen what it's like? Nothing but spineless children, mewling and crying. Each generation weaker than the last."

"Weaker," he repeated and kissed her wounded arm. "Yet they still wounded you."

"Enough!"

Bibi hadn't intended to hurt him or humiliate him, but that's exactly what she did. Her heart darkened. J'harr's language left her lips. And then Harlan was sliding across the floor, through the door, his skinny legs squeaking and robe flapping as he came to a stop in the foyer.

With a wave of her hand, the doors slammed shut.

Yes, she'd been rough and impulsive, traits unbecoming of a woman of her stature and station. But those damn intruders had really gnawed into her patience. Rats, indeed.

Besides, she needed silence for this next part.

The heirloom chessboard measured three feet by three feet, a thing of grim beauty. The frame was carved of old-growth redwood, deep and rich in texture. Copper and brass filled in the accents, sourced from ship fittings and patinaed by the decades. Inlaid Mother of Pearl demarcated the lines of the game board, sixty-four mirrored squares perfectly polished and reflective. The game pieces themselves were chiseled and whittled from the very stones and tidal debris of her beloved cove: inky-black stone against sun-bleached driftwood.

The game had been in play for decades, and years often passed between moves. No matter how she had tried to move the pieces, they always reset to the last session.

A reminder of the Larchmont debts.

With a wave of her wounded arm and a few words in that forgotten tongue, the blinds descended and shadows consumed the room. Bibi placed her palms on the chessboard's edge. This next part dampened her spine, always.

Sometimes, the reflection below the pieces matched Bibi's own face.

Sometimes, it showed her true form.

Tonight, it simply vanished altogether.

With a quiver in her voice—half nervous and half struggling against the pain in her arm—Bibi spoke the words that lived in her heart.

"*Aska em'mollosh ar'dukar gorrjimika. M'fore's gallax quoraska em'mollash.* Light of my lights, I need your wise sight. Something is blocking my vision."

For a moment, nothing happened. Just the *pitter-pat* of rain and her own echoing words. The mirrored game board revealed only darkness, oily and deep.

First, a tiny white worm inched through the shadows. Then another. Soon, a dozen more squirmed and blossomed. Starbursts now, some blue and gold, others flickering crimson and green. Gaseous clouds swirled and vanished.

She wasn't sure if she was piercing the depths of the sea or looking beyond the edge of the cosmos.

Then, a black-violet eye.

Her eyes.

One of thousands now blinking open from beneath the game pieces. That eye, it turned to regard Bibi as a whale might look upon a single plankton drifting past.

With a *scritch* of stone upon glass, a single chess piece moved. A driftwood knight, his noble features rubbed down from decades of play.

"Yes, I know," Bibi said. "But what are they concealing? Why can't I see it?"

The chessboard shook and several pieces moved, one after another. A black bishop slid two paces closer to the game's crowded center. Another driftwood knight skipped over a pawn. Bibi kept track of each move and exchange, new plays emerging and old plays collapsing.

And there it was: a piece she had overlooked.

A humble driftwood pawn.

It seemed impossible that she hadn't tracked this piece, yet it was just a few squares away from the far side of the board. If the pawn reached the edge, it would achieve promotion, becoming any piece that it wished: a rook, a knight, a bishop, or even a queen.

"No, that's not possible. It's not..." Yet as Bibi rewound every move, she saw the strategy appear: that driftwood knight protecting the pawn at each turn, distracting and defending.

From the board's reflective black depths, a thousand eyes blinked.

"Wait, there's another way." Bibi slid one of the black knights into a new position. She swapped out a driftwood pawn for a black bishop. She moved a rook three spaces ahead. Yes, that unlocked new opportunities.

Then, there it was: a trade. Her own black knight exchanged for that driftwood knight protecting the pawn. Yes, that would work.

For the first time in years, the board spoke in response. *"Mmm... Don't lose sight of the endgame. There's more in play than your son."*

A piece toppled and rolled down the game board, *tickity tick*. It came to a stop in an errant glow, J'harr's light hitting it in such a manner that Bibi understood the message.

The piece was a rook, black and polished. A purple sapphire sat atop its battlements, inlaid and sparkling. But at this angle, with the glow passing through, Bibi saw it for what it was: a lighthouse... and a lens.

"A risky play." She returned the rook to its spot, where it loomed near the pawn at the far edge of the board. "I trust your vision is better than mine. Otherwise, we're both going hungry."

"I have... contingencies."

And so do I, Bibi thought.

One by one by one, the eyes winked out of existence. Bibi gazed at her reflection lined with decades of burden. This face, it might be a mask, she supposed. But if she played things right, she would soon wear a crown.

From her desk she withdrew some paper and a fountain pen. Then she scribbled a name. Yes, she had one more invitation to extend.

Then she'd need to find her repugnant son, wherever he'd shuffled off to. The great game of Greywood Bay called for a trade.

46

W hile his date studied the dinner menu, Kyle Comerford took a moment to check his reflection in the accent mirror beside their booth. With a lick of his finger, he tamed a curl of hair, then smoothed down his collar. He stretched his arm across the booth's partition, stealing a glance at the waitress's skirt and the curves underneath.

Yeah, he liked Bertolucci's. It was pricey and went heavy on the oils, but he could usually score a phone number if he hinted at a good tip. College girls. They really were so eager to please.

"Sorry I'm taking so long," Melanie said, turning the page. "I just can't decide. What are you ordering?"

He covered his mouth and stifled a yawn. According to that seduction guru on YouTube, feigning boredom put your date on the back foot. Made 'em think they'd done something wrong and would have to catch up.

"Oh, so many good choices," he said. "What's catching your eye?"

Melanie licked her lips. "It's between the veal piccata and the tortellini al... prosciutto. Am I saying that right?"

She was, but he shrugged. "Eh, close enough." Then he added, "Wow, looks like someone's hungry."

She scowled as if she'd chewed something unpleasant.

"I mean, go for it," he continued. "Nothing like a woman with a healthy appetite, right? Good for you."

He closed his menu and let his words sink into her mind. He could see it now: her crinkled brow as she reconsidered, her doubting eyes drifting down the page and stopping at *insalata*. Perhaps this date might not cost him an arm and a leg.

Even better, wine went far on an empty stomach. Another life hack he'd picked up from the internet.

He broke off a piece of herbed bread and smeared it through the oil and balsamic. Chewing, he considered what compliment to give, settling on something low value, like her bracelet.

"Oh this? Thanks." Her fingers touched the bangle self-consciously. "It was my grandmother's. She ran that little shop on Main with the crystals and..."

He nodded and smiled but quickly tuned out. The small talk he could mostly handle on autopilot. Nod. Mirror her body language. Repeat the last few words to confirm understanding.

"That eclipse party at the pier?" he said. "I might check it out."

Yep, he gave himself good odds of getting lucky. He just needed to turn a few screws—balance the compliments with the negs—to make her feel like she was maybe reaching a bit out of her lane.

After all, he did have a six-pack, and he'd been going light on the liquids all week. He wanted her to gasp if he took off his shirt.

No, he told himself. *When* he took it off.

"I'll order us a refill." He flagged the waitress with the good hips and gestured to Melanie's wineglass.

"Oh, thanks." She drank the last third in a hurry and held out her glass.

As the waitress finished her pour, he flashed a smile but got a curious squint in return. Was that a wink? Nah, probably not. There it was again. Was she flirting with him? It wouldn't be the first time he wound up two ladies and set them against one another.

"I like your tattoo." He pointed to the snake curled around her forearm in a loop. "'Don't tread on me.' Nice."

"Actually, it's Ouroboros." She wiped the wine bottle. "You're thinking of the Gadsden flag and that stupid rattlesnake. Ouroboros is alchemical; it means change."

"Well, you learn something every day. Let me guess: you're studying agriculture."

"Chemical engineering. Doctoral." She blinked. "So, are we ready to order or...?"

After a quick deliberation, Melanie said, "I'll take the Insalata Tricolore. Dressing on the side."

The waitress turned her gaze on Kyle, and there it was again, that bemused glint to her eyes. "Sir?"

"Hit me with that Risotto alle Ostriche-y." He folded his menu and passed it to her. "And you can tell the chef to add a few extra oysters."

"Extra order of oysters," she said. "Got it."

He almost corrected her but figured, *Fuck it, why not?* He'd earned good overtime keeping the seniors in line at the granny pad. His man juice could use the boost since taking that pledge not to fap. He almost pitied the next lady to get a blast of his batter.

As the waitress headed off, he turned his full attention to Melanie. "So, tell me about yourself. Three details... and go!"

"Wow, three details. Um... Well, I'm honest—"

"Honesty's important."

"Yeah. And if I'm being honest, I'd want to know if I had something in my teeth."

"Totally. I hear you. What else?"

"It's your teeth. You've got..." She grinned and pointed to the left side of her mouth.

Damn, so that explained the waitress's funny look. Quietly seething, he checked his reflection in the mirror, sliding his tongue across his teeth and sucking in a few times.

"Right," he said. "So anyway, you were saying—"

"Still there." She winced. "Sorry, but you've got a nice smile."

He gave her his best close-lipped smile and excused himself. "Hold that thought."

He left his Corvette key fob on the table, making sure the shiny logo faced his date. Peacocking: another trick that influencer had taught him.

As he walked across the restaurant, a curious idea tickled his mind.

Was *she* negging *him*? Women were crafty, sure, but was she actually sending his tricks back? Maybe she'd read the same book.

He paused outside the bathroom door as a commotion caught his ear. By the front of the restaurant, a man stood—a big man—wrapped in filthy clothes with an odd tint to his skin.

Kyle watched as the server said something, probably telling the bum to get lost. And yet the man's gaze swung across the restaurant, searching, scouring, then landing on Kyle.

Those fucking eyes...

Why the hell was Kyle's sphincter constricting?

Because he's crazy, Kyle thought and made his way into the bathroom. Just another Lost Coast head case falling through the cracks. Hell, another few decades and he'd probably end up at Pacific Manor.

"This town," Kyle muttered, checking his teeth in the mirror. There it was, a stubborn piece of rosemary wedged between his incisors. He scraped it out and flicked it into the sink.

Then the door swung open.

The bum stood there, shoulders taking up the whole frame. Christ, he was huge.

And sick.

Loose skin hung, sallow and crinkled, a kid in his father's clothes. A mad gleam flashed in his eyes. And his mouth...

His lips parted in a cavernous smile, toothless and rancid and speckled with mud. A voice burbled from deep in the bum's gut. "You've got... something... that I need."

Kyle stared, stupefied, struggling to implement all those lessons he'd learned: When a rival sizes you up, only betas back down. Always wait five seconds before responding. A man apologizes for nothing.

Instead, he simply muttered, "Sorry... What do you need?"

The bum reached back and locked the bathroom door. His sick lips opened wide, wider, until a wet voice burped two simple words: "Your... body."

The smile stretched until raw fissures split his cheeks. Snakelike, his jaw fell open. And Kyle—a man who desperately followed rules about what real men do—now quickly betrayed his most holy tenet of all: a real man never cries.

But that's exactly what he did.

He screamed as the hands seized him, slippery yet impossibly strong. Shrieked as they pulled him tight into a lover's embrace. Something heaved within the bum's chest, and Kyle thought of a damp sack of eels. He twisted and squirmed, his squeals hitting octaves he didn't know he could reach.

Yet the man's enormous palm simply clasped Kyle's face and turned it to his own. He was going to kiss him.

No. Something far worse.

Inside that broken mouth, a hand opened up. Then an arm wriggled forth. And something behind it—*beyond* it. Something so much *more*.

It all exploded forth and surged between them—surged *into* him— and Kyle found himself tumbling backward, sliding down a slippery chute of his own consciousness. Screaming and fleeing inward.

There was another within, someone surging the opposite way. A man that looked—oddly enough—like the bum himself. They locked eyes as they passed. Kyle, crying out into the dampness. That bum— sane and healthy—sliding past and ejected like an unwanted passenger.

Then: darkness. A muddy pit of confusion with wet, toothy walls. Above, a glimpse through eyes that Kyle owned yet no longer controlled. Visions of the restaurant passed by, bathed in a seething black-violet light.

First the bathroom and the whimpering bum on the floor. "W-W- What happened? Where am I? What's g-g-going on?"

Then a glimpse of Kyle's own reflection in the mirror, more of a loose mask than a face. His lips shifted as he broke another rule—alphas never show teeth when they smile.

But that's what he was doing. Puppet-like, his hand ran a tender finger across those pearly whites, something greedy in its touch. This was a nightmare, yes; that's what he clung to from this pit of submission. Didn't everyone have bad dreams about losing teeth?

Banging at the door, followed by voices. "Sir! Sir!"

With a smooth turn, the perspective swung to the left. He was opening the bathroom door now. Stepping out into the restaurant's hall. Line cooks and waitstaff crowded the narrow corridor beneath some Italian song he'd never learned. A manager backed up and gasped as the keys fell from his hand.

Kyle moved through them all, into the dining area, where dozens of heads turned his way. His vision swung and centered on one woman in particular, bathing her pretty face in his black-violet gaze.

"Melanie," he tried to say. "Please do something. Call somebody. Help!"

She sat dumbstruck and rooted to the booth. "Kyle? What happened? Are you okay?"

"No, I need help," he cried out. "Please call the police!"

Those words never left his mouth.

The muddy cavern rumbled, and the teeth chattered and clicked. "Everything's... fine."

Kyle watched his hands reach past her and pluck something from the table: his keyring and fob. That purple gaze studied the little Corvette logo, then something dangling beside it.

A security key that opened every door at Pacific Manor.

47

As Aiden tucked his green Forest Rangers shirt into his khaki work pants and cinched his utility belt, Maura's patience faltered. Each click of his buckle echoed in the townhouse, amplifying her annoyance and breaking her concentration.

"I swear to God," Aiden said, "if you leave the apartment, I'm speed dialing Mom and Dad. They can fly home and play babysitter. Got it?"

She nodded, hardly looking up from her phone. Ever since the beach party, Aiden had been up her ass. Which was fair, she supposed, since their parents were riding his. Still, it sucked to be under his eye, like they were kids again and he was stuck babysitting her. Didn't he have some hikers to rescue?

"Hello? Earth to Maura." He rapped on the door, his rucksack bumping against the frame. "This is the limit of your freedom."

"What if I get hungry?" she asked.

"There's food in the fridge. DoorDash or starve, I really don't care."

He was almost gone when she called out, "Bro, quick question!"

He turned around, her perfect older brother who made perfect grades and never got grounded. With all the tools, he reminded her of a pack mule. "What?"

"Does Smokey the Bear know you stole his outfit?" she asked. "Or do the two of you coordinate fashion?"

He gave her two middle fingers and kicked the door closed.

Smiling to herself, Maura glanced at the phone as another text message arrived.

ZELDA:

> Still w/ grandparents, can't break free.
> Checked photos?

ALI:

> Working on it w/ Elrond. Need help.

MAURA:

> Not Elrond, YOU! Elrond's just code. You're smarter than him.

ALI:

> Elrond is life. Elrond is future. But yes fine we'll do it together.

Zelda's status updated:

> in church, FML DND.

With a ping, the phone signaled Ali's file transfer was finished. A folder opened up, filled with hundreds of photos they'd captured in the Historical Society. Sometimes, she admired how fast Ali's mind moved. Geez, was she really catching feelings for him?

ALI:

> Gave you chat access to Elrond. Be gentle with him.

Maura found some fresh spinach and slices of turkey in the fridge, rolled them up, and poured ranch into a dipping bowl. Armed with enough protein and greens, she settled back on the couch. They had work to do.

Swiping, she scanned the old photos. Some were dimly lit and others were out of focus, but most were usable. Elrond's image-to-text function made searching old articles a breeze. And yet, after thirty minutes of her turkey wraps, she wasn't seeing many connections.

The Historical Society.

The town's rich history.

Bibi Boyle, or whatever had worn her skin and tried to chow down on Ali.

Then she saw the man Zelda met—Ben Thomas—smiling at the camera from a black and white clipping. His photo was taped to some sort of form, *Greywood Gazette Classified Submissions*. Below, the submission read:

> *Missing Person: Reward!*
> *Help Find Ben Thomas, a postdoc who went missing sometime during January. All local avenues have been exhausted. If you have any information, please call...*

January, 1998, Maura thought. Why did that year ring a bell? She swore she'd seen something in the museum.

"Elrond, what happened in Greywood Bay in January of 1998?"

The little wheel spun on the screen. Then:

> There doesn't appear to be any significant events in Greywood Bay from the sources I can access. Try consulting local archives, newspaper records, or the community historical society for specific events that don't make it into the broader records.

"Useless." She couldn't believe she was talking to one of Ali's creations.

She studied the classified form, the word *SPIKED* scribbled in red ink. She'd seen a movie once where a reporter fought with their boss to identify a serial killer.

Spiked...

"Elrond, who was the editor of the Greywood Gazette in 1998?"

While Elrond scoured the internet, Maura scrolled through several more photos.

There was Ben Thomas again, with the same smile and stance. It was no longer a black and white closeup but a color wide shot. The original photo.

He stood at the edge of the pier, the bay behind him. A woman in her mid-twenties leaned into him, holding a churro while the seagulls looked on enviously. The couple were in their own world: Ben smiling at the camera and the woman smiling at him. Maura knew that look, even if she was struggling with her own feelings lately.

That was love in their eyes.

Elrond pinged its response.

> The editor of the Greywood Gazette in 1998 was Harlan Boyle. He co-founded the newspaper in 1977 and remained involved until it was purchased by Lost Coast Publishing.

Boyle. Harlan and Bibi.

She asked, "Elrond, who owns Lost Coast Publishing?"

> I'm sorry, I can't find any available public records.

A dead end. She repositioned on the couch to keep her knee from bouncing. Another swipe back to the classified page as she scoured the form for more clues.

Paid: Check
Status: Refunded
Name: Thorpe, J

She studied the photo of Ben Thomas and that woman with love in her eyes. Thorpe? The name tickled her mind, vaguely familiar. Damn, it seemed like half this town was connected yet tucked behind a wall of amnesia.

She took a photo of the woman and said, "Elrond, age this photo up thirty years."

Like most of Elrond's work, the first result was useless. It turned the woman into a zombie. The second result wasn't much better, just different. It had turned her into a painting, like *Whistler's Mother*. The fourth result was the worst of all: her face simply had the word *thirty* tattooed all over it.

But the third result was close enough to scratch that itch.

"No way," Maura muttered.

She'd last seen Ms. Thorpe at the mall, several weeks ago. Her hair was gray in a streak down the side. Her eyes bore a haunted sparkle. She'd been reaching toward Zelda, talking about...

Phones, Maura realized. A phone that was ringing.

She called Ali immediately, and he answered on the first ring.

"Prove you're not a ghost," he said.

Maura scoffed. "What?"

"You always text, and I just found some super freaky shit. Prove you're not a ghost or I'm hanging up."

"You cried at the end of *Avengers: Endgame*."

"That's not... Look, everyone cries at the snap. So, why are you blowing me up?"

She hesitated, knowing that Ali was already in as much trouble as she was. Still, she had to leave the apartment, and she needed a reason. "Come Christmas shopping with me."

"No way. I'm so broke my cash card is dividing by zero."

"You can borrow some money. I just need an excuse to hit up the old mall."

Ali agreed, and Maura gathered her things. She locked up the town-house and rushed down the path. Halfway to the garage, her feet halted.

Because of the man by the bike racks.

It wasn't just the dark jacket, weathered from too many seasons of rain. Nor was it his pants, worn loose and high, as older men sometimes did, one knee pressed to the ground as he crouched. Or the flashlight in one hand and the Swiss Army knife in the other. Mostly, it was the dried mud and grass on the bike tires he examined.

That was Maura's bike.

The Historical Society, she thought. Of course it had cameras. How could she have been so naïve?

The man turned toward Maura, eyes narrowing in the cool afternoon light. Her mind faltered. If she doubled back, that would draw his attention. She pressed on, heart pounding but her pace steady. She slipped her phone from her pocket and held it to her ear, the device cold against her skin.

"Alright, Dad, I'm just around the corner—meet you at the curb." She spoke just loud enough to be heard. "Yep, coming out now."

She kept her walk measured, confident. As she passed the man, his gaze hooked onto her and she shivered. Beneath the harsh overhead LEDs, it almost looked like his shadow was stretching across the pavement—elongating and distorting. No, impossible. Maura caught a glimpse of fingers splitting and unfurling and reaching for her and—

Then she rounded the corner. With her heart hammering in her chest, she broke into a desperate sprint, her footsteps echoing off the townhouses.

She didn't stop running for miles.

⁂

ONE HOUR AND TWO BOBA TEAS LATER, MAURA AND ALI entered Vinyl Countdown. They spotted Ms. Thorpe stocking used CDs at the back of the store. She exuded a broken energy, eyes like a tired mouse surrounded by cats. As they approached, Maura wasn't sure what to say. Part of her worried those haunted eyes might be contagious.

She cleared her throat. "Ms. Thorpe?"

"We're not hiring," the woman said. "And if you're looking for cheap records, try Urban Outfitters. Everything here's the real deal."

"Actually, we're here about Ben Thomas," Ali said. "We just... Well, we've got a few questions."

The woman didn't say anything, but her fingers began shaking as she organized the CDs, *tickity tickity tick*. Then her shoulders sank and her eyes drifted to the phone in Ali's hand.

"Ben Thomas," Ali repeated. "You've heard of him, haven't you?"

She closed her eyes and something like a smile flashed on her face.

That same smile from the photo, Maura realized. Beautiful, but worn down by the years.

"Of course I have," she said softly. "But this is the first time in three decades I've heard his name."

She brushed past them, shuffling to the front of the empty store. Ali and Maura followed close behind.

"We have questions," Maura said.

Ms. Thorpe turned the *OPEN* sign around and locked the door. She said, "So do I."

48

Chester Halgrove was folding a sheet of aluminum foil when it hit him: another number murmuring deep in his mind. He closed his eyes. There, among the floaters crawling upon the back of his lids, the countdown echoed.

Twenty-four hundred.

Well, he supposed he'd better tidy up.

He spent the next few minutes organizing his apartment. He placed two foil figures on the windowsill, one facing the dark courtyard. Another three on the bedside table. He removed the sheets and the pillowcases, then folded them. He placed the last four figures atop each stack, little presents in the center of his bed.

In the bathroom, he waited for his bladder to begin its slow release. He squeezed a final dollop from the Colgate tube and brushed his teeth. He surveyed the sink and shelves: an empty shampoo bottle, mouthwash drained to the last drop, and a single piece of toilet paper clinging to the roll.

Like the backcountry camping of his youth: leave no trace.

Still, there was a loose end, a temptation to back out.

A new number murmured: *Fifteen hundred.*

He unscrewed the towel rod and studied the tired reflection in the mirror.

Who was this old figure staring back? When had he traded his wavy, blond locks for this wispy, gray mop? Even now, he could still feel his sister's hand pulling him into the redwoods. "Chessie, come quick! Come see the lights that I've found!"

"Almost there, Mabel," he muttered into the emptiness of the bathroom.

Then he swung the towel rod and shattered the mirror.

He swept the mess into a plastic bag, dumping toiletries and medications, then tying it off. He left it there in the corner beside the empty paint cans.

Six hundred and sixty-five.

He found the Pacific Manor regulations pamphlet in the drawer beneath the TV. He'd never read the damn thing and had no intention of starting. He tore sheets loose, crumpling them and placing them in a mixing bowl from his kitchenette. He fetched the fresh steel wool from under the sink. He dropped it in the bowl with the paper.

Four hundred and eighty-one.

He dragged the only chair he owned to the center of the crummy apartment and placed the bowl in his lap.

He didn't have to wait long.

The sound of the key turning in the door was familiar, a rattling clink made by the Pacific Manor's nurses or caretakers or the cleaning lady that came on Wednesday. Tonight, a unique form lingered in the hall, reeking of sour mud and decay.

"Well, come on in," Chester said.

Over the past several months, he had observed each of the resident aides: Ms. Tan and her smoking habits; Mr. Parnell, who always nodded but never listened; Freddy, who listened and smiled kindly and often.

And Mr. Comerford, who spent his evenings swiping right on his phone, locking doors and clocking out early.

Most of all, he knew Mr. Comerford did not have a limp.

"Close the door, then," Chester said. "It's chilly."

Mr. Comerford shuffled in and locked the door. His skin hung lumpy and ill-fitting, a loose sack over conflicted bones and a back that hiccupped and twitched. Droopy eyes scanned the apartment, taking in the foil origami figures. Thirty-nine little men and women standing at attention.

"Look at these." Mr. Comerford let out a wet cough as violet steam burped from his lips. "You think you brought... your friends."

"And she's brought one of her puppets," Chester said. "Go on, Grant. Cut the strings and take off that mask." He waved his hand as if to say, *Get on with it.*

For a moment, the two stood there staring at each other. Chester, in his chair as his tired heart went *lub dub, dub dub.* And that grinning *thing* wearing Mr. Comerford's skin.

Three hundred and twelve.

Mr. Comerford's smile stretched wide, wider, too wide. Chester winced as the man's throat distended, and two muddy arms pulled themselves from his ruined mouth.

It was painful and messy, as most births were, and not without spasms and moans. With a final quiver, dirty limbs crowned their way past split lips and spilled across the floor. Whimpering, Mr. Comerford collapsed and curled into a ball. Chester pitied the man, even if he was a prick.

A wet form rose, ochre and clay molding itself into a perversion of human shape. Broken teeth sprouted through the murk, beading fingers and rimming sockets. Smoldering purple eyes bloomed and blinked within a head so narrow and lopsided it looked ready to collapse.

And yet there lived terrible power here, a grotesque infusion giving structure and strength beyond bones and muscles. Dripping and rigid, Grant's muddy form rose.

One fifty.

The wet visage said, "Look at how the years have ruined your flesh."

Chester's eyes rose up Grant's body. "Congratulations on becoming... whatever this is."

"This?" The shambling form took a muddy step forward. "An echo of Ascension. Too perfect for this world. Too... unstable. But in hers, I have... dominions."

With damp fingers, he plucked a fallen molar and pressed it back to his cheek. Just one of dozens that gave him the face of a bear trap.

"You and those stupid teeth," Chester said. "What's the deal with them anyway?"

Grant traced a sopping finger along the kitchenette counter until it came to a foil figure standing watch. "My therapist once asked me the same thing, and you know what I told her?" He flicked the figure into the sink. "I never gave it much thought."

"You always were a shallow pool."

The thing paced the small apartment, boneless legs limping and dragging, smokey eyes scanning all 388 square feet. "The town's madman, Old Chester the Molester, entombed and forgotten. Your friends are gone."

Grant pressed a brown finger onto the windowsill, crushing another foil figure.

"Was it worth it?" he continued. "Turning her down and ending up here? Even these walls are tired and pathetic."

Chester closed his eyes, letting the pins and needles in his fingers dance their way up his left arm.

Seventy-five.

"Answer me," Grant croaked. "Was it worth it... you ruined sack... of ligaments and bone?"

Chester's eyes fluttered, the darkness behind his lids bleeding through to the edge of his vision. Were the lights always so dim in his suite? Was that flickering painting always so bright through the wall?

"Yeah," Chester said. "It was worth it."

Something like disdain twisted Grant's loamy face. "You know, I was jealous that she wanted you, a nobody without oaths or ancestry or sacred blood. Another lunatic in the asylum. For the longest time, I was *envious.* But I owe you my gratitude. In the end I just had to work harder for her... blessing."

A smirk curled Chester's lips as his gaze swept over Grant's grimy form. "That's one way to call it."

"That's the only way," he snarled. "When you've hunted the far shore of her creation and tasted the endless feast she provides—when you've bathed in her light... All of this?" He waved his fetid hand in dismissal, little pieces spattering the floor. "You and your tricks and stolen knowledge—it's not even a scrap that falls from her table."

Thirty-two.

"I've seen her dogs that fight over scraps." Chester coughed and squeezed his numb knee. "At least they know their place. But you, you're just another servant, one of countless that came before. Sure, you're clever. Just not clever enough to know when you've lost."

He raised his right hand and made a sign, two circles with his index finger and pinky. Grant took a lumbering step back, smoldering eyes darting to the little foil figures. Then...

Nothing.

A single foil figure teetered and fell, so quiet it could have been toppled by a soft breeze.

Grant's infected smile returned, stretching his sludgy face. "Your totems are empty and spent." He pinched the foil figure and dropped it at Chester's feet. "Your ghosts no longer answer. Oh, is she going to have fun with you."

He drew closer and closer, teeth chittering with excitement around a maw within maws. And deeper inside: a hole that stretched to the Nether itself, hungry and infinite and bathed in her glow.

Ten. Nine. Eight.

That smile...

Yeah, Chester knew that terrible smile.

It stretched all the way back to that rainy night at West Pine Psychiatric. Grant, smiling as he locked the patients in the basement. Smiling as Chester cried out. As time folded over itself and his failures chased him, years and decades all blurring together. That smile... always there.

It wasn't going to be the last thing Chester saw.

"My ghosts are all gone," he whispered as a distant knot tightened in his chest. "Because we made peace with each other. But you... Grant Larchmont... You'll never see her wretched world again. This room is a tomb... and you'll be here... forever."

Three. Two. One.

Chester drew in a breath—his final breath—and his heart fluttered beneath ribs he thought might just collapse, empty and spent. But no. It was something else.

In this moment, his heart was brimming and grateful.

For all he had seen and learned in his life.

For the ghostly and the cruel and the arcane rites that bent reality itself.

For the few that believed him and gave him such strength.

And yet, in this moment he fell back on a matter of science, one he had learned while renovating that old house children feared.

Steel wool might be metal, but it conducted electricity and it burned well in a pinch.

His numb fingers found Ms. Tan's stolen e-cigarette battery and pulled it from his pocket. He pressed it into the bowl—into the steel wool—and watched as a field of stars ignited. They danced and swirled, a galaxy held in his hands. As the crumpled paper caught fire, he willed his tired arms to raise the burning bowl overhead.

He couldn't smell the smoke or feel the warmth of this world, but he could see the confusion twisting Grant's muddy face. Then, the shrieking smoke alarm above. And the pop and hiss of sprinklers.

In a wet spray, droplets spattered the room, the furniture, the very walls that Grant had mocked as pathetic and tired. Walls now oozing and sliding and collapsing.

Because they weren't walls, but brown builder's paper, painted and taped. The real walls—the ones Chester had paced and measured—revealed themselves beneath soggy paper, a manifesto of symbols scrawled in waterproof paint.

There were swirling words that meant *enclosure* or *prison*. Words that meant something like *eternity* in the twisted tongue of the All. Words Chester had never finished translating, nor had those who came before him. Powerful words and stolen words, sentences and commands. They wrapped the room in their meaning, glowing brighter and brighter.

Grant twisted and turned at their unveiling, scurrying away. Yet water cascaded down him, brown rivulets slithering and dripping. Muddy chunks slid free from his body. With little *tinks* and *clinks*, his teeth—his precious teeth—salted the floor.

Shrieking, gurgling, he tore at the walls until his hands melted away and his feet sank into viscous pools. On dissolving knees, he shuffled toward the window and stretched a dirty nub to the dark light of the moon.

If he could just make it. If he could...

A wet creak, then his head tumbled from his shoulders and burst on the floor. His body inched past, a trail of filth flattening beneath the torrent.

Grant's smoldering eyes were the last piece of him to vanish, twin cinders of violet blinking out of existence. In that moment it might have felt like there was someone else here, looking back through that light at old Chester Halgrove. Something seething with the rage of the ages.

But Chester was no longer looking.

He sat in his chair, one hand clutching his chest as the other hung limp and loose. Fading murk and countless teeth surrounded his splayed feet, and above, cool water he no longer felt dripped past his dimming eyes.

But he wore a smile on his lips.

49

Zelda pretended to listen to her grandmother and Uncle Alejandro as they discussed the accomplishments of cousins she hadn't seen in several years. Marta, who was headed to Yale on a scholarship for young civil servants. Beninga, serving the church in Cuernavaca as a youth outreach coordinator. Sandra, Alejandro's eldest, apprenticing at the family import-export business in El Paso.

"You know, there's always a place for you, Zelda," Uncle Alejandro said. "Family comes first."

She smiled, trying to ignore the ringing phones, which skipped between the restaurant's front desk, the back, and the kitchen.

Phones no one else acknowledged.

"Zelda, your uncle just made you a generous offer." Her grandmother reached past the dinner rolls and patted Zelda's forearm. "Were you listening?"

"No. Not really." Zelda scratched at her neck. "It's just... My mind's kinda elsewhere."

"Oh, and where's that?" Uncle Alejandro asked. "Video games? Boys?"

"*Seguramente and a pensando en drogas,*" her grandmother said.

A posh family at the next table glanced over. Despite dressing up, she felt out of place. The fancy plates and gold foil napkins. The menu she could hardly pronounce. And her, in her church service best: a crushed velvet skirt, denim jacket, and a pixel art scarf. Uncle Mark never made her go out for fine dining.

"No, Grandma, I'm not on drugs." That definitely got the neighboring table's attention. "But if I was, I'd probably say something... like —*shit...*"

The pain was instant and icy, a spike through her chest stealing her breath. For a few beats of her heart, the restaurant spun. Every tooth rattled in her mouth, and she tasted...

Mud.

Why the hell did she have mud on her lips?

It was the necklace most of all, the pendant pressing heavy against her skin, its weight anchoring her to this moment as the frigid spike faded and something else took its place.

A void.

Zelda knew.

Somehow, she knew he was gone.

"We need to leave." The chair fell over as she stood up. "I need to see Chester."

Her relatives stared as if she'd just asked for a unicorn. No, she needed to go this very minute. Maybe she was wrong. Maybe she could do something. Maybe...

"Guys, c'mon, please. I need to go, now. It's an emergency."

"Zelda, we just ordered," Uncle Alejandro said. "Can't it wait?"

"*Drogas,*" her grandmother said. "See, I told you."

Even her grandfather offered his usual detached gaze. No, this wouldn't work. Whatever she said, they wouldn't listen—they never did.

So she ran out of the restaurant.

As the door swung shut on Uncle Alejandro's shout, she realized she needed to put distance between her and them. She bolted down Main Street, took a right at Ocean Way, and another right down the alley beside the vegan bakery. She passed a group of students smoking cigarettes on the sly, and she heard giggling.

"Whoa, nutcase alert," Arianna called out. "Run, psycho, run!"

Two blocks later, she crouched by a dumpster and ordered a rideshare, paying the fee to have it arrive extra fast. As she climbed in, she spotted her grandmother hurrying down one side of Mayfield Lane while Uncle Alejandro jogged the other way.

There, in the back of that Prius with some stranger's music playing, it occurred to her that she could do things like this: just walk from her grandparents. Maybe this was what growing up meant. There would be consequences, sure, but perhaps she had more power than she thought.

Ten minutes, three miles, and five ignored phone calls later, the shingled roof and scraggly willows of the Pacific Manor Assisted Living Community came into view.

"No," she whispered. "No, no no."

The ambulances were parked nose-in near the entrance, fire trucks flanking them. A pair of police cruisers idled, lights painting the facility windows in blue and red. Residents and caregivers huddled against the afternoon drizzle, little murmuring hordes here and there. But it was the man on the stretcher that sent a gasp through the crowd.

Mr. Comerford lay, one hand clutching the stretcher rail, the other pressing a bandage to his face. Beneath the dressings and cervical collar, his jaw hung open, red and raw. Confused, beady eyes darted about, like he'd just woken up.

"Chester!" Zelda pushed her way to the front of the crowd. "Chester Halgrove, is he okay?"

A cop stopped her at the steps. "Are you family?"

"What? No, I'm—"

"You'll have to move back. Fire suppression created a hell of a mess. Go on now."

"Hold up." A caregiver stood guard at the door, his big arms crossed. Yet kind eyes gleamed over a face wrinkled with smile lines. His nametag read *Freddy*. "You must be Zara or—"

"Zelda."

"Zelda, that's right. You know Mr. Halgrove. He sure talked about you a lot."

"Talked...?"

Freddy hesitated, yet his eyes had already told her the story. He shot a glance back to the facility, where firemen uncoiled hoses as someone rushed past with a mop.

"Is he...?" Zelda felt something rising inside her that wanted to be unleashed as a scream but came out as a whimper.

"I'm sure sorry," Freddy said. "How'd you get to know Mr. Halgrove?"

"He's my—he *was* sort of my teacher. I just..." The words thickened in her throat. "I wasn't a very good student."

"Naw, I'm sure you made Mr. Halgrove happy."

"Chester," she said. "He liked to be called Chester."

Freddy laughed. "Yeah, you're damn right he did. Probably give me five kinds of hell for calling him that."

At the far side of the crowd, where the facility met rock-laden paths and winding bushes, a young boy with striking blond hair stared at her.

Those eyes.

Zelda knew that gaze.

The boy gave her a nod—*come over here*—then walked off around the bushes.

A hundred feet later, and she found him in the facility's gardens, strolling among the damp flowers and shrubs. Even at her fast pace, he remained just out of reach.

"They're bringing me out now," the boy said. "I didn't want you to see it."

"But... shouldn't I be there for you?"

"You are."

The boy ran his finger down a dewy camellia, the pink petals gently bowing. Then he stepped around a wind-twisted birch. When Zelda caught up, he was on the other side of the patio, the foggy bay behind him.

"Chester," she shouted. "Why are you so... young?"

The boy looked down at his hands as if seeing them for the first time. "Am I? Hmm..."

There was a noise from the far side—doors slamming shut—and then a van circled the parking lot before merging onto the road. She knew what was inside. The thought of Chester alone and carted off misted her eyes.

"That's just a body," the boy said. "One with too much time under J'harr's dark glare. It's funny, you know? I don't think I ever saw myself as an old man. Maybe none of us do. Maybe that's why these hands are so smooth."

"I'm just…" She wiped her eyes with her sleeve. "I'm so fucking tired of everyone leaving. It's bullshit. It's not fair. It's—"

"Fair? There's nothing fairer than death. It's the one thing we owe, and we face it alone. That I got to see so much… Well, maybe that was a blessing among a lifetime of curses."

"People should know what you've done for the town."

"The wrong ones do. The right ones rarely will. That's how it's worked down through the centuries."

"Centuries?"

The boy came to a stop at a series of sculptures: anchors and nautical armaments and driftwood, all arranged like totems and pyres. It held the mossy look of something erected and soon neglected.

"You're part of it now, Zelda. The newest link in that chain stretching beyond our world. Beyond time."

"But I don't know what to do," she said. "I can't even keep my life together, and it's just… boring and basic."

"No, there's nothing boring or basic about you. But the cost… The light that you carry, it'll cost you so much. This town and its horrors, they'll swarm like leeches to blood or—"

"Maggots," Zelda said. "Like maggots in your heart."

"Mmm-hmm." The boy nodded. "But your enemies, shit… You asked me when we stepped into the All. Your reflection, what it looked like when you're older?"

"I did. I do."

The boy nodded, a smile pursing his lips. "Fierce."

Zelda found herself returning the smile as warm tears streaked her cheeks. "Thanks."

"Your enemies are in for one hell of a storm." The boy's gaze rose as a chorus of birds circled overhead, their calls merging with the whistling winds through the trees and the murmuring bay. "You hear that?"

"Warblers," Zelda said. "Ali could probably tell you what type."

"That's not it." The boy closed his eyes. "My sister. Funny, I haven't heard her singing in years."

For a moment, they both stood there. Zelda, with her fourteen years in this world and the impossible weight of it all. This boy, an echo of Chester Halgrove. Both swaddled by the murmuring wind and the waves, the song of this town that they loved. Both bound by its horrors.

She wasn't sure when she'd closed her eyes, but when they opened, the warblers had flown off, the sky had darkened, and the garden stood empty.

"Chester?"

As she said his name, a cool finger touched her neck, and something slid down her chest. She lashed out to catch the necklace, but her fingers were cold and clumsy. The bottle glass pendant struck a path stone, shattering into blue fragments. In that moment she knew he was gone—truly gone—and the town was all the dimmer.

Cursing, she fumbled for the necklace. The breeze caught the smaller shards, whisking them off as if they'd never existed.

And then she saw it—the sculpture garden—truly noticing the pieces for the first time. Among the carved driftwood totems and thick nautical chains sat glass bottles, the same shade of blue as the pendant.

She remembered his words back at the birthday party: "It'll come off when it's ready."

And there, in the center, like a treasure from the video games she loved, sat a wooden trunk. Beneath rust and a dozen shades of lichen, the box seemed nearly invisible. Pieces of blue bottle glass wreathed its lock, offering a glimmer of color among the old wood.

One piece was missing, the same shape as the pendant.

The gesture came to her fingers, the silent word to her mind. The lock fell open as if some key had clicked into place. Slowly, she lifted the lid and peered into the darkness.

Upon a bed of sand and shells, rimmed by countless pieces of smooth bottle glass, rested a plastic bag containing a rectangular shape. She didn't know what it was as she lifted it out, not at first. Only that it was heavy, perhaps ancient.

And powerful.

Carefully, she peeled back the plastic, revealing aged leather, rich and patinated. Gilded accents adorned the book's cover: twisting geometric patterns and spirals winding inward, reminiscent of the very shapes Chester had drawn with his fingers. A musty scent gave way to something deeper: the aroma of forest groves and freshly cut wood, the smoke of fires and cured meats. She ran her finger down the rigid spine, and voices whispered around her.

Words in a language not of this world.

The All Tongue.

Despite its age, the spine did not crack as she opened the book. Yet the trees rustled and the wind let out a low sigh. With a delicate touch, she turned page after page.

She recognized Chester's handwriting in the back. His cursive that rose and fell, wavelike upon the unlined paper. There were diary entries covering decades. Some went into great detail, while others were mere statements.

Avoid Mount Marsden after sundown.

The mine at Garber's Hollow... old wound opening up?

Diagrams interspersed the entries: sculptures with three arms and ambiguous faces; gears and contraptions, each accompanied by little notes to himself.

J'harr breaks their memories again and again.
Give them new form and ask for their help.

Further back, the penmanship shifted. It was no longer Chester's but someone else's, their cursive refined and elegant. Precise lines mapped the neighboring mountains and coastal contours. Notes adorned the side:

I closed a new wound at Leeman's Retreat, but another

opened just as fast. How many servants does she have in this town?

Even further back now, where ballpoint gave way to fountain pen ink and then tools even older. Zelda could almost see dip pens and inkwells in candlelit rooms.

A droplet of rain landed on the page, smearing several letters. She closed the book, pausing to study the first page, so aged that the words were mere shadows. There, on the yellowed paper, was a name she remembered:

The Diary of Arthur Cummings.

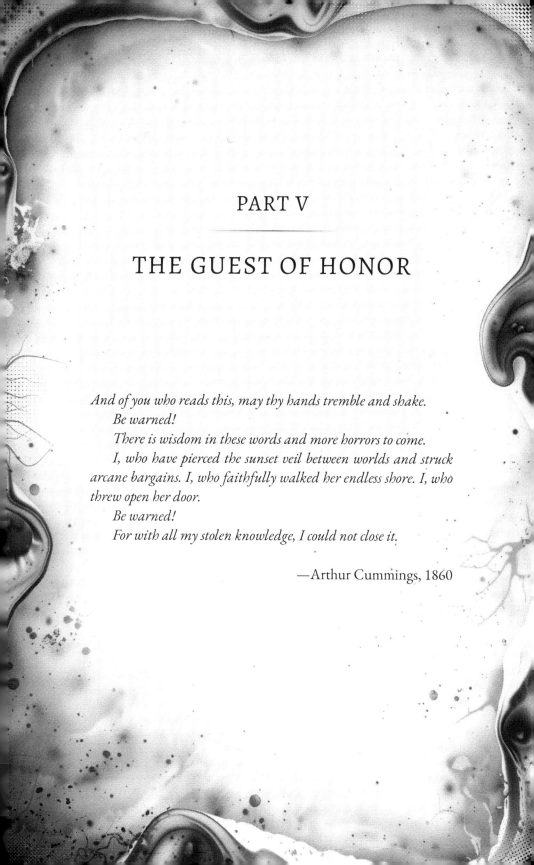

PART V

THE GUEST OF HONOR

And of you who reads this, may thy hands tremble and shake.
   Be warned!
   There is wisdom in these words and more horrors to come.
   I, who have pierced the sunset veil between worlds and struck
arcane bargains. I, who faithfully walked her endless shore. I, who
threw open her door.
   Be warned!
   For with all my stolen knowledge, I could not close it.

—Arthur Cummings, 1860

50

When the phone call from Alejandro came in, Mark braced for another ass chewing. Maybe a dig at his employment and the tutoring gigs. Perhaps some new legal threat. He never expected to be told they'd lost Zelda. That she'd simply run off after church. Nor did he expect to be asked if he knew where she went.

"She said something about a friend," Alejandro said. "Charles or Lester or... I don't know. She ran out, just like that."

Yeah, Mark had a pretty good idea where she'd gone, and the Find My app confirmed it. He ended his tutoring session early, apologizing and telling Sasha he'd make it up next week. She wished him a merry Christmas and was out the door in a blink.

As he drove across town, he replayed Alejandro's conversation in his head, wishing he'd said something witty and cutting. Something that put a little humility in the Ruizes.

"Funny, it's almost like teenagers have a mind of their own."

"Guess losing nieces runs in the family."

Or maybe, "Looks like it's your turn to be captain of the 'Lost Zelda Club.'"

But what he'd offered was a simple reassurance. "Don't worry, Alejandro. I'll pick her up and we'll figure this out."

The Pacific Manor parking lot was busy for a Sunday. Emergency vehicles idled as firemen rolled up hoses. When Mark saw the cops, his back bristled and his tongue went sticky and dry.

What the hell did you do, kiddo?

He spotted Zelda sitting curbside, alone, clutching a plastic bag and an old book. He was about to yell when he saw her streaked mascara. He pushed back his frustration, reminding himself that she was in that uncanny valley of adolescence. Trying so hard to look older yet under-lining her tender youth.

Their eyes met, and he knew what had happened.

Wordlessly, he wrapped her up in a hug. He had questions—and he sensed there would be consequences from the Ruizes—but for now he just listened to the rumbling of the sea. He found it soothing. Maybe old Chester Halgrove had, too, here, at the edge of the continent. At the end of his life.

"Thank you," Zelda whispered. "For being here."

"That's what I do." His eyes fell to the plastic bag and the old book inside. "You gonna tell me what that's about?"

"To be honest, I'm really not sure." She ran her finger over it, some-thing darkening in her eyes. "Uncle Mark, you remember when you said I could tell you anything? Did you really mean that?"

He stepped back, his gaze lingering on the uncertain shadows playing across her face. "Of course. Anything you need."

"It's just... When we get back to the apartment, I'll tell you. But it's not anything." She took a deep breath. "It's everything."

FIFTEEN MINUTES LATER, MARK TURNED THE STOVE ON AND brought the water to a boil while Zelda took a seat at the kitchen table. He only realized how hungry he was on the drive back, their silence broken by repeated calls from the Ruizes.

Yes, Zelda was with him.

Yes, she was okay.

Yes, she needed a little space to mourn the death of... Well, he wasn't sure what Chester truly was. Only that he had helped a lot of people. That he was important to her.

Now, as Mark chopped vegetables and prepped the pasta, he could see Zelda's eyes faltering, her voice growing hesitant.

Was it drugs or something worse? Had she gotten mixed up in grooming or put nude photos online? Every horror story from PTA meetings and nervous parents now screamed through his mind.

"You won't believe me," she said. "You'll think I'm crazy and I probably am, but I just think it's time."

And then she told him.

About the summer and her connection to Chester.

About the fire and the ravenous pups.

About this fall and the winter, the maddening whispers of a dark force they had thwarted.

She-Who-Consumes.

Xooloocotiq'r.

J'harr.

She told him about the ghosts: Mrs. Saperstein, Detective Brown, and all the eleven dead from the fire of Raven's Valley. How they followed her, growing stronger, bleeding through.

Mark realized he'd stopped chopping the mushrooms, and the knife hung loose in his fingers.

"Do you..." He paused as his sanity pushed back. "That woman with the burned baby, the jogger. Do you still see them?"

"All the time," she whispered. "Sometimes they follow me here."

"To the apartment?"

She nodded. "And sometimes in."

Then he was pacing, opening the fridge and searching for a beer, something strong to really smooth out his shakes. Yet he remembered he hadn't bought any in months. Maybe there was a straggler in the very back, just past the ketchup and ranch dressing.

"Uncle Mark?" Zelda's voice, so quiet he almost didn't hear it. "I knew you'd think I was crazy."

His body stiffened and his eyes clamped tight. As the boiling pasta grew soggy, Maya's words echoed in his thoughts, clearer than he wanted to admit.

"The veil festers and widens."

"Ajar... A jar... J'harr."

Because how could you tell someone the improbable? The impossible? Something your entire reality had been built on denying?

Trust, he realized.

Yes, maybe every rational neuron in his brain screamed against it, but it was trust that gave Zelda the courage. The trust that her words would be heard.

"No," he said. "You're not crazy at all. I've seen things, too. Impossible things."

As he spoke, his body relaxed and a great calm overtook him. It was his turn now, and he told her everything.

Her mother appearing in Madrid one midnight in spring.

How he knew she was gone before Alejandro called with the news.

Things with no explanation he'd tried to dismiss.

With each new fact, Zelda's eyes glistened and her shoulders shook. It was like a burden was being lifted from her, stone by stone, word by word. God, how long had she carried this weight?

"So, you moved across the world," Zelda said, "because my mom's ghost asked you? That's... pretty badass."

Mark felt his cheeks warming. "I came because Maya asked. But I stayed because of you, kiddo. And if half of what you've told me is true, well, I'm not as nearly as badass as the other person in this room."

Her eyes drifted to her shoes as a smile curled her lips. He liked that smile and wished he saw it more often. "Who said there were only two people in this room?"

Mark's heart fluttered as he scanned the dark corners of the apartment.

Then Zelda winked.

"I never should have shown you those scary movies as a kid," he said. "Probably turned you into some sort of antenna."

"Maybe you were training me and you didn't know it."

The pasta boiled over and sizzled the stove. "I can't even think straight enough to cook a grilled cheese, so we're ordering pizza." He turned the burner off and dumped the soggy pasta in the sink. "But first, we need to be very careful, okay? If word gets out—"

That's when the front door opened, flooding the apartment with afternoon light and a cool breeze. From the kitchenette, Mark could only see the silhouettes, but he knew who they were.

"Breaking news, Zelda-rooni," Ali huffed. "This shit goes, like, so much deeper... than we thought. We're talking illuminati level... but with NIMBYs and death."

Pushing Ali aside, Maura noticed Uncle Mark and she froze in place. "Uh, he means... Wasn't that a great movie, Ali?"

Mark eyed the three teens, their expressions dancing between hesitation and horror. He understood at once he wasn't the first to find out Zelda's secret.

"Great," he said. "So, who else knows about this?"

51

Of all the awkward conversations she had imagined having with her uncle—the bad grades, the boyfriends or girl-friends, the first time she might learn how to drive—Zelda never guessed it would involve Ali and Maura debating the supernatural over an extra-large pizza.

"Maybe it's like a black hole bending space-time," Ali said. "The phone calls. You seeing Chester as a kid. The Everything—"

"The All," Zelda corrected.

"Whatever. My point is, maybe he saw himself as old 'cause he was past the event horizon. Stephen Hawking 101. It's too bad I wasn't there to test him."

"Are you seriously bummed you couldn't probe an old man?" Maura asked.

"I'd be respectful." Ali raised his phone and scanned a page from Chester's old book.

Zelda watched Uncle Mark's gaze bouncing between the three friends. He rubbed the bridge of his nose. "I can't believe we're actually having this conversation."

"Oh! Did you tell him about the sculptures?" Maura poked her, then pointed to Uncle Mark with a crust of pizza. "Zelda made these sculptures move during the fire."

Zelda squirmed. She didn't like being the center of attention. "It was Chester," she said. "And the dead from that hospital. I just asked them for help."

"The dead," Uncle Mark repeated. "You just... asked for their help?"

She shrugged.

"I can see I've got my homework cut out for me." He washed his slice of pizza down with a long sip of Diet Coke.

"And speaking of homework," Ali said and snapped another picture of the book. "Tell them about crazy old Thorpe."

"She's not crazy," Maura said. "She just... hears things no one else does. Like phones ringing for thirty years."

Zelda winced. Those calls had only been coming for a week, and they'd taken a toll. Sometimes, she twitched in anticipation. She knew others were starting to notice.

"Right, Ms. Thorpe," Maura said. "So, here's the deal: you ever heard of Fat Morgan?"

"*Fata Morgana*," Ali corrected.

Maura turned to him. "Do you want to do this?"

"I'm feeding Elrond this Necronomicon." Ali turned a page and took another picture. "Besides, you know I can't multitask."

"Okay, Fata Morgana," Maura said. "It's like a mirage over water. You know how ships can appear all weird on the horizon? This Ben Thomas dude was studying stars and light bands and how it all interacted. Greywood Bay is a hotspot. No, seriously, Google it. I remember them telling us old mariner tales as a kid."

"Mariner tales?" Ali laughed. "Sorry, keep info dumping, Ahab."

"Guys, you're losing me," Uncle Mark said. "What does that have to do with ringing phones?"

Zelda said, "Ben Thomas and Ms. Thorpe knew each other, didn't they?"

"Knew?" Ali asked. "She was crushing on the guy more than my Maur-bear crushes on me."

Maura said, "The only thing crushing on your bird bones is gravity."

"Deny it all you want," Ali said, turning another page, "but the facts are more obvious than a fart in a car."

"It's a miracle you three get anything done." Uncle Mark sighed. "Okay, this Ben guy... He's the one you saw in the lighthouse?"

Zelda nodded. Even though she'd spent less than an hour in there, time had felt different, distorted. Maybe it was Ben's confusion that had warped things. Or J'harr's maddening presence.

Or maybe Ali was right—the All was warped and time-dilated, something her mind struggled to understand.

"So Ben gets some last-minute research grant," Maura said. "He cancels their date, ghosts, and never returns. Eventually, she starts looking for him, and that's when things get weird. It's like he never existed."

"The spiked story you sent me," Zelda said. "Someone erased him from the town's history."

"Like that mind-wiper thing in *Men in Black*," Maura said. "How would you even do that?"

Zelda didn't like the way Uncle Mark's eyes were darting about. He was here, but not entirely. "When did you say this was?" he asked. "Ninety-five—"

"Ninety-eight," Maura said. "Guess what else happened that year?"

Ali swiped his phone and turned it toward them. The headline: *Oil Spill Mars Coastal Migration; Rogue Tidal Surge Claims Lives of Cleanup Volunteers.*

"There's more," Ali said. "Elrond had to dig deep. Pre-internet, yo."

"The horror," Mark said. "So, you think it's connected?"

"Nineteen sixty-five." Ali swiped his phone to another headline: *Faulty Wiring Blamed for Swimming School Deaths; PG&E Perplexed.*

"This goes back centuries, Mr. F," Maura said. "Mine collapse. Sawmill disasters. Fur trappers slaughtering natives and natives slaughtering each other. Zelda, did those sailors have British accents?"

"Sailors?" Uncle mark asked.

"That's why she went into the water," Ali said. "She wasn't trying to delete herself but—"

"Ali, c'mon." Maura nudged him.

"Right, check it." Another swipe as he passed them his phone. It was some sort of telegram:

FROM: JOSEPH LARCHMONT
TO: MESSRS. CUMMINGS
** HMS VINTNER'S PRIDE SUNK OFF POINT GREY-
WOOD MIDNIGHT 1859 // ACCUMULATED WINE
VAPORS IGNITED BY CARELESS LANTERN // VIOLENT
EXPLOSION OBSERVED // LOCALS REPORT FIRE OFF
COAST // NO SURVIVORS // CARGO LOST // AWAIT
YOUR RETURN **

"Every town has accidents," Mark said. "That doesn't mean it's cursed."

"Fist bump for team skeptic, Mr. F." Ali held out his fist, but Uncle Mark let it dangle. "Anyways, that's what I said, too. But then Maura said..."

Maura rolled her eyes. "Don't do the finger guns, please."

He did the finger guns.

"Ugh. What I said was, 'Look at the dates. What else happened around then?'"

"An eclipse," Zelda said.

"Whoa, nice sleuthing, Nancy Drew," Ali said. "How'd you figure that out?"

"If I was J'harr, I'd turn off the lights," Zelda said. "Easier hunting in the darkness."

They all studied her, as if it wasn't quite the answer they'd expected. "Yeah, that's not unsettling," Ali said.

"She's right." Maura turned her attention to Mark and Zelda. "And that's not the half of it. See, you guys didn't grow up here. And, Ali, you didn't move here until third grade."

"Someone ate their gatekeeper flakes for breakfast."

"What I mean is, they have streets for every founding member. A local goes to Congress and they get a library in their honor. I sang that stupid lumberjack song so much in preschool I still hear it. But sometimes, unless I really think hard, I can't even remember the fire or that creep who started it all."

"Lloyd," Zelda said. "His name was Lloyd."

"So that begs the question," Maura continued. "How much of our history is real? And how much is being hidden?"

Uncle Mark took Zelda's plate and began cleaning up. She wasn't sure how much he believed, but something was still moving behind his eyes, a mental filter trying to sort through the impossible. Maybe adults needed more encouragement because they'd built their lives on a rational foundation. And now his world was collapsing.

"Uncle Mark, what is it?" she asked.

"Tides of darkness on her day of black night," he whispered.

"What's that?" Ali asked.

"Something my sister told me." He hesitated, then added, "After she died."

"Dude, your family is awesome," Maura said. "My dad just lectures about civil rights and my mom spends the money."

Zelda surprised herself with a smile. She'd never thought of it that way, but perhaps Maura was right.

"You said something about light," Uncle Mark said. "And this place, the All. If these Historical Society wackos wanted to let J'harr's light out... Would they use something like a lens from a lighthouse?"

"Already looked into that one, Mr. F," Ali said. "But according to Elrond, they decommissioned the lighthouse thirty years ago."

Uncle Mark closed his eyes and whispered, "Sláinte."

"Slawn-cha?" Maura asked. "What is that?"

"It's how the Irish say cheers."

Zelda sensed what Uncle Mark was going to say before he said it, and his words chilled her to the bone.

He asked, "What if they brought in a new lens maker?"

52

W ith the sharp tang of adrenaline on his tongue, Mark walked quickly across the Heartwood courtyard, his heart pounding as Ali and Maura hurried to catch up.

"Mr. F, I just want the record to reflect I disagree with this plan," Ali said. "You really, like, need someone with our set of skills."

Mark slowed by the mailboxes, shooting a glance back at the other apartments. For now, the drizzle kept the basketball court clear. No one was in earshot.

"He's right, Uncle Mark," Zelda said, slowing down.

"He can be the grand champion of *Jeopardy!* for all I care," Mark said. "Zelda, you're with me. Ali, Maura, you need to go home and stay with your parents. I'm not risking your safety; it's really that simple."

"This isn't our first rodeo," Maura said. "Zelda even locked a monster in a basement—"

"After you stabbed it," Zelda said.

"Harpooned it, technically," Ali added and made a thrust. "Pokey-poke. Mr. F, you should have seen it."

"No, I shouldn't have," Mark snapped. "You know why? Because you were supposed to be at the library, not fending off... whatever."

"Oops," Maura muttered.

Mark took a deep breath and tried to center himself. "Look, this isn't *Stranger Things*. You're not going to ride your bikes and fight evil with quirky banter."

"Burn," Ali said.

"No, facts," Mark continued. "You're kids, okay? And if half of what you've said is true, you've drawn the attention of some dangerous people. I'm not letting you get hurt on my watch. Not any of you." He tapped his phone and held it up. "See this timer? In ten minutes I'm calling your parents. You better be at home doing something normal, like popping zits or playing video games."

"Uncle Mark, please," Zelda said. "They can really help."

He glanced at the leasing office, where Mr. Glendale was arguing with a tenant, probably some leak or broken appliance he hadn't fixed. "Fine. That lens maker—McDonald or whatever—find out where he's staying and text Zelda his address."

"That's like, super basic," Maura said.

"Good. Then it shouldn't take you very long." He held up his phone. "Nine minutes and counting."

"Dang, Mr. F," Ali grumbled. "And just when we were finally bonding."

"We can bond another time. For now, Zelda..." He chirped the car's remote.

A few minutes later, they were merging onto De Los Santos Boulevard, the late-afternoon rain picking up and the wipers matching his pulse. Yeah, Mark knew they needed a better plan. For now, he just needed to keep Zelda safe. If half of what he'd learned was true, he'd already been derelict in his duties. What kind of guardian was he?

Phones ringing for thirty years.

A monster in the basement wearing the skin of an old woman.

Forgotten tragedies and missing people, as if the town had digested their memories.

None of it made any sense. Even the feeling at city hall, as if he'd forgotten something by the police station. Detective Brown, he told himself. That was her name. And then he pushed past the mental fog and she emerged, clear as a day without clouds.

"Unbelievable," he mumbled.

"What?"

"Nothing." He took a left onto the crosstown expressway. "Have they found something?"

"Still searching." She tapped her phone. "But it looks like McDermott got a grant through the university, so—"

"University, got it."

He turned the wheel, signaling and crossing over two empty lanes. He was a few hundred feet from the off-ramp when red and blue lights smeared the rear of the car. A shrill chirp of the siren tightened his knuckles.

"Damn," he muttered. "Bad time to get pulled over."

"Uncle Mark, there's something I forgot to tell you," Zelda said. "There was this guy at the Historical Society. Maura said he was, like, the head of the police."

"The police chief? This just keeps getting better."

Mark slowed the car and signaled his intent to pull over. He scanned for lampposts, storefronts, any well-lit spots. Yet all he saw were tall fences and closed gates, foggy streets that ended in warehouses. They were at the edge of town, between the industrial parks and university offices.

"Put that book away." He eyed the rearview. "Just... stay calm."

She slid the old journal beneath the seat. "I am calm."

He had to admit she was as cool as a cucumber. He'd been speaking more to himself.

Another glance in the rearview, where the cop still sat in the cruiser. Did it usually take this long? Maybe they were just running his plates.

Or maybe they were calling others...

He needed to say something to reassure his niece. "Y'know, the last time I got pulled over was with your mom."

Zelda's eyes sparkled in the shadows. "What happened?"

"I was visiting for the holidays. You were maybe eight or nine. Maya, she'd gone to a protest in Sacramento but called to say she was spending the night to see Taylor Swift. That was the code for 'come swiftly' because she'd gotten arrested. J.C. was busy with your grandparents, so I picked her up."

Mark warmed at the memory. The lies he and J.C. had to coordinate to keep the Ruizes in the dark. The bail Mark had helped post and how fast he'd driven the next morning. The McDonald's breakfast he'd brought for the ride home, hashbrowns that Maya gratefully ate as they put the state capital behind them.

"We got pulled over before the freeway," he continued, "and sure enough, your mom recognized the cop. He'd been at the protests, just on the other side. She pretended to flirt, said she had a thing for police."

"Gross."

He shrugged. "She gave him a fake number, and we got off with a warning. That was it."

As he spoke, the smile tugged at his eyes. Maybe it was the late-afternoon glow off the rain. Or maybe it was the fact that he sometimes struggled to remember Maya's face. If this J'harr-thing was devouring memories in this town, well, he'd burn the whole place down just to see more of his sister.

"Mom always talked about you like you were her hero. If she came to you, Uncle Mark, maybe that's why."

The words hit him like a gut punch. He squeezed the wheel to keep his eyes clear. "I don't understand how it works; I wish I did. But maybe that's where you come in." He glanced at the rearview. "Here he comes."

The policeman—a baby-faced guy in his late twenties—tightened his rain jacket and drummed his fingers down the car. Mark put the dome light on so they could all see each other.

"G'evening, folks," he said. "You know you cut through two lanes before signaling?"

Mark grimaced and gave his best "oops" face. "Sorry, Officer."

The man leaned down, peering into the vehicle. He chewed gum and carried a bored energy, like he might be looking for something more. Even though Mark hadn't drunk in over two months, he wondered if the edible might show up in a blood test. How would he explain that to the judge?

"I know you," the cop said. "Where do I know you from?"

As his eyes scoured Zelda, Mark noticed her shrinking into her hoodie.

"She gets that a lot," he said. "One of those faces, like—"

The cop slapped the roof, the echo startling its passengers.

"Raven's Valley!" the cop said. "I was one of the first responders. You were in that tunnel. And you..." He poked Mark's shoulder. "You were carrying her. Shit, I remember now. They said you helped those people escape."

Mark slowly released the breath he'd been holding. "It was a team effort, right, Zelda?"

She nodded. "We had lots of help."

"What a pair of aces, the two of you. Look, I'm really sorry about this, but I already wrote up the ticket. Just go before the judge, contest it, and I'll be sure not to show up."

"Oh, I've got a thing about judges," Mark said.

"No, really, it's three hundred bucks and a point on your license. Just show up on that date there at the bottom. I'll be, uh, 'preoccupied.' Promise."

Mark signed the ticket, stating he would show up on the court date next month. As he watched the officer hurrying back to his car, it occurred to him that he wasn't sure if they'd be here next week or ten counties away.

"That was weird," Zelda whispered.

"First time I've been bribed by a cop." He gave her knee a nudge as he put the car into drive. "Look at you with your fan club."

Ali texted them an address at the western edge of campus, a series of townhouses reserved for visiting scholars, postdocs, and fellows. A plan started to crystalize in Mark's mind, not perfect but clearer. He needed to keep Zelda safe, but he sensed she wouldn't like it.

For now, he parked in the visitor's lot near the address, Zelda following as they made their way beneath the cool glow of lamps, past rows of bikes and lawn signs protesting the latest Middle East conflict.

A group of shaggy-haired grad students hung out on the covered porch of a townhouse, a few reclining in hammocks while others grilled hotdogs. The college football game blared from a TV.

"Y'all want a brewski?" the one with the tongs asked Zelda.

"Y'all want to spend Christmas in lockup?" Mark said. "She's fourteen."

Zelda shot a curious glance back as they passed.

"Anyone who calls a beer a brewski is not to be trusted," Mark said. "What's the address again?"

"Unit 44. There."

The postdoc townhouse was cozy but modern, teak and bamboo accents blended with concrete and glass. Mark rang the doorbell and waited.

"What do we tell him?" Zelda whispered.

"Working on it." He rang the doorbell again.

Nothing.

After another moment, he glanced back across the paths and spotted the students grilling up dinner. Time to make peace.

"Hey," he said. "Any of you guys know Mr. McDermott? Postdoc, shaggy hair, Irish. We're... friends from out of town."

"Rock on," the guy with the tongs said. "But I've never heard his friends call him 'mister.'"

"That's because my uncle's being polite," Zelda said. "We're not friends, not yet. But we're about to save him a ton of money on some lens he's designing. If you know him, he's probably told you about it, right?"

"Uh... Maybe."

"The thing is, it's time sensitive," Zelda continued. "We need to get in touch and he'd be bummed if he missed out and, like, we had to tell him his neighbors were super unhelpful."

"Man, there's zero chill coming from your side of the fence." He passed the tongs to one of the others and took out his phone. "Henry... Henry... No go, amigos. I don't have his number."

Great, Mark fumed. "Is he in class, or—"

"Nah, dude, he's gotta sing for his supper. He had some bougie event and got dressed to the nines, jacket and tie. They even sent a limo. Y'all missed him by a half hour."

Mark's nostrils flared and his jaw tightened. Shit, it was like Ben Thomas all over again: history repeating. They'd need to move fast. He thanked the students and hurried back to the parking lot.

"You know where that is?" Zelda asked.

"I've got an idea."

Zelda stopped at the car. "Then we have to warn him."

"That's the plan," Mark said. "Now climb in."

While Zelda went around to the other side, he typed out a quick text message and hit send. He had a drive ahead of him, a dozen miles up the coast. He wasn't looking forward to it. Most of all, he knew Zelda wouldn't be happy when they stopped.

53

Z elda tried to read her uncle's expression, but his eyes remained fixed on the road ahead. The campus gave way to ranches and stables, then hills and the occasional hiking trail crossing the misty asphalt. She texted Ali and Maura.

> Heading up the coast. Larchmont castle I think.

> Need help?

> Not sure. Standby.

As the road grew curvy, she tried to ignore the nervous whisper inside, the one that said they still didn't have the full picture.

Point Greywood Lighthouse.

Ben Thomas, missing for thirty years and mostly forgotten.

And now Henry McDermott, some physics geek with a fascination on optics and a few patents on glass. Even Elrond had failed to explain it. Sometimes it felt like the unseen world was always ten steps ahead.

A notification flashed on Uncle Mark's side of the car. He shot a quick glance at his phone, then locked the screen.

"You know I love you, Zelda," he said. "You do know that, right?"

The statement blindsided her, sucking the air from her lungs. Yeah, of course she knew. It was just...

Awkward.

Uncomfortable.

Like her skin constricted as the words fled down her throat.

Tell him, she told herself. *Say something nice.*

"Anyway," he said, "being your guardian has been the greatest joy of my life. I mean, it's been a challenge, too, but that's not your fault. Well, not mostly."

She swallowed. "Why are you telling me this?"

He turned his blinker on and crossed a quiet road where the murmuring ocean grew louder. "Because being a guardian means you have to prioritize the safety of others. Sometimes, in order to do that, you disappoint the people you love."

She studied her shoes in the dark footwell. "You don't disappoint me."

Another signal, another turn, and the car slowed down. "I'm pretty sure I'm about to."

There was something familiar about the rattling gravel beneath the tires.

No...

Then she saw him, Uncle Alejandro, waiting at the end of the Airbnb's driveway beside their rental car. Grandma Ruiz stood in the walkway, bathed in the warm glow of the porch light. Even Grandpa Ruiz loomed in the house's wide picture window, a friendly shadow waving softly.

"No, no please, Uncle Mark," Zelda said. "Please, I need to come with you. I *need* to help."

"You've already helped more than you could ever know." He unlocked the door. "But like I said, I'm not putting you in danger."

She slammed the door's lock. "I can do things. Please, I know what we're up against—"

"We have no idea what we're up against, okay? We've got pieces, that's it. I'm not dragging you into something we don't understand."

Again, he unlocked the door. Again, she locked it.

"Please..." She could feel her voice beginning to break. Dammit, not now. "I'll be good. I won't get into trouble or break any rules, I promise. Please don't leave me."

"Hey, listen to me." Taking her face in his hands, he wiped a strand of hair from her eyes. "You've always been good, even when you haven't. You're my sister's daughter, and she'd be damn proud of every fight you've taken on. But sometimes, you gotta sit one out."

He reached past her and unlocked the door. Then Uncle Alejandro's hand fell on her shoulder. She could smell her grandmother's perfume, heavy in the salty bay air.

"C'mon, Zelda, let's have a fun night," Uncle Alejandro said. "We're not that bad, are we?"

"Cariño, hace frío," her grandmother said. *"Por favor, entra. Estamos preparando la cena, y hay fuego en la chimenea."*

Then they were helping her out of the car, guiding her up the driveway. Some sort of unspoken glance passed between the adults.

"Uncle Mark!" she shouted. "What if... What if something goes wrong or something happens or—"

"Stacey has my info. But, Zelda, don't worry, okay? I'll see you tomorrow. We'll meet up for brunch."

Alejandro gave Uncle Mark a cool nod while Grandma Ruiz took her elbow, leading her up the driveway, up the steps, and into the warm glow of the house. They were right: there was a fire going and the smell of Mexican hot chocolate filled the air, sweet with just the hint of the chili powder she loved.

Yet this house, with its spacious rooms and wide windows, the tall ceiling and beams, it felt more empty than their cramped apartment at the edge of town.

"Nos diste un susto al escaparte esta tarde. Come, help me with dinner."

They even had her overnight bag and her skateboard, still lying by the door from when they'd left for church. Then her stomach dropped when she remembered what she'd left behind.

The old journal.

"Shit," she muttered.

She took her phone out to call Uncle Mark, but not a second later, Alejandro snatched it from her hand.

"What are you doing?" she asked. "I need to call Uncle Mark—"

"This is a reset," he said. "That's what this is. No more running off and catching Ubers. We're starting at zero and rebuilding."

"You... You don't know what you're doing."

"Si, sabemos," her grandmother said. *"No vamos a perderte otra vez."*

Alejandro tucked her phone into his pocket. "Uncle Mark might love you, but he's let you go feral for too long. You're under our roof, under our watch, and we're going to start practicing good manners."

54

With a double tap of the brushed metal pump, Bibi cupped the lotion into her palm and savored its scents: jasmine and neroli with just enough ylang-ylang to balance the citrus and flora. Beneath it, delicate traces of frankincense and spicy cardamom. She rubbed the lotion on her arm, wrist to elbow, imagining it settling with all the other scents her flesh had acquired over the decades.

There was Guerlain's Jicky, and Joy by Jean Patou. There was Chanel No. 5, of course, a vintage bottle she still kept from the first production. And while its contents had been long replaced—not even the finest perfume lasted a century—it still delighted her to see the bottle on the shelf beside her vanity mirror, a friendly memento among her vast collection.

Yes, she had earned much in her years. Why not surround herself with these treasures? New money shouts. Old money whispers. But ageless wealth, it tips the scales from the shadows.

Tonight, she settled on a more modern scent: Baccarat's Les Larmes Sacrées de Thèbes, a gift from her insufferable publisher for some milestone she'd long forgotten. As she dabbed her pulse points, her mind drifted to tomorrow.

She was tired, yes; that much her aching bones told her. Too much time had passed since their last renewal of vows. She would need a new challenge for the next season, something less creatively taxing.

Maybe politics or rare commodities speculation. Maybe neuroscience, probing the depths of the mind. She had long wondered why her son had turned out as he had.

Like his heart had been born empty and waiting to rot.

At the thought of Grant, the vanity lights flickered.

Her benefactor was waiting.

"Oh, you'll have to wait," Bibi said. "Some of us still have appearances to keep up."

She hurried through the rest of her routine—the foundation, the concealer, the powder and bronzer and blush. With her brow razor, she cleaned up her left eyebrow, then her right. She was nearly done when the wound on her forearm quivered and her fingers slipped.

She didn't feel the brow razor's bite, nor the rip of her skin. But she did see the seam opening up on her forehead, a plum fissure that caused her eyelid to droop.

For a moment, she simply stared at her reflection: a slipping mask concealing wormy structures withering among mutation and decay; the bloody brow razor in her trembling hand; a glimpse of her undercoat, offending her like an unwelcome guest.

In a lashing strike, she thrust her hand into the antique glass. Her reflection splintered, as did her knuckles.

Fuming, she pressed her thumb against her broken fist. She gave herself five sobbing breaths for her own self-pity.

She needed only three.

Because her laughter came now, one breath at a time. This mirror, yes, it had wounded her skin and a few bones underneath. A mirror that once sat in a queen's summer palace and held royal reflections.

Now, this mirror would be forever scarred by her outburst. The world could be bent. Priceless things could be broken. But she would be mended and wiser, a true living antique.

Soon, they would all be mended.

And if that wasn't power, it didn't exist.

The vanity's Edison bulbs pulsed, that oozing black-violet glow chasing off the warm amber. She could feel her skin drinking it in, pores opening like a million mouths, parched and suckling. She didn't need to see her reflection to know what was changing, yet her fingers rose to her forehead, tracing her brow.

The wound had filled itself in.

"Thank you," she whispered.

"Mmm... We have complications... to discuss."

Dressed and refreshed, she took the private elevator down to her study. As before, she waved her hands and let the words flow through her—words her human tongue could not form. The blinds descended, cutting off the moonlight.

She found the chessboard, reviewing each piece and its placement, pleased to see the game was proceeding as planned.

And yet...

That pair of knights they had traded, why was one still standing?

She placed her hands on the edge of the mirrored board. J'harr's darkness pooled underneath, subsuming her reflection.

One eye.

Two eyes.

An oily sea of infinite cruel glares.

"What is this?" Bibi demanded. "We made a trade, or did you forget?"

The board remained still, the eyes unblinking.

Bibi moved the driftwood knight to the edge and off the board, yet the piece grew heavier, heavier. With a squeak of wood and glass, it shot from her fingers and reset its position.

"No, that's not... That's not fair. The exchange was made, my son for that old rat Halgrove. That was the trade; I felt it."

J'harr said nothing.

"Unless..."

She saw it now, another opening. A bishop, blocking her assault. A rook, shielding a queen. And that pawn, it would move closer and closer to the edge of the board, gaining promotion and then—

"The other knight is still in play," she whispered.

She had been so focused on that one knight she had never noticed the other. Guarded by the rook, it had felt nonexistent, a simple nuisance. But now...

"Oh, there you are," she whispered. "How did we miss you?"

The eyes finally blinked as she put her finger on the right piece and slid it over several squares.

Her rook.

If she traded it willingly, the loss brought the knight into the open, exposing both him and the pawn. Separate and alone, they would be easier to pick off. Yes, she saw new moves opening up now. Moves that would ripple down through the decades.

"Remember," J'harr whispered, *"there is only one god in this room."*

Light stretched across the dark study, chasing off that sea of cruel eyes. "Mrs. Boyle?" Mr. Osmond said from the door. "Your guests are arriving."

"Let them in."

Bibi smiled at her reflection looming over the mirrored board with its unknowing pieces moved by her knowing hands. J'harr had been right. No, she wasn't a god. But to the pieces she lorded over, well, was there really much difference? She had time on her side. And with enough time, she could make any play that she wished.

55

Mark left his car a half mile down the vineyard road, tucked behind an antique wagon loaded with casks and a sign promising weekend wine tastings and organic produce. He ducked under grapevines, following the furrows and weaving his way up the terraced hill. The misty rain had given way to a starry sky speckled with clouds and a cool lunar glow. In the moonlight, the dormant vines glistened and dripped.

He wasn't sure what his next step would be. Most of his life had been a series of quick improvisations and pivots.

The company he founded with his classmates in the final months of grad school.

The funding they kept acquiring at the eleventh hour with too many clauses.

The collapse and the self-exile and the years spent abroad.

His feet squished through the damp soil. When he thought of it now, he almost laughed—forty-four years of blundering onward, from returning home to take care of his niece and build a new life to now ducking beneath grapevines to prevent a near stranger's death. He'd never had a clue what he was doing.

Only that this was the right thing and he at least had to try.

Fifteen minutes later, he emerged by the gravel driveway and court-yard, sticking low by a stone wall. A dozen cars sat parked around the fountain, some modern and sleek, others elegant and old and exquisitely cared for. A Rolls Royce from the forties shared space beside a Mercedes Maybach, so new the dealer plates were barely dirty.

And there it was, a limousine, parked near the front door. He hoped it wasn't too late for McDermott.

Crouching in the shadows, he gave his ears several minutes to listen to the night. The rustle of scavenging animals through the grapevines. An owl tucked high in a mossy oak. The distant murmur of waves beyond the cliffs. And the din of voices inside the mansion.

Whatever event was occurring inside, it lacked the decorative festivity of the fundraiser. No red carpets or gloved attendants. No glowing sconces imbuing the walkways with light. Straining, he could hear music, but he sensed it was recorded, with no live band in attendance.

"C'mon, Mark, you can do this."

Keeping low, he followed the stone wall, until it joined a garden and a yard larger than the entire Heartwood Apartments. Sculpted bushes surrounded subtly lit statues. A Rodin in bronze featured two lovers intertwined in a kiss. A balanced mobile by Calder rotated slowly. Near a koi pond, a fusion of wood and stone featured carved holes that whis-tled in the wind. Mark sensed he was staring at more wealth than he'd ever known, a private collection with an audience of one. God, he wished Stacey could see this.

Sticking to the ample patio, he skirted the mansion's perimeter.

Then he heard it: a round of applause, muffled yet distinct. It came from three doors down.

Carefully, slowly, he peered over the stone sill, the indoor light searing his eyes. The guests were in the drawing room, roughly a dozen or so. Most had their backs to the window.

He saw hands clutching wineglasses and cocktails. Wrists banded with gold and fingers glistening with gems. Laughing, an older woman swept a shawl over her shoulder, the distinctive golden-brown of vicuña sheening beneath the light.

And there, near a grand piano and the center of attention, stood

McDermott. Even from a distance, his rented tuxedo, with its boxy fit and bulky shoulders, clashed with the partygoers' bespoke attire. Poor guy, Mark thought. He was the focus of a dozen faces, drunk on their smiles but oblivious to the hunger in their eyes.

McDermott finished a toast and raised his glass. Then a dozen others raised theirs. Mark's stomach soured as he caught a glimpse of Councilman Brand standing near the bar, his grin sharklike and amused. How deep did the rot truly go?

Just get in and warn him, Mark told himself. *Just a few minutes, that's all it takes.*

As the conversation shifted gears and the chief of police spoke, McDermott tapped the butler and made a gesture: *Where's the bathroom?*

The butler led him out of the drawing room as a memory surged through Mark's head. Those towels with the vineyard crest. The gold-handled sinks. Yeah, he remembered that bathroom. Even better, he remembered the patio door at the far end of the hall.

Mark watched from the shadows as McDermott ambled down the hall, marveling at the tapestries before disappearing into the bathroom.

Holding his breath, he pressed down on the handle. Warm air caressed his face, rich with the scent of spices and meat. Beneath it lingered the subtlest suggestion of sour rot and decay.

Someone said something from the drawing room and everyone laughed. The music picked up; Duke Ellington's "It Don't Mean a Thing (If It Ain't Got That Swing)" filled the room with lively piano before bursting into full big band rhythms. Mark stepped lightly, timing his movements to the roar of the brass.

He found McDermott washing his hands. He gave Mark a friendly nod as he entered. Christ, the guy was barely thirty, his eyes full and his skin youthful.

"Evening," McDermott said. Then his gaze drifted down.

If the dark hoodie and black joggers hadn't given Mark away, his muddy shoes certainly did. McDermott's gaze darkened.

Mark, who had rehearsed a dozen different speeches and dialogue trees over the past thirty minutes, now found his mouth gumming up.

What should someone say at such a moment? He did the only thing he could think of: he forced the words out—the whole truth—as insane as it was.

"Listen to me. I don't know how else to say this, but those people out there, they're not who they say they are. I know they hired you to build that lens for the lighthouse, but that's not all they want. I'm pretty sure they won't let you leave here tonight. In fact, I'm pretty sure they're going to do something awful to you."

The color fled from McDermott's face. "Something awful, like...?"

"Like, sacrifice you to appease some crazy god they all follow. I know, I know. It sounds insane—"

"Hold up." McDermott stared, stone-faced and still. With each blink, his eyes darted to a different corner of the room. "What are you saying? They're some sort of cult?"

Mark could feel the disbelief emanating from the man. Even the bathroom, with its high ceiling and space, now felt suddenly cramped.

"That's exactly what I'm saying," he said. "You need to go, now."

McDermott moved quickly, leaning in and—much to Mark's surprise—wrapping him in a tight hug. "Thank you," he whispered. "I knew it. I fucking *knew* it."

Pulling back, Mark almost laughed, yet the fear on McDermott's face was real, as real as this moment. "You believe me?"

"Brother, you have no idea the weird shit that I've seen. Tide pools turning into gnashing mouths and bloody ships that keep sinking. That butler that slinks around like a ferret? I swear that old codger has eyes in the back of his head. Three of them, right here." He tapped the base of his neck.

Mark let out a low chuckle, realizing now how tense he'd been for the past several hours.

"And that lens they commissioned?" McDermott continued. "Fucking craziest specs I've ever followed. I should have known when its refractive index was inverted, but they just kept throwing more funding my way."

"What does that mean?"

He took his wineglass off the sink. "Water, air, glass, they all bend

and distort light. That lens I designed, it doesn't project light outward;
it absorbs it inward, like—"

"Like it's being swallowed?"

"Swallowed, right. That light room should be warm, but it's cold,
always." McDermott glanced at the door. "So, how do we do this?"

"Down the hall, there's a patio door. It's open. You go first. I'll
count to sixty—"

"Better chances." He opened the bathroom door and peered into
the hall. "Shit." He closed the door and pressed his finger to his
lips. *Shh...*

A moment later, a shadow stopped at the door. A knock, then an
elderly man's voice echoed from the other side. "Sir? Is everything
okay?"

"Doing well, Jeevesy; just freshening up. The Limburger didn't
quite agree with me."

"Would sir care for an antacid?"

"That'd be great, thanks. I'll find you in the, uh, drawing room."

"Very well."

The shadow moved away from the other side of the door.

McDermott whispered, "I'd stand you a pint once we're clear, but
I'll be fucked if I'm spending another night in this town." Then something creased his brow. "You should head off as well, mate. I've got a bad
feeling about tomorrow."

"What about the lens? Can they even install it without you?"

McDermott cocked his head. "Brother, it's already active."

Mark's heart fluttered and his throat tightened. "But at the
fundraiser, I thought—"

"Just some bullshit antique Mrs. Boyle pulled out of storage. A
party prop. That lens I designed—the real one—we installed it weeks
ago." Then he opened the bathroom door. "All clear. Good luck to you,
whatever your name is."

And with a quick turn and a careful squeeze, he slipped out into the
hall.

Mark studied his watch, each second heavy and slow.

The lens. The lighthouse. That night he saw Maya for the first time
in months.

"I slipped through a wound only meant for one way."

Christ, McDermott was right. He had to get Zelda out of Greywood Bay. He'd stop by the Ruizes' Airbnb, pick them up, drag them if they protested.

And they always did.

But first, he needed to put this grotesque manor behind him.

Holding his breath, Mark pushed the bathroom door open, inch by inch. To his left, the hall ended in a large double door he knew led to the drawing room. To the right, the dark patio, not thirty feet off.

Stacey's morning jogs had trained him to be light on his feet, and he walked each step in silence. When this was over, he was going to kiss her, take her with them, tell her that, in many ways, she might have saved him.

He was thinking of her when he pushed the handle down and the floodlights came on.

A half dozen guests stood on the patio. They clutched wineglasses and cocktails, bemused grins on their faces. One plucked an olive from her martini.

Six sets of eyes, all focused on him. Waiting and smiling and—

Mark doubled back, where thirty feet of dark wood and tapestry lined halls now filling with guests.

They smiled hungry smiles, eyes glinting with amusement. One by one, they began to clap as both sides closed in.

"It is truly a thing of wonder, is it not?" The crowd in the hall parted as Bibi squeezed through. "J'harr works in mysterious ways, indeed. But she always provides." Another step, then another. "I did try to warn you, Mr. Fitzsimmons: this town truly isn't for you."

They came from all sides. Grinning elders in fancy suits and fine gowns. Councilman Brand and the chief of police. That old lady that ran the farmers market, always yelling at Zelda to get off the skateboard. A dozen faces Mark knew, all grinning and drawing closer, closer. Jesus, there was even Adam Fitch, his colleague from Neumann Prep—and that last fact broke his heart.

"Sorry, Mark," Fitch said. "But we've been here long before you. We'll be here long after, too."

Ten feet. Eight. Seven.

He could smell their perfumes and lotions; they'd gone heavy tonight. Because the rot, he realized, it had been all around him; these rotten ones thriving in plain sight.

Maybe the gentry did run the town, but that didn't mean he had to play nice.

With a sharp, desperate tug, he ripped a tapestry from the wall, all eight feet of Larchmont nobility. He didn't care about the thick fabric; it was the brass rod he was after.

Hoisting it and swinging, he aimed his first blow at the host. In a quick slash, he wiped that placid smirk off Bibi's face. A muffled shriek, then she crumpled.

The next swing caught Councilman Brand in the shoulder, a sickening pop that echoed off the walls. Grunting, the heavy man stumbled back.

"Stay away!" Mark shouted. "Stay back!"

But they kept coming, a wave from each side. He swung and thrust, yet they were laughing now. Some whispered to each other and giggled.

His arms trembled as he poked and prodded, each blow growing clumsy and wide. When he missed that damn butler by inches, hands seized his back. Then palms and fists, unbreakable grips pressed against him and wrenched the rod from his hands.

Someone squeezed the back of his knee, and his legs shuddered and folded. He fell to the rug.

Then someone forced him to look up. How the hell were they so strong?

Mark knew he had struck Bibi hard, but his mind recoiled at what he saw. Because that wasn't human flesh or muscle there, glaring back from beneath her torn, ruined face. Whatever it was, time had twisted it into a mass of seething tumors bursting with wormy fingers, all twitching and gray.

From her one remaining eye, the Bibi-thing blinked that same dismissive gaze. There was no kindness living in there, only a bitter greed, cruel and insatiable.

The smell, the writhing gray lumps bursting from her cheeks, and the laughter; it was all too much for his senses. A husky noise fled his lungs as someone yanked his head back.

"Save your voice, Mr. Fitzsimmons," the Bibi-thing croaked. "We'll have need for it soon. You're our guest of honor, and you owe us so many screams."

56

Without her phone, time moved at a different pace. Zelda spent dinner listening to her grandmother and Alejandro discuss the family business in El Paso while her grandfather napped by the fireplace. She feigned interest, but her focus soon drifted to worries of Maura and Ali. And, most of all, to Uncle Mark. She stifled a yawn.

"I know it's not that exciting," Alejandro said. "Cotton, denim, synthetic fibers. But, Zelda, import-export is good money. If you ever want to see the family business in action, well, we'd be happy to show you."

She gave him a flat smile and started cleaning up the plates. The only business she'd been interested in was the video games her father designed. And lately, even those had lost their sparkle. Maybe Dr. Rhonda was right. Maybe she was depressed.

She found some magazines on travel and read them, dog-earing a few pages on Spanish fashion. Regions like Andalusia and Galicia and the Balearic Islands captured her imagination. She envied the stylish women in the photos, lounging on the warm beaches and backlit by the sun. Summer never seemed further away than in late December.

She excused herself and went to bed early.

For three hours, she lay in bed fully clothed, listening as the house fell to silence. She counted the seconds until they became minutes, the minutes turning to hours.

At midnight she climbed out of bed, gathered her jacket and backpack. In socks, she tiptoed down the dark hall, past the main bedroom where her grandfather snored like a flooded engine. She'd put her shoes on outside.

She crept across the dark living room, still warmed by the fire's embers. She wasn't sure what her next move would be. They were at the edge of town, surrounded by empty hills and scattered rentals. If she could find a store or flag down a car, she might have a chance to call Ali or Maura or Uncle Mark.

She slid the front door latch open slow, slowly. She steadied her hand on the knob.

"It's midnight, *mi querida*. Where do you go?"

Zelda closed her eyes as her body went rigid. Her grandmother had been sitting in the dark corner, just waiting for her.

"Is it drugs?"

"What?"

"*Drogas?*" The chair groaned as her grandmother leaned forward and turned on the lamp. "Are you on drugs?"

"Of course not."

"Then, is it a boy?"

Zelda scoffed.

"I don't understand why you make such a noise. *Ven. Siéntate conmigo.*" She patted the couch beside her.

Zelda didn't want to come or sit. She didn't want to be in this house with these people and the confusion they brought. Yet, she remembered Uncle Mark's words: how her grandparents showed their love in different ways, how they needed to get along.

So Zelda sat close to her grandmother but not beside her, which seemed to wound her.

"I would like to speak to you something," her grandmother said. "It is a... How do you say? *Tengo algo en el alma que necesito desahogar.* Like, a confession of my heart."

Zelda blinked, unsure if she was supposed to respond or not. When her grandmother's hand reached out, she almost pulled back. Yet there was sincerity here, and vulnerability too. Things she'd rarely seen in her *abuela*'s stately persona.

"Okay," Zelda muttered.

"For a long time, I have trouble understanding you. I think I still do. I know you is having trouble, too, when you see me, yes?"

Zelda glanced down at her socks. She didn't want to answer but she was too tired to lie. "Yes."

"You are fourteen," her grandmother said. "Sometimes, you feel like a girl and sometimes a woman, no? For me, this is... discomforting."

"Discomforting?" Zelda felt the words emerging, soft yet furious. "How do you think I feel?"

A squeeze and a gentle pat on her wrist. Her grandmother leaned closer. "*Lo siento*. My English is... *nunca ha sido bueno*. What I mean is... I envy you. Is this the right word? Envy?"

Zelda swallowed. "I don't know."

"When I was your age, my family, we had very little. No property or nice clothes. *Nada*. My father, he was a *vaquero*, like a cowboy or ranchman. Sometimes, he go away for months. I remember... he had such a smell, like leather and oils and the stables. I used to be ashamed of him, maybe like you are of me."

"I'm not ashamed." But there was a small part that always had been. Her grandmother, with such straight posture and rules. It felt like every room she entered held its breath.

"You are just like Juan Carlos," her grandmother said. "Lies are difficult to hide on that beautiful face."

Zelda turned away and stared at the bookshelf. She didn't want to hear about her parents and how she reminded others of them. She knew this. She saw them every time she looked in the mirror.

Her grandmother asked, "Do you know the *quinceanera*?"

"A fifteenth birthday."

"*Sí*. But then, when I was your age, it was much more. Like a celebration of womanhood. My father, he showed me magazine pictures of the dress he had ordered, and when it came, I was the happiest girl in Veracruz. It was..." She closed her eyes and her fingers curled, tracing little shapes in the air. "Ivory with delicate lace. Long sleeves embroidered with pearls that shimmered. The skirt was wide, and oh how it flowed. All the boys tried not to stare, but when I twirled, that dress danced only with me. To be young and free... such a dream."

Zelda felt a smile pull at the corner of her lips. She had thought the same thing when she saw herself in that vintage dress. For a moment she had felt so alive in it, then so naïve to have worn it to a beach party.

When the evening soured, it became a reminder of her childish ambitions.

"What I didn't know," her grandmother continued, "was that my father had arranged for me to meet another family—a family who made fabrics and sold them into Texas. My *quinceanera*—even that special day and that dress—had been to match me with a husband so my family could prosper. It was like a *subasta*, an auction I didn't know I had entered."

"Wait," Zelda said. "Grandma, you had an arranged marriage? Fuck that. I would have—"

"Would have what?" The embers glistened in her grandmother's eyes. "Run? Where am I going? I had no money. Even that dress was decoration. No. I had one choice, to accept it and make the best future for my family."

"That's so messed up."

"That's life, *mi querida*. But I was fortunate, too. Your grandfather, he is kind and decent. Knowing how it turned out, I would do it the same. Most things, but not everything."

Zelda leaned forward. "Not everything?"

Her grandmother's gaze drifted to the floor. To a place far beyond. Her lips struggled with the words.

"I put too much pressure on Juan Carlos," she whispered. "I drove him away. Drove him across half the country where he met your mother. I know I can be... overbearing. I tried to protect him. And now..." Her voice cracked as she swallowed. "He haunts me, my dear J.C. I wonder if he would still be here if I hadn't tried to keep him so close."

While her grandmother wiped her eyes, Zelda tried to give form to a feeling she'd buried for three seasons.

"You blame me for his death," she whispered. "After the memorial, I heard you say it. 'If Zelda hadn't gotten in trouble, they'd never have been on that road.' You blame me, don't you?"

"Yes."

A single word, so quiet it was almost never spoken at all.

"I did," she continued. "And I know in my heart that I'm wrong."

"I wish I could take it back, Grandma. I think about it every day." She felt something steeling inside her, giving strength to her words. "But it's not fair to treat me like that."

"I know... And I'm sorry."

"Then why do you do it?"

"I don't know. It's..." She waved her hand. "Maybe I wanted a daughter but had only boys. Maybe I see you and your freedom and all that you have. I envy it. And maybe I think, 'If I could protect her, I'd stop being haunted.'"

"Grandma, you can't protect me forever."

"No, not forever." She squeezed Zelda's hand. "But can't you understand why I try?"

Zelda supposed that she could. On every trip she'd taken to her grandparents' house in El Paso, she'd seen her father's childhood bedroom, kept the same way as when he'd left for college. Maybe it was like Dr. Rhonda said. Sometimes people talk around the truth. Zelda was so tired of it all.

"You need to be nicer to Uncle Mark," Zelda said, her voice firm and even. "This fighting, it's not bringing us together. It's driving us apart."

"I know. And I'm sorry. Tomorrow, we set things right in this family. We'll have Uncle Mark over for lunch and we'll talk. Okay, *mi querida*?"

Zelda nodded. "You'll work things out?"

"*Sí,*" she said. "I would like that very much."

Zelda studied her grandmother, seeing something new in her. No longer the cold matriarch, but a woman, wounded and scared. Someone still grieving the death of her son. Someone struggling with the world and all its changes.

"Get some rest, please," her grandmother said. "My back aches from sitting in this chair."

Zelda returned to the bedroom, buzzing with nervous energy and struggling to keep her thoughts in line. She had stood up to her grandmother, not by defiance but empathy; she'd opened her ears and her heart.

Now she listened to the sounds of the house. She yawned once, telling herself to wait a half hour before deciding whether to sneak out.

She never yawned again and was asleep within minutes.

57

W hen the sack was yanked from his head, the first thing he noticed were the casks lining the musty stone walls. He blinked and sucked in a lungful of damp earthen air. Oak and fermentation, the tangy bite of grapes with subtle notes of tobacco and spice.

A wine cellar. Of course.

The next thing he saw was his colleague at Neumann, Adam Fitch. "Hey, Mark, this is quite the awkward situation, isn't it?"

Mark tried to rise but found his feet strapped to a chair and a leather band tight on his waist. He tugged and twisted as something metallic clinked behind him.

"Yeah, they've got you fastened in a horse harness. I'd tell you not to squirm, but you'll be doing a lot of that, too. Unless you play nice. You'll play nice with me, Mark, won't you?"

"He won't." The voice came from a shadowed alcove between vats. Even in the dim light, Mark could make out the guest's tuxedo. "We all know a troublemaker when we see one."

"Troublemaker? What is this, detention?" He turned his glare on Fitch. How many faculty meetings had they spent together, bored and joking their way through some new administrative presentation? "C'mon, Adam, whatever this is, you're not selling it."

Fitch sighed. "What this is, Mark, is the final day of your life. And what you say determines how many pieces you spend it in."

"He'll break," said another, a woman with thin wrists and a dress fine enough for the Oscars. "In the end, they always break."

Mark squinted, pulling the shapes from the shadows and really seeing the rest of the cellar for the first time.

There were machines and devices, things of antique design for bottling and corking, for curing and crushing. A bench full of pliers and clippers and saws, some as long as his arm. A brazier burned dimly, coals warming a poker laid across its grill.

"See, here's the deal," Fitch said. "You answer a few questions honestly, we make your remaining hours pleasant. You don't, well..." He gestured to the implements. "Make sense?"

"They're coming for me," Mark said, forcing a chuckle to his throat. "And coming for all of you. They're on their way now."

Laughter from the shadows. Something inhuman curled in the back of Fitch's throat and glimmered oily violet.

"Please," Fitch said. "We've been doing this for centuries. By dawn they'll barely remember your face."

He reached down and lifted an object, turning it over in his hand. When the brazier's glow danced down the leather spine, Mark's stomach twisted.

The old journal, damn.

"We found this under the passenger seat," Fitch said. "Mrs. Boyle may be our elder, but her sight has its limits. Pay attention now, I'm only asking once. Who gave you this book? Who else has seen it?"

Mark drew in a breath and let his mind wander. He forced his face to shift through expressions: confusion, frustration, resignation. He needed to sell them on his lie. And to do that, he needed to sell himself.

"He's stalling." Bibi spoke from behind him, her voice raspy and clicking, as if her jaw didn't quite work. Rancid breath warmed the back of his neck. "Perhaps some pressure will loosen his tongue."

"I'm just thinking." Mark shook his head. "The guy who gave me that book, he was Austrian, a painter. I met him on the internet. He knew all about your AARP coven; he's been studying you for years."

"Liar," Bibi whispered.

At first he thought it was a finger on his shoulder, yet it stretched longer and longer. Lined with milky eyes, the gray tentacle stroked his neck and slid under his collar, worming its way down his left arm.

"Your aura betrays you."

"My aura? Wait, did Professor Trelawny send you? Oh, I remember now." Mark shivered as the tentacle constricted around his bicep. "The guy, he had a beard and a walking stick and this long pointy hat. He was looking for hobbits—"

With a sharp jerk, the tentacle squeezed and flexed, shoving his left hand out onto the table. With a sidelong glance and a shiver of revulsion, he realized the protuberance was coming from Bibi.

From an orifice in her chest.

"Start with the pinky," she said. "And make him watch."

Fitch moved fast, his hand lashing out and pulling a bizarre contraption from the shelf. Mark's eyes danced over the shapes. A crank handle, metal rollers with teeth, and some sort of small bucket.

An antique grape crusher.

Shit.

It turned out Fitch was correct. Mark squirmed and tugged, but there was no breaking free. The tentacle straightened and flexed. God, he'd never felt such strength.

Without any fanfare at all, they pulled his left hand and fed his pinky the cold, metal rollers. Placid and calm, Fitch turned the crank. His eyes never left Mark's.

"No. No, no, NO—"

The pain came, so blinding and sudden Mark's entire body burst into sweat. He screamed. Or at least, he thought he might have. Too many senses fired all at once.

The vibrating crunch of bones.

The lightning bursting before his eyes.

The distinct blur of his pinky, simultaneously pressed together and chewed apart between the wet metal teeth.

He wasn't sure if he passed out or simply retreated deep inside. He only knew that Fitch was telling him now to look at it—"Look at what you've made us do to you, Mark"—and they were prying his eyes open and holding up his ruined finger, bone jutting through split muscle—*no, no, no*—while his brain simply went to a white void.

"Yep, he's in shock," said the distant voice of Councilman Brand.

Bibi sighed. "Doc, you know what to do."

The doctor was in his early sixties, the kind of How Do You Do Neighbor? face that Mark had seen a thousand times. Yet in the cellar's shadows, his eyes flashed oily and violet. With a pop of a leather bag, he produced a vial and waved it under Mark's nose. With a deep whiff of ammonia, the world slammed back into focus.

"Now you listen up, son," the doctor said. "In this here bag, I've got everything you can imagine and plenty you can't. Stuff to stop your pain or heighten your nerves. We can stretch every miserable second out to an hour. I've got tools to take you apart and put you back together. And if that ticker of yours decides to quit ticking, well, I've got enough epinephrine to jumpstart it again and again. You follow?"

"Answer him," Bibi whispered in his ear as her tentacle lifted his chin.

"I... un-du-du..." He swallowed, realizing he'd clenched his jaw so tight he'd drawn blood. "I understand."

"Well, good," the doctor said. "You'd be surprised how much you can remove of a person with the right tools and talent. And we've had a long time to practice, haven't we?"

A few chuckles from the shadows. Someone lit a long cigarette off the brazier's heat and grinned with too many teeth.

Mark spat. "I... I bet you... enjoyed all that practice... you sick fucks."

The doctor gave him a friendly pat on the shoulder. "It ain't for our enjoyment, son; it's for her glory." He gestured upward. "But it's also a perk of the job."

Mark's head tilted, and the world dimmed. He must have blacked out again because the ammonia was under him now and the doctor had a stethoscope pressed to his chest. The casks wobbled and the bricks shuddered, as if the whole cellar was quivering in delight.

"Mark, let's try this again, shall we?" That was Fitch, his face swimming at the edge of perception. "Who gave you this journal? Who else has seen its contents?"

"It's just... an old stupid book."

"Lies." Bibi leaned in behind him, her wormy lips against his right ear. "You may be too simple to know what it is, but you know what it isn't. Tell us: who gave this to you? Who put you onto our scent?"

Zelda, Mark thought. Sweet Zelda out there on her own. So much stronger than she knew.

But these people—these *things* of cruel inquisition—could anyone endure such torment?

No, he realized. He would die by their hands. They would ruin his body in their search for that old book's new owner.

"Ah, I can see it forming," Bibi whispered. "Just tell us."

Zelda, his niece. He closed his eyes and could see her face, so clear it was almost there. He smiled.

Then he pushed her memory down a hall in his mind, to a door of discomfort he locked deep away.

"Fine," he muttered. "The name... is Yu."

"Yu?"

He was a dead man; Mark knew this. They were right that he still had many screams left in his lungs.

But he also had nine fingers as well. He raised two in particular, the middle ones on each hand.

"Mr. Yu." Mark laughed. "He's a Vietnamese cowboy. Yu, as in, fuck you and the horse you rode in on."

Bibi's grasp coiled and tightened around his shoulders. Whatever she said to Fitch, Mark's ringing ears never heard it. But his eyes... They widened as Fitch slid a pair of pruning shears into the brazier's hot coals.

58

A warm caress on her cheeks pulled Zelda from a night of bizarre dreams into the day's sunny glow. She rolled over, checking the bedside table for her phone.

Empty.

Then she remembered: Alejandro. The midnight talk with her grandmother. Brunch with Uncle Mark.

Yawning, she took in the smoky scent of bacon filling the house. Maybe they were making huevos rancheros. She certainly hoped that they were.

She made her way down the hall, rubbing her eyes as light bloomed in funny through the windows.

"There she is." Uncle Alejandro placed cups around the dining table. "Glad you decided to join the living."

"Why didn't you wake me up?"

"A teenager that didn't want to sleep in. That's a first." He smiled and began placing the napkins. "Your grandmother told me about the midnight prison break. We figured you'd want some rest."

Zelda turned to the windows with their wide view of the ocean. The fog had burnt off early. For the first time in weeks, a blue sky stretched across the horizon.

That light... Why was there an odd quality to it?

She asked, "What time is it?"

Alejandro checked his watch. "Quarter past eleven."

"What?" Zelda's heart beat faster and her eyes widened. The eclipse. "Oh my god, it's almost time."

"Relax," he said. "We wouldn't let you miss the big show. Here." He handed her some silverware and went into the kitchen.

Her grandmother brought in a steaming plate of eggs and gave Zelda's shoulder a gentle pat. "Huevos rancheros, your favorite."

Zelda spotted the magazines she'd read last night, dog-eared pages still open to Spain and the beautiful fashion. Then she saw the place settings.

There were only four.

Four cups. Four sets of silverware. Four chairs.

"Where's my uncle?" she asked. "Grandma, you said he was coming. Where's Uncle Mark?"

From the kitchen doorway, Alejandro mimed toking a joint and gave Zelda a wink. But her grandmother just shrugged and laid out the store-bought tortillas. *"Mi querida,"* she said. "Who is this Uncle Mark?"

No.

The silverware fell from Zelda's hand as the words stuck to her throat. She forced the sticky horror past her lips.

"Uncle Mark," she said. *"My* uncle Mark. You know who he is."

But the confusion wrinkling her grandmother's face said otherwise.

"Oh, Mark," Alejandro said, as if he hadn't thought of him in years. "Last I heard he was in Spain. Was he coming?"

No, no, no...

Zelda rushed to the window, breath jagged, a knot tightening in her throat.

The light...

A muted sun dangled in the late morning sky, cold and weak. Drawing toward it through a veil of haze, the dark moon loomed. Even the dappled sunlight seemed altered through the nearby trees, the leaves sending mottled, toothy shadows across the ground. To the north, faint auroras rippled and stretched along the bay's silvery surface.

Creeping tendrils of black-violet light.

The eclipse was almost upon them.

"My phone," Zelda said. "Give me my phone. I need to call him."

"Now hold up, Zelda," Alejandro said. "We'll give him a ring after brunch—"

"I said give me my phone!" she screamed and slammed her palms on the table. The plates rattled and a glass of orange juice fell over. Her grandmother jumped. "Listen to me. Something really bad is going to happen. We need to get out of here, now. Drive me to the vineyards and I'll give you directions."

She was the only one to move at all.

The others stood, not quite sure what to say or do. Then her grandfather began silently dabbing the spilled orange juice with a napkin.

"Zelda," Alejandro spoke slowly. "I don't know what craziness you're up to, but I'm tired of it. All of us—we're done with this disrespect, this... whatever it is."

"Fine, okay, we're all done with Zelda. Just *please*, take your phone out. Good. Now, look up Uncle Mark's number. You see it?"

Alejandro's brow creased as his thumb stopped moving down the screen. Something familiar narrowed his eyes. "California area code," he said. "Huh, that's a... Greywood Bay address."

"Call him, you'll see."

"Zelda," her grandmother said. "*Siéntate*, please. Let's talk this over."

No, she was done talking because they weren't listening; they never had. The only person who did was now half-forgotten, which probably meant...

She pushed the idea away. There wasn't time to talk; no time at all. Just time for action now, now, now.

With a quick swipe, she snatched Alejandro's phone right out of his hand. "Hey, what the hell?"

She raced across the room and down the hall, her family calling out, shouting, then hurrying after her. She slammed the bathroom door and locked it. If she could just have a second to call, to find out, to—

Alejandro banged on the door. "Zelda, have you lost your mind? What the hell's going on? C'mon, open up."

As the doorknob jostled, she paced, nervous fingers moving on their own. She wondered, if it worked on Bibi in the basement, would it work here as well?

Yeah, it actually did.

With a flick of her wrist and several quick gestures, she traced the locking symbol above the door's handle. The lights flickered. Alejandro's voice receded behind a mute curtain. The door grew still and silent.

Think, Zelda, think.

She scrolled down Alejandro's phone and tapped Uncle Mark's number.

Ringing...

Ringing...

Then his voice answered, as if he was out of breath. "Who... is this?"

"Uncle Mark? Where are you? What happened?"

There was a pause on the other end, then a sound like something was cupping the phone.

"I'm not sure who this is, but..." A deep breath. "Run! Get out of here! Listen to me, you need to leave—"

A muffled grunt, then a struggle as the phone was yanked from his hands.

Silence, then:

"Zelda Ruiz, is it? It's so nice to formally meet you."

That voice, she recognized it. It had spoken in city hall. It had mocked them from the dark depths of the Historical Society. Now, it murmured into her ear, sibilant and smug and dripping with malice.

An echo of J'harr.

"You're an interesting one," Bibi continued. "You should have forgotten him, too, yet here we are. I guess some bonds are harder to sever. I'm afraid time is short, young Zelda, so I'll make you a deal, the same deal we offered that fool Halgrove. I can tell by your silence you knew him, didn't you? Old Chester, with his brain full of ghouls."

Zelda struggled to say something, anything, but the fear froze her in place.

"Goodness, child, I can sense your terror; it's only natural. In time, we can temper that, too. We can teach you many triumphs of the flesh.

So, let's make this easy, shall we? Tell us where you are, and we'll bring you into the fold. We could use some new blood. It's the best offer we've made in, oh, quite a few decades."

Bibi inhaled, wet and rattling. Somehow, the rot filled Zelda's nose, burning her senses and blurring her vision. She could feel Bibi, almost beside her in this bathroom.

"Ah, I can sense the rejection coming to your lips," Bibi said. "Pity. You're as stubborn as your uncle."

Zelda's fourteen-year-old body clenched, tighter than it had on any wrestling mat. Her uncle, Mark. Who had moved across the world for her. Who had lied to keep her safe. Who was now on the verge of being consumed and forgotten.

Hearing his name from such rotten lips gave her all the courage she needed. She found her voice growing strong as the tides.

"I'm just like him," she said. "So save your pity, old woman. I'm coming for you."

She hung up the phone, shivering and shaking. With trembling fingers, she sent Ali and Maura a group text:

> Borrowed phone. It's Zelda. Calling now
> please pick up.

Maura answered on the first ring. "What's up with the new digits?"

Zelda told her as much as she could, as fast as her cracking voice could speak. The eclipse. The phone call with Bibi. Her grandparents and the vacation house she was stuck at.

And most of all, Uncle Mark.

"Who?" Maura asked.

"Think about my apartment, okay? Someone else lives there. He's got brown hair, mid-forties. You said he was cute and I hit you. Then—"

"Ah, my heart," Ali said in the background. "Are you having an emotional affair?"

"Shut up, Ali," Maura said. "Sorry. Speakerphone. We were studying."

"Studying anatomy," Ali shouted. "Operation: Make Out City— ow!"

"Tell me you remember him." Zelda squeezed her nose. The world was tilting and she was running out of time. "It's like Detective Brown and Ben from the lighthouse and all those messed-up tragedies. Please, try to remember him."

"I remember Mr. F," Ali shouted. "I set Elrond to remind me of everyone I know once an hour."

Zelda sensed both her friends crowding the phone.

"Right, your uncle," Maura said. "So what do we do?"

"I don't know," Zelda said. "But something bad usually happens, right? Where would people be gathering?"

"Coogan's Wharf," Maura said. "There's a huge viewing party going down."

"Zelda, we're on it," Ali said. "What about you?"

She studied her reflection in the mirror over the sink, then turned on the hot water. "Me? I think Chester gave me everything that I needed."

Then she hung up.

With the steam filling the air and fogging the mirror, her eyes rose to the overhead lights. She needed darkness. Then her fingers began tracing symbols on the damp glass. Curves and sharp corners. Little spirals dripped as Chester's voice filled her thoughts.

"Lesson two: light isn't always your friend."

Faster and faster, the symbols came to her finger. Words that she didn't quite understand. Words that were a part of him once, and those before him as well. Words, now flowing through her fingers and given meaning by her desperate heart.

"Please," she whispered, "I'm asking for your help."

It came as a flicker and a buzz, each bulb winking out one by one by one. The darkness bloomed around her, oily and sheening and bleeding through the bathroom's tiled walls.

She was miles from the vineyard, too far to run on her own.

But that didn't mean she couldn't get there.

Because if Chester could leave Pacific Manor, perhaps she could go even further.

"Lesson three," she whispered. "Sometimes the fastest path is a shadow."

As she wiped the mirror, the darkness peeled off like loose scabs. They flaked and crumbled and slid free from the world. She saw...

Nothing.

Well, nothing at first.

Only the dim light from the hallway creeping under the shaking door. Then, a body slammed against it—Uncle Alejandro, really throwing his shoulder into it now. Through a gap in the curtains, a sliver of eclipse light poured in. The moist mirror, glinting in the celestial glow. A stale flavor grew on her tongue as it all came together.

Then she saw what was missing.

Her reflection.

She stood at the sink, the last of the scabby shadows falling from the wall. The steaming mirror, a portal to a room behind her. She looked into that mirror—through it—as Alejandro broke the door open and stared, confused, at the phone resting beside the sink in the now empty bathroom.

She'd done it, she realized. She'd entered the All.

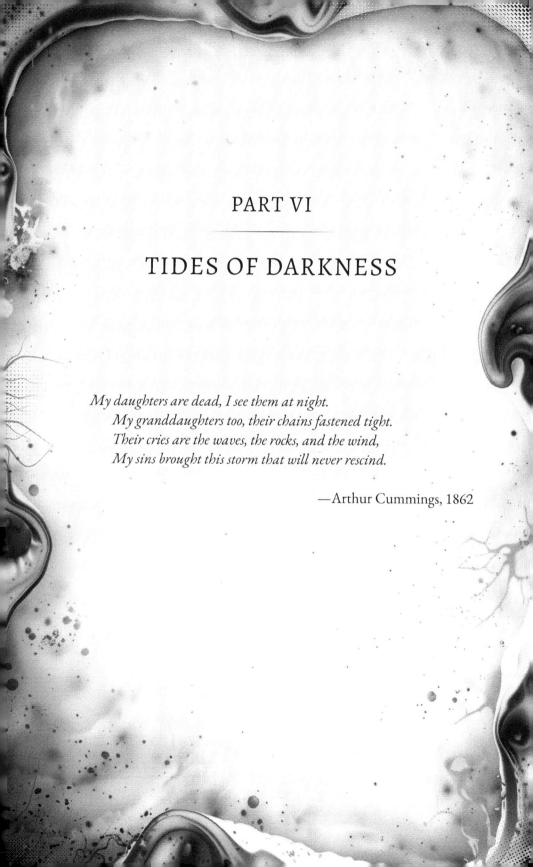

PART VI

TIDES OF DARKNESS

My daughters are dead, I see them at night.
My granddaughters too, their chains fastened tight.
Their cries are the waves, the rocks, and the wind,
My sins brought this storm that will never rescind.

—Arthur Cummings, 1862

59

Among the shadowed folds and caverns of the sack that echoed his own endless screams, Mark dreamed deeply, reaching for moments of comfort among the tunnels of pain.

The midnight rain in Madrid, and how it captured the moonlight on the cobbled streets.

The salty-crisp breeze of Greywood Bay, the first time they drove down from the hills.

Stacey Layne, smirking as he carried an armful of tampons to the register. "You're pretty green at this, aren't you?"

Yeah, he was. But he was grateful as well. For every small kindness she'd shown him.

Then the sack was pulled from his face, gently for once. Stacey vanished, leaving Mark to blink the darkness aside. His left eye was so swollen it didn't open. His right leg shivered and twitched. They'd taken turns hitting him and cutting him, pouring wine down his throat and choking him to the edge of blackout. He wasn't sure if that was before or after they'd cut off two of his fingers, joint by joint.

"You're a tough son of a gun," the shadow said. "I mean that in the best ways. It's been a long time since I've seen anyone get under Beebs's skin."

Another blink and the shadow came into focus. A white mustache. Friendly eyes.

"The Monopoly Man," Mark sputtered.

Harlan Boyle smiled. "That's pretty clever. I guess I do see the resemblance. Here."

He poured a cup of water and pushed it across a table slicked with blood, sweat, and plenty of tears. Mark studied the empty wine cellar. They were alone.

"It's not a trick, I promise." The old man took a sip from the glass.

The moment it was back on the table, Mark seized it with shaking, bandaged hands. He raised the cool glass to his lips and drank deeply and greedily. His dry, ravaged throat shivered at the cold touch. And then it was empty. Trembling, he tried to place the empty glass upright, but it slipped.

Hard to hold anything with missing fingers.

"Thank you," he muttered after finishing a second glass.

"I'm afraid I'm not here with a Get Out of Jail Free card," Harlan said. "You will die. Very soon, in fact."

Mark gave his harness a tug. Still locked. "You say that like you don't own this place."

"No, just married into it. But none of us own what you see. Only J'harr. The rest of us, well, I'm afraid we're all in her debt."

"Slaves," Mark muttered.

"Slaves," Harlan repeated. "And today, she comes to collect. As she has for centuries."

A shiver overcame him and Mark felt the chair he was strapped to wobble as he shook. Even his nerves were failing.

When the fit passed, Harlan produced a tiny glass vial with clear liquid inside. "Doc Mitchell had me on some cocktails over the years. They temper my fits." He held the vial up to Mark's good eye. "This is opium, mandrake, belladonna, and a few others. You know what they do?"

"Lights out, I suspect," Mark said.

"Lights out, indeed. I've been stockpiling for this day. You will be awake for the renewal, I'm afraid. But this'll dampen the pain at its fiercest. I'll slide it in your mouth, here."

The man's finger's probed Mark's swollen mouth, tucking the glass between his molars and cheeks.

"Wait until after they bind you, but before the first cut. Bite down and grind. The glass will hurt going down, but what comes after will hurt less."

Mark tongued the vial and spoke out of his left side. "Or you could just let me go."

The brazier's dim coals glistened in Harlan's tired eyes. "I'm afraid," he whispered. "That's what it is to get old. I'm afraid of her judgment. Afraid of all that I'll lose. All of us chained to our debts, and none more cowardly than me."

Light bloomed behind him as a door opened. Harlan shrank as a familiar shadow drew across the cellar.

"Dear, tell me you've had some luck with our guest," Bibi said. "I'm bored of this nonsense."

Mark felt Bibi's wormy touch upon his shoulder. Were those hands or claws clasping his skin? Were those fingers or tentacles stroking his hair? He could only see a twisting shadow on the wall playing tricks on his broken senses.

Harlan asked, "You're not going to tell us who gave you the book, are you?"

Mark let out a dry laugh that turned into a cough. After all the pulling and tearing, all the wounds and mutilation, he still hadn't given them what they'd wanted. Hearing Zelda's voice on the phone had only strengthened him. It was amazing, this fortress one could build on a foundation of spite.

"He's a businessman from Spokane," Mark coughed. "They call him Nonya Business."

"You have quite the mouth, Mr. Fitzsimmons," Bibi said. "I think we'll leave it on when we peel the skin from your face."

She took the old journal and dropped it into the brazier, stirring the coals with the poker. Mark watched with silent horror as smoke rose in thin curls. He couldn't help but feel like something tremendous was being destroyed. Not just a book but lifetimes of secrets studied and learned at terrible cost.

Then the sack descended over his eyes, but the dreams did not follow. Only the feeling of being lifted, carried, placed on a cart, and hauled through rooms and halls, each echoing with different sounds.

Wheels clattering upon stone.

Then wood.

Then softly upon rugs.

Then, the rocky bumps and shifting dirt of a cavern redolent of the salty breeze.

An elevator rattled and descended, and soon the dampness washed over him. The ocean. Yes, it shivered his skin, crisp and windy. Waves murmured beyond the black veil. He was on sand now, the wheels sinking in and catching. A final tug, and he was pushed upright as hands yanked the sack from his head.

The first thing he noticed was the odd quality of light. The sun hung at noon, yet the sky was as dark as the hour before dawn. And the moon, a dark sliver drawing closer and closer.

The eclipse was beginning.

The second thing he noticed were the guests.

They stood on Persian rugs and lounged amongst cushions set upon a raked beach. They wore suits and jackets, fine gowns and shimmering dresses. They clutched mimosas and Champagne while the butler made the rounds with a tray of shrimp cocktails. Beneath a marquee tent sat a buffet table lined with fresh lobster, caviar, and a whole suckling pig.

Like it was a damn garden party.

"Here we go, Mark." Fitch and two others took his shackles and gave the harness a tug. "Please remember, I did try to make this easier on you."

With a yank, the chain behind him cinched and clicked into something. Mark turned, his stomach souring at the slanted black stone set among the sand.

An altar.

They had him on a fucking black altar.

There were rings in six places at least, two already threaded with chains. There were locks as thick as his finger. Most of all, there were grooves in the stone that formed bizarre symbols, the same ones he'd seen in Chester's book.

Mark twisted and jerked, but the chain dragged him back like a tired dog.

"C'mon, Mark," Fitch said. "You really think we haven't perfected this by now? I'll let you in on a little secret." He leaned in and whispered, "The last guest to break free was before the invention of airplanes." Then he winked.

Fitch was right, of course. No matter how Mark fought, they simply pulled one chain after another and physics did the rest, splaying him out on the cold altar, limb by limb. A few of the guests watched with amusement, yet most seemed bored.

They'd seen this before, he realized. Ben Thomas, and others.

Sore and exhausted, Mark could only lie on his back with his head hanging loose. He could no longer see the sky from his upside-down perspective, but he didn't need to. The cove waters reflected the eclipse, a dimpled mirror of rolling waves.

"It's almost time," someone said.

As the wind died down, the waves grew softer and smoother. Soon, they vanished altogether. The cove took on a mirrored polish, reflecting the darkening sky and a moon cutting through the sun.

He saw it now. There was something within the sky's reflection. Something behind it. Something *beyond*.

J'harr.

Black-violet tendrils stretched over the cove's waters, filaments so thin he could hardly see them. Next came the eyes. One, two, a dozen and more. They opened up, a blanket of shimmering pupils beneath the water's surface, mesmerizing and infinite. With each blink, the world darkened and her eyes grew clearer, clearer.

There, on the softening horizon, two worlds began to meet until the boundary smudged from existence. Piercing them stood a proud structure rising from the shoals.

The lighthouse.

It quivered and twisted. It shivered and pulsed. Where its once-solid foundation gave unwavering structure, the darkening base expanded. Stonework and skin, metal struts and wet muscle. It all conjoined in an unraveling tower that pierced the horizon, above and below.

Ali had been right, Mark realized. Just not in the way he imagined.

It wasn't a black hole, yet it was still ravenous—a monstrous proboscis, unliving and relentless, piercing the fabric of this world, eager to suckle and gorge.

A mouth of J'harr.

"Friends," Bibi said. "Gather round, you know the drill."

The guests meandered over, sipping their cocktails and chewing hors d'oeuvres. A few offered Mark smiles. Someone ran a gem-studded hand across his bruised flesh.

There was Councilman Brand and Doc Mitchell.

There was the chief of police.

A dozen faces, some exceptional and others ordinary, all darkening as the eclipse shadowed their skin. The only one missing was Harlan.

Mark tongued the glass vial, moving it from his cheeks to his molars. One bite. That was all it would take.

Yet his mind rebelled. This wasn't how his life was supposed to end, butchered here on a beach. He should be shopping for Christmas gifts. He should be jogging with Stacey. He should be trying to be a better boyfriend, a better guardian.

His jaw hesitated over the glass, just a moment too long.

Fitch lashed out, fingers shoving their way into Mark's mouth. Mark bit down and shook his head, gnashing and pulling.

The glass didn't break.

But Fitch's skin certainly did.

Screaming, Fitch recoiled as his torn fingers hung in strands of red wetness. He balled his other hand and punched Mark, sending sparks across his vision.

"Yeah, he's a clever one," Councilman Brand said. "Been dealing with him for months." He patted Fitch on the shoulder. "Hang tight. She'll patch you up better than the doc."

With the tilting world, Mark could only watch as Bibi plucked the glass vial from the sand. "My husband always had a weak stomach for this part."

He wasn't sure when she had produced the hooked blade, but it was long and thin, an unnerving shade of dark metal. Its serrated edge sparkled in the shadowed light, designed not just to cut but to torment.

A purple gem adorned the pommel. In the eclipse's dwindling glow, Mark swore the gem winked.

An eye.

A wretched eye peered out from the pommel.

Time thickened and oozed through his ruined senses now. The smooth waves, slowing in this cove of infinite reflection. Motes of dusty sand, suspended in the air forever. Even the wind held its breath.

Only his heart quickened, drumming faster and faster, in time with the pulsing lighthouse and the voices.

Because they were chanting now, a dozen shadowy guests all swaying and muttering. They turned their eyes upward. In an inkblot explosion, color bloomed from the lighthouse. It filled the cove waters below and the dark sky above.

A color so sickening his mind went numb.

First came the cold fires of deep space, so electric and ultraviolet he blinked back the tears. Next came a red, deep as the richest Burgundy wine. Sour brown followed, like the hidden caves of earth where blind horrors burrowed and squirmed. Then the aquatic green of tide pools teeming with life. And grays of driftwood and fog and ashen memories stolen from his mind. And black, a greasy decay without borders.

Mark stared at the maelstrom bathing the hidden cove, subsuming the horizon. There was wonder and terror within it. So much beyond earthly knowledge. He saw time unraveling, a light that carried more than colors and shadows but the horrors of eternity itself.

Hell, he realized.

Not some Sunday school vagary, but the mouth of true hell itself. A prison of torment to give shape to a dead god, wardened by her followers and their chants.

Bibi raised her hand skyward. "Light of my lights, hear our prayers through the veil."

The others swayed, singing a reply no human throat could produce. *"Glima dil'im, sky'une voka'rr zathule n'ga vey'eel."*

"We gather in your glory on this day of black night."

Their fingers began undoing buckles and loosening ties. *"Verin zar'hane v'ghar'alor thraale dur zarikrind dakhal nakte."*

"As we break this body before us, may your dark glare grow bright."

With moans and gasps, they unclasped silver bracelets and pearl necklaces, diamond earrings and gold watches. *"Zhal verin kreshe thor-jim'ka korushe, sklar'leen d'har zur glarik zarbrige."*

"As his screams kindle your furnace, may our world feel your touch."

"Zhal ghis skrems'khane d'lure vzaruke, sklar'leen dorle zur tha'kün." Moans filled the air as the clothes slid down trembling bodies, suits and gowns piling in the sand at their feet.

"And with your blessing, may your endless splendor renew us."

"Da're verine bez'in, verine renude in d'har zo'quan for'sheen."

Bathed in the glow, they ran their shaking fingers over nude flesh. Old skin and age spots. Wrinkles and scars. A dozen quivering bodies dropped to their knees in the throes of something between delight and discomfort.

"J'harr!" they screamed. *"J'harr! J'harr!"*

Then, as Mark's mind desperately reached for every inch of sanity on this maddening beach, a new hell erupted before him.

The partygoers—all twelve of their ecstatic nude forms—reached up and peeled the flesh from their bodies.

Molting, he realized.

What emerged defied physics and biology, even Mark's unblinking eyes. Some burst into writhing bundles of tumors and quills, scabrous forms of many legs and no arms. Others unfurled wings, bat-like and veiny above columns of chitinous shell. A few were simply too alien for his mind to assemble: a crystalline cocoon floated, hardening amber encasing organs pulsating inward, an infinite fractal. With an inhuman screech, bulbous bodies and twisted limbs ripped away the last of their human husks.

They turned to him, reptilian and alien and something else altogether. Countless eyes burning with J'harr's seething glow.

And Mark, he felt himself molting, too. Shedding not his skin but his connection to all that he knew, all that he loved, and all that anchored him to a world of logic and reason. Tipping into the mouth of hell where timeless screams filled the winds.

This was how oblivion felt, he realized. To be devoured—body, soul, and something even deeper.

His very memory itself.

Yes, he was screaming now, and the blade hadn't yet touched his skin.

He had always been here on this beach.

He had been screaming forever.

60

Stacey finished her thirteenth mile in record time, jogging the final few hundred feet at a slow, comfortable pace. Her legs burned and her lungs screamed. Yet few things felt as good as the tingling high at the end of a run and the breeze off the bay.

She checked her watch, pleased with her heart rate and splits. She might qualify for Boston if she kept it up.

What displeased her was the feeling that had chased her for each mile.

It began as she ran past the Heartwood Apartments, a sense that she'd forgotten something, something important. She'd called Pavarti to check if she'd left the stove on, a heater, anything really. She knew the answer was no.

Pavarti's reassurance did little to silence the fear: *You've forgotten something, something important.* Despite her steady pace, every mile grew lonelier.

As if someone was missing.

She dodged a bus full of Chinese tourists and crossed Sunset, finishing her cooldown at Coogan's Wharf, just as planned. She bought a pair of viewing glasses and a fresh churro from a hawker by the pier. While he fried the dough, she stretched her sore legs on a guardrail.

That nagging worry...

Hadn't she had a running partner these past several months? Someone much slower who tried to talk, always interrupting her podcasts?

Mike or Marshall or...

Switching legs, she leaned against the pier's railing, really stretching her hamstrings. Then something moved in the waters below.

Beneath a floating Pepsi cup and a layer of ocean scum, a crab scuttled in the muddy shallows. Dirty clouds swirled around its odd shell. A deformity or... What was that?

Blinking, Stacey watched the crab vanish beneath the pier.

With a muddy bloom, another crab emerged from the silt. She leaned over the rail, the dim light playing off the surface like an oil sheen, mesmerizing and hypnotic. The barest hint of colors whose names she didn't know.

Marty or Mitchell or...

The crab scurried and turned, and then she saw it again: the shell's unsettling pattern.

Three more crabs emerged in silty clouds, marching in jerky formation before skittering beneath the pier. Stacey leaned even further out.

There were dozens down there. Dark skittering crabs crowding the piling, circling and burrowing, scratching and clawing. In the odd glow and sheening distortion, the patterns on those shells looked human.

Like screaming faces.

"Here you go, Ms. Layne."

"Thanks, Miguel." Stacey took the warm churro and slipped her glasses on, finally peering up at the eclipse. The sun was already vanishing behind the dark moon, sliver by sliver.

What had the ancients thought at such moments? Had they been reverent or fear-struck? She couldn't help but feel a blanket of awe wrapping around her

Sure, Greywood Bay had its problems. Sometimes she felt like she was fighting too many battles at once. But for now, she was grateful to be here at the continent's western edge, beneath this cosmic spectacle.

Grateful for the darkness in her life.

And for the light.

The crowd, however, she could do without. She'd never seen so many people gathered at one place in this town. And she could do without the seagull stalking her, its greedy eyes on her churro.

"Shoo." She waved it off, but it only circled and followed.

A teenager shoved past her, lanky and fast. Then another, broad-shouldered and strong, bumped her. Maura turned back, breathless and red in her cheeks.

"Sorry, Ms. Layne," Maura panted. "You really... need to... get away from here."

Stacey smiled at the girl she'd known since she was in Neumann Pre-K. Yet there was something on Maura's face, something she'd rarely seen on the football fields or wrestling mats.

Fear mixed with panic.

"Maura, what are you talking about?"

"We got a call... from Zelda."

Ali rushed over, his backpack half open and a dozen colored sticks in his hand. "The bad people have Mr. F," he said. "They're gonna do the mind wipe-y thing. *Men in Black. Men in Black!* Seriously, just get away from here. Trust us."

Then he grabbed Maura, and they both hurried down the pier, shoving their way through the crowd.

Mr. F.

Stacey's mind locked up and her feet remained frozen in place. That hungry seagull seized the moment and snatched the churro right out of her hand. She didn't even flinch.

Zelda.

Mr. F.

There was a connection, one that put her fingers in motion. She unlocked her phone and scrolled through the recent calls and texts.

Fitzsimmons, Mark.

There he was, Zelda's uncle and her... boyfriend. Yes, she could see him now in her mind, his face hazy at the edges and fading. They'd made plans to go jogging this morning. How the hell could she have forgotten someone so important?

Staccato pops rang out down the pier, where a group of Chinese tourists split apart and backed off. Maura was shouting at the crowd to disperse, to look away from the eclipse, to go on and leave.

Another pop and a series of shrill whistles. There was Ali, but he wasn't shouting at all. He clutched Roman Candles and aimed them at the feet of confused tourists, chasing them away from the pier.

61

In a kaleidoscope of shifting bricks, peeling wallpaper, and old rusty pipes, the All merged together, and Zelda found herself standing in a house of confusion, a house of bent time. Paisley-patterned walls fused with a cabin's log beams. A radiator hissed beside an elk-skin rug. In the kitchen, an old Frigidaire shared space with a gas oven, the door open as moldy roast sizzled upon a bouquet of rot. And in the living room stood the fireplace her grandparents had spent the evening next to.

Behind it all, a TV hissed, its black and white screen painting the walls in static patterns.

"—not an emergency but a natural phenomenon. We apologize to our viewers for the disruption."

Zelda hurried down a hall, halfway through the living room, when she realized she wasn't alone.

"I'll see what I can do about dinner, love," a woman said. "And I'll take care of the baby."

The young woman squatting by the TV could have been a poster child for a decade long past. She wore a full-skirted dress cinched at the waist, with a polka-dot pattern down to her knees. Gorgeous red curls curtained slender shoulders. Rosy cheeks and pink lipstick filled out her face.

Yet there was an unhinged desperation as she adjusted the TV's antenna and tuned its knobs. "I told you, honey. I told you," she muttered. "I expect things to be taken care of when I get home. Just what the hell is it that you do here all day?"

Another twist. The static worsened.

Chester's warning echoed, "If they can see you, they won't ever forget."

Slowly, quietly, Zelda tiptoed past the woman, toward the front door. Then: a tinkling sound at her foot, then a clanging.

The baby rattle she'd kicked came to a stop at the foot of a dead body.

The man lay askew in a recliner, his suit stained crimson. Half of his face was twisted in a grimace of surprise. The other half speckled the wall.

"Why isn't the dinner ready, Cheryl?" the woman said. "Why is Jessica always crying?"

The woman—Cheryl—jerked the antenna back and forth, back and forth, her fingers red and trembling. A voice seeped in between TV stations.

"—this is Point Greywood to base. Over. Point Greywood to base. Do you copy?"

With a scream, Cheryl reached over to the table and raised something dark and metallic. Even in the twisted acoustics of the All, the revolver's peal was deafening. Zelda screamed as the woman filled the TV with bullets.

The hissing pop of the dying TV filled the room. Somewhere, a baby cried.

Cheryl turned her tear-stained face toward Zelda.

Damn, she saw her.

"It never ends," she whispered. "It. Never. Ends."

She raised the revolver and pointed it at Zelda.

"You'll see soon enough."

As she swung her aim past Zelda, both their gazes stopped on the same object. But only Zelda closed her eyes. Because an image burned its way into her mind as the barrel lit up the room.

A crib.

One shot boomed out. Then another, followed by the heavy thump of a body hitting the floor.

Silence stretched on.

Oh God, why did she...

From the darkness beyond Zelda's clenched eyelids, the static-laced voice returned. "Well, folks, it looks like we're getting reports of interference for our station affiliates up north."

Zelda opened her eyes.

The TV was on, no bullet holes or broken glass marring its screen. Behind a warped curtain of snow, a football game flickered. The cry of an infant returned.

"Dang it, I thought you said that TV guy was going to fix the darn thing."

The man in the chair rose, no longer dead but simply inconvenienced. He passed Zelda without giving her a glance, then kneeled before the screen.

"Harold, you really should see this." Cheryl's voice drifted in. "It's quite something. You *need* to see this."

She stood on the porch, her polka-dot dress billowing in the stale breeze of the All. Eyes upturned and as wide as a child's, she whispered, "Me? Yes, of course I know where he keeps it. Are... Are you certain? Well, I suppose he has been awful moody."

"Cheryl, dammit, make yourself useful and gimme a hand; I'm missing the second half."

Cheryl brushed past Zelda with a soft "excuse me." She walked right past Harold, too, who shouted, "And I thought we agreed on having supper ready—"

The gunshots echoed out and Harold fell back in the recliner, that same stupefied look on half his face. The infant wailed and wailed. Had it always been wailing?

"I'll see what I can do about dinner, love," Cheryl said and began twisting the TV antennas. "Don't worry, I'll take care of the baby."

Zelda sensed how the rest would play out. Hurrying onto the porch, she heard gunshots confirm the hellish script's ending.

But she forgot it within seconds.

Because her eyes rose skyward, like Cheryl's. The woman had been right; it really was something to behold. Something so terrible Zelda's jaw went slack. The Ruizes would never have known it, but they'd rented a house with one hell of a view.

Greywood Bay loomed as a fractured panorama of horrors reflected through the All.

To the east, flames swept down from the dry hills, golden threads engulfing Raven's Vally. This summer's fire.

To the south, a lumberyard shuddered and collapsed, piles of logs rolling over screaming workers and crushing trucks.

Northward, outposts of stone and wood came under assault by native people, their battle cries filling the air. Severed heads topped wooden spikes while fur-clad frontiersmen kicked over totems and set teepees aflame.

To the west, steamboats splintered and sank as boilers exploded. Great schooners crashed upon rocks, spilling cargo and wailing sailors into violent waters.

Dozens. Hundreds. Perhaps thousands or more. Misery and tragedies piled upon each other and played out in torturous loops.

The All.

Zelda understood it now.

It was the town's tragedies, collected here all at once.

Her body froze, terror gripping her muscles as new horrors emerged.

In the town square, a group of shouting ranchers shoved Chinese merchants up a rickety gallows. With cruel efficiency, they tightened nooses and pushed them forward to the cheers of a mad crowd.

Down Main Street, an old bus careened through a farmers market, crushing stalls and vendors alike.

Where Coogan's Wharf met Sunset, the old anchovy canning plant collapsed in on itself. Steel beams and roofing twisted as the structure slid down a muddy incline and into the bay.

The atrocities looped again and again, a never-ending symphony of suffering.

Looming over it all, like the roots of a feeding tree, tendrils ascended until they reached a twilight sky filled with the dark star and her eyes: J'harr.

With each new loop, her tendrils quivered, and her eyes brightened —a blood-gorged tumor, fed by the All.

Then her dark glare swept over Zelda, shivering her skin and softening her thoughts. A single eye narrowed and focused.

"Mmm... I warned you, little child, yes I did. You're no conqueror, not even a guest. This land is mine... and my foundation is ravenous."

Zelda felt other eyes upon her now, cold gazes dotting her skin. At the edge of the woods, three malnourished kids glared with dead, envious hunger.

"Warmth," they muttered.

Down the road, tortured faces rose in an overturned church bus, pressing their desperate cheeks to the cracked glass.

"Warmth," they chanted. "Warmth."

A wounded native brushed past her, his confused eyes meeting her own. Then came the fur trader with his bloody knife.

"Warmth," the fur trader grumbled. "Warmth. Warmth."

J'harr's dark glare was upon her, inside her, washing over her mind in black-violet shadows. Dissolving the very world around her. *"Run, little child. My prisoners see you... and they hunger."*

Zelda's eyes closed on their own. Yes, she could turn around, leave this town behind. She knew—somehow—that J'harr would clear the way. Phones would stop ringing. The whispers would fade. Even her twitching fingers might finally rest, no longer drawing the dead into her life.

Yes, she only needed to take a single step back.

But she remembered Chester's words in the garden, her reflection in the All. How did she look?

Fierce.

She forced her eyes open. Forced herself to meet each and every haunted pair that looked back at her. The fur trader, the dead kids in the woods, so many others, too, emerging from the fractured landscape.

The All. It's like a record and we are the needle.
We don't move through the All.
The All moves through us.

"Hey!" Zelda shouted. "Hey, everyone! Over here!"

The wounded native twitched, but something changed in his eyes. His tortured gaze softened.

"Over here!" she shouted. "All of you!"

Limping, the bloody native reached out a trembling hand. She wasn't sure what he said, but he repeated it again and again. It sounded like a question.

Then came the fur trader, his knife shaking in his grip. "You... You behold me, child? You remember me?"

"No, I don't know you," Zelda said. "I don't remember any of you. But if you'll let me... I'll try."

Slowly, nervously, the fur trader reached out. Their fingers connected. It was cold—his touch—colder than anything Zelda had ever known. It slid under her skin.

Her body arched and twisted, every instinct resisting and screaming out to pull back.

We don't move through the All.
The All moves through us.

The frigid touch of centuries of death moved up her arm now, up into her shoulders. Her breath grew heavier, sharper, leaving her lungs in frosty gasps.

We don't move through the All.
The All moves through us.

Then it was inside her, crystallizing deep in her chest and forming a frozen cage around her heart.

So cold. So cold. So cold.

Because that's what it was to be forgotten. To have existed. To have been snuffed out.

The memory came to her as the simplest of things: a street sign. One she'd skateboarded past daily on her way to school: *Anderson Lane.*

Next, an old plaque on a rock at the edge of a park, something she'd leaned her skateboard against: *John William Anderson established the first trading post here in 1824.*

And a fading store at the forgotten end of the mall, where a bearded pioneer made up a logo: *Anderson Trading Company*.

She laughed. Because the memories weren't gone, not entirely, just transformed by time. Little actions still rippling down through the centuries. The town was tortured, yes, but as long as it existed, its history lived on. There were memories everywhere; she'd just never known how to look.

So cold. So cold. So...

"So warm," the fur trader said. "Funny, I'd forgotten how warm it feels... to be remembered."

With each shivering beat of her heart, the icy cage in her chest melted. High above, a hungry tendril sizzled and broke free and withered from existence.

She carried the light; that's what Chester had said. She'd long thought it a warning. But it wasn't. Because with the right light, one could do quite a lot.

Perhaps they could warm up a small part of this town.

"I see you," Zelda shouted. "I see you all. Help me remember."

There were others now, so many more hungry dead emerging from the smoke and fog. A fireman, his suit half-melted to his skin. An old woman, her body wrapped in seaweed. Cheryl with her polka-dotted dress and Harold with his loosened tie and a crying infant in his arms.

"Warmth," Cheryl said.

"Warmth," Harold repeated.

Even the native held out his hand and spoke the word in his own tongue.

She met their touch with her own. She let their memories flood her mind, feeling their torment and terror, their confusion and cold touch. They crowded in and almost crushed her.

Almost.

More tendrils sizzled, little filaments crumbling and decaying and burning off like the morning fog. The sky shuddered and twitched. From the dark cosmos beyond, J'harr's eyes squinted.

"Ah, look at you, Zelda Ruiz, so proud of your pruning. But I've carved voids through worlds that would shatter your mind. I was ancient before light touched your skies."

She was right; Zelda knew it. There were thousands of tortured souls here, perhaps more. Countless lost and forgotten, limping or shuffling or crawling their way through the All.

Sophie Saperstein and Diana Betancourt emerged from the woods. Randall, that security guard who Tased Chester, shuffled out from a burning basement. Dozens more emerged from the fog and smoke. There was Detective Brown, too, giving Zelda a slight nod that filled her with courage.

"Mmm... you think yourself a protector? You think yourself strong. Go on, child. Tug on my roots and see how deep they're dug in."

They drew closer... Closer.

Zelda, who had craved what so many her age wanted—to be left alone—now found herself turning to others. Making room for them. She met the sorrowful gaze of the dead. She opened her arms and opened her heart.

"I don't know if I can carry you all," she said, "but I'll try. I just need you to carry me, too."

62

Ben Thomas knew the touch upon his cheek the moment he awoke: a wretched black-violet light. He didn't know how he knew this. Only that some deeply scarred part of him—a primal instinct rutted into his soul over decades—understood the sick caress of such colors.

And what its arrival meant.

He lay in his bed, shivering. He clenched his eyes. Despite his deep faith in science, he prayed.

And still that light encroached. It crept through the bedroom walls where the words *I CANNOT LEAVE* were etched in never-ending reminders. It oozed through the beams of the ceiling, now twisting and shaking. It separated the very bricks of the lighthouse.

Now, it seeped through the skin of his eyelids, bathing his mind in looping torments: shipwrecks crashing, a sky filled with eyes, and a circle of inhuman shapes on a beach all chanting.

"Glima dil'im, sky'une voka'rr zathule n'ga vey'eel."

His soul was worn down, nearly spent. He no longer had the energy to call for help, for no one answered. This was his prison; his fearful body knew it.

A prison forgotten by all.

Then he heard her voice, so soft he almost mistook it for the groaning lighthouse. A girl's voice he remembered from so long ago. It was a quiet voice.

But it was powerful as well.

Ben threw off his blankets, raced out of the bedroom and down the winding stairs.

"... to Point Greywood. Can you hear me?"

He threw open the radio room's door and grabbed the mic. His voice shook as he answered the transmission.

"I can hear you. I can hear you loud and clear."

"Ben, listen to me. I need you to open the door. Can you do that?"

He wiped his moist eyes. "Yeah, I can do that."

He raced down the stairs, past bricks shaking with that warning: *I CANNOT LEAVE.* Past infinite words he never remembered writing. Down stairs his body knew. His mind spun with disbelief, because he was crying now, laughing too, and he didn't care. Someone *had* heard him.

After so long, someone answered his call.

With a slide of the latch and a twist of the handle, he threw the lighthouse door open.

Then he recoiled.

Because there wasn't one person here, but dozens. A dead-eyed audience stood upon the rocks and damp soil, upon the very steps that led inside.

A beautiful woman with red hair and a polka-dotted dress.

A fireman, burn-scarred and smoldering.

A leather-clad native with battle-weary eyes and bloodied skin. And so many more.

They stared at him now—sailors and factory workers, the young and the old—eyes bright with determination that he envied.

And then they turned, something rising behind them, above them. With tender hands, they reached up and passed a young woman over them.

They carried her forward.

Yet he sensed that she was carrying them, too. In their own way, they were all carrying each other.

Her mismatched shoes came first. Her skinny legs followed. With gentle hands, they placed her down on the threshold of the lighthouse. Ben knew her, this girl from his dreams. He even remembered her name.

"Zelda. You came back for me."

"Told you I would."

"I thought I was alone."

Her ephemeral smile filled him with hope.

"No, you're not alone," she said. "Not anymore. Take my hand. We've got the town with us."

63

Entering the lighthouse, Zelda felt the very structure shudder and bend. Bricks squirmed and rattled as railings twisted free from the posts. The walls breathed while eyes peered between cracked concrete and stone. Even the air grew putrid and warm, the breath of the dead.

Because this wasn't a lighthouse, not on this side of the All. It was a living *thing*—an organ—alien and spiteful and hungry. An appendage of J'harr—both connected yet separate—no more a lighthouse than Zelda's own teeth. This tower, this effigy, was merely the form her mind filtered through sanity's prism.

But if it was an organ, Zelda wondered, could it be wounded? Perhaps even blinded and starved.

Yes, she had just the place in mind.

She turned to the ghosts crowding through the door. "Can you help me to the top?"

The dead townsfolk looked up. As their gaze swept the tower shaft, the structure trembled. Blocks of stone crumbled and fell. With a groan, a crushing slab broke free from the wall and tilted toward her.

Then it teetered and paused.

There, crouching against it, the fireman, Harold, and Detective Brown held it back.

"Go, Zelda," the detective said. "We're all with you now."

Zelda squeezed past them and up the spiral steps. Looking down, she caught a final glimpse of the three—struggling, struggling—before the wall finally collapsed.

"Hurry!" Ben shouted.

She shimmied along the wall and around the collapsed hole outside the radio room. The doorframe sprouted teeth and lashed out with dozens of thin tongues, coiling her wrists. The radio room shook, tiles cracking to form a gnashing maw. From deep within, J'harr's hungry pups circled and growled.

Then the native and the fur trader pulled Zelda back. They swung their blades, hacking and slicing the coiling tongues apart. With a shiver and a shriek, the doorway distended, swallowing them before sealing itself off.

Another floor, where the stairs stretched and doubled.

"Fifteen!" Ben shouted. "It's a trick of the mind. There's fifteen steps, then the landing. Close your eyes. I'll take you there."

As his cold hand clasped her own, their memories entwined. She was standing on the pier at Coogan's Wharf, the wind in her hair as a college student squeezed his palm. She was smiling, posing for a photo before sunset.

And Ben, she could feel his eyes peering out through her own.

Seeing the missing-person newspaper ad with the word *SPIKED* scribbled in red.

Seeing that very photo of himself on the pier, Janice Thorpe's name on the signature line.

Seeing her sad, desperate eyes, three decades older in the mall as she asked Zelda if she heard the ringing phone.

And the sadness as Zelda lied and said no.

Then they were at the top of the stairs. The legion of dead was thinning out, shadowy hands pulling them back down the steps. The tower fought back with everything it could: walls parting to release hungry pups, the floor collapsing underfoot, railings twisting into barbed tongues. Yet through it all, the dead pried the lantern room open.

Held the door open for Zelda.

Ajar. Ajar. Ajar.

"I remember," Ben said. "I think I knew it this whole time. I just didn't want to admit it. I lost her the moment I canceled our date."

"I'm so sorry," Zelda said. "She never forgot you."

Somehow, the smile that crossed Ben's face broke Zelda's heart into pieces yet mended every crack. Somehow, she was stronger because of it. Stronger because of them.

"Go!" He strained, holding the door open against the tearing fingers of black violet. "Go and let go!"

The stairs fell away and the walls sagged. Like a cinching knot, the lighthouse twisted in on itself, crushing Ben and a dozen others.

But not Zelda.

She let go of his hand—let go of them all—and stepped into the lantern room's oozing glow.

For a moment—or an eternity perhaps—Zelda drifted within an inky liminal void. She sensed something before her. Stretching her hand out, she brushed the darkness aside.

Then, light.

She found herself looking out—looking at... what was this? Herself, she realized. A mound of green objects rolled past her hand. Little vegetables, each growing rotten at her touch.

Impossibly, Zelda looked at herself.

This was not a reflection—the Zelda peering back—but herself nine months and two haircuts younger. She had a childish twinkle in her eyes. The dark glare of J'harr hadn't found her.

Then her uncle Mark peered back, too, wrinkling his nose. "Ah, good eye, Zelda. See? You're a natural."

This moment, she recognized it. A spring day in Whole Foods a week before her suspension. They had been shopping and she'd seen something deep in the produce.

Something like fingers stretching back.

No...

Then the darkness split. Shadows unraveled into vibrant beams, splitting and refracting as colorful threads. They bent and spread. They speckled the walls of a cozy room in pastel patterns. They slid over futons and cushions and across a shrine, then settled upon the crossed legs of a woman locked in meditation.

Annie Paxton, Zelda's neighbor, who always had some gossip to share with her parents.

Annie Paxton, who had strong opinions on auras and feng shui and the healing properties of crystals.

Annie Paxton, who nearly tore herself to pieces climbing through Zelda's bedroom window.

Who had warned that something was coming.

As J'harr's hue shadowed her face, Annie's widening eyes met Zelda's through time. "My gods," she whispered, "what have they done to you, child?"

Zelda felt her skin stretching, tearing, her body becoming a billion filaments of shadow and light. Her mind spun loose, unanchored in a storm of endless time.

Was she the dark shape Ali's drone captured that summer day as they played in the park?

No...

Was she the reflection Sophie Saperstein saw in a mirror as she watered her hanging fern and leaned too far on the ladder?

Please no...

Was she a glint of light on the window of her family's overturned car, her mother reaching back on that terrible day?

No. No. No.

Zelda's mind reeled in the darkness, impossible questions tearing open loops in her thoughts.

Had she brought herself here by trying to warn others?

Had she been haunting her own past?

Had she been trapped here forever, a prisoner of her own crumbling mind?

Psycho.

Zombie.

Zelda.

But no.

She had Ali and Maura, Ms. Layne and Chester. She had her grand-parents, too, with their flawed love. She had dozens of dead souls behind her, infusing her with their trust, carrying her forward as she carried them, too.

She had Uncle Mark, who needed her now most of all.

And that was it. With a whimper, the last of the black violet peeled away, and she found herself in the lamp room. Twelve feet of glass loomed in the center, brass frames clutching curved prisms around a central lens, hungry and pulsating with shadows and light.

Like the lighthouse itself, Zelda knew what she looked upon was more than optics and glass. It was a heart and a hole, an eye and a finger. It was a mouth, greedy and feeding. And it was a wound most of all, one rancid and festering and bridging both worlds.

Surrounding her, a dozen wide windows offered a 360-degree view. The endless ocean and the rocky coast that she loved. Cliffside estates and that hidden cove. Far below—so far it spanned worlds—a circle of inhuman creatures gathered around a black altar, where a man's shape lay splayed, squirming and chained.

Zelda, who had once thought her parents invincible, realized she'd fallen into the same misgivings about Uncle Mark. Now, as she saw him bruised and battered, the rage burned inside her, stiffening her back and giving movement to her fingers.

J'harr, with her sky full of eyes and infinite dark glare. Zelda turned her own glare right back. Then she said, "If you're so hungry, you better eat quick."

She didn't know all the words Chester had written or studied. Maybe someday she would. But he'd shown her a few, and for now, it might be enough.

Raising her finger over the first window, she traced a symbol in the salt-frosted glass. Four little curves and two lines. She said the command, not with her lips or her throat—not at first. She brought it forth from that place of warmth deep in her chest. Her voice, soft in one world, roared here in the All. For others spoke with her, through her lungs and her lips and her heart most of all.

The All Tongue.

Yeah, Chester was right; it was fierce indeed.

It cracked prisms and glass, and it snuffed out the dark light.

64

With J'harr's blessed glow caressing her skin, Bibi Boyle savored this threshold moment; renewal was at hand. One hundred and seventy-four years. Each borrowed hour knotted her true flesh, twisting her hidden structure into something she no longer understood. A being above human frailty and form. A being *beyond* it.

And perhaps one day soon, a being beyond time itself.

As the rejuvenating beams swept over her, she watched those knots and tumors fade. Another sweep of the light, and her human skin emerged, youthful and effervescent and dimpling in the breeze. Yes, she felt it: five decades more, maybe six. Like the eclipse, her body was in perfect alignment.

Another sweep, and the garbled moans of old throats and cancerous lungs gave way to cries of laughter and joy. Young voices filled the crisp, salty breeze.

Doc Mitchell shed his vestigial wings. Mrs. Rutherford's quills shrank and retracted into her smooth, strong spine.

Councilman Brand's crystalline shell cracked and shattered, amber shards revealing his full cheeks and cleft chin. She'd almost forgotten how handsome he was, like those silver screen stars they'd once known. She'd be sure to seek him out in the orgy that always followed.

Yes, she'd try new things for this fresh season ahead. No more writing simple stories for simple minds. She'd grown tired of it just as she'd tired of preserving the town's history for those who only thought of tomorrow. As she'd tired of buying up land and toiling the soil. Tired of pressing grapes and fermenting wine. Tired of sending bottles and casks off to the world's farthest corners.

There were decades ahead of her now; so much more to learn and to become. But first, time to pay their blood debt in screams.

She ran her finger over the blade, testing its edge on her supple skin. It would cut deep; it always had.

She pressed her youthful palm against Mr. Fitzsimmons's palpating chest, considering where to begin. The kneecaps, perhaps, with their rich bundles of nerves. Maybe an eye, just to hear him shriek as she took him apart. She smiled, remembering his curt words.

Yes, his tongue would do nicely.

She was pressing the blade to his lips when she saw it: a curious flicker across the mirror-black cove. She hesitated, her eyes rising to the lighthouse.

There it was again, the dimming of J'harr's light.

Like someone had painted over one pane of glass.

A second pane darkened, then a third. She squinted, her flawless vision narrowing in on the lantern room, where the silhouette of a young woman traced a symbol against the salty glass.

"No."

Zelda, she knew the All Tongue.

Bibi shrieked, "No, wait—stop her!"

She didn't feel the blade tumble from her hand. She didn't feel anything above her wrist, except that pain beside her thumb that had plagued her for years. She fumbled around the cold sand for the knife, but her vision grew hazy in the cove's dimming light.

"She's blocking... our light! Move!"

Bibi stumbled down the beach until a sharp pain wracked her ankle and white fire bloomed before her eyes. The sand rose up and smacked her, knocking a wheezing breath from her lips.

"Sss... Stop her!"

She cradled her crooked ankle as varicose veins bulged to the surface of skin fast-bruising and peeling.

"Stop her!" she wanted to scream. "That girl is blocking our light and J'harr hasn't fed. Stop her, you fools!"

But now her words were heavy and wet. Teeth tumbled from her gums, a dozen bloody pebbles salting the sand. A drooling cry: "Thop... tha... guuurl!"

There was no one upright to stop her.

Councilman Brand rolled and gasped, his blistered lips making little O's.

Fitch wriggled and crawled toward the shoreline, wet ribbons dripping from his face. "My eyes! What happened to my eyes?"

And Mr. Osmond—her dear faithful butler—tried to hoist Mrs. Rutherford up but found his own arms degloving.

They screamed with dry throats and dusty lips as Point Greywood grew dimmer and dimmer. And there she was, the young girl framed by one final window and J'harr's ravenous light. Zelda Ruiz was the last thing Bibi saw before seventeen decades caught up. Before her eyes rotted to dust and poured down her face.

But it wasn't the last thing she felt.

J'harr's servants—the mewling crabs of her nightmares—were hungry. Even Bibi's ruined ears could hear them rising from the cove's waters. Cooing and chattering *clickity click, clickity click*, the starving chorus scurried through the darkness, louder and louder.

No, she couldn't see those tortured faces bursting from the seams of their shells. But she could feel their claws and their pincers. And she could hear their lips against her ears, whispering two final words: *"Time's up."*

65

Of the many grotesqueries to emerge from the cove's mirror-black waters, Mark's eyes instinctually clamped, and his mind consigned the skittering human-faced crabs to a place of oblivion. Because if he looked any longer, he might draw their attention. If he met their maddening gaze, his thoughts would surely shatter.

The screams of the partygoers reached a raspy crescendo as the beasts feasted. Then, like the rumble of a passing storm, they faded. He was left to the cove's murmuring waves and a growing warmth on his battered cheeks.

He opened his eyes.

The eclipse was almost over.

The world brightened.

The only traces of the guests were the piles of clothes shed in ecstatic transformation. Fine jackets and dresses. Priceless bracelets and rings. Even that very blade that had nearly ended Mark's life. They all lay in scattered piles, the decades catching up. In a swirl of dust and rust and unraveling threads, the salty breeze carried them off.

With a tug, the brittle chains fell from his wrist. Another yank, and he freed his ankles. Limping, he made his way past the rotting bar, just another piece of driftwood bleached by the decades.

It took him ten painful minutes to work his way across the tide pools and down the shoal. He'd never seen the old lighthouse up close. As he crossed into its shadow, he noticed it looked weathered too, one storm away from collapse.

He spotted Zelda making her way down the muddy slope in the eastern shade of the tower. He stumbled and hurried, but he was fairly certain they'd broken two of his toes with the hammer.

Still, he tried.

Zelda raced to meet him halfway down the shoal. Her skinny arms wrapped around him, and they shivered together in the breeze. It was good, one of the greatest things he'd ever felt. To reach for his niece and find her reaching back even faster.

He tried to thank her, but the tears were flowing now. His tired vocal cords could only speak in hoarse whispers. Still, she understood.

"Uncle Mark, your face. Your fingers. Oh my god."

"It's nothing." She ran her fingers over his bruised cheek, beneath his swollen eye. "Nothing I couldn't handle." Then his knees wobbled, and he stumbled and fell.

She caught him and dug her shoulder beneath his armpit. "C'mon," she said. "We'll help you."

Her strength shocked him. "We?"

She glanced back at the lighthouse, where the eclipse was in its waning moments and the sun grew bright. Her gaze rose to the lantern room, the windows cracked and frosted, dusted black by the decades. A bird circled the tower and settled on a sagging railing.

"We," Zelda repeated. "I think that's how it works. We all carry each other."

66

Neither Mark nor Zelda had a phone, so they made their way up a flight of rickety stairs, took an old elevator, and followed a shadowy cavern whose musty scents put a sheen on his skin. They'd carted him through this very tunnel on the other side of the eclipse.

Occasionally, his legs locked up and his body seized. He shook for minutes. Zelda held his hand until it passed.

"I'm probably dehydrated," he said. "Don't worry."

She nodded, but he sensed she didn't believe him. He didn't believe himself either.

Inside the once-opulent manor, walls dripped with decay and decades of mold. Lichen coated the paintings and moss dangled from doorframes, curtains of billowing rot. Even the floor groaned, so they stepped lightly, scaring the occasional rat.

They only found one body, near mummified and resting in a rusted chair upon the very balcony Mark had first spoken with Bibi. The corpse sat facing the lighthouse, tatters of a black smoking jacket wrapped around a sunken leathery frame. Tufts of white whiskers dotted the dead man's upper lip, drifting off like cotton in the breeze. For a moment, old Harlan almost looked like he was smiling.

Then his dry body collapsed and the breeze carried him off, bone dust and rich fibers over a cove brightening in the glow of midday.

THEY FOLLOWED THE FAMILIAR RINGING OF MARK'S PHONE through room after room until they found the wine cellar's entrance. He lingered, the scent of torture wafting up from the darkness. As he touched the banister, his legs locked and the shakes overtook him. He couldn't go any further.

"Would you—"

"I'll get it," Zelda said. "Stay here, Uncle Mark."

He squeezed his fists and closed his eyes, a welcome blanket of shadows among the pain wracking his body.

"We've been doing this for centuries."

"We've had a long time to practice."

"Look at what you've made us do to you, Mark."

He must have blacked out, because Zelda was standing over him now. She held his phone in one hand and something dark and misshapen in the other. The old journal.

"Sorry, kiddo. They found it in the car."

She nodded, cracking the burned spine and thumbing through the ashy pages. Only pieces near the center remained. Whatever it had contained—the diagrams and drawings and entries dating back centuries—it was beyond any hope of salvage.

"It's just..." She glanced at the wine cellar. "There were other things in there. They tried to get you to talk, didn't they?"

He smirked. "They tried."

He unlocked his phone and checked the recent calls. He dialed the top number.

Stacey answered on the first ring, breathless. He could hear wind and commotion in the background. "Hey. I've been trying to reach you. I just..." She hesitated. "It's weird but... Weren't we supposed to go jogging this morning? We were, weren't we?"

"Sorry, I forgot." He leaned against an old chessboard and sighed. "Actually, I had a weird kind of morning."

"Tell me about it. I'm watching the cops arrest Maura and Ali. He was shooting fireworks at tourists on the pier. Where's Zelda?"

"She's with me."

"And where are you? You sound different."

"No, I'm just tired. Teenagers, right?" He winked at Zelda. "But if you aren't busy, we could use a lift."

"Of course. And, Mark, listen, it's cheesy, but... I dunno. Watching the moon and the sun and our little planet do their dance, I guess... Well, I missed you. I feel like sometimes I keep you a little too far away, you know? Anyway, I'm rambling. Where can I pick y'all up?"

Even with one eye swollen shut, Mark turned so Zelda couldn't see the tears spilling down his cheeks. "Larchmont Vineyards," he said.

"Sorry, where?"

"Larchmont Vineyards," he repeated. "We'll meet you in the courtyard."

"Got it. It's just... Is that north or south? I've never heard of the place."

PART VII

THE PROTECTOR & THE GUARDIAN

Let the earth reclaim my flesh and ill deeds. Let my sturdiest creations collapse beneath the forest's embrace. May the soil scour my name from these lands. May the mushrooms feed on my lament.

I retreat now, deep into the ancient groves, where the Light of Lights no longer soothes but scalds.

Eagerly, I build my tomb of absolution.

Gratefully, I await my final blanket of rot.

What hells have I brought to this peaceful, lost coast?

—Arthur Cummings, 1864

67

Mark spent three days rotating between surgery and the orthopedic ward and fighting off infection. On his left hand, his pinky had been amputated to the proximal phalanx, leaving nothing above the knuckle. His middle finger fared a little better; they'd cut it off at the middle phalanx.

The doctors did what they could, but without the missing fingers to reattach, there were only wounds to be debrided and assessments to be made. The skin grafts were harvested from his abdomen and inner forearm, locations that matched his tone and would heal with minimal scarring. Hours after the surgery, he stared at his odd hand from a warm haze of painkillers, amused he could feel phantom fingers flexing with joints he no longer possessed.

"You've suffered considerable trauma, Mr. Fitzsimmons," the doctor said. "This will be a lengthy recovery, with regular PT and exams. I hope you understand what you're facing."

"Not really." He pinched the bandaged gap between his index and ring fingers. Weird. It almost tickled. "But you can talk to my niece. I've deputized her with power of attorney."

The doctor smiled at Zelda. Yeah, they knew her already. She hadn't left his side since they'd arrived.

THEIR STORY—HASTILY CONCOCTED IN THE THIRTY MINUTES
it took Stacey to find Larchmont Vineyards—soon fell apart. No one
believed he'd been injured while attending a winemaking class. Not with
two months of sobriety behind him. But for the moment, no one
pushed the issue either. His wounds bought them some grace.

There were so many wounds.

While they had prepped him for surgery, Zelda caught a glimpse of
bruises and burned skin on his chest and his sides. Purple hickeys lined
his shoulders and spine. She thought of the suckers and tentacles in the
Historical Society basement. She thought of those inhuman forms on
the beach. And the rusty tools she'd found in the wine cellar: pliers and
hammers, chisels and tongs. A pair of charred bones in the ashy brazier
near the burned journal.

Bones about the size of two fingers.

No, she wasn't leaving the hospital until Uncle Mark left as well.
The staff knew that fierce look in her eyes.

The Ruizes picked up on it when they visited. Especially Uncle
Alejandro, who looked at her differently and kept more quiet than
usual. He didn't stay alone in the room with her.

But he did return her phone.

SWIMMING IN A COCKTAIL OF PAINKILLERS AND ANTIBIOTICS,
Mark dreamed he was walking upon a reflective chessboard. He carried a
shield. As he moved between pieces, his shadow stretched long—a
bright shadow—and it bathed a wooden pawn in its glow.

He wasn't sure why, but it reminded him of Zelda.

Then he screamed himself awake, tearing at wormy fingers coiling
tight to his arm. Something stringy hit the hospital floor. His vein
burned.

Shit, he'd pulled out the IV.

Gathering his senses, he scanned the empty room, searching for
shapes among the shadows.

Bibi.

Fitch.

Councilman Brand.

A dozen of the Greywood Bay gentry.

He had seen them, bitterly watching from beyond that chessboard's edge, their skin sloughing off to reveal inhuman forms. Yet with each breath, their memories evaporated. The more he tried to recall, the more he realized he wasn't even sure what color Bibi's hair was. Or whether Fitch had taught science or math.

He found five fingers on a tray beside his bed near Zelda's homework. Each was soft and pink in the moonlight. He picked one and turned it over in his bandaged palm.

Sample prosthetics. Cute.

He limped his way to the bathroom and winced through a midnight piss. He flushed the toilet, glad Zelda was gone for once. He found himself crying in the dark.

The things they had done to him over twelve hours. They hadn't just broken flesh and bone, but something deeper. He wasn't sure what it was, or if he'd ever recover.

He told himself he had to. For her. For each other.

He left the bathroom light on, the safe glow of his own lighthouse in this storm of pain and discomfort.

He found Maya sitting in the chair Zelda had spent the past several days warming. Even in the moonlight, she was a picture of death: rigid flesh speckled with decay, a complexion as lifeless as the floor. Yet her eyes still sparkled, twin embers of warmth. They met his in the darkness. Her pallid lips stretched into a smile, soft and grateful.

"Hey, sis," he said.

She turned the bedside lamp on for him.

And then she was gone.

Mark's fever broke within minutes.

RESTLESS AND AWAKE, HE THOUGHT OF LEAVING. MAYBE THE hospital, or maybe Greywood Bay altogether.

This isn't your town.

These aren't your people.

Whatever you think it is that you're building, you're mistaken.

It took him a few moments to put on his hospital slippers. In the hall, he found Zelda standing in the cool glow of a moonbeam by a door at the end of the ward. She looked tiny, swaddled in her hoodie, hands buried within.

"How you feeling?" she whispered.

"Good. Better actually. How long was I out?"

"Sixteen hours."

"Seriously? At least I didn't sleep through Christmas."

"The doctor said it's something called neurogenic shock. Oh, and they left some artificial fingers to check out."

"I saw. You know, maybe I'll just lean into the look." He raised his wrapped hand. "You kids can make up a name for me, like Dr. Claw or —*fuck...*"

He squeezed his hand until the shivers passed and the searing pain dulled to a low throbbing. Sadness dampened Zelda's eyes.

"I'm really sorry, Uncle Mark."

"Listen to me. You've got nothing to be sorry about, okay?"

"I could have been faster—"

"Or you could never have come!"

A night nurse leaned out from the station and shushed them. Mark put his wounded arm on Zelda's shoulder and steered her to an alcove.

"I went off on my own like an idiot. What's one of the basic rules of *Critical Mass*?"

"Never play a healer?"

He let out a low chuckle. "No, but that's close."

He couldn't quite remember Bibi or the others, but he could now see J.C., sharp in his mind's eye. Mark had been visiting Alder Glen for the holidays. They'd gotten buzzed off a bottle of *orujo* he'd brought from Spain. Thinking back, he realized it had been exactly three years to the very hour. While Zelda and Maya had slept, J.C. passed Mark his phone, excited to show him this new game his company was making. And he'd said—

"The first rule of *Critical Mass*," Zelda whispered. "Never solo what you can do with your team."

The father's words from the daughter's lips.

"Your dad was pretty proud of that part," Mark said.

"Yeah. He really was."

Mark glanced to the hall and the door beyond, where the sign read *BURN WARD*. He said, "Feel like telling me why you're here? And why your hands are shaking inside your hoodie?"

Zelda's gaze drifted over the empty hall, stopping occasionally as if something else met her eyes.

"It's complicated."

"More complicated than a coven of interdimensional cultists, or whatever they were? C'mon, Zelda. We need to trust each other. Open communication, from now on."

"Okay. It's just..." Her hand slid the burned spine of that book out from inside her hoodie. She flipped through the ruined pages. "I'm not sure what I'm supposed to do."

"Whatever it is, we'll figure it out. I don't care if that means leaving tonight. We'll do it together. Deal?"

"Deal. Except for one thing." Her eyes hardened. "We're not leaving, Uncle Mark. Greywood Bay is our home."

68

To an electronic remix of "O Holy Night," Mark watched his niece open her final Christmas present: a gift certificate to Anderson Vintage, a sewing kit, and a coffee-table book on mid-century American fashion.

"If it's too old-fashioned or cringe, we can return it," he said. "I wasn't sure—"

"It's awesome." Zelda ran her finger over the cover and turned through the glossy pages. "How'd you know I like Vivian Maier?"

"How else? I had Ali hack your phone." He flagged down the waiter for more coffee. Uncle Alejandro's eyes lingered on Mark's hand and the dressing that concealed the true depths of his wounds.

"Speaking of Ali…" Stacey reached for some breadsticks. "Guess whose mom I bumped into this morning at city hall? That little stunt didn't go over well with the tourism board." She dipped the breadstick in the oil as her curious stare lingered on Zelda. "I sometimes wonder what adventures you kids get into. But I'm not sure I want to know the answer."

Zelda shook her head. "Probably not."

The meal passed in a blur of polite conversation: what classes was she taking this winter term? What was her favorite subject? What clubs was she joining?

The Ruizes did most of the talking, which was fine. Even five days later, Mark's vocal cords still ached. And sometimes, when the Christmas songs grew quiet, he could hear his screams echoing in that dark, musty cellar.

Zelda slid a small box across the table. "Your present, Uncle Mark."

With clumsy hands, he fumbled with the ribbon but soon got it open. He caught a nervous glimmer in Zelda's eyes.

Yet when he saw the box's contents, his voice hitched in his throat and the restaurant's lights grew misty and haloed.

Cuff links.

She'd found him a pair of cuff links with old Spanish coins on the face.

"If you don't like it, we can switch the coins out. I ordered, like, a ton of different coins."

He ran his hand down the post and toggled the closure. "Hold up. You made this?"

She nodded. "I spilled some resin on the carpet, so the deposit might be screwed."

"Zelda, language." Her grandmother pinched her shoulder.

Yet there was a playfulness to the gesture. A year ago Zelda might have bristled at the touch, but colder things than her grandmother's fingers had been on her lately. Besides, there was a flash of kindness in the old woman's eyes. Maybe it had always been there, and Zelda just needed to look for the signs.

Mark removed his blazer. "Now I know why you told me to dress up."

Alejandro helped him fasten the cuff links through the convertible cuff. Mark nodded his thanks and turned them over for the table to see. Even Grandpa Ruiz let out a whistle.

***

CHRISTMAS LUNCH GAVE WAY TO MID-AFTERNOON DESSERTS. When Alejandro ordered a sweet wine, Mark found his cravings getting the better of him. He excused himself, went to the bathroom, and stopped by the bar on the way back. A glance around a fern confirmed it: he was out of the table's line of sight.

"Rémy Martin VSOP, neat please." The words left Mark's lips and the bartender gave a comforting nod. "Oh, and the bill for the window table."

When the cognac arrived, Mark savored the aroma drifting from the snifter. Ripe fruit. Vanilla. A hint of toasted oak. He opened his eyes to see Grandpa Ruiz beside him, his credit card already on the payment tray.

"Sorry, boss," the bartender told Mark, "but he was quicker on the draw."

Grandpa Ruiz gave Mark a friendly pat and signed the credit card slip. *"Un día a la vez,"* he said. *"Ni más, ni menos."*

Then he tossed the cognac in the fern.

One day at a time. No more, no less.

Beneath a canopy of Christmas lights and garland-wrapped lamps, Main Street sheened in foggy dampness. The Methodist church at the corner of Cummings and Vine was hosting a potluck, Roman and his family waving from a grill steaming with meats. Somewhere far off, birds called out from the low-hanging mist.

Mark held Grandma Ruiz's elbow while Alejandro brought the rental car around. As the door opened, Mark caught a glimpse of luggage stacked in the back.

"Wait, are you guys leaving?" Zelda asked. "I thought you were staying for the New Year?"

Grandma Ruiz smiled. "Uncle Alejandro misses his kids. And for me—*este clima está muy frío.* Too chilly."

While Zelda and her grandparents said their goodbyes, Alejandro gave Mark a knowing nod. "I really tore into you at the hospital, didn't I?"

Mark's shoulder stung as he shrugged. "You care about Zelda. You did what you thought was best."

"Yeah, I don't know. To be honest, I'm glad to get going. I've had a killer headache since I arrived. They're not putting something in the water here, are they?"

Not exactly, Mark thought.

Their gaze turned to Zelda, giving her grandfather a hug. "How do you do it?" Mark asked.

Alejandro smirked. "What, raising girls?"

"Raising anything. What's the secret?"

For a moment Alejandro said nothing, just nodding as if some private joke were playing out in his mind. "The secret, I think, is that there isn't any secret. Just a lot of gray hairs."

That was the last thing Alejandro said to Mark before he climbed behind the wheel of the rental car. Grandpa Ruiz settled in the back against a pillow and closed his eyes. He'd probably be snoring before they hit the coastal highway.

Only Grandma Ruiz lingered, fighting some internal battle. She took Mark's bandaged hand and led him a few steps away.

"*No te creo,*" she said. "What happened, I don't believe you. But if I ask, I will only get lies."

Mark fought his desire to say something, but he doubted his words would change her mind. They never had.

"There is still much to discuss with Zelda's well-being," she continued. "But for us..." Her gaze softened. "The other night I wake up and find Juan Carlos sitting there, by side of my bed. He was real, *tan real como tú eres para mí ahora.* He was... how do you say? Like a *paradoja*—both young and old at same time. This wasn't first time I see him, no, no. But I think... I think it might be the last."

She wiped her eyes. Even though it pained his wounded hands, he let her squeeze them.

"You think I'm crazy? Maybe I am. But do you know what he told me?"

Mark shook his head. He had no words, only his ears to listen with and his heart to try to heal the family's wounds.

"My son, he said, 'You need to stop worrying, Mama. Our Zelda, she's in good hands—the best hands. Even if those hands are missing a few fingers.'"

69

As the events preceding the eclipse began to fade and time marched forward, Zelda and Mark settled back into their familiar routines. Students arrived at the apartment to be tutored in Spanish or to have their essays corrected. Zelda caught up on late assignments and worked on extra credit. She was taking an interest in the town's history.

Sometimes the two of them talked openly, and sometimes they kept a few secrets to themselves. Occasionally, Mark would catch Zelda's eyes lingering on things: an old painting in city hall, an empty chair in their apartment, a window or mirror.

And sometimes Zelda asked him how his physical therapy was coming, or if he needed help opening a jar. He insisted he needed to learn to navigate the world with eight fingers. She refused to call him Dr. Claw.

But every now and then, she could hear Uncle Mark through the paper-thin walls, waking up with a scream and crying softly in the night. He slept with the bedside lamp on, always.

WHILE MARK PRACTICED HIS FINGER EXERCISES, A CERTIFIED envelope arrived with a postcard of a lighthouse and a handwritten note: *If you're on my side of the world, I owe you a drink.*

As his eyes scanned the postcard's location and the green, rugged coastline, a faint smile touched his lips.

Fanad Head, Donegal, Ireland.

McDermott made it home.

"Sláinte," Mark whispered.

AFTER SEVERAL DAYS OF SILENCE IN THEIR SHARED CHAT group, Zelda read a headline in the newspaper that she just needed to share: the Historical Society had burned down overnight.

She ran down the two flights of stairs and knocked on the Hadids' apartment door. Ali answered yet lingered inside.

He had lots of homework, he said, and thirty-five more hours of community service for creating a public disturbance. He was grounded into the next century. Mrs. Hadid watched from the kitchen as the scent of chicken biryani and lentil soup escaped through the door.

It was the first time Ali's family didn't invite Zelda in for a meal.

THEY CHATTED OCCASIONALLY OVER THE BREAK, ZELDA'S messages to Ali and Maura staying unread for longer and longer. Their parents probably blamed her, in one way or another. She supposed they were right. Since she'd met them this summer, they'd gotten into a lot of trouble together.

What none of them knew or ever found out—what the city's structural engineers discovered and quietly handled—were the anomalies discovered beneath Coogan's Wharf and the pier. Somehow, several key pilings had splintered and rotted to near failure.

As if hundreds of creatures had been chewing on the old wood and then migrated elsewhere.

IN A NEAR-EMPTY MALL AT THE EDGE OF TOWN, JANICE Thorpe closed her store early. It was New Year's Eve, and she was tired. The only customers for the past hour had been a group of tourists who mostly browsed and took selfies. Records and CDs were good for likes on social media, but they barely covered rent. She wasn't sure how much longer she could keep the place open.

But at least the phone wasn't ringing. In fact, as she turned off the lights and locked the door, it occurred to her the old pay phone hadn't rung in over a week.

Funny. A small part of her actually missed it.

She spotted a teenage girl in a vintage jean jacket and mismatched high-tops waiting by the fountain.

Standing, the girl said, "I owe you an apology. My friends and I, we were in the mall a few weeks ago."

"I remember them." Janice pulled her jacket tight and glanced around. This was probably a prank and they were filming her from nearby. Kids could be so cruel. "So where are they?"

The girl shrugged. "In trouble. They set off some fireworks at the pier and they're pretty much grounded."

"I read about that on Nextdoor. Didn't know that was them."

Then, it happened: the old pay phone's shrill bell echoed through the near-empty mall. It tightened her shoulders and shattered her focus. What the hell had they been talking about?

"It's okay," the girl said. "I hear it, too."

Six little words, yet they turned Janice's world on its head.

The years of therapy and medication. The doctor's visits. All the phones she'd removed from her home, from her business, from her life.

And all that had cut her off from.

She had to force her reply out. "You're not fucking with me, kid?"

The girl tapped her fingers in time with the ringing phone. "It's always the same message. 'Point Greywood to base—'"

"'Do you copy?'" Janice smiled. "What's your name?"

"Zelda," she said. "But don't worry about me. Why don't you tell me about Ben Thomas?"

THEY WALKED TOGETHER, JANICE IN HER LATE FIFTIES AND this strange teenage girl with eyes so inquisitive for her age and a voice quieter than most. Yet Janice soon found herself doing all the speaking —really talking for the first time in years—because it was the first time someone listened and believed her.

She told Zelda about meeting Ben in a symposium he taught on the physics of light dispersal. How he tutored her, helping her understand advanced concepts with patience. And how when she dropped out of grad school, Ben didn't consider her a failure like the other students. Sometimes, the smartest choice was to walk away.

That was a good thing, too; since she was no longer a grad student, he worked up the courage to ask her out on a date. She said yes on the spot. In her heart, she'd been waiting for months.

As they walked down the streets of Greywood Bay, she could almost see Ben's shadow here, alongside them. Their first date, where a cup of coffee became dinner. Where dinner became drinks. And then drinks became a stroll to the pier and a park, and before they knew it, it was sunrise and they'd walked the whole town and back.

Like time had simply stopped for them both.

Sure, Janice had other relationships over the years, and even an ill-fitting marriage. But she'd never connected with anyone as deeply. A glimpse of a future, stolen and erased.

Then Janice realized where they were: the corner of Sunset and Coogan, the wharf spread out before them. The Ferris wheel and gift shops. The food stalls with cotton candy. Workers at the edge of the pier affixed metal struts to the pilings.

Mostly, it was the memory that stopped her feet.

This was where they had their final date. Where they said goodbye but hadn't known it back then.

"I should head home," she told Zelda. "I'm sorry. I've taken up too much of your time."

The pier was packed with New Year's revelers: young couples holding hands, youthful and laughing. This wasn't her place, not anymore. It would be a half-hour walk to her duplex, and she didn't like the breeze here anymore.

"This is going to sound weird," Zelda said, "but I heard about your New Year's plans. Ben was supposed to meet you here, wasn't he?"

The girl's words dazed her. She hadn't gotten to that part. She hadn't told anyone about that in years. "How'd you know that?"

Zelda nodded to an old sticker-covered pay phone at the northern edge of the pier. "Because Ben told me."

Janice scoffed. This was a prank; she knew it. Yet the girl's kind smile calmed her nerves. One hesitant step at a time, Janice followed her to the old pay phone.

"I don't understand," she said. "Is he alive?"

Zelda answered, not with her lips but with an empathetic blink that confirmed her fears. Yeah, Janice knew; she'd known for three decades. But in this moment, the pain was fresh and her knees wobbled.

"Hey, hey," Zelda helped her to her feet. "It's okay. He told me it's okay. But I think he'd rather tell you himself."

The girl did the strangest thing, just a few quick gestures against the dusty glass with one hand—an infinity sign bisected by three lines and dotted in four places. Her other hand tapped her heart.

Then, the phone rang.

Janice's body locked up. All the thousands of ringing phones through the years, and now she was too nervous to answer. "What do I say?"

Zelda shrugged, and it occurred to Janice she was asking a fourteen-year-old girl for advice. Somewhere down the pier, a group of college kids cheered as someone won a prize at balloon darts. Beyond, the sun was beginning to set, the final rays of the final day of the year scattering, warm and golden.

"What do I say?" she repeated.

"I don't know," Zelda said. "Maybe you both say goodbye. And everything else."

With the bay winds tussling her hair and youthful laughter serenading her down the pier, Janice put the broken phone to her ear. When the voice spoke, a smile illuminated her face.

"Hey, Ben," she said. "What took you so long?"

She was worried her words might fail her.

They did not.

NEARLY A DOZEN MILES UP THE COAST AS THE BIRDS FLEW, a lighthouse ushered in a starlit evening at the edge of the continent, at the edge of this world. Bottles lazily clinked against rocks, scaring a crab into a damp hole. The soil around the tower's foundation—long bare of vegetation—showed signs of new growth. Seeds carried by gull droppings and the swirling breeze gave rise to green sprigs. Nature was catching up on lost time.

Here, on this misty patch of land, the angles stretched and echoes lingered impossibly long. The lighthouse door—a dented slab of metal welded shut decades ago—concealed two floors of poured cement. These weren't the only barriers starting to crumble. Even the radio room —long empty—was filling with shorebirds. Despite the strange shadows and the sense that something else was here, the shorebirds felt at home and built nests.

In that same room—but not the same lighthouse—a man listened to the voice he had been calling out to across time. He smiled and he laughed. He told her he was sorry; he never should have canceled their date. He never should have left to search for a star that didn't exist when he had something better.

What was she like now? he wondered. This woman he had known for only a few months when their future seemed intertwined. How could years have passed all at once?

Hell wasn't just a place, but a place of forgetting. Now, her voice was his way out. He could feel the connection fading, the signal breaking apart. Yes, it was time to hang up.

Time to let go.

He said goodbye and laid down the radio. He ascended the lighthouse to a room of cracked glass and symbols. The lens, broken from both sides. The seething light of his nightmares, snuffed out. Through the salted windows, the ocean loomed far below.

And the rarest of occurrences: Fata Morgana *and* shadow bands together. They painted the world in impossible hues.

Reds so vibrant they danced like Christmas ribbons upon the water.

Oranges as deep as the poppies growing along the coastal highway.

Yellows and pinks on the crest of each wave, precious gems only for him.

And something else—a green he'd never seen before, as emerald as the earrings he'd wanted to buy Janice for their fifth date or their sixth. When he had more money. When his research was done.

When.

A storm gathered from the east, not of clouds or wind, but feathers and wings. A swirl that soared over the old-money estates and dove along the cliffs. That danced over the tide pools and secret coves.

There were black oystercatchers with bright crimson bills. Western gulls as white as ice. Caspian terns and peregrine falcons and tufted puffins all flying together. And in the rear, the orange-crowned warblers. A flock so numerous the light dappled and darkened.

Ben smiled and closed his eyes, yet he could still see it all. The far horizon, a reflection so vibrant and perfect there was no ending or beginning, just shadows and light and a merging of worlds.

As the sky darkened and the colors faded, he was with them now— the greatest migration—soaring over Point Greywood and its empty lantern room. Yes, he was flying wherever they went—north or south or somewhere else.

Somewhere *beyond*.

70

On the first day of the winter term, Zelda scooped up her skateboard and backpack and slid down the apartment's railing. She waited outside Ali's apartment, too nervous to knock. After a few minutes, she hurried around the side and checked the bicycle cages.

His bike was gone.

She stopped by Maura's townhouse and discovered the same.

"Mmm... I told you there would be consequences," J'harr murmured. *"But you didn't listen."*

"Shut up," Zelda said.

She was getting better at ignoring the whispers. After all, she'd had practice with the ringing phones.

She skateboarded alone, aware of occasional glances from other students as she drew closer to campus. A few even pointed her out to their friends. She was getting better at ignoring them, too.

At the edge of the fields, by a car, an upperclassman shouted and waved her over. "Hey, I owe you an apology," Sam said. "What we did at that party, that was big time fucked up."

Zelda glanced around. She didn't see Finn or the others, yet she half-expected Arianna to jump out of a bush. Then she remembered Bayview's classes started last week.

"Listen, I want you to know that I'm sorry," Sam continued. "I guess... I don't know. People do dumb things to impress their friends. Or more like assholes that weren't really their friends at all."

Zelda thumbed her skateboard wheel. "Okay."

"So... we're cool?"

She shrugged. "I guess."

"Good. Great. Well, I'll catch you around sometime, Zelda Ruiz." Then he cinched up his backpack and locked his car. "Oh, and that dress you wore to the party? I never told you, but it was super awesome."

Zelda nodded. "I know."

She made her way to her locker as the first bell rang, switching her skateboard for a biology textbook and leaving her lunch on the shelf. When she closed the door, she found Ali and Maura standing there, awkward and nervous.

"It's the Zeldster 5000," Ali said. "Sorry we couldn't meet up over break."

"Or this morning," Maura added. The big girl glanced down at the floor and Zelda knew the bad news was still coming.

"So, we're like... not supposed to hang out anymore," Ali said.

Zelda swallowed. "All of us, or...?"

"Our parents talked to each other," Maura said. "It's bullshit, but... well, we've gotten into a lot of trouble together."

"I've gotten you into a lot of trouble," Zelda said.

"Same difference," Ali said. "Plus, I'm not really built for fighting ghosts or cults or... whatever."

"We've got to start focusing on college," Maura said. "My folks are freaking that it's going to, like, hurt my chances since we keep getting arrested."

"Detained, yo," Ali said.

"But maybe we can hang out at a party," Maura said.

Zelda forced a smile to her lips. "Yeah," she said. "At a party."

"Or track in the spring," Ali added. "I'm making Maura try out for the harpoon team."

"Javelin, Ali," Maura said.

The second bell rang, and the students hurried down the hall to their classrooms. Zelda went to the left, and Ali and Maura walked right. Then Ali doubled back and rushed over.

"Wait! I totally blanked, but I need to AirDrop you this stupid book."

"What book?"

"That old creepy journal, remember?" Ali swiped on his phone and tapped. "I only scanned like part of it, but it keeps making Elrond crash. This Necronomicon can't get off my phone fast enough. Here."

Zelda's heart raced as the file transfer came through: *FreakyAncient-TerrorTome.pdf*. There were over a hundred pages at least, nearly half the old journal.

"Alright, folks, let's go," Mr. Knowles called out, doing a sweep of the hall. "Zelda, you coming or what?"

She went to thank Ali, but he was already walking off with Maura, toward their first class. Zelda's heart hurt in this moment, yet something brought a flat smile to her lips.

Maura and Ali were holding hands.

ZELDA SPOTTED AN EMPTY SEAT AND MADE HER WAY TO THE back of the classroom. She ignored that Albert Einstein poster glaring at her with worm-ridden eyes. As she squeezed between desks, a few students stared, as if she was sick and contagious.

"Don't worry," Elliot leaned in and whispered. "It doesn't last too long."

"What doesn't?"

"You know, the rumors."

As her classmates talked and caught up, something tickled at her thoughts. What the hell was she forgetting?

She was by herself in the back of the classroom. Maybe this really was a preview of the years to come. Maybe J'harr was right.

"Mmm... So much more than you know. Only one of us has seen the future. Alone... Alone... Alone..."

Then two teachers stopped at the door: Mr. Knowles and her uncle. They exchanged words. Then Mr. Knowles laughed and entered the room. Uncle Mark lingered at the door, just long enough to spot Zelda and give her a wink.

Alone?

No, fuck that. She wasn't alone.

Not yet.

Not now.

And for this moment, that was good enough.

It was only when Mr. Knowles began taking attendance that she realized what was wrong. He taught earth sciences, not freshman bio.

"Hey!" She raised her hand and asked, "Where's Mr. Fitch?"

Twenty-three sets of eyes turned to her, confused and curious. Even Mr. Knowles cocked his head.

"Who?"

"Mr. Fitch, he…" Zelda hesitated, his name lumpy on her tongue. A few students shifted in their seats, as if his memory was almost there, so close… and then so far away.

She lowered her hand. "Nothing. Forget it."

And they did.

71

The thing about bureaucracy was that it worked slowly, but it still worked. And when it found holes, well, it moved a little quicker.

Like the acres and acres of land around Greywood Bay owned by trusts no one could untangle. Or the laborers who had been paid to pick grapes at a vineyard that didn't quite exist. At least, not in any shape to produce wine. And dozens of old, ramshackle houses and estates and condominiums, deeds signed by names forgotten by most.

But not by all.

It was on a Tuesday evening when the city council checked a section in its municipal charter and discovered an embarrassing oversight: they were short by one council member. The vacancy, laughed off and dismissed at first, was soon confirmed by a bewildered city clerk. It sent a murmuring ripple through the chamber.

Then Mark Fitzsimmons pointed something else out: *Municipal Bylaw 33.b-201.*

"Upon a city council vacancy," he read into the podium's mic, "Greywood Bay citizens are empowered to nominate an interim council member to serve until the next general election. This community nomination overrides all internal appointment mechanisms by the mayor or council."

A few council members sighed as their evening just got a lot longer.

"Mr. Fitzsimmons," the vice-mayor said. "I'm not sure it says anything about a self-nomination. But rest assured, we'll have the clerk double-check the bylaws."

"Actually, it's not for me." Mark glanced back at Zelda and Roman, Pavarti and several others seated among the Raven's Valley families. Even a few of his former students were still showing up. "Stacey Layne has been a fixture of the community for years," he continued. "I know it's more work for her, and I'll probably get an earful in a few minutes. But I'm sure she'll be great. If she accepts, that is."

It wasn't often that he saw Stacey blush, but it made his heart race. As he returned to the seat between her and Zelda, she shook her head.

"Oh, you bastard," she muttered. "I don't know how you did this, but you've released the kraken."

"I was kind of hoping that I had."

She stood up and addressed the council and the few dozen citizens in attendance. "If the community wishes, then yeah, I'll accept the nomination for interim council."

"I'd like to add my name as well," Mr. Abernathy said. "The city's been turning a blind eye to the raccoons, and it's high time we get down to business."

Twenty minutes later, Stacey won by a landslide.

FROM THE BASE OF THE TRAIL, MARK WASN'T SURE WHERE they were headed, only that Zelda had insisted they come here today. She had something to do. And something to show him.

As the trail crested a hill and they passed between a pair of fire-scarred redwoods, that's when he sensed what was coming: this was Raven's Peak. Looking at the valley below, he struggled to imagine there had ever been homes down there. The demolition trucks and cranes, the empty pits and fences. An entire community, scraped out of existence.

"Look at that," he said. "It's just... empty."

Zelda stopped at a boulder surrounded by charred stumps. "It's not empty at all. It's festering."

Then she loosened her backpack.

The letter and the package both arrived the day before last, delivered by a probate administrator. It was only a single page, handwritten on Pacific Manor stationery, notarized, and witnessed by someone named Freddy. The letter read *Zelda Ruiz gets it ALL*.

That "all" turned out to be a simple box urn containing Chester's ashes and a deed to his property just past the edge of Raven's Valley—a junkyard half-melted and an old Victorian house so smoke-damaged it still smelled like a campfire. Even from here, they could see its boarded windows and fences teetering on the edge of collapse. The house looked like a money pit, Mark thought. They'd probably have to take it down to the studs.

And yet the winter rains had cleansed the valley. New life was taking hold. Perhaps with time and their care, it might look like something they hadn't felt in months: a home.

As Zelda opened the box urn and pulled out the bag of Chester's ashes, Mark asked, "Should we say something?"

"I don't know what to say."

For a moment even the wind grew still and the hum of demolition machines faded.

She took a deep breath. "You were a link on a chain. You did your part, Chester. I hope I can do mine."

"You will." Mark placed his hand on her shoulder, his phantom fingers itching. "You can. You already have."

They watched the wind carry the ashes off fast, a fine gray powder that soon joined the fog and the cool winter breeze blowing in from the sea.

When it was done, Mark started back toward the trail. Zelda did not follow.

"Uncle Mark, there's another reason I came here. The real reason. At the hospital, at the burn ward, you said communication was important."

"It is."

"We have to trust each other."

"We do, Zelda."

"There are some people that didn't make it out of the fire," she said. "They're still here. I think they're stuck and we need to do something."

"Do what?"

She unlocked her phone and opened up a document. She turned the screen toward him. At first, he wasn't sure what he was looking at. Strange symbols and diagrams. Old words in an even older script.

The book Bibi had burned. "How the hell did you..." Then it clicked. "Ali scanned it. Clever."

"The thing is, I don't know what I'm doing," she said. "I'll probably screw it up. But I could use your help."

Mark didn't like the fear in her eyes. He wanted to keep her safe, to be her guardian. But maybe she needed to be something, too—something to others. Maybe the duties that bound them meant leaving safety behind.

"Of course I'll help."

As she smiled, he saw in her a glimpse of totality. Not just a four-teen-year-old girl on the cusp of becoming a woman. Not just an awkward teenager trying to rush into the future. Not just his sister's reflection. Or J.C.'s. Or her grandparents'. He saw both tenderness and strength, fear and fortitude, and so much more.

The world had been unfair to Zelda, burdening her with pain and loss. But maybe it was training her, too. And if so, he'd be there for her. Wherever they were headed.

"Okay, let's do this," he said.

Squatting, she began tracing those bizarre symbols in the soil. A triangle here. Two circles there. Something like a spiral and more.

With each stroke of her finger and each new line connecting the design, vague shimmers crept in at the edge of his vision. A bird took on a different hue, its feathers sticky with oil. A mossy redwood began to cinder at its base. And the sky, patched with scattered fog only moments ago, now hung behind a darkening blanket of—

Smoke.

Was that smoke forming over the sun?

"Take my hand," Zelda said.

He clasped her warm palm in his, and for a moment, her eyes glistened at the touch of his missing fingers. They each had their own scars. Maybe life had been training them both.

As she wrote something on his wrist with a pen, he asked, "What's this?"

"Lesson one," she said. "Some chains are for protection."

As she resumed her line work in the dirt, he realized the patterns surrounding them formed something like a circle. He marveled at the design when a man ran past them in short summer joggers. Where had he come from? And where was he going? The jogger glanced back, and Mark's stomach soured.

The man's eyes were two smoldering holes.

"What's going on?" Mark asked.

"It's hard to explain," Zelda said, "but this is the All. And we're going to start cleaning it up." She wrote a final symbol in the dirt. "Lesson two: sometimes we need to chase our own ghosts."

Then the peak of Raven's Valley—and Greywood Bay itself—peeled back to reveal a landscape terrible and beautiful, humbling and heart-breaking—a dreamscape, time-twisted and living, where forgotten histories played out beneath a sky bleeding in colors without name.

Mark's mouth fell open at all that he saw.

72

D r. Rhonda St. James welcomed her second-to-last patient of the day into her office and gestured to the couch. She was tired, her blood sugar was low, and a malaise had settled over her these past several weeks. She reminded herself even therapists fought their own mental battles.

But for now, she put on her friendly face. She liked Zelda Ruiz, even if the young woman played her cards close to her chest.

For the first ten minutes she asked probing questions and listened, finally pulling a few sentences from her.

"I'm sorry to hear about your friends," Rhonda said. "How does that make you feel?"

Zelda shrugged and stood up, her eyes drifting to the window and the street outside. Her neutral posture hinted at a storm churning within.

"How do I feel? My only two friends can't hang out because I always get them in trouble," she said. "Their parents hate me. It's two weeks into the winter term and I'm eating lunch by myself. Oh, and coach has me riding bench because our team can't afford another disqualification."

"I'd feel pretty lousy," Rhonda said. "And if that's how you feel, well, that's perfectly natural."

The words seemed to soothe Zelda, and after a moment she sat back on the couch. Sometimes that's all therapy was, just acknowledging the validity of emotions.

And yet something still troubled Rhonda. It wasn't what Zelda had said, but what she'd spoken around. A void her words had uncovered.

"I'm just confused about why you blame yourself," Rhonda said. "Earlier, you said Ali and Maura, they set off the fireworks, right?"

"Right."

"Weren't they on their own?"

Zelda squirmed, her right finger making strange little gestures, like she was tracing those nervous patterns again and again.

"No, I wasn't there," she said. "But that doesn't mean it wasn't my fault."

"How so?"

"Nothing. Forget it." Zelda caught Rhonda's gaze and covered her fingers. "I'm just tired. Uncle Mark and I took a trip, and we're still recovering."

"Oh, that's good. Trips are important. Where'd you go?"

Zelda reached out for a jellybean from the bowl on the coffee table. For a moment, Rhonda glimpsed discoloration on her forearm.

Was that a fresh bruise?

"It was more of a staycation." Zelda's sleeve fell, covering it up.

Rhonda glanced at the clock and did her best to hide her frustration. This was going to be one of those sessions where little got said and the doors remained hidden.

Yet that void...

Maybe it was time for a Hail Mary. A bit of sour mixed with the sweet.

"You know what phrase I hate?" Rhonda waited, but Zelda just shrugged. "Safe space," she continued. "That phrase implies the world isn't safe when the truth is we're statistically safer than we've ever been. But, Zelda, this room is a safe space. I just feel like we're in a holding pattern. You know what that phrase means?"

"It's when, like, planes are trying to land."

"When they're waiting for permission to land. You don't need my permission. These sessions, if you're not getting anything useful out of them, I'll tell the judge you don't need them. Because in my professional opinion, you probably don't. But if you need something or just someone who'll listen, you've got to give me something to work with."

With the honey laid out, it was time for something bitter. She chose her next words carefully.

"Or just keep lying," Rhonda continued. "You wouldn't be the first."

Zelda's eyes narrowed. It was like she had just returned to this room. "I'm not lying."

"Apologies, I misspoke. What I mean is..." Rhonda leaned forward. "One of my patients told me she lies for a living, but she does so to process the truth. I like that. 'Cause the real world—the heavy shit we deal with at school or at home—sometimes it's all distorted, hard to see what's underneath. Like a poor reflection. If a patient needs to make up a story, talk around the truth, hey, safe space, remember?"

Zelda's nostrils flared. "I really hate that phrase, too."

Rhonda smiled but left it at that. She'd said her piece, opened a door, and given her patient all the permission she could. She had other tools in her toolbox, but no energy to go digging. Mostly, she hoped Zelda could be kind to herself. The girl seemed to carry so much.

After a long silence, Zelda said, "This whole town's a bad reflection. People can't see what's on the other side."

"Denial pays my mortgage," Rhonda said. "Most people don't know they're in it. But it's part of the journey to a healthy mind."

"Or maybe they shouldn't know."

Interesting, Rhonda thought. Finally, a glimpse through the keyhole. "What do you mean?"

"Maybe what's on the other side," Zelda said, "is something so terrible it can't be let out. Something alive and alien, festering in the town's wounds. Something ancient, and obsessed, feeding on evil and pain. Maybe it's something a few people have tried to hold back. Something that cost them everything. Maybe there's, like, places where those wounds are weak and the scars are fresh. And maybe even this town's history is confusing. People and events swallowed up and forgotten, except for a few who remember them. Maybe this paradox chews at those people, growing like mold between the walls. And they say nothing because... who would listen? Who would even want to hear it? A therapist? A counselor? And most importantly, who would believe them?"

The words had all poured out, like a pressure release valve long shaking and finally twisted open. Just as fast as her patient had spoken, Zelda's expression hardened. She stuffed her hands into her hoodie.

"But that's just a story," Zelda said. "A lie to process the truth. Safe space, right?"

Rhonda cleared her throat. "Right. Of course."

She adjusted her clipboard and covered her palm. Her hand didn't stop shaking for the rest of the session.

LIGHTHEADED AND DRY-MOUTHED, RHONDA SAW ZELDA OFF and asked her final patient to give her a few minutes. She told him she needed to eat.

Mr. Fitzsimmons didn't notice the bowl Rhonda carried, a wooden antique that had sat on her shelf for years, unused and dusty.

Until now.

She locked the shared kitchen door behind her and turned off the lights. She removed the bowl's lid, carefully placing it in the sink. Hands trembling, she turned on the faucet.

She cursed herself for being so blind that she'd missed the omens.

The mark on her patient's arm wasn't a bruise, but a burn. The malaise that had come over Rhonda, it must have begun around the eclipse. Zelda's fingers, those weren't motor stereotypic compulsions at all. And the wounds in the town... Oh, yes, Rhonda knew them quite well.

She had even widened a few.

At the window, a single warbler stared back, blinking with oily, amethyst eyes. She met the ill-omened creature's eyes, then closed the blinds. Yes, she saw the signs now for what they were; they were in trouble indeed.

Unless...

Using her phone's flashlight, she watched as the cold water filled the bowl's mirrored cavity, base to rim. Her eyes grew heavy. She turned off the faucet and flashlight. She needed utter darkness for the next part.

And so much courage.

As she thrust her face into the scrying bowl, the frigid water assaulted her, clenching her shoulders and urging her eyes to clamp shut. She forced them not to blink.

Because the mirrors, they showed more than a shivering reflection now. They expanded.

First, with darkness. Then, a shadowed cavern thick with old-growth roots and rocks and bioluminescent fungi twinkling in the depths. There, in that dank, sunken vault, upon a forgotten throne of brambles and bones, a sleeping figure turned his mossy face toward hers.

"Who... am I?" his earthen voice moaned. *"Who... are you?"*

Her shaking hands gripped the bowl's rim, so close and yet distantly far off. She trembled in his ancient presence.

"And why... have you disturbed my rest?"

Rhonda opened her mouth and let the cold waters rush in, reeking of minerals and soil. It filled her and moved through her, giving form to unspeakable words.

"Arthur Cummings," she said. "I think I've found you a new vessel."

AFTERWORD

It's a curious thing, how a novel comes together. Sometimes the chapters write themselves, words becoming sentences, sentences turning into paragraphs, paragraphs forming scenes, and then chapters and stories. Sometimes you can see the chain connection, and it's as clear as a day without haze. Other times, there's so much nebulous mystery, you might as well be wandering through the foggy redwoods, brushing damp ferns aside and struggling to see your fingers through the mist.

By the summer of 2023, the first draft of *Tides of Darkness* was mostly written... or so I thought. As a reward, my wife, our dog, and I embarked on a road trip along the Lost Coast. We stopped at old sights and new, wandering misty beaches, exploring adorable towns, and visiting ancient groves where our pup gleefully marked every towering redwood he could find.

While having breakfast at a "brunch club" perhaps a bit beyond our financial strata, a woman in a salmon-colored blazer loudly complained about the tour buses, the out-of-towners (us, of course), all the new money, and the new ideas. Perhaps some of her complaints were warranted—I don't know—but it was her manner, so *insistent* that things were better before. Before what? I wondered. Airbnbs? The internet? Electricity?

In that moment, Barbara "Bibi" Boyle walked right into the story, and damn if she wouldn't leave. Hell, she'd probably organize a hearing.

Or carve me up on an altar.

One of the joys of writing such villainous characters is that they truly surprise you.

Did I know Bibi would be a cozy mystery writer? Not at first. But the minute Mark was in front of her bookshelf, it made sense. Here was an Angela Lansbury who knew where all the bodies were buried.

Did I know Bibi would send a grieving mother child-size coffins on the birthday of her dead kid? Of course not. But the moment Bibi imperiously shoved her way into the story, I knew the centuries had taught her plenty of cruel amusements she'd deploy.

As a writer, sometimes all you can do is set up the chessboard and let the characters make their moves. Zelda and J'harr. Mark and Bibi. Ben and Debra. Old Chester Halgrove and the various vessels for Grant Larchmont—they all took over, often in surprising ways. I believe that's where the real magic happens. Sometimes, I'm just sitting there, hallucinating and documenting the plays. If those plays surprise and delight me, chances are they'll delight you as well.

Thanks, as always, to my fantastic editor, Bodie Dykstra, for wrangling my errant commas and helping to refine my prose. I promise I'll try to dangle my participles less publicly. Thanks to the team at Damonza, who did another wonderful job on the design. Yes, books are judged by their cover, and they do some of the best in the business. A huge thanks to Tom Jordan for the audiobook. I consider him the voice of my words.

The following people have offered great help, suggestions, or simply listened to me vomit out ideas and nodded along: Tom & Sarah Rey, Mike Keane, who always offers great advice at a time I need it most, and the members of Ghoulish Gains, who have been insightful in their creative and business suggestions. Thank you, all of you.

Thanks to my Beta Readers who keep my facts in line & chime in when I wander off. Special thanks to Dr. Santos, Kay Clark, Matt Quinn, Chelle Pak, and Joanna Brody for going above and beyond. Thanks to Justin Boote for lending his flesh to a certain muddy body swapper. And thank you to my wonderful Street Team who share my words with the world. I'm the worst marketeer imaginable, and they truly help out. Y'all rock! Plus a huge shoutout to the Facebook community Books of Horror. They're refreshing glass of water among the parched wastelands of social media. My heart and bookshelf thank them. My wallet does not.

As always, thanks to my wife Marissa, who listens to me patiently on walks when I babble endlessly about "servant crabs with the faces of people" and stays up late at night reading early chapters. If you've read something you loved in this book, she undoubtedly had a hand in shaping it.

And thank <u>you</u>, dear reader, for continuing to follow Zelda and Mark, and visiting this strange, wounded town at the western edge of the continent, at the edge of this world.

More wounds are opening and the door is widening.

Ajar. A'jar. J'harr.

ABOUT THE AUTHOR

A child of the eighties, Andrew Van Wey was born in Palo Alto, California, came of age in New England, and lived as an expatriate abroad for nearly a decade. He currently resides in Northern California with his wife and their Old English Sheepdog, Arthas.

When he's not writing Andrew can probably be found mountain biking, hunting for rare fountain pens, or geeking out about D&D and new technology.

For special offers, new releases, and a free starter book, please visit andrewvanwey.com

facebook.com/andrewvanwey

instagram.com/heydrew

goodreads.com/andrewvanwey

bookbub.com/authors/andrew-van-wey

amazon.com/author/andrewvanwey

ALSO BY ANDREW VAN WEY

Novels

Forsaken: A Novel of Art, Evil, and Insanity

Head Like a Hole: A Novel of Horror

Beyond The Lost Coast

By the Light of Dead Stars

Tides of Darkness

The Black Lantern

The Clearwater Conspiracies

Blind Site

Refraction

Collections

Grim Horizons: Tales of Dark Fiction